P9-DTS-592

The first novel in an
original new paperback series
—"Wagons West"—
about the first
great wagon train westward.

INDEPENDENCE!

WAGONS WEST

INDEPENDENCE!

**PROUD, PASSIONATE MEN AND WOMEN
CAUGHT UP IN THE GREAT ADVENTURE OF
AMERICA'S WESTWARD DRIVE . . .**

CLAUDIA HUMPHRIES,
a young widow with a fiery temper
who meets her match in Sam Brentwood.

SAM BRENTWOOD,
the wagonmaster, a weathered veteran and
mountain man and a close friend to Whip Holt.

MICHAEL "WHIP" HOLT,
who gets his nickname from the whip he
carries, which he wields with expert accuracy.

CATHY VAN AYL,
Claudia's sister, married to a man her
father's age, to whom she has never been close.

TONIE MELL,
a frontier-wise young woman who wears
buckskins and shoots and rides like a man.

DR. ROBERT MARTIN,
a middle-aged widower who joins the wagon
train in the hope of easing his grief.

BARON ERNST VON THALMAN,
an Austrian nobleman and ex-cavalry officer,
who joins the wagon train for adventure.

★★★★★★★★★★★★★★★★★★★★★★★

EMILY HARRIS,
a widow who is traveling to Oregon seeking
a new life for herself and her boys.

LENA CALDWELL,
who travels with her father
and her illegitimate baby, hoping
to be able to forget her past.

TERENCE MALCOLM,
a twenty-year-old Easterner who has
been told he is dying from consumption.

TED WOODS,
a blacksmith, a giant of a man
whose uncontrollable temper
frightens him, as well as others.

CINDY,
a former prostitute from Louisville
who wants, above all, nothing to do with men.

STALKING HORSE,
a Cherokee Indian and consummate
scout, who is Whip Holt's
closest friend and companion.

DANNY,
a former bound boy, who has run away
from a cruel and unreasonable master.

CHET HARRIS,
Emily's oldest son who,
with Danny, alternately assists the
men and gets into mischief.

HENRY ST. CLAIR,
a wily British agent, whose
assignment is to prevent the wagon
train from reaching Oregon.

★★★★★★★★★★★★★★★★★★★★★★

WAGONS WEST ★ VOLUME I

INDEPENDENCE!

DANA FULLER ROSS

BANTAM BOOKS
TORONTO · NEW YORK · LONDON

INDEPENDENCE!

A Bantam Book / February 1979

2nd printing .... *March 1979*	5th printing .... *October 1979*
3rd printing .... *August 1979*	6th printing .... *December 1979*
4th printing .. *September 1979*	7th printing .... *March 1980*

Produced by Lyle Kenyon Engel

ISBN 0–553–14115–5

Published simultaneously in the United States and Canada

Bantam Books are published by Bantam Books, Inc. Its trademark, consisting of the words "Bantam Books" and the por-
trayal of a bantam, is Registered in U.S. Patent and Trademark
Office and in other countries. Marca Registrada. Bantam
Books, Inc., 666 Fifth Avenue, New York, New York 10019.

PRINTED IN THE UNITED STATES OF AMERICA

16 15 14 13 12 11 10 9 8 7

INDEPENDENCE!

I

"I disagree with you, Mr. President," Sam Brentwood said. "I think you're dead wrong."

Andrew Jackson averted his face so his visitor wouldn't see his grin, and stared out of the window at the thick coating of white snow on the neat lawn. Winter had come early to Washington City, his last full winter in the White House. He reflected that, in the more than seven and a half years he had spent as President of the United States, few people had dared oppose him to his face. Sam Brentwood, of course, was afraid of no one and always spoke his mind.

Composing himself, Jackson turned back to the man he had summoned from the distant frontier town of Independence, Missouri, and studied him in the unexpectedly strong sunlight that had streamed into the President's office in the wake of the snowstorm. Sam wore well, in spite of the wrinkles at the corners of his eyes and a skin that, after years in the Rocky Moun-

1

tains, resembled old leather. Sam had to be close to forty now, the President thought, remembering him as a seventeen-year-old scout back in the winter of 1814–15, when he had contributed so much to Jackson's celebrated victory against the British at the Battle of New Orleans. Sam hadn't gained an ounce in all those years. His life as a hunter, trapper and guide kept him fit.

"You're taking a short-sighted view, lad," Jackson said, speaking in the gentle tones he reserved for old and trusted friends.

"The hell you say, sir!" Sam was still vehement. "When I pulled into Independence with the season's load of furs from the mountains and found your letter asking me to come here in a hurry, I dropped everything. If I'd known you were aiming to destroy the West I'd have taken my time."

Jackson couldn't keep a straight face any longer, and laughed heartily.

There was no malice in Sam's return smile, but he shook his head. "I'm damned if I'm joking, Mr. President. You can go for days at a time in the Great Plains without seeing another soul. Just like you can spend weeks alone in the Rockies. And you're asking me to fill up the West with settlers."

"Not exactly. I'm trying to organize my last major campaign before Martin Van Buren takes over this job of mine in March. If I can get the financial backing of men who have a vested interest in the West—and I believe I can—I'm asking you to lead a covered wagon train out to the Oregon country on the Pacific.

2

Or at least to take it as far as you can, and get somebody else as wagonmaster for the rest of the trip."

"You know how the Indians are going to react when they see hundreds of strangers coming into their territory in wagons?" Sam said.

Andrew Jackson nodded. "I reckon. At least some of them will be unhappy until they find out we mean them no harm. That's why I need a man with your experience in charge, Sam. You served with me against the Choctaw in Tennessee and the Seminole in Florida when they were ornery, and you helped work out the treaties that were as fair to them as they were to us. So you understand Indians."

"Maybe so, Mr. President." Sam Brentwood could be stubborn when he made up his mind. "But I hate to see the West get filled up with people."

"So do I," Jackson replied quietly. "But there's no choice. Immigrants are still coming here from the Old World faster than the cities and towns of the East can absorb them. We're the only viable democracy in the world, and there's only one way we can expand—by moving people westward."

Sam sighed, realizing that, like the President, he had to accept the inevitability of national growth. "I suppose so," he said grudgingly.

"There's still more behind all this," the President said, "and I'll thank you to regard it as highly confidential."

His tone as well as his words caused the lean visitor to sit upright. "Yes, sir!" he said.

"The claim of the United States to the Oregon territory is unclear and muddled." Jackson spoke soberly now, his eyes clouded. "Great Britain has a claim every bit as valid as ours. So has Imperial Russia. They were the first nation to occupy Oregon, but they pulled out when we and the British began to contest it. Pulled out a little too fast and too easily to suit me."

"What you're saying, Mr. President, is that this country is in a battle with two of the world's most powerful nations."

"It could be three of them if Spain should decide to press her claims. But London and St. Petersburg are worrying me, not Madrid. We've fought the British twice in the past sixty years, and we could whip the Redcoats again. However, wars are a luxury a young nation really can't afford. The British have the world's strongest navy, plenty of manpower and all the money they need. The Russians aren't as well off, but they're still rich and strong. We need everything. Manpower. Factories. More agricultural products. Meat on our young bones."

Sam nodded, seeing the problem for the first time from a new perspective.

"Every American," Jackson said, "automatically expects us to stretch from the Atlantic to the Pacific."

"Well, sure." Sam himself thought in no other terms.

"If the British or the Russians can establish a solid foothold first," the President declared, "that's the end of America's dreams. The British can start moving from west to east, using Canada as a base for their operations. They can take the Rocky Mountains. They can even move into the Great Plains, and we'll have another major war on our hands if we want that land. We could be pushed all the way back to the Mississippi River."

Sam was starting to forget his objections to the settlement of the West.

"We have one natural advantage over London and St. Petersburg. We're closer. By thousands of miles." Jackson was emphatic. "It will be difficult for the British to occupy the Pacific Northwest, and even harder for the Russians. I'm not saying we can just walk in. But we can send our people as settlers, first by the hundreds and then by the thousands. Once they've established homesteads and built towns and roads, British and Russian claims won't amount to a pot of burned beans. If America really intends to fulfill her destiny and become a great nation, our citizens have got to go into Oregon. There's no two ways about it."

A handful of mountain men might prefer isolation, Sam realized, but the needs of the country as a whole were paramount.

"Much as we need settlers in Oregon," the President continued, "we're not asking them for favors. I'm told that not even Tennessee and Kentucky have land that rich, forests as full of game or rivers as crammed with fish."

"So I hear, sir."

The President stared at his visitor in ill-concealed dismay. "You just hear, Sam? You don't actually know Oregon?"

"No, sir. I've done no traveling the other side of the continental divide. But I won't let you down, Mr. President."

5

"That's good to hear. How well do you know the town of Independence?"

"There isn't all that much to know, sir. It has a general store and a couple of taverns."

"That's going to change. The settlers bound for Oregon will need a supply base, and we aim to build up Independence. Would you be willing to act as wagon-master of the first train as far as Independence, and then stay there to organize a depot for later trains?"

"I'll do anything you want, Mr. President."

"Thank you. Now, once I find a guide who'll take the first band of settlers from Independence to the Pacific, I'll be ready to start talking to the financiers."

"I have your man," Sam Brentwood said.

Jackson leaned forward in his chair.

"Mike Holt is my friend. Out in the Rockies he's known as Whip because he can do things with a bull-whip as a weapon that you wouldn't believe. He's still in his twenties, at least ten years younger than I am, but he's been a hunter and trapper for a long time. He knows the Great Plains and the Rockies as well as I do, and he's friendlier with the Indian tribes out there. And he's gone through the Oregon territory at least twice."

"Do you suppose he'd be willing to replace you at Independence?"

"I think he'd do it for me. And I know he'd ride a log down the Colorado River rapids if you asked him to do it. You're his idol."

"That's comforting to hear, even if I question his judgment," Jackson said. "Where can he be reached?"

"If he hasn't already brought his furs down from

the mountains to Independence, he'll be arriving there mighty soon. Just looking out these windows tells you the whole country is going to have an early winter, and Whip Holt is no more inclined to freeze to death up in the mountains than I am."

"Send for him, Sam. Tell him I want to see him, and the Government will pay his expenses. But put no details in writing. We can't take any chances if we hope to beat the British and the Russians to the punch."

Sam nodded.

Suddenly the President of the United States sighed. "I'll tell you another secret, Sam," he said, looking forlorn. "When I leave office in another three months I'll go back to my property outside Nashville and rusticate. Meanwhile you'll be on the road with a wagon train, you and this fellow Whip Holt, if he works out as you think he will. You'll be having all the fun. And between us, Sam, I envy the living daylights out of you!"

"I'm not a vixen, I'm not a witch and I'm not an overbearing woman!" Claudia Humphries spoke quietly, as befitted a New England lady of the 1830s, but her voice carried far beyond the confines of the Long Island farmhouse kitchen. "I'm a former schoolteacher, I have the misfortune to be a widow, and I refuse to be buried in a premature grave beside my husband or to let other people manage my life for me! And that's final."

As she marched up and down her brother-in-law's kitchen, her kohl-rimmed green eyes alight and her shoulder-length blonde hair tousled, not even her voluminous silk dress and petticoats could totally conceal the lithe figure of a twenty-seven-year-old woman in radiant good health. She not only meant every word, but seemed to be speaking the truth.

Claudia's relatives realized that she was extraordinary, just as her friends and neighbors in New Haven claimed. There was no one else in the world quite like her. Daughter of a widower, she had reared herself and her little sister Cathy before making the mistake of marrying a man who not only had her father's servile temperament, but also suffered from an appetite for liquor.

In Claudia's opinion there were no contradictions in her nature. Intelligent, hard-driving and sensible, she had been horrified when her late husband accused her, in a drunken stupor, of wanting to be the man of the family. Untrue! She was a woman, first, last and always, and proud of it. Since that day, she'd gone out of her way to emphasize her femininity, using cosmetics liberally and wearing clothes that most New England ladies considered much too revealing. Claudia's reaction to their criticism was characteristically blunt: If her detractors had her charms they wouldn't hide them!

She considered herself self-sufficient. Having managed Papa's affairs for a long time, she had taken charge of her husband's business when he himself proved incompetent. It was Claudia's private conviction, zealously guarded, that men were little better than bumblers, inferior beings all.

Occasionally she revealed her innermost attitudes without realizing it. A New Haven physician, who had known her for a long time, tried to put it in a nutshell:

8

"What Claudia needs is a man who can handle her. But I doubt if the good Lord ever created a man that strong, that wise and that patient."

Certainly her relatives couldn't restrain her. Her younger sister, Cathy van Ayl, who was twenty-one and resembled her, was the mistress of her own home, at least theoretically, but she knew better than to reply. Long familiar with Claudia's temper, she could only shudder.

Claudia pointed a slender finger at her middle-aged brother-in-law, Otto van Ayl. "You're neither my father nor my husband, so I won't permit you to dictate what I do."

Otto sighed. Married to Cathy for four years, trying in vain to earn a decent profit from his farm near Montauk Point on the eastern tip of Long Island, he had enough trouble trying to handle a spirited wife young enough to be his daughter. Attempting to control Cathy's fiery, sophisticated sister also, was way beyond his capacity.

"You can sell this place and take Cathy anywhere you please. Kansas City, the Ohio Valley, even the wilds of Illinois for all I care. But I'm not going with you!"

Otto rubbed a hand across his balding head. He'd never known anyone like her. "I didn't ask Gil Humphries to make me the executor of his will or to put me in charge of his wife's business, and for the past couple of years, ever since he died so suddenly, I've been sorry he did. But the law is the law and I have no choice."

"Indeed you do," Claudia was swift to respond.

"You can sell your farm, if that's what you want, and go west. Settle there, if that's your fancy. But allow me to manage my own property. My house in New Haven is snug, my woolen mill earns me enough to pay my bills, and I'm content."

Otto refrained from pouring himself a drink of brandywine from the decanter on the shelf, and helped himself instead to more tea. "You're intelligent," he said, "for a woman. You must have the brains to understand that the law won't let you keep either the mill or the house under your own control. They've got to be supervised for you by a trustee who's a man."

Claudia glared at him. "I wonder what Mrs. Thomas Jefferson thought when her husband neglected to write that all women are created equal, too." Claudia began to pace again, her hips swaying slightly, neither knowing nor caring that she was the epitome of outraged femininity. "Be sensible, Otto. You know very well that for all practical purposes I've been in charge of the mill and the house. I was doing that long before Gil died."

Otto disliked being crossed. "You're the one who's got to be sensible," he said. "Suppose Cathy and I find us a new property a thousand miles from here. No court of law is going to believe I could keep an eye on what you're doing, not from that distance. And the judge would be right. If our system is wrong, change the system." He added, dryly. "But till you do, women aren't allowed to direct their own business affairs, and that's that!"

Otto smiled with a satisfied air. How smug he looks, thought Cathy, like always when he made a conclusive point. That was one of the problems of being married to Otto van Ayl: he was so seldom wrong. All the same, he didn't seem much like a husband; he reminded her of Papa, whose friend he had been. She couldn't feel close to him. They hadn't been intimate since their wedding night, which had been a disaster for both of them. She knew such thoughts were disloyal, however, so she put them out of her mind. In the present instance she happened to agree with him, although she wouldn't dare admit such a thing to Claudia. There was no telling what her sister might do if she really lost her temper.

Claudia was fighting for self-control and gradually winning the battle. She poured herself a cup of tea and sipped it before she spoke again. "Rather than go off into some godforsaken wilderness," she said, "I'd prefer to marry again. There must be some man I could make an arrangement with."

Cathy was so shocked she couldn't remain silent. "Claudia! You wouldn't marry a fortune-hunter."

Her sister's shapely shoulders rose and fell. "I'm not likely to tempt a fortune-hunter. I'm hardly all that rich."

"She isn't marrying anybody," Otto said. "Because she'd need my permission as the head of the family, and I'm not going to give it. Claudia, you're forcing me to act like the villain in that foolish play we saw in New York last month. And I don't like it."

"Well, Otto, you're trying to force me to leave my home for a wretched life in the wilderness, and I don't like it either," Claudia said, glaring at him defiantly. "I'm aware of your predicament here, Otto, and I sympathize with it. I know the soil on your farm is poor, and salt air isn't good for your crops. You want to sell out and buy a big piece of land where the soil is rich. More power to you—and to Cathy. But it isn't fair to insist that I join you."

"I'd be much happier without your nagging, I'm sure," Otto said drily. "But I've got to earn my fee as your husband's executor."

Cathy dared to intervene again. "How do you know you wouldn't like it out west, Claudia? You've never been there."

"It's different for you, dear," Claudia replied with asperity. "You were young when you and Otto got married, and you've lived on this isolated farm ever since. But I'm accustomed to the finer things of life, and a little comfort. I enjoy the lectures at Yale College and the theater in New York. I certainly don't look forward to the prospect of hunting for elk or moose—or whatever wild beasts there may be in the Ohio Valley."

Otto chuckled. "You'll have to go out to the real wilderness, all the way to the Rocky Mountains, before you'll find elk and moose."

Claudia tried to cover up her ignorance. "You know very well what I mean. It's become the fashion to be uncouth these past seven and a half years, thanks, no doubt, to President Jackson. But, I can tell you, Andrew Jackson isn't *my* version of the ideal President, and I'll be very pleased when Martin Van Buren takes office. He's a gentleman."

"God help this country," Otto said, "if women are ever given the right to vote."

Cathy had to laugh. Claudia smiled, too, but her

12

green eyes were cold as the winter waters of the Atlantic.

"Mock me if it gives you pleasure," Claudia said, "but I make you a solemn promise. If you force me to pull up my roots and make a ridiculous journey to some place where no one else lives, if you insist that I live in a cabin like those of the poor Scottish immigrants in Tennessee, if I'm forced to eat wild onions and tough boar meat—well, Otto dear, I won't be alone in my misery."

The President was speaking, and when Andrew Jackson raised his voice people listened. When he pounded the table with his fist they paid attention to every word.

It was a cold morning in January 1837, and there was no other sound in the conference room of the White House except the crackling of the wood fire in the hearth. It didn't matter that the old man was leaving office in another two months and retiring to his Tennessee farm. His was still the dominant voice in America.

Even his chosen successor, the rotund President-elect Martin Van Buren, was maintaining a respectful silence. So were the bankers from Philadelphia, New York and Boston, men who had been feuding for years with Old Hickory but who had responded quickly when he summoned them to this meeting. Grouped together at one end of the long table were three men who already knew what the President wanted:

John Jacob Astor, reputedly the wealthiest man in America. He had made a fortune in fur trading in the Pacific Northwest, and it was said that he controlled large quantities of New York real estate. Like Jackson he was elderly. And although he, too, could pound a table when necessary, he was quiet—at least for the moment.

General William H. Ashley, Astor's arch-rival as a fur trader and millionaire and, like Jackson an old Indian fighter. Both men had made fortunes in the Oregon country, and ordinarily they took great pains to avoid each other. Now, however, they were united in a common enterprise.

Jedediah S. Smith, Ashley's associate, looked somewhat out of place in this august gathering, and doubly uncomfortable in his expensive clothes. Smith was the only man present who actually knew the Oregon country at first-hand, having made a number of explorations there. He disliked all meetings, but the President had demanded that he attend this session, so he came.

"Gentlemen," Jackson said, "the future growth of the United States is in jeopardy right now, on the shores of the Pacific Ocean. Make no mistake about it. I've called you here because something has to be done. We can't wait any longer to act."

No one moved a muscle.

"In the past few years," the President continued, "we've persuaded Spain to give up her claims to the Oregon country. We've also signed a treaty with Imperial Russia, who has pulled out of the territory. But under the terms of the peace treaty we made with Great Britain at the end of the War of 1812, we and the British control Oregon jointly." His gnarled fist thumped the table again. *"Joint control is no control. Either that country becomes part of the United States, or the British will annex it and incorporate it into Canada. Those are the two alternatives."*

Pausing for effect, he looked in turn at each man present. "I aim to make the Oregon country a part of the United States."

His listeners applauded spontaneously.

Jackson gestured for silence. "We can't do it with troops, because the territory is too far from our population centers. We can't do it through diplomacy at this point, because the British won't listen to us any more than we'll listen to them. There's only one way we can gain a hold out there and keep it: to have settlers take actual possession of the territory, establish their homesteads and live there."

"Can't the Congress pass a bill to encourage homesteaders, Mr. President?" A banker made bold to ask.

Old Hickory glared at him. "That's exactly what we cannot do. We'd be violating our treaty with the British, and none of us wants another war with them. The United States Government is obliged to stay out of this situation—officially, that is. But there's nothing to prevent private citizens from banding together and sending homesteaders to the West. Mr. Astor, tell them the plan we've concocted."

John Jacob Astor leaned forward in his chair. "We propose to form a company for the purpose of settling the Oregon country. We'll advertise in newspapers all the way from here to the Mississippi, telling people

15

there's rich, free land available to them. Then we'll send out a covered-wagon train, the first of many, and give financial assistance to those who need it."

One of the Bostonians was puzzled. "I don't understand what you mean by a covered-wagon train."

President Jackson grinned.

"It's a new way of traveling," General Ashley explained. "In the limited trade the Spaniards allow us on the Santa Fe Trail, we've been sending goods by covered wagon. That is, wagons with canvas stretched over them and held above the wagon surface by big hoops of wood. If such wagons can protect merchandise they're even better for people."

"How many people could go on one of these trains?"

"As many as want to," Astor said.

"And how long would the journey take?" another banker wanted to know.

Everyone looked at Jedediah Smith.

"A minimum of two years," he said slowly. "Maybe as long as three. It depends on the weather, the mountains and the Indians."

"Mr. President," a New Yorker said, "we gather you're asking us to invest in this program."

"I'm asking you to invest in the future of the United States."

Astor felt compelled to soften the curt answer. "It'll take time for any investment to pay off. But real estate in the Oregon country will be worth as much—eventually—as the fur trade has been for Bill Ashley and me."

Astor's words struck Jackson on a raw nerve. The antagonism he felt for the wealthy Astor flared anew.

16

"I'll let you people worry about your profits," he said harshly. "My only concern is the natural expansion of this country across the continent from the Atlantic to the Pacific. Profits be damned."

John Jacob Astor may have been the only man in the room who wasn't afraid of Old Hickory. "Unless investors can be assured of making a reasonable profit," he said coolly, "you'd better send the troops out there now, Mr. President. That's the only other way you'll take the Oregon country. And without actual settlers—families who'll take the land, cultivate it and hold it—your troops will never succeed. All you'll do is drag us into another expensive war with Great Britain."

The President's eyes blazed—always a danger sign, but he remained civil. "If I'd wanted to send troops to the Pacific," he said, "I wouldn't have called you here, Astor. Or any of you. I know what's needed to take and hold land, and I don't require lessons from fur traders and bankers. I know you're here because you want to make money. What I'm trying to tell you is that there's a damn sight more than money at stake. What we accomplish or fail to accomplish will have a direct effect on the future of the United States for hundreds of years to come. I hope that even you businessmen have the vision to see it!"

There was a long, uncomfortable silence.

The discreet Martin Van Buren felt compelled to enter the conversation, even though he had long deferred to Jackson. "What the President is saying, gentlemen," he declared smoothly, "is that we can expect serious trouble over this venture."

"What kind of trouble?" a Philadelphian inquired.

"Surely you don't expect the British to accept our settlement of the Oregon country without a murmur," the President-elect said. "The British are proud. They aim to be the most powerful nation in the world. They know the Oregon land is rich. They also appreciate the value of the fur trade, the magnificent timber and the superb fishing."

"Are you suggesting," a New Yorker asked, "that London will send a military expedition all the way to Oregon?"

Jackson's snort indicated his disgust.

Van Buren hastened to reply before Old Hickory exploded. "The British don't want a direct challenge any more than we do. They'll try to thwart us in some way, you can be sure, but we don't know how they'll go about it."

"Then the possibility exists that a war with Britain could develop."

"Certainly," Jackson said, "even though neither side wants it. The stakes are high."

"We may be in for problems with Imperial Russia, too," Van Buren added. "They signed the treaty I negotiated as Secretary of State only because we exerted great pressure on them. Czar Nicholas is a proud man —and you can depend on it that he wants to recover Oregon. He may be something of a bumbler as well as a despot, but he's got some able advisers. And I don't see St. Petersburg giving up all that territory without another struggle."

"What I don't understand," the Bostonian said, "is why so many people should covet that wilderness."

President Jackson's temper had reached the boiling point again. "Maybe one of you Westerners will explain to this gentleman from the East—who seems to know nothing except how to balance his infernal ledgers!"

Jedediah Smith was quick to respond. "I've never seen land so fertile anywhere else, not even in the black-earth farmlands of Illinois." He spoke with sudden passion. "And the climate is perfect all year 'round. If there's ever been a land of milk and honey anywhere on earth, it's the Oregon country."

Jackson took charge of the meeting again. "We don't aim to let parties of innocents wander out across the plains, the deserts and the mountains by themselves. That would be foolish. They'll be escorted every inch of the way."

Van Buren spoke again. "The whole country will be watching. We realize that. And if this first group succeeds, others will follow—in large numbers. If it fails, we may as well give up our claims to the Oregon country and let the British take the whole territory."

"We see this journey taking place in two stages," Jackson explained. "First, a wagon train will start out from the East, and we hope it will attract people along the way, thanks to newspaper advertising. In addition, we aim to set up a takeoff depot at Independence, Missouri. And from there the pioneers will go into the wilderness."

A Philadelphia banker cleared his throat. "Isn't there great risk involved, Mr. President?"

"Hell, yes." Jackson looked at him coldly. "When I migrated from South Carolina to Tennessee, I walked behind my donkey cart all the way. I fought rattlesnakes, Indians and some of the meanest critters this side of Hades, but I'm none the worse for it. Besides, we have good men to act as escorts. One of my own lads, who served under me at the Battle of New Orleans, has agreed to act as the train commander as far as Independence. I can vouch for Sam Brentwood. He'll stay on at Independence and run the depot there. And he's recruited a mountain man to take charge of the party the rest of the way."

"I've traveled through the Rocky Mountains with Mike Holt," Smith said. "We've fought the Indians side by side. And a few years ago we had one hell of a fight with the Russians. One winter we damn near starved together. Mike Holt is a good man." Anyone who knew Smith realized he could offer no higher praise.

The President glanced at John Jacob Astor, who nodded.

"I believe in this program," Astor said, "and I'm convinced it'll make money for everyone concerned. I also believe it will win the Oregon country for America. I'm pledging an initial investment of four hundred thousand dollars."

The sum was so large the bankers were stunned.

"I'm putting in a quarter of a million," General Ashley added before they could recover from their first shock.

"I'm not all that rich," Jedediah Smith said, "but I'm pledging one hundred thousand dollars. The West has been good to us, and I know this is one investment I won't regret."

20

One by one the other bankers offered their pledges, too. Some were reluctant, others showed a genuine interest in the project and still others were content merely to follow the lead of men as shrewd as Astor and Ashley.

Andrew Jackson had no intention of allowing even one to escape. He stared at each banker in turn until a commitment was made. By the time the meeting ended the new company had received promises of almost two million dollars in capitalization. Approximately half of this sum, it was explained, would be used to build the depot in the little village of Independence, and to stock it with the supplies and provisions the travelers would need on their long journey across the wilderness.

When the meeting ended and the visitors departed, Martin Van Buren remained. "You brought it off, Mr. President, just as you said you would," he said with a smile.

"This is my final legacy to you, Martin—and to the American people," Jackson said. "The next step will be for folks to respond to the advertising. Then it'll be up to Sam Brentwood, and this young Holt fellow after him, to lead those brave pioneers to the promised land."

Free, Rich
LAND!
in the
Oregon Country
New Homesteads for all!

The arthritic pains in Sam Brentwood's hip were intense as he limped to a table in a dark corner of the New York waterfront tavern, but he ignored them. A man learned to live with pain, and at the age of thirty-nine Sam was no stranger to discomfort. With his graying hair and lined face, he looked much older than his years. The bullet wound he had suffered at New Orleans had contributed to that, and so had the scars he still bore after his torture by the Kiowa tribe.

At first glance Sam looked like a city dweller, in his dark broadcloth suit, half-boots and white shirt and stock. But his hands were those of a man who had known hard physical labor. His skin was that of a man who had lived most of his life out of doors and, most of all, his eyes told their own story. Clear and gray, they were the eyes of a fighter, a man who had tasted life to the full, a man of many experiences who

22

had been forced by necessity to pass judgment on his fellow humans in order to survive.

So a stranger who studied him would take him for a frontier dweller, not realizing that he had been born in this part of the country. But his past was very private. Not even his few close friends knew all of it.

Just before the beginning of the nineteenth century, when he had been a small boy, his mother had deserted his father and run away with another man, never again to be seen by her husband or son. So Pa had taken Sam out west, and he had grown to manhood in the wilds near the Mississippi River.

Only since he had come east at President Jackson's request had Sam thought about those days, buried in his memory almost four decades in the past. After all, he had been standing on his own self-reliant feet for a long time. But, he realized, many of his attitudes grew out of those dark days of early childhood.

For example, he hated "ladies," particularly those who put on airs and wore fancy clothes. He found them no better than the whores who, from time to time, took care of his physical needs. On the other hand, he went out of his way to be polite to ordinary women, particularly cooks, chambermaids and others who had to earn their living. Not that he'd ever marry one. No woman would ever hurt him the way his Pa had been hurt. Actually, just being in the East now made Sam uneasy, although he could face an entire herd of stampeding buffalo without flinching.

The Eastern Seaboard was too civilized now, boasting theaters and inns, elegant dining places and shops that might rival the best that London and Paris could offer. But Sam made no apology for the curved, bone-handled knife he carried in his belt. He was one of Andy Jackson's cubs, a veteran of more battles than he cared to remember, and New York footpads who regarded him as an easy mark because of his limp hastily changed their minds when they drew closer to him.

The barmaid took it for granted that he wanted whiskey, and stayed out of his reach because she assumed he would try to paw her. Sam surprised her on both counts, treating her with elaborate courtesy as he ordered a small mug of non-alcoholic ginger beer. When he smiled his thanks he looked far younger than his years.

Everyone in this rough establishment—sailors and dock workers alike—gaped at the younger man still in his twenties who arrived to join Sam Brentwood. The heavily tanned Mike Holt was almost painfully thin and towered above everyone else in the tavern. He wore his usual soiled buckskins, disdaining the clothes that New Yorkers regarded as proper, and when he removed his broadbrimmed hat he revealed a shock of pale, blond hair. What caused the most stir, however, was the coiled bullwhip looped casually around his belt. It seemed a natural part of him, like the moccasins that were molded to his feet.

Holt slid into a chair opposite Sam, moving with effortless ease. Then he lived up to the barmaid's expectations by slapping her lightly across the buttocks as he ordered a glass of whiskey.

"You're late, Whip," Sam Brentwood said.

Whip Holt had the grace to flush beneath his tan. "I can find my way through a blizzard in the Rockies," he said, "but I get lost in this town. I'm blamed if I know why I had to come here in the first place."

Sam sipped his ginger beer. "You can head west again in a few weeks," he said with a grin, then sobered. "Andy Jackson wanted you to join me for a spell at the start of this expedition, and when General Jackson gives an order it's got to be obeyed."

Whip was well aware of his friend's opinion of the great Andrew Jackson, and wanted no dispute. Sam was the one man he knew who could beat him in a fistfight, wrestling match or free-for-all.

The barmaid saved him the need for a reply by bringing his drink and favoring him with the broad smile that most women bestowed on him, sooner or later. Whip raised his glass to his companion, then downed its contents in a gulp.

"You and Jed Smith got me into this fix," he said, "but I reserve the right to quit after I see how you make out between here and Independence."

"I can't say I look forward to acting as a nursemaid to misfits, dirt farmers and God only knows what else we'll dredge up on this trip. I wasn't cut out for the life of a nanny. But I reckon the settlement of the Oregon country will be worth a few headaches," Sam said.

Whip brooded in silence. "It's the most beautiful land there is. Mountains of fir and spruce and pine. Wild onions and berries waiting to be picked. So many salmon in the Columbia River you can almost scoop them out with your bare hands. There's no call there

25

for dirt farmers, or for towns that will be big and ugly as this one is, either. Oregon ought to be left the way it is."

"That's not what Andy Jackson wants," Sam said, and so the issue was settled. "We'll find us an inn where we can stay overnight, and tomorrow we'll go out to Long Island and start to work. There's a farmer out there by the name of Van Ayl—the first to answer Mr. Astor's advertisement. We'll show him how to fix up a covered wagon nice and cozy. And soon as he's ready we'll start our caravan on its way."

Whip sighed. "I wish I was hunting elk in the Ute Mountains."

"You'll be back there soon enough—which is more than I'll ever do again with my ailing hip."

Whip was abashed. "Sorry, Sam. I didn't mean to—"

"No harm done, boy. Even a stupid old stallion knows when his time to turn out to pasture has come. I told Andy Jackson that this is my last job before I find me a quiet place to live out my days." Sam reached into a fat purse he'd been given earlier in the day at John Jacob Astor's office, selected a gold coin and placed it on the table.

He and Whip were unaccustomed to city ways, and neither realized, as they waited for their change, the stir that the purse and gold coin created. Significant looks were exchanged, silent signals were given and when the pair left the tavern and moved out into the alleyway beyond, they were followed by a half-dozen burly men who quickly surrounded them.

The leader planted himself in front of Sam, blocking his path. "I'll take that purse you're carrying," he said. "Hand it over, or you'll limp on both legs."

Sam's response was rapid and violent. His fist lashed out with great force, smashing the robber full in the face, and the man went down.

Another man drew a pistol from beneath his cloak. Before he could use it, however, Sam was wielding his knife with unerring expertise, slashing his assailant across the hand.

The man howled in agony and dropped his pistol.

In the meantime Mike Holt demonstrated how he had earned his nickname. He uncoiled his bullwhip quickly. It cracked only once—and a third robber screamed in pain. On the second crack, another man dropped his pistol and ran, a red welt forming across his face.

The remaining two men beat a hasty retreat down the alley.

The entire encounter had lasted barely thirty seconds.

Sliding his knife into its sheath, Sam calmly nudged the body of the unconscious gang leader with his toe. "Reckon we ought to find us an inn in a better neighborhood for the night," he said, hobbling along at Whip Holt's side. "I'm a mite tired out this evening, and I don't want my sleep disturbed by rowdies."

II

A discreet sign attached to the door of the building facing St. James Park in London identified the premises as the offices of the Empire Trading Company Limited. It was the only building in the neighborhood that wasn't a private dwelling.

On the ground floor, clerks worked quietly at ledgers, dipping their quill pens into ink jars, filling page after page with neat rows of figures. Subordinate executives were housed on the second floor.

Only in the large room on the third floor, overlooking the park where a cold winter rain was falling, were there hints that the Empire Trading Company might be other than what it appeared to be on the surface. A portrait of England's monarch, William IV, hung in solitary splendor on one wall, near a glass case containing a pair of dueling pistols and several swords.

To anyone in the know, the presence behind the desk of Sir Edwin Knowlton was a certain indication that this establishment was actually a secret branch of His Majesty's Service. A quarter of a century earlier, when he'd been young, Sir Edwin had insured the loyalty of Canada to the Crown during the War of 1812. Now white-haired and austere, he had just returned from lunch at his nearby club. Having consumed a dozen oysters, broiled partridge, saddle of lamb and a bottle of excellent claret, he was in an amiable mood. As subordinates who saw him regularly knew well, however, Sir Edwin's temper could flare up at any moment.

But the younger man who sat opposite him showed no sign of discomfort. Solidly built and in his thirties, Henry St. Clair had spent a full decade in Sir Edwin's employ, and had earned his spurs. They were colleagues, not master and servant, and St. Clair didn't even bother to ask permission before lighting a West Indian *segaro*.

Sir Edwin disliked the aroma of burning tobacco, but was inclined to humor one of his more accomplished operatives. "I trust you've enjoyed your leave?"

"Very much, Sir Edwin. I've spent most of it right here in London, catching up on the theater and civilized eating places. I felt I owed it to myself, after spending two years in the jungles of Latin America."

"You're ready for a new assignment, I hope."

"Of course, sir."

"I regret you'll see no theater for a long time to come, and you'll have to toughen your palate."

St. Clair shrugged. Experience had taught him that rain always follows sunshine.

"What do you know about the Oregon territory?"

"Nothing, Sir Edwin—except that we and the Yanks are parties to an awkward joint-occupation arrangement there."

"Precisely. The problem is that no one is actually occupying most of the country. A tiny band of Americans belonging to some religious group has established a little settlement somewhere or other in the wilderness, and we have a small garrison at Fort Vancouver. That's the extent of the occupation on the part of both nations."

"Are we going to beat them to it?"

"No, Henry. I was in favor of trying to, but the Colonial Office doesn't think the idea is feasible. Now that the Americans are sending a large, well-financed wagon train out there, we're forced to take a different approach." Sir Edwin smiled at his visitor. "You'll join that train and use every means at your disposal to disrupt it."

St. Clair whistled. "Sabotage is nasty business."

"Indeed. You'll be free to carry out the details as you see fit. Let me know by tomorrow what you'll need in the way of funds, and be prepared to sail for Plymouth the following day."

"So soon?"

"The wagon train is already being formed. And . . ." Sir Edwin said, speaking slowly, "I regret to say that you won't be working alone. I've been notified by the Imperial Russian Legation that St. Petersburg is also assigning an agent to work toward the same end."

St. Clair groaned. "The bloody *Cheka* is so inefficient and sloppy!"

"I've never been fond of the Russian secret police

myself," Sir Edwin said, "but I scarcely need to remind you that Czar Nicholas is His Majesty's ally."

"How closely must I cooperate with this *Cheka* idiot?"

"Just enough to justify the glowing reports I shall send to the Prime Minister and Foreign Office. If the Russians offer you any real help in crippling the wagon train, you'll want to accept it. Ultimately, however, you'll want to be rid of the *Cheka* agent. We're not in business to advance the cause of the Czar."

St. Clair smiled, but his eyes remained hard. "It won't be the first time we've played that game. Who is the Russian representative, sir, and where do we meet?"

"Don't ask too much of St. Petersburg." Sir Edwin's smile was wry. "I've been given no details. Presumably you and their agent will have to locate each other on the wagon train."

"It's going to be difficult enough to carry out this mission without stumbling over some bumbling idiot of a Russian," St. Clair said. "After I've finished this job I hope you'll consider me for a desk assignment right here at headquarters. Ten years of working abroad is a long time."

"Do what's expected of you," Sir Edwin said, "and prevent that wagon train from reaching Oregon. If you succeed, you can plan on spending the rest of your career right here."

The *chargé d'affaires* of the Imperial Russian Legation in Washington City looked out of his window at the wet, muddy road that the Americans called a street, and wondered when it might be paved with cobblestones. The dignity of the Legation demanded a pavement, but so far the State Department had blandly ignored his requests. "General Valichevsky expects us to perform miracles," he said to his companion, referring to the problem in Oregon. "But we are diplomats here, my dear Tarnoff, not magicians."

Baron Tarnoff, a high-ranking *Cheka* official who had come to the United States on a special mission, was unmoved. "The Czar himself has taken an interest," he said. "He signed the treaty when he was new to the throne, and he feels the Americans and British have taken unfair advantage of his lack of experience. He would very much like to see the Oregon territory under our sovereignty."

"I share that wish, as does the Minister," the *chargé d'affaires* said. "But we have no agents on our staff, and we find it difficult to find an experienced operative on such short notice."

"Four members of the Imperial household staff who have disappointed His Majesty in recent months have been sent to Siberia," Baron Tarnoff said.

The *chargé's* hand shook slightly as he picked up a sheaf of documents from his desk. "The best I can offer you is the young woman who came to see us three days ago—provided she can be persuaded to accept. And provided General Valichevsky keeps in mind that she is a rank amateur."

The *Cheka* representative snapped his fingers. "The pertinent details, please."

"Her name is Antoinette Melichev, born twenty-three years ago to Ivan Melichev, a court jeweler to the late Czar Alexander. Melichev and his wife, Olga, continue to live in St. Petersburg, where he's a commercial jeweler in a shop near the Summer Palace. The girl was sent to America as a small child, and moved with her aunt and uncle to the frontier in the West, where she grew up. She now calls herself Tonie Mell."

Baron Tarnoff's gesture was impatient.

The *chargé* spoke more rapidly. "A year ago I received a letter from the girl, saying her parents had applied repeatedly for visas to join her here, but had received no reply from the Ministry. She inquired whether she could hasten the procedure. I sent a letter to St. Petersburg, but so far there has been no reply."

"That's not surprising," the *Cheka* official said. "It sometimes takes ten to fifteen years before we issue visas—if at all."

"I know that, my dear Tarnoff. But the girl has learned American ways and she is impatient. Three days ago she arrived in Washington City and came to the Legation in person. I didn't see her myself, but left instructions that she was to return today. She seems to offer our only hope. She's been waiting for several hours to see me."

"See her." Baron Tarnoff was decisive. "And use her!"

"Even though she's an amateur, and her loyalty to His Majesty may be questionable?"

"We utilize the tools at hand," Baron Tarnoff said, stalking to the door and pausing there. "Thank God she appeared when she did. You surely know how to handle her. Apply the right pressure, and she'll be loyal." He left the room and vanished down the corridor.

The *chargé* sighed, picked up a small silver bell with an ivory handle and rang it. When a servant in Imperial livery appeared, he said, "Send in the young lady who calls herself Tonie Mell."

Any diplomat who had spent a number of years in the United States would have known that the young woman who entered the office was from the West. The blonde highlights in her short, red hair indicated long exposure to the sun. She wore no cosmetics or jewelry, and her awkwardness in handling her full skirt and petticoats as she curtsied showed an ignorance with such frivolous attire.

She was lean and wiry, with work-roughened hands, and at first glance she resembled a boy. But the *chargé*, who appreciated women, was quick to note that her breasts, although small, were perfectly formed, that her waist was tiny and that the legs that flashed when she rose from her curtsy were long.

"You are Antoinette Melichev," he said, addressing her in Russian as he waved her to a chair.

"Tonie Mell," she replied in unaccented English. "I've been waiting a long time to see you, and I reckon you know why I'm here."

"Indeed I do," he said, also speaking in English. "In fact, the delay was caused by a discussion of your parents' case. Some of my colleagues have been wondering why any subjects of His Imperial Majesty would want to leave Russia."

"My aunt and uncle like it here, and so do I," the

girl said, speaking in the blunt manner of the American West. "My mother and father like what we've written to them about this country and want to join us."

"It's the policy of Czar Nicholas to permit his subjects to immigrate only under special circumstances."

Tonie Mell was dismayed. "Is their application being turned down?"

"Not necessarily," the *chargé* said smoothly. "Their status depends on how anxious you are to have them join you."

She became fervent. "I want it more than anything else in the world!"

"We shall soon see." He consulted her dossier, which a subordinate had prepared. "You live in Missouri?"

"My uncle and aunt own a ranch near the village of Independence, and that's where I was brought up."

"You do housework there?"

She shook her head, tousling her short hair. "Mostly I ride herd and go hunting with my uncle. He always wanted a son, I guess, so I've been kind of a substitute." She smiled easily. "Out our way there's more need for ranch hands than cooks."

Perhaps she was better qualified for the mission than the *chargé* had dared to hope. "You ride and shoot?"

Tonie Mell couldn't help laughing. "I grew up in the saddle, and I can handle any gun made." She spoke without false modesty.

He nodded. "You've heard of the wagon train that's being organized for an expedition to the Oregon territory?"

"Heard of it?" She sounded envious. "I've been reading everything I can find out about it in the papers! I'd do most anything to join them."

"Perhaps something can be arranged," the *chargé* said. "Suppose we provide you with funds for a wagon, supplies and a team of fine horses?"

The unexpected generosity made the girl suspicious. "I already have a gelding I raised from a colt. I rode him here all the way from Independence."

"Keep your horse, by all means. You'll need a strong team to pull your wagon. And," the *chargé* added, "we'll also give you a purse to pay all your expenses."

"Why would you do this? And what does it have to do with my parents being granted an exit visa from Russia?"

"Do our bidding, and visas will be given to Ivan and Olga Melichev. Refuse to do it, or fail, and they'll never be permitted to leave the motherland."

Her green eyes were unwavering. "Just exactly what are you aiming for me to do, mister?"

The Imperial Russian *chargé d'affaires* was emphatic. "The wagon train must never be allowed to reach Oregon."

Stunned, Tonie grew pale beneath her tan. "You want me to be a traitor to the United States?"

"For your parents' sake," he replied, "we hope you'll be loyal to the land of your birth."

She began to tremble, and grasped the arms of her chair to steady herself. "I wouldn't believe this if my uncle and aunt hadn't told me about the terrible things the *Cheka* does!"

"Our secret police, like our diplomatic service, is devoted to the cause of the Czar Nicholas. When he was new to the throne, soon after he succeeded his late brother, may God bless him, the Americans and the British pressured him into abandoning his claims to the Oregon Territory. Now he wants only what is rightfully his."

As Tonie became increasingly aware of her own dilemma, she was engulfed by a feeling of despair. Her uncle and aunt hadn't exaggerated when they told her about the ruthlessness of the secret police, the callous disregard that all Imperial Russian officials showed for the natural rights of the Czar's subjects.

The *chargé d'affaires* increased the pressure. "If you refuse to work with us, the loyalty of your parents to Mother Russia will be suspect. I'm sure you wouldn't want to be responsible for their deportation to Siberia."

In spite of her incredulity, Tonie knew he meant what he said. She was relieved that she had left her rifle and pistol at her lodging house, because if she had either weapon with her she'd be tempted to put a bullet between his eyes.

"Help us," the *chargé* said, "and we're prepared to deal compassionately with your parents. Refuse, and they'll pay the consequences."

Tonie hadn't cried since she was a little girl, but she found it hard to hold back the tears. She was trapped, caught in the conspiratorial web of a backward and conniving government that cared nothing about its people.

"If you tell the American authorities about this conversation," he continued, "I'll deny it. And the State Department will choose to believe me, because the growing trade between Russia and America makes it desirable for both nations to maintain good relations."

She wanted to defy him. Only the knowledge that her mother and father would be forced to pay the price for her temerity caused her to clamp her jaws together.

"Which will it be, yes or no?" the *chargé* demanded. "I must have your reply."

Tonie had no alternative. She loved the United States, the only country she knew, but she loved her parents more. And she knew that they'd never survive the rigors of life in Siberia. No longer able to meet the man's gaze, she lowered her head and whispered, "Yes. I'll do what you ask."

The *chargé* tried to hide his exultation. "You won't regret your decision, and neither will your family," he said. "You'll be given funds this afternoon, before you leave. Then you must be on your way without delay."

The girl nodded, too ashamed to speak.

"Now I can reveal that you won't be alone. The British also are sending an agent to join the expedition. Work with him when you learn his identity. But always remember you're in the service of Czar Nicholas, not William of England."

Tonie despised herself for being weak. It was ironic. She had dreamed of joining the wagon train, but in coming true that dream had turned into a nightmare.

"You've never been married?"

She was jolted anew by the unexpected question, and felt her face become warm. But she merely shook her head, telling herself that it was none of his damn business if she was still a virgin.

"Before you leave, we'll invent a story for you," he said. "But keep your own name. You lack the experience to use another. You've lived in the West, but be vague about where. Present yourself as a widow who's going to Oregon to begin a new life. And always, *always,* find new ways to delay the journey and cause trouble for the wagon train."

Until a few minutes ago Tonie had relished everything in life, but now she could only wish she was dead.

In spite of Claudia Humphries' protests, the die was cast. Her house and the mill in New Haven were sold. She'd accepted payment in U.S. Government securities, which she regarded as so many scraps of paper. She had cashed in one to buy herself a wagon and a team of horses; if she had to travel west, and there seemed to be no escape, at least she wouldn't be forced to live and sleep in the very same wagon with her sister and brother-in-law. The vehicle that would be her new "home," together with the horses that would pull it, were already in the Van Ayl barn.

As hard as Claudia tried to accept the inevitability of her new future, she couldn't do it. Thanks to laws made by men, she had no control over her inheritance, no voice in the determination of the way she would live. Her own wishes counted for nothing. Like a small child or a slave she was forced to bow to the judgment of Otto van Ayl, whose mentality society regarded as superior to hers simply because he was a male and she was a "helpless" female.

In her present frame of mind, Claudia knew that

even the slightest incident might trigger a violent outburst of temper—which would only prove to Otto that even the most sophisticated of grown women was still just a little girl. Somehow she must gain the upper hand over her emotions. But the knowledge that she would soon be heading west only soured her spirit.

Cathy and Otto had gone to the village to conclude the sale of their house and to make some last-minute purchases, so Claudia was alone. Most of her belongings were packed, but she felt restless. She wandered from room to room, accompanied by Quincy, her shepherd dog.

When she heard a sharp tap at the back door of the farmhouse, Claudia looked out through the window before she went to the door. Two men were waiting, the elder in a rusty black suit and the younger in dirty buckskins. Both looked so disreputable that she took the precaution of removing Otto's pistol from a cupboard drawer to carry with her. It was always best to be prepared.

"Who's there?" she said as she approached the door.

"Sam Brentwood and Whip Holt, ma'am. We've come to arrange with Mr. van Ayl for the wagon train."

Claudia sighed. Her fate couldn't be avoided. She was surprised to see that Quincy, usually on his guard with strangers, was wagging his tail. Wishing she could send the two men away, she opened the door.

Sam Brentwood patted the dog as though they were old friends, then grinned at the young woman. "Ma'am," he said politely as he took the pistol from her hand, "firearms don't do much good unless they're properly prepared for use." He cocked the weapon, then offered it back to her.

Claudia was as angry with herself as she was with him. Refusing to touch the pistol again, she glared at him. "Be good enough to wipe the mud off your boots before you come inside!"

For a moment Sam Brentwood stared at her. With her cultured accent, genteel gestures and fancy airs, she sounded like a great lady. But her eyes were rimmed with kohl and she wore rouge on her mouth, just like the tarts he'd known in river towns out west. And the way her snug-fitting dress clung to her body put ideas into a man's head that had no right being there.

The combination of qualities he saw in her—or imagined he saw—were bewildering. He was willing to bet his mother had been just this sort before she vanished with her lover. Hellfire, this woman—half fancy lady, half fancy harlot—was just about the age his mother had been when she'd disappeared, in her late twenties. Sam felt an unreasoning surge of anger, but did his best to conquer it. It was absurd to want to humiliate a woman who was a total stranger to him.

Claudia felt his eyes boring into her, and was outraged. Somehow it was typical of a man to think he could treat a woman with an insolent lack of respect, expecting her to be grateful, perhaps, because he showed a spark of interest in her. What arrogance!

"For the second time," she said crisply, "please wipe the mud off your boots!"

"Yes, ma'am." Sam obeyed with alacrity, Whip following his example. Still holding the pistol, Sam couldn't resist taking aim at a lone, dead leaf suspended from the branch of an elm tree at the far side of the front yard. He squeezed the trigger, and when the smoke cleared away the leaf had vanished.

Claudia was impressed by this feat, but refused to let him see her reaction, since it was obvious to her that he'd shown off for her benefit.

"This gun has too much of a kick for a lady," he said. "I recommend that you use one that's lighter and smaller."

"Maybe I have one in my gear," Whip said.

Were they laughing at her? "Thank you all the same," she said frigidly, "but I don't really approve of pistols and the like." Closing the door behind them, she realized she had to be hospitable. "May I offer you something to eat?"

"That's right kind of you, Mrs. van Ayl," Sam said.

"Mrs. van Ayl is my sister. My name is Humphries."

"Well, now." Sam was appreciating her appearance, as most men did. "So you're Mrs. Humphries. Mr. van Ayl wrote that you were going on the wagon train with us, but as he said you were a widow, I kind of had it in my head that you'd be much older and plainer."

Perhaps he intended the remark as a compliment. If so, there was no time like the present to put him in his place. "I can't apologize for my age, and I believe that any woman who deliberately makes herself look plain is guilty of false modesty."

Whip Holt was enjoying Sam's discomfort in dealing

with this sharp-tongued young woman. He chuckled quietly.

Claudia removed a smoked ham from the larder, placed it on the table with bread, cheese and butter, and then set a jug of hard cider between the pair. "My sister and brother-in-law should be back soon, so help yourselves."

"I'd best put our horses in the stable first," Whip said. "Where is it?"

"In back of the house, of course." Claudia was irritated by the question.

He hurried off, carefully closing the door behind him.

Sam Brentwood, alone with the young woman, couldn't help staring at her. Her beauty was enhanced by her cosmetics, and her silk gown, revealing a ripe figure, made him realize how long it had been since he'd last had a woman.

Not even attempting to check himself, he reached for her.

Outraged, Claudia slapped him hard across the face, angered because Quincy continued to wag his tail as though nothing out of the ordinary had happened. "Get your hands off me!" she cried. "What do you take me for?"

Sam was aghast. Although her attack had caused him no physical pain, he realized that he had made a mistake. He went on to compound it. "I didn't realize you were a lady," he said.

He was adding insult to insult, and she tried to sweep past him. Under no circumstances would she make a long journey across the continent in the company of such a man.

He blocked her path. "Ma'am," he said, "I apologize. In my part of the country, there's two kinds of women, and I got confused into thinking you were the other kind."

Claudia could see his contrition was genuine, but she was not mollified. "But the very *second* we were alone you grabbed me. Do I look like a harlot?"

Even in this embarrassing situation he could not dissemble. "Well, ma'am, out my way the fancy women all wear silk and paint their faces."

In spite of her anger she wanted to laugh. This seemingly hard-bitten westerner had acted out of ignorance. "I don't pretend to be high-born," she said, "but I can assure you that in this part of the United States a great many ladies of quality wear silk dresses and use cosmetics."

His ears burned as he shuffled his feet. "If you'll give me half a chance to become better acquainted, Mrs. Humphries, you'll discover I don't go around trying to kiss ladies."

She looked at him, biting her lower lip.

Sam now had the suspicion that she was laughing at him because of his innocence, and he felt even worse, but he forced himself to meet her steady gaze. "Ma'am, I'm sorry as all hell I thought you was a harlot. I didn't know the way ladies look hereabouts. But I'm not the least bit sorry I thought you was so pretty that I couldn't help reaching out for you."

Claudia was flattered.

"We're going to be on the trail together for a long time, ma'am, and I'd rather be friends than enemies. What do you say?" He extended a hand.

She realized she had to shake hands with him, even though she couldn't completely forgive him, now or ever. But she managed to force a smile.

At that moment Whip returned from the stable. Aware of the tension in the air, he quietly poured himself a mug of cider, raised it in a silent toast and drank.

Sam Brentwood was one man Claudia would never forget. Some day she might even enjoy telling the story of his incredible naiveté.

Sam sniffed the contents of the jug, then shook his head. "If it isn't too much trouble, Mrs. Humphries, I'd rather have milk or tea, or just ordinary water."

"You don't drink, Mr. Brentwood?"

"I can't, ma'am. Liquor doesn't agree with me, and I always used to feel sorry after it made me do such damn-fool things, so I gave it up."

Claudia was both astonished and pleased by his candor, and as she went to the wood-burning stove for the teakettle she softened a trifle her hostility toward him. "I'm aware of the problem," she heard herself saying. "It was drink that killed my husband."

Sam's nod was grave. "It's rotten medicine for those who can't handle it. My friend Mike Holt here can drink any ten men under the table, but after just a swallow or two I wouldn't rightly remember my own name."

She handed him a cup of tea, then decided to pour one for herself. He was younger than she'd realized, and his honesty was refreshing. "You have courage."

"No, ma'am, common sense. It's like my bad hip. Pretending it's all right doesn't make the stiffness go away." He ate slowly, savoring his food. "This is fine bread. You must have baked it today."

It was Claudia's turn to be frank. "My sister made it. I always had a hired girl to do my cooking for me."

"Sam is one of the best cooks there is," Whip said. "Maybe he'll give you lessons on the trail."

"Sure." Sam looked at her and smiled.

All the circumstances that Claudia disliked about the coming journey flashed before her vision. "If I have my way," she said, speaking with almost explosive intensity, "I'll never learn to cook anything!"

The two men exchanged glances, and Whip raised an eyebrow.

"You're aiming to spend your time just riding in the wagon with the Van Ayls?"

"Certainly not! I'm traveling in my own wagon."

Sam ran a hand through his graying hair. "Who's going to drive it for you?"

"I'll drive myself, naturally," she said with contempt. "I've been handling horses all my life, and I assure you I'll feel safer if I'm holding the reins than if Otto van Ayl is sitting on the boards."

"Well, now," was all Sam could manage.

Whip wanted to laugh, but thought better of it. Independent-thinking women were troublemakers, and he was relieved that he wouldn't be on hand during the first part of the trip. Sam Brentwood would have his hands full with this ornery widow.

"I appreciated your honesty when you told me about your drinking, Mr. Brentwood," Claudia said, "so I'll return the compliment. The only reason I'm going west is because I have no choice. I hate the whole prospect. I don't care about farming. I have no interest in seeing uninhabited country and I loathe the very thought of traveling through the wilderness."

Sam patted the dog, who was stretched out on the floor between them, as he tried to absorb what she said. "When you take the right precautions," he said, "there isn't too much to fear in the wilderness, ma'am."

"Who said anything about fear?" Claudia was scornful. "I don't like being uncomfortable, that's all."

If she were to come face to face with a cougar in the Rocky Mountains, he thought, the beast's instinct would prompt it to flee. "Are you taking this dog?"

"Quincy goes everywhere with me. We look after each other." Claudia stopped short of saying that she and the shepherd, as a team, were self-sufficient.

Sam Brentwood was far more sensitive to the feelings of others than most of his acquaintances realized. He understood precisely what this high-minded young woman was saying, and he decided to clear the air immediately rather than wait until complications developed. "You say you know horses, ma'am, so I'm sure you realize they do their best work when a team pulls together."

She waited warily. She had no idea what he was trying to tell her.

"The reason I'm making this haul for Mr. Astor and the others," Sam said, "is because I'm an old friend of Jed Smith's, so I couldn't rightly refuse when he and Andy Jackson asked me to do it."

Claudia had no use for President Jackson or any of his rough crew.

"Being a wagonmaster makes me responsible for everybody in the party," he continued, and there was no humor now in his pale eyes, "but they're responsible to me, too. It's a mighty long way from here to the Missouri River. Fifteen hundred miles as the crow flies. And we aren't crows, so we'll be doing some extra meandering. The only way we'll get there is if we all work together in harness."

She wished Quincy would stop inching closer to the man. "Just what are you trying to tell me, Mr. Brentwood?"

"Nobody, including me, is going to hold a gun to your head and make you roast a side of beef, Mrs. Humphries," he said. "If you don't like cooking that's your right, and I reckon there'll be plenty of ladies in the train who'll be glad to cook for us all. But you'll still be given chores to do, I can promise you."

She bristled.

He went on quickly, before she could reply. "Quincy will have his jobs, too." Smiling to remove the sting from his words, he scratched the shepherd behind the ears.

Claudia made no comment. Neither this man nor anyone else could force her to do anything against her will, but she saw no need to make an issue of it before she learned what he meant by chores. There was no sound in the kitchen but the slow, steady thumping of the dog's tail on the floor.

The tension was still thick when Otto and Cathy van

Ayl returned home a short time later, Otto struggling with a satchel so heavy he could scarcely carry it. He was delighted to see the newcomers. Placing the satchel within easy reach, he peppered them with questions about the upcoming journey.

Cathy, always shy in the presence of strangers, finally asked a question of her own. "How soon will we leave?"

Whip Holt hadn't been able to take his eyes off her. She was far prettier than her sister, he thought, and a good deal softer, with no arrogance in her. How unusual that such a lovely girl should be married to such an old man. "It all depends on how soon you're ready to go," he said. "Have you stretched your canvas over your wagons yet?"

"We have the wood for it," Otto said. "Good, seasoned willow. But we want the covers to be waterproof, so we've been waiting for you to show us what to do."

"That shouldn't take more than a couple of hours," Sam said, "and if you stash away your gear tonight you'll just have your mattresses to throw in tomorrow morning. That way, we can get an early start."

"There's no need for that," Claudia said. "The Orient Point ferryboat sails once a week, and leaves tomorrow at noon. It'll take us across Long Island Sound to New London, and from there we can take the road to Albany."

Sam was startled by her commanding words, and he wondered if he was actually the wagonmaster of the train. Unfortunately, her advice was sensible. That'll give you more time to pack all the things you have here."

"Most of them will be left behind," Cathy said. "We sold them as part of the property."

Otto explained. "I figured it would be wrong to take more than we need, and there's just so much can be squeezed into a wagon. So I took cash instead, which I always prefer."

Claudia showed the guests to the room they would occupy that night, as Cathy began to prepare the last meal she would cook under this roof. Otto took his satchel outdoors.

Whip Holt returned to the kitchen. "I thought you might need some help, Mrs. van Ayl," he said.

Cathy blushed deeply. This hard-bitten giant had fascinated her from the first moment she'd seen him, and she was astonished that anyone so masculine should offer to help her out in the kitchen.

Whip smiled, aware of her confusion. "Suppose I scrub these potatoes for you. Then, after your fire dies down a mite, I'll start roasting the beef. And don't open those jars of pickled onions and beets. They pack easy and they'll keep on the road, so take them with you."

Cathy accepted his help with a quick, shy smile. Otto never did anything for her other than chop firewood and bring it into the kitchen. She even pumped her own water.

Whip worked efficiently and rapidly. He wasted no time, but didn't seem to be rushing.

"You're a very good helper," she said.

"When a man spends as much time on the trail as I have, traveling through the mountains all the way to the Pacific, he learns to make do for himself."

She had no right to question him. Still, she was curious. "It must be a lonely life," she ventured.

Whip shrugged. "It's the only life I know. Besides, no wife would want to live on the trail. Some day, if I get the wandering fever out of my blood, then maybe I'll settle down. I love it out there. There's no place on earth like the Oregon country." His eyes shone.

"I hope I like it as much as you do," Cathy said.

"Nobody can help liking it," he assured her. "The mountains are high as the Rockies, with snow on the peaks the year 'round. Forests stretch out far as human eyes can see, and they're filled with game. You can blame near scoop salmon and trout out of the rivers with your bare hands, and the water is the purest and best tasting there is."

"Aren't the Indians dangerous?"

"Not if you treat them right. They're willing to share the country with us if we don't cheat and steal from them."

He sounded so casual about Indians that her fears were somewhat allayed. The presence of Whip Holt would be comforting in dangerous territory. Though she didn't share Claudia's distaste for the new adventure, she would have been content to remain on Long Island, in spite of her dreary life there and their lack of friends.

"Here, let me attend to that," Whip said. As he took the roast from her, their hands touched.

Her whole body tingled. She felt as though a jolt of electricity had shot through her, a reaction as startling as it was sudden. She realized that she was strongly

52

attracted to this stranger, and the discovery horrified her.

Whip was feeling unusual stirrings, too. He had lived with an Indian girl in the mountains, and occasionally he'd paid brief visits to prostitutes, but he'd never before been drawn to a lady. But there was something special about Cathy van Ayl, and an unexpected magnetism was surely at work.

She was feminine and desirable—but she was also a married woman, and so beyond his reach, no matter that her husband was a cantankerous old goat. She was still the man's wife, and he had to respect her position. He'd known hunters and trappers who boasted of fooling around with other men's wives, but they filled him with contempt. Though he could kill when necessary with neither guilt nor remorse, he knew he could never live with himself if he took unfair advantage of a young lady's innocence and trust.

Edging away as he placed the meat on the fire, he was glad he'd be leaving the party in a few weeks' time, once Sam had the group well organized. By the time he rejoined them on the Missouri River next fall, he should have the proper rein on his feelings.

"While supper is cooking," he said, "maybe I can help your husband cover his wagon."

"I'll show you the way to the barn," Cathy said, taking care not to look directly at him again.

Otto van Ayl was hammering boards into place on the floor of his wagon as they joined him. He seemed to be taken aback. Whip curbed the impulse to watch her as Cathy returned to the house, and forced himself to concentrate on bending the willow rods and fastening them to the sides of the wagon in a shape that resembled a horseshoe. Otto observed him, then went to work with a vengeance, too.

As Whip nailed the struts into place he wondered why Van Ayl had been so upset as they entered the barn. Real fear had been on his face, yet he'd only been engaged in an ordinary chore, securing loose floorboards. That task was still unfinished as he worked on the stays.

All at once it dawned on Whip that there was something different about the floor of this wagon. He didn't want to seem suspicious, but when he stepped back from the wagon to inspect his own handiwork, Whip examined the boards more carefully. Suddenly he knew.

This wagon had double flooring. An entire new floor had been placed over the original base. This was odd, particularly since there seemed to be a space three or four inches deep between the two floors. Pondering as he went back to putting the hoops in place, Whip noticed the satchel that Van Ayl had carried from the house. It was open now, and a quick glance told Whip that it was empty.

All at once, Whip knew what had happened: the farmer had built a second, false floor in order to hide his valuables between them. A man had the right to protect his property in any way he saw fit, but Whip concluded that Van Ayl was being foolish. Wagons were fragile. They could be smashed or otherwise wrecked on the long journey across the continent. A favorite trick of Plains Indians was to shoot flaming arrows into the carts of trappers, and it was likely they'd use the same technique against covered wagons. Not only would Van Ayl's wagon be burned to the ground, any paper money hidden in it would go up in smoke, too.

What Van Ayl had done was none of Whip's business. If he elected to conceal his fortune—large or small —that was his own concern. But the way he'd chosen to hide it was so foolhardy, Whip figured it would be a disservice to remain silent.

"Mr. van Ayl," he said, taking a deep breath, "you're making a big mistake. This double flooring doesn't give you anywhere near the protection you think it does."

Otto van Ayl was shocked. "You've seen what I put underneath?"

Whip nodded. "Your wagon could break down, or be destroyed, or bust up on a river crossing, or burn to bits. And that could mean the end of your money."

The older man became agitated. "I've spent a long time planning how to make my wagon the way I want it. And there's no better way to protect what I've put in there."

"You're wrong," Whip said. "Sam Brentwood has ordered a special wagon that we're going to be picking up in a few days. It'll hold everything: ammunition, firearms, spare wagon parts and harnesses. Emergency food supplies, too. It's so solid and so heavy it'll need a team of four horses to pull it. Talk to Sam. I'm sure he'll let you keep your money in that wagon. It will be safer there than anywhere else."

Van Ayl wasn't convinced. "All that stands between

me and starvation," he said, "is what I've spent my whole life saving. If you think I'm going to trust it to a man I just met today, you're crazy!"

Whip shrugged. "Hellfire, Mister, it's your money. Do what you please. I was just trying to help."

Van Ayl turned on him. "You were snooping. That's what you were doing."

It was difficult, but Whip managed to control his temper.

"You've got to promise me something," Van Ayl said.

"What's that?"

"Don't tell anybody what you've seen."

Whip nodded, but made a mental note to reveal to Sam Brentwood what he had just learned. The wagon-master had the right to know everything of importance about his train. Furthermore, President Jackson had warned Sam to expect trouble on the long journey—and to prepare for it. Sam wouldn't need any extra complications.

"Most of all," Otto van Ayl added, "I don't want my wife or her sister to know."

It was impossible for Whip to hide his surprise.

"My wife is so young and giddy, she'd spend every last penny if she knew I had it."

Whip had judged Cathy van Ayl to be as sensible as she was pretty. Nothing about her indicated a giddy nature.

"If I let her have money, it would seep through her fingers like water." The farmer's eyes gleamed, and his mouth was small and tight.

Studying him, Whip Holt couldn't help deciding that Van Ayl was a miser.

"Promise me you won't say a word to Cathy!"

Whip was disgusted. "I promise." It wasn't enough that such a young, attractive woman was married to a man old enough to be her father, she was also married to a miser. Whip couldn't help sympathizing with Cathy van Ayl. Because she was the kind of girl he had always wanted to marry, he couldn't refrain from wanting to help her. Then he told himself to mind his own business. Cathy was a married woman, and that was that.

III

A raw March wind ruffled the chilly, blue-green waters of Long Island Sound, and there was no hint of spring in the air. Claudia could have told Sam Brentwood that winter was inclined to linger longer here, but she preferred to volunteer no information whatsoever to a know-it-all.

Sam's thoughts as he stood on the deck of the ferry would have surprised her. He reflected that Long Island, New England and many other parts of the United States were remarkably similar. Most houses and shops here were one or two stories high, made of clapboard and whitewashed—just as they were in the Ohio Valley. Which, come to think of it, had been settled by New Englanders.

"What town is this?" Sam asked, as the ferry drew close to the shore. "New Haven?"

Claudia's reply was lofty. "New Haven," she said, "is a city of twenty-five thousand people. This happens to be New London, which has only ten thousand."

Sam grunted his thanks and turned away from her. In spite of his good intentions, he wasn't sure he could tolerate this lofty lady with such exquisite manners— plus the cosmetics smeared on her face. Just once he'd like to scrub away all her makeup.

Feeling his eyes on the back of her head, Claudia automatically stiffened. If he touched her again, she told herself, she'd hit him twice as hard. Some men understood nothing but physical violence.

"This is New London, folks!" the ferry operator called, throwing a line to his mate on the dock.

They came ashore at the foot of State Street, the main thoroughfare. Sam, dressed now in the buckskins that would be his uniform on the journey, organized the line of march.

He placed Whip at the head of the column. The "train," this early in the trip, consisted of only two wagons. Otto and Cathy's was first, with Claudia's close behind them. Sam, his rifle in a sling and a pistol in his belt, moved constantly from the front of the column to the rear, then back to the front again.

"When we get a dozen wagons or more," he explained, "we've got to be ready for problems every minute of the day. Wheels will fall off and axles will break. Then we've got to stop the whole wagon train until it gets fixed. Later on, I'll find some riders to spell me, but till I do I'll oversee things myself, and there's no better time to start than now."

The man was conscientious. Claudia had to admit that. Although she was still smarting over his initial insult, she had to admit that he was now the soul of

courtesy. Perhaps he wasn't as common as she'd supposed. Perhaps he'd simply made a mistake. Still, she
couldn't picture him at a New Haven dinner table with
her friends. He simply wouldn't fit in, and she told
herself she wasn't being snobbish in feeling so.

Claudia looked around her. New London was Connecticut's principal seaport, with merchant ships from
many nations in the harbor. But if its inhabitants were
accustomed to strange, foreign sights, they lived none-
theless in a staid New England community, and the
pioneers had created an immediate stir. The two covered wagons were unlike any vehicles the townspeople
had ever seen.

A man fishing from the wharf called out, "Where
you heading?"

"Oregon," Sam replied.

Oregon! That single word had a galvanizing effect.
Onlookers poured out of State Street shops and mar-
kets, as all the windows in the buildings along the street
were opened and occupants leaned out to watch the
little procession.

For the wagon train was an indication of what was
to come. Thanks to the publicity generated by newspaper advertisements, everyone in town knew about
the expedition to the far Pacific. And a boy in his teens
expressed the wish of many of his elders when he
called out wistfully, "Take me with you!"

Harnesses creaked and wheels clattered as the ungainly wagons bounced on the cobblestones. Small
children ran alongside, peering at the occupants, whose
progress was further impeded by barking dogs. Whip,
already proceeding at a crawl, had to slow the minia-

ture caravan to a snail's pace on the half-mile ride to the head of State Street. Well-wishers called out their greetings:

"God bless you!"

"Have a safe journey!"

"May God ride with you!"

Claudia smiled and waved. It was exciting. She remembered as a child seeing President James Madison passing through town in a carriage. He, too, had smiled and waved.

Several young men, entering into the spirit of the occasion, mounted their horses and escorted the little procession out of town for several miles. When the bolder blades tried to flirt, Claudia maintained an aloof but pleasant attitude. Cathy was enjoying herself thoroughly.

Cathy's attitude changed abruptly, however, when one of the men called out, "Ask your Pa if I can court you, honey!" Otto spoke to her in an angry undertone, and thereafter she stared straight ahead, pretending to disregard the playful young men.

At first, they averaged almost twenty-five miles a day, a speed Sam said was miraculous. "Once we start adding new folks," he said, "we'll do well to make ten miles a day."

Quincy had taken to Sam. Ordinarily Claudia trusted her dog's judgment, but it irritated her that Quincy could accept this boor as a friend. Of course no dog could be expected to discern the refinements that a lady found attractive in a man.

One afternoon they halted for the day around 4:00 near the bank of a wooded lake. Each night, Sam insisted they make camp near water, and he always made certain there were woods nearby. Firewood and water, Claudia learned, were essentials. No wagon train could do without them.

As Whip fished in the lake, Otto gathered firewood and Cathy began to cook supper. Before Sam went to join Whip, he took time to speak to Claudia. "Seeing you don't plan to do any cooking, you can fetch the water."

Claudia was tired, but she knew it was only fair to do her part. She bit back a retort and accepted the tasks in silence. Thereafter, both morning and night, she transported the water. After several days her muscles hardened and she found that she could comfortably carry two buckets at the same time. She found a grim satisfaction in performing her tasks. Sam Brentwood, she felt, had deliberately humiliated her by assigning her to such a demeaning task, and she wouldn't forgive him for it.

Quincy's preference for the wagonmaster annoyed her, and one day she tried to break the animal of his new attachment. But for the first time Quincy refused to obey her, and she was forced to leave the dog be. At night, however, Quincy continued to sleep at the entrance to Claudia's wagon, guarding her. Then, even Sam might have encountered problems had he chosen to come near, but he took care to keep his distance. Clearly the austere wagonmaster, polite to a fault, was atoning for his initial error. In spite of herself, Claudia couldn't help wishing he would sometimes forget the rift between them and treat her like a woman.

The caravan continued to attract the same kind of

attention it had received in New London. Claudia got most of the attention and although she knew it was her own fault she stubbornly refused to change her ways. She continued to use rouge and kohl, partly out of habit and partly, she privately admitted, to defy Sam Brentwood.

Her clothes, as she well knew, were totally unsuitable for the journey. Her dresses, made of silk, linen and broadcloth—some of them lace-trimmed, some requiring full petticoats—were all wrong. Eventually, she knew, she'd have to buy cotton and muslin and make herself some more suitable dresses.

She was in no rush, however. Sooner or later, she'd cure Sam Brentwood of his mistaken belief that anyone who wore such clothes was a strumpet. The memory of her initial encounter with him continued to annoy her.

She quickly developed the habit of wearing a broad-brimmed, feathered hat on the road. When they'd been made for her, these hats were intended for far more formal occasions—a reception given by the Governor of Connecticut or perhaps a tea in honor of a distinguished visitor to Yale College. But Claudia had discovered that the hats protected her face from the sun, and she wore one each day. It didn't matter to her in the least that they were unsuitable for travel by covered wagon. And although any passerby who cared to assume she was a pioneer was entitled to that opinion, Claudia knew better. She despised Otto van Ayl for forcing her to make this interminable journey into the unknown.

She was worried about Cathy, who seemed as interested in Whip Holt as he was in her. Not that she could blame her sister. Holt was personable, quiet-spoken and respectful, a gentleman, in fact, even though he earned his living as a hunter and guide. If anyone was to blame it was Papa, who, when he'd given her in marriage to Otto van Ayl, had thought only in terms of Cathy's financial security. Otto, with his narrow opinions and avariciousness, cared no more for Cathy than for any of his other possessions, and Cathy was starved for affection.

Holt didn't appear to be the kind of man who would take advantage of her situation, but there was always the possibility that, sooner or later, he'd give in to temptation. Claudia didn't trust any man. And she hated to think what Otto might do if his wife became involved with another man. Cathy was his property, to be treated as he saw fit, and Claudia didn't doubt that he would sell her into indentured service if she was unfaithful.

But for the present, at least, Claudia preferred not to interfere. A candid talk with Cathy could wait. Holt had indicated he'd be leaving the caravan soon, and Claudia hoped he'd go before he became too involved with Cathy. Meanwhile she was keeping watch over them, feeling apprehensive every time she saw them exchange quick, guilty glances. It was astonishing that Otto remained unaware of what was developing. Claudia could only assume that he was too full of self-satisfaction, now that his dream of going west was coming true.

When they reached Albany, Sam led his small train straight to the U.S. Army depot located on the banks of the Hudson River. His own special wagon, built according to his specifications, was waiting there. Long and heavy, it needed four sets of wheels instead of two. Its baseboards were made of weathered oak, in order to carry the greatest weight.

Andrew Jackson had given orders—since confirmed by Martin Van Buren, who had now taken office as President—that the wagonmaster was to be given the supplies he needed. Rifles, pistols, gunpowder and shot took up the least space. Spare wheels, axles, tools and harnesses were bulky, as were the barrels of salt fish and smoked meat, ordinarily used as Army rations, that would be kept for emergency use in the event the wagon train ran out of food. There were spare pots and skillets, too, as well as spades, shovels, other tools and many coils of rope. Sam Brentwood was preparing for any emergency.

He carefully inspected the team of four work horses that would pull the special supply wagon, and had a long talk with Abe Ellis, the hired driver. A taciturn, middle-aged man with a wife and children in Albany, Ellis was making the trip only for the wages. As soon as a member of the expedition could replace him, he would return to his family. In his younger days he had made two trips by wagon to the Ohio Valley and a third to Tennessee, where he had been captured and tortured by Cherokees. Two fingers of his left hand were missing as a result of that experience. He loathed all Indians.

"When I see one of them bastards," he said, "I shoot."

Sam knew Ellis would have to be replaced before they reached Indian country. Most Indians who lived

66

east of the Mississippi River had been tamed, but they were still dangerous when provoked, and Ellis seemed just the sort of man who could do the provoking. But Ellis would be fine for the first part of the journey. He was solid and reliable, and he knew horses. The special wagon would be in good hands.

They spent two days in Albany while the wagon was loaded under Sam's careful supervision. Claudia, who had little to do, spent most of her time wandering about the town. She was not impressed. Albany should have had something of the flavor of New Haven, even the excitement of New York and Philadelphia, but it didn't.

There were warehouses on the waterfront and a number of small factories operating here and there, but the atmosphere was rural rather than urban. Farmers brought their wares into a large, open-air market, ignoring the snowbanks that hadn't yet melted.

Late in March the pioneers left town and started westward toward Syracuse. They had hardly reached the outskirts of Albany, however, when they saw a wagon awaiting them at the crossroads. As Sam called a halt, a rider in buckskins raced toward the caravan on a gelding.

Claudia, whose wagon had been given first place for the day, observed the slender young man with reddish-gold hair, a rifle across the pommel, bend low in the saddle as he galloped. Not until the youth reined in his gelding did Claudia realize, with a shock, that the rider was a girl.

"I'm Mrs. Mell," the young woman said, almost stumbling over the unaccustomed "Mrs." Smiling to cover her self-consciousness, she added, "Tonie Mell."

Tony was a man's name. Claudia stared at her, disliking this tomboy on sight. She had to admit, however, that the girl's figure beneath her buckskins was very trim. She wore no cosmetics, and her hair was absurdly short.

"How do." Sam and Whip spoke at once.

"How do," Tonie replied. This time the broad grin was genuine. These two men were her kind of people. "I'm a widow," she said, hating herself for the role she was playing. "I've read about this expedition, and I'd like to join you. I want to start a new life."

Sam passed immediate judgment. "Welcome," he said, and introduced the girl to the others. Then, as they started forward toward her waiting team and wagon, he asked casually, "You come from out West?"

"Uh-huh." Tonie was deliberately vague, as she'd been ordered.

"What part of Missouri do you hail from?" Sam said.

"Who says I come from Missouri?"

"No need to say so," he replied. "I can tell it from your accent."

Tonie realized it would be dangerous to dissemble. "Independence. I grew up there."

Sam nodded pleasantly. He assigned her a place at the rear of the train, behind the special wagon. Anyone who could ride as she did was a valuable addition to the party. He suspected she might even know how to use the rifle she carried. In any case, he felt at ease with her; a girl who had grown up on the frontier could be helpful in many ways.

Tonie climbed onto her wagon, her gelding walking beside it on a long lead. It had been absurdly easy to join the train. She hadn't been forced to show any of the false documents the Russian Legation had prepared.

She was deeply ashamed of deceiving these people. Except for the high-nosed blonde in the silk dress, who looked as though she was on her way to a garden party, the pioneers seemed to be decent and honorable people. How would they act if they found out her true purpose in joining them?

She knew well enough what Sam Brentwood and Whip Holt would do. She'd known many men like them. Her instinct told her that Brentwood could be cold-bloodedly ruthless if the occasion demanded. He'd put a bullet through her head if he found out she was a traitor to the United States. Well, that would be one way to end her misery, not that she wanted such a drastic solution. She hated the assignment she'd been given, but she didn't want to die.

As always, her common sense came to her rescue, restoring her natural sense of balance. Anyone who'd lived for years at the edge of the wilderness was by nature a pragmatist. Each day had to be lived for its own sake. It was pointless to worry about tomorrow when tomorrow might never come—thanks to Indian raids or natural catastrophe. With luck, Tonie reflected, she might yet find some way to resolve her terrible dilemma.

Late that afternoon Sam called a halt in a pleasant stretch of woods beside a swift-moving river. As Tonie unhitched her work horses and let them browse, she noted with amusement that the uppity blonde was already fetching water from the stream. It was good to know that her ladyship didn't think she was above a little hard work.

Mounting her gelding, Tonie rode forward to where the men were standing. "Sam," she said, "I'm going to exercise my horse for a spell. He gets restless if he doesn't work up a sweat. While I'm about it, maybe I could bring us back some supper."

Sam's level gaze was thoughtful as he looked up at her. There was no time like the present to see if she could like up to the promise of her background and appearance. "Do that," he said.

Tonie cantered off into the woods.

Sam knew one thing: She sure as hell could ride. He helped Whip erect some crude barriers to prevent the horses from straying off into the woods. Then, as he started back to the camp, he saw Claudia walking ahead of him carrying two buckets of water. She moved easily, with no apparent strain, and he realized how much stronger she had already become. Although she still kept her distance, she no longer acted as though she suspected he might pounce on her at any moment, and that was an improvement. His basic faith in human nature, essential to anyone who lived in the wilderness, made him hope that she would some day be willing to bury the hatchet. Perhaps a friendly gesture might speed that day. He caught up with her and relieved her of one of the buckets.

"That's very kind of you," she said.

"Just don't let it spoil you, ma'am," he replied with a grin.

Claudia changed the subject. "Who's the new girl?"

"We'll find out soon enough. I don't rightly know her yet myself." Sam nodded in the direction of a flock of geese, flying low in formation northward. "Damnation! A goose or two cooked over the fire would have been tasty tonight."

They heard the crack of a rifle in the distance.

"Could be," Sam said, placing the buckets on the ground near the kettles, "we'll find out about Tonie Mell sooner than I thought."

Claudia noted that he was already calling the tomboy by her first name. When they heard another rifle crack ten minutes later, Sam said, "I reckon she missed those geese."

In a quarter of an hour, Tonie rode calmly into camp. Hanging from her saddle were a large wild turkey and a plump goose. In a natural, offhand way, she handed both birds to the wagonmaster. "Here's supper," she said.

Rejoicing inwardly, Sam nodded. "Not bad shooting," he said.

"Not too bad," she replied. "Here, let me get them ready for the fire. Easterners don't know how to cook wild fowl and that can ruin the flavor."

Watching the girl obliquely, Claudia decided she was too talented to be real. She certainly didn't know how to make herself attractive. And she certainly wasn't a lady.

Not that it mattered to people like Sam Brentwood, Claudia thought, immediately wondering why she should care what opinion he formed of anyone. He and

Whip Holt were primitives who wouldn't even know which fork to use at a dinner party. They were ignorant of the finer things in life.

Sam Brentwood was entitled to lead whatever life he chose. It was none of her business what he did. So why should she care? She had to admit that she was a little bit interested in the man, if for no other reason than to provide relief from the tedium of the journey.

Well, it was probably wrong to look back over her shoulder at the kind of life she had led in the past. Spring was in the air at last, and with the approach of a new season she could at least admire the scenery.

As the little train made its way through the forests of central New York, approaching Syracuse, the trail was narrow, just wide enough for the wagons. The early spring wind filled the woods with the smells of the salt springs that were the basis of the growing prosperity of the town of Syracuse. These had been the hunting grounds of the Onondaga Indians for many generations.

The low-hanging tree branches forced Claudia to remove her hat, and she had to concentrate on her driving, keeping the horses on a tight rein. Her wagon had fallen a short distance behind the others. Quincy napped on the boards beside her, tired after spending several hours keeping up with Brentwood's horse.

Suddenly one of the bay geldings shied violently. Quincy was on his feet in an instant, his ears erect, a low growl emanating from deep within him. Before Claudia could stop him the dog leaped to the ground. Only a few feet away, she saw a wild boar emerging from the underbrush. It was a hideous-looking beast at least three feet high and weighing more than two hundred and fifty pounds, with tiny red eyes and short, bristling hair. The shepherd was poised to attack.

"Quincy! Come back here!"

Claudia was terrified. Her dog was no match for an animal with the speed and power of the boar.

The dog paid no attention. The boar lowered its head to charge. Claudia jumped to the ground. Somehow she had to protect her pet.

The wild boar turned to face his new adversary. Quincy pulled up short and began to bark, the sound making the boar even more aware of its danger.

As Claudia looked into the small, evil eyes she realized she had nothing to protect herself with, not even a knife. She knew Quincy would attack for her sake, but he'd be killed for his gallantry, and she herself would be helpless.

Instead of charging, the boar began to inch slowly toward Claudia, obviously hoping to draw near enough for a final charge before the dog attacked him. For the first time in her life Claudia was so frightened her mind went blank. In trying to save her dog she'd condemned them both to death.

All at once the boar charged. Two hundred and fifty pounds of furious wild animal hurtled toward Claudia. At that instant, a shot broke the silence, and the boar seemed to rise several feet into the air before crumpling to the ground, a bullet hole in its chest. Quincy continued to growl, even though the beast was dead.

For a moment, Claudia was so weak that she thought she might faint, but she managed to compose herself.

Sam Brentwood approached her, his pistol still in his hand. "Reckon we'll be eating roasted pig for supper," he said in a calm voice.

Claudia's pride wouldn't permit her to thank him in so many words. But perhaps she could show her appreciation in some other way. "Under the circumstances," she said, trying to match his casual tone, "the least I can do is cook the meal." If Tonie Mell could cook supper, so could she.

Sam grinned at the young woman, stroking Quincy's head, quieting the dog. Nothing in his attitude indicated that she had capitulated to him. "We'll call an early halt for the day, then," he said. "Wild pig needs a lot of roasting before it gets tender enough to be tasty."

The man who joined the wagon train in the farm-market town of Syracuse, Henry St. Clair, was extraordinary. In his early thirties, solidly built and so handsome he was almost pretty, he wore clothes and boots tailor-made for him, he slept in a real bed fastened to the floorboards of his luxuriously appointed wagon and he carried an expensive, English-made rifle, chased silver scrollwork decorating its stock.

He'd read everything available about the explorations of the Rocky Mountains during the past decade, and he could discuss the customs of a dozen Indian nations west of the Mississippi River, none of whom he'd ever encountered. His larder was stocked with smoked hams and ox tongues, barrels of beef in brine and salt fish. And, to the astonishment of Sam Brentwood, he carried several cases of wine he'd imported from France.

"My life was so dull," he said, offering his only explanation for joining the caravan, "I wanted a bit of excitement."

Whip Holt was contemptuous of him, and scarcely bothered to conceal his reaction. Sam Brentwood, as always, kept his feelings to himself.

As a British agent with long experience in the arts of espionage and sabotage, St. Clair had no doubt of his ability to create incidents that would slow down the progress of the wagon train to a crawl. He was particularly interested in the special wagon, but he didn't want to act too soon. The caravan was still too close to the cities and Army depots, where precious supplies were easy enough to replace.

First, he had to learn the identity of his ally, the Russian agent. Methodically he went through the group. Sam Brentwood? Impossible. Whip Holt? Never. Tonie Mell, the girl who acted and dressed like a man? Laughable. All three were frontier dwellers, with boundless faith in the future of the United States.

Abe Ellis? Perhaps, but he seemed too ponderous, too slow a thinker. Agents, even those hired by the Russians, had to be mentally alert. Otto van Ayl was an unlikely candidate, too, and his pretty wife was too young, too inexperienced. Assuming the Russian representative had already joined the caravan, which wasn't necessarily the case, that left Claudia Humphries. She was sophisticated, alert, intelligent and certainly the most likely prospect. She deserved cultivation, but an experienced agent knew better than to move too rapidly. Subtlety and caution always paid dividends.

St. Clair was polite to the Van Ayls and courteous to

the guides and Tonie, but at mealtime he devoted himself almost exclusively to Claudia. He took delight in discussing Shakespeare's plays and Milton's poetry with her, and he could quote long passages from the Bible, reciting them with the dramatic gusto of an actor.

Claudia felt at home with him at once. He reminded her of professors she'd known at Yale. He was a man of erudition and refinement, and he added a new zest to the days on the trail, no matter that he was a trifle effete. But, she had no interest in him as a man. He rode behind her, and made a point of helping her carry water without neglecting his own duties of gathering firewood.

Claudia noted, however, that he wasn't assigned to sentry duty on the nights when they made camp far from any civilized community of consequence. This was a duty that only Sam and Whip shared. Did they lack confidence in Henry St. Clair? It was typical of men accustomed to danger to trust only their own kind. In any case, she didn't care. Henry, with whom she was already on a first-name basis, made the trip almost pleasant.

For example, he offered her delicacies from his larder. Her own taste in food was simple, but she took token portions so she wouldn't hurt his feelings. Occasionally when he opened a small bottle of wine at supper, she took a glass, not because she really enjoyed the taste but because she could see that her acceptance annoyed Sam Brentwood.

"Even in my drinking days," Sam said one evening, "I never could stomach that stuff."

"It's an acquired taste, I suppose," Henry replied politely, inhaling the aroma of his wine.

Whip had almost nothing to say to the newcomer, and Otto van Ayl seemed uncomfortable in his presence, too. Cathy dutifully avoided him. To Claudia's continuing distress, Cathy seemed to have eyes only for Holt.

Going south from Syracuse, they made their way into Pennsylvania, where they were scheduled to pick up newcomers in the rolling hill country west of Harrisburg. It was the height of spring; trees were budding and farmers were busily plowing, but Claudia was bored by the long days of jolting along in the wagon. Though her muscles were no longer sore, it was always a relief to stop for the night.

When Whip announced that he would be leaving them at their next stop, and going on alone, Claudia was relieved. He and Cathy exchanged so many looks at mealtime that Claudia found it difficult to pay attention to the conversation Henry St. Clair directed at her.

Sam wasn't familiar with this part of the country, and Whip was ignorant, too. But their instincts seemed unerring, and they always chose pleasant campsites. One or the other would go into the woods, as did Tonie, and come back with game. Or they caught fish or bagged ducks and geese returning north after the winter. Claudia had to concede that they were skilled in the ways of the outdoors, but they were also uncouth barbarians. Sam had saved her life, to be sure, but that didn't mean she had to be friendly with him.

Claudia was learning to appreciate fresh fish and

game. She was grateful for the hunting and fishing that provided relief from the monotony of their staples: flour, bacon, oatmeal and smoked ham, pickled beef and salt fish.

On their second night in Pennyslvania they stopped to make camp in a large clearing beside the shore of a small lake. The water was warm enough for a swim. The ladies had the privilege of going first, and both Claudia and Cathy enjoyed the luxury of soaking in the water for a long time. Tonie, who couldn't swim, bathed alone in a shallow area.

By the time they returned, the fire had been laid and lighted. As the women retired to their wagons to dress, the men trooped down to the water, Quincy following along.

Impulsively, Claudia opened one of her leather clothing boxes and changed into a frilly gown with eyelet lace at the collars and cuffs. Occasionally, she felt she owed it to herself to dress like a lady in something fine and frivolous.

She emerged from her wagon to find Cathy and a furious Tonie Mell tied together back to back on the ground. Before she could scream for help, strong hands grabbed her, a gag was stuffed into her mouth and she, too, was thrown to the ground.

Knowing she was helpless she made no struggle, but watched her captors carefully. There were five of them and they were thorough, two standing guard with drawn pistols on the path that led to the lake as the other three went through the wagons. All were rough, bearded men in shapeless linsey-woolsey. They searched the wagons quickly, displaying the expertise of professional thieves.

They knew better than to take either firearms or horses—both hanging offenses, and they paid no attention to clothing or other personal belongings. Claudia, her mind functioning in spite of her fear, could only pray that Quincy, who was with the men, would sense the danger and bark an alarm.

"I got something, Ned," one of the quintet called. "This here wagon has a false bottom."

Two of his companions joined him without delay, and in a few moments Claudia heard the sound of floorboards being wrenched up. There were muted shouts of delight, and soon the three men emerged, stuffing gold coins into their pockets. They had found even more than they hoped for, and all five men lost no time in leaving.

"Thanks for the hospitality, girls," one of them said. "We'd show you some real lovin', but we got to clear out before your menfolk come back." Then they vanished into the forest.

Claudia tried to free herself, to work the gag out of her mouth. Her failure only increased her frenzy. The wait for the men's return seemed interminable, and she had no way of judging whether five minutes or a quarter of an hour passed before Quincy came running into the clearing, then raced back toward the lake, barking furiously.

Sam Brentwood was first to arrive, running quickly in spite of his stiff hip. He took one look at the women, then hastily slashed their bonds and removed the gags.

Cathy was weeping hysterically. Claudia didn't wait to be questioned as the men crowded around her.

"We've been robbed by five men. They took off that way." She pointed toward the woods. "They found the false floor in Otto's wagon and stole a lot of money."

Otto van Ayl ran to his wagon. When he saw what had happened, his face went deathly pale. "I had four thousand dollars hidden away," he said, his voice shaking. "I can't tell how much they took."

"Were the men mounted?" Sam asked.

"They had to be." Tonie's anger made her inarticulate.

"They may have left their horses somewhere else," Claudia added, "because they left on foot."

Sam picked up his rifle. "Let's go," he said to Whip. "We'll start off on foot, and come back for our horses only if we have to. No, Tonie! You stay here!"

"I'm coming with you," Henry St. Clair said. He ran to his wagon to get his expensive English rifle.

Sam and Whip were somewhat surprised, but wasted no time arguing with him. They expected no real help from him, but saw no point in trying to stop him. They rushed to the woods. Henry followed them at a run.

Claudia made no attempt to recall Quincy, who had followed Sam Brentwood. She tried to console Cathy and Otto, who sat on a fallen log, dazed, his trembling hands covering his face.

Sam Brentwood had taken the lead, with Quincy at his heels. There was just enough daylight left so he could read signs that were invisible to most men. A broken twig here, a footprint on matted grass there, told him all he needed to know. He moved so swiftly that Henry St. Clair, bringing up the rear, had to hurry.

Henry noted that his companions moved quietly as

they moved forward through the woods, and he tried to emulate them, but the task was too much for him. In spite of his long experience as an agent, the deep forests of America demanded special techniques. Twigs snapped under his feet, and once he tripped on a hidden tree root, causing Whip Holt to glare at him over his shoulder. He was doing his best, St. Clair reflected, and they shouldn't expect more than that.

Daylight gradually faded, but Sam seemed to have night vision that was extraordinary, and kept on the trail. Sometimes he paused, crouched low and placed his ear to the ground. Then he nodded, sprang to his feet and started forward again, the arthritis in his hip causing him no noticeable difficulty.

Henry assumed he could hear the robbers' footfalls on the earth and marveled at the man's talents. Some day, he thought, he'd have to persuade Brentwood to teach him the trick.

"We're gaining," Sam said in a low voice after one such pause. After his next halt he merely pointed through the trees. Whip nodded. Both men cocked their rifles and Holt unwound his ever-present bullwhip from his waist. Henry moved forward warily, doing his utmost to make no noise. When a low growl was heard from Quincy, Sam put a hand on the dog's head, and the animal appeared to understand, becoming silent.

Sam and Whip seemed to communicate silently. Sam and Quincy began to make a circle on the left and Holt did the same on the right. In the dark St. Clair could see that the dog's ears were erect; the robbers couldn't be far ahead.

St. Clair himself appeared to have been forgotten.

Uncertain which of the two men to follow, he walked forward in a straight line.

It was so dark that he almost stumbled on the robbers before he realized how close they were. They had paused to rest briefly in a small clearing. Three of them were sitting on the ground, as the two others leaned against a tree. It occurred to St. Clair that his companions might be using him as a decoy, although he couldn't understand how they could have planned it without talking. The robbers, realizing a stranger had blundered into their midst, cocked their weapons.

Henry froze.

Then the bullwhip sang through the air and wrapped itself around one man, pinning his arms to his sides and causing him to drop his pistol, as he screamed in pain. He was jerked off his feet.

One of his companions caught sight of Whip Holt and raised his pistol, intending to shoot him. But Henry St. Clair came to life, his rifle spoke, and the man dropped to the ground. Sam Brentwood fired at almost the same moment, and a third robber staggered and fell.

The remaining two men raised their hands above their heads.

"Drop your guns!" Sam called, coming into the clearing, a snarling Quincy beside him.

The brief struggle was ended. Two of the robbers were dead, the other three apprehended. Sam tied their hands behind their backs. Otto van Ayl's money was safe.

"There's a town up ahead," Holt said. "I reckon we can turn these vermin over to the constables there and let the undertaker come back for the bodies of their friends."

The three men were marched forward, Quincy staying close, ready to pounce if one of them tried to escape.

Sam clapped St. Clair on the shoulder and said, "You did all right."

IV

After the abortive robbery, Henry St. Clair enjoyed a new status. Sam Brentwood and Whip Holt accepted him as an equal, Otto van Ayl was grateful to him and sought his friendship, and Cathy became less shy in his presence. There was a significant change, too, in his relations with Claudia Humphries. More self-confident, less inclined to quote from the classics, he openly paid court to her. Her feelings toward him were unchanged, but she accepted his attentions. They helped to pass the time around the campfire.

Henry told them something of his background. "As a boy," he said, "I was sickly and spent most of my time reading. Then, as I grew older, I began to spend more time out of doors. I'm a good swimmer, if I do say so. I've hunted in Scotland and the Black Forest of Germany, and I fancy I'm not too bad a shot."

"Plenty good enough to take over from me," Sam

told him. "Tomorrow you can go out and bag our supper for us."

Otto van Ayl had counted and recounted his money before replacing it under the false flooring of his wagon. Sam still thought he was making a mistake. "Your fortune will be safer," he said, "if you pack it in a saddlebag and put it with your other belongings. That way it won't be so obvious. Or let me carry it in the special wagon for you."

Claudia was forced to agree with him. "That's true, Otto," she said. "It didn't take those robbers long to find that double flooring. Other people may notice it, too, and get curious."

But Otto stubbornly rejected their advice. "If you folks just keep your mouths shut, I'll have no problems. It was bad luck that the thieves found my hiding place, but it won't happen again. I'm going to build me a fine house and buy a dozen head of cattle when we get to the Oregon country. I can't take any chances of losing my money along the way."

After awhile, they spoke no more of it.

Late one afternoon, when they halted for the night, Henry surprised Claudia by inviting her to go with him while he hunted. Sam promptly intervened. "She'd tear her clothes to shreds on brambles," he said. "If she wants, we'll cure the hides of the next couple of deer we shoot, and she can make herself some proper hunting clothes. Meantime she'll need to learn how to shoot."

The idea of handling firearms, much less becoming a proficient shot, hadn't occurred to Claudia. But she had a reason for accepting the challenge, and she couldn't help looking at Tonie Mell, who was standing nearby.

Then Tonie made that challenge irresistible by laughing. Her meaning was obvious: it was ludicrous to think that the great lady could be taught how to shoot.

Claudia stiffened at the sound of that laugh, color flooding her face. Who did that half-girl, half-boy think she was, anyway? "I take it you're amused, Mrs. Mell," she said, her New England accent flatter than ever.

Tonie's temper flared, too. She realized it was dangerous to make an open enemy of anyone in the caravan. She knew she'd be wise to call as little attention to herself as possible. All the same, she had conceived an intense dislike for this woman who wore fancy clothes, made up her face and put on airs. Claudia Humphries had never been openly condescending to her, but the woman seemed to go out of her way to treat Sam Brentwood with a remoteness that verged on contempt. And here he was, making up to her.

"Mrs. Humphries," Tonie said in a Western drawl even thicker than usual, "some folks can do things that other folks can't. It's a wise woman who knows her own place."

Sam Brentwood observed the two women in astonishment. Even the debonair Henry St. Clair was surprised by the depth of feeling they both showed. Neither man understood why there should be bad blood between them, but Henry promised himself to remember it. Such hostility might turn out to—be useful.

"What *is* my place, Mrs. Mell?" Claudia demanded coldly.

Tonie's slow shrug was insulting.

Claudia turned quickly to Sam. "I very much appreciate your offer, Mr. Brentwood."

Tonie's smile broadened.

Sam knew he was caught in the middle of a tug-of-war between these two females. He wished he was back in the Rocky Mountains, stalking an elk. Women were beyond him. Claudia was so high-class he never knew quite what she was thinking, and although he felt far more at home with Tonie, she was far more complex than he'd imagined any one woman could be.

"I assume," Claudia said, "that you'll teach me how to shoot."

It had been the farthest thing from Sam's mind. As wagonmaster he had only tried to prevent a greenhorn from going hunting with Henry St. Clair, who should have known better than to ask her in the first place. Now, there was no graceful way to back out. Claudia was prickly enough already, and he knew he'd have his hands full even if he found some excuse to evade the responsibility she was thrusting at him.

"Sure, ma'am," he said, trying to express an enthusiasm he was far from feeling.

She realized he was less than happy. "When may I have my first lesson?"

"Right now, while Henry and Tonie here go off to find our supper."

Henry departed on foot, and Tonie rode off on her gelding without so much as a backward glance.

Sam led Claudia to a secluded spot, some distance from the camp. There he explained how his rifle functioned. Then he taught her the way to hold it. "Always keep it snug against your shoulder so the recoil doesn't knock you down," he said. "Take your time sighting and, when you fire, be sure you squeeze the trigger. Never jerk it."

He placed a pine cone on the stump of a fallen tree, moved a hundred feet away from it and showed her how to load the rifle, then told her to shoot.

Claudia sighted the cone down the long barrel, braced herself and squeezed the trigger. The explosion deafened her momentarily, and the acrid odor of burned gunpowder made her cough. What caused her the most chagrin, however, was the realization that the pine cone was still intact. "I want to try again," she said grimly.

Sam had thought it likely that she'd lose interest after firing one shot, and he was impressed by her determination. He showed her how to clean the rifle and reload.

After six shots she still hadn't hit the cone. "That target's too small," she said.

He took the weapon from her, reloaded with practiced ease and raised the rifle to his shoulder. Then he fired, and the pine cone was gone.

"If you can do it, so can I!" Claudia said angrily.

She was a real hellion, he thought. "I reckon you've had enough for one lesson," he said. "You're not afraid of firearms any more, and that's progress."

"I want to shoot again tomorrow," Claudia said.

He had underestimated her determination. Now she probably wouldn't be satisfied until she became an expert shot. She was more complicated than she seemed. Though she was pretty, spoiled and bad-tempered, there was more to her than that.

Whip Holt announced at breakfast the next morning that he was taking leave of the company immediately. "I've got me a hankering for the taste of elk liver," he said, "and the closest place I'll get any is the Rockies, so I'll be on my way. I'll see you next year in Missouri."

As he shook hands with each of them in turn, Claudia was almost sorry to see him leave. He was quiet and unassuming, although it was evident that he could be violent when the occasion demanded. But he was a lot less abrasive than Sam.

"Be careful, Mr. van Ayl," Whip said to Otto before turning to Cathy.

Their fingertips barely touched.

Claudia saw the sheen in her sister's eyes, and hoped no one else—least of all Otto—was aware of it. It was plain that Cathy had fallen in love.

"Take care of yourself, ma'am," Whip said. "I'll be counting the days and months till we meet again."

Claudia realized that he loved her. She felt sorry for both of them. Otto van Ayl didn't know what it meant to love anyone.

"Good-bye, Mr. Holt," Cathy said, her voice so low it was almost inaudible. "Don't take too many risks while you're off by yourself."

"I'll do my best, ma'am," Whip said, and walked to his horse. Sam joined him for a final, private word.

Then Cathy became furiously busy cleaning the breakfast dishes in the water Claudia had brought her. She didn't look up from her work until Whip Holt was gone.

Before they could break camp a new arrival unexpectedly joined them. In a small wagon drawn by a team of tired horses, he'd been trying for several days to catch up with the train. Today, he'd been traveling since long before daybreak.

At first glance Terence Malcolm wasn't much of an addition, and his story only confirmed his appearance. He was twenty years old, he said, and suffering from consumption. His doctor had told him he'd probably die within the year. So he'd sold his small property and answered the advertisement, because he wanted to see something of the West before he died and maybe even enjoy a share of adventure.

Claudia liked the expression in his eyes, and she was upset when Sam told the newcomer he'd take his admission under advisement.

As they began to break camp she approached the wagonmaster.

"You can't turn that boy away," she said. "It would be cruel."

Sam could barely restrain his anger. "Ma'am," he said, "I don't practice cruelty for its own sake. We're going to be joined by a great many people in the next couple of weeks, and it'll be hard enough to get them all working together. We can't afford to be slowed down by a boy who's suffering from consumption. It's my duty to think of everybody else."

"Mr. Malcolm can't be as weak as he looks," she replied. "Not if he's been alone on the road trying to catch up with us. Give him a chance, at least. There'll be time enough to drop him later on."

Sam held his tongue and agreed. It was easier than arguing.

Terence Malcolm was waiting for Claudia when she returned to her wagon. "I couldn't help hearing what you said," he told her, brushing his sandy-blond hair from his bright, watery eyes, "and I'm mighty grateful to you."

"Take your place in the line behind me," she said. "We don't have far to go today, because we're meeting some people from Pennsylvania and New Jersey. If you feel you're too tired to go on, just let me know. I'll find an excuse to stop for an hour or two."

Young Malcolm shook his head. "There's no way I'm going to drop out," he said, "not after all the weeks of planning and all the trouble I've gone through to get this far. I'm going to keep going if I have to pull my own wagon."

Claudia knew then that her original estimate had been right. "I know you'll make out fine," she said. "That's why I spoke up for you the way I did."

His quick grin told her she had won his friendship.

Sam Brentwood had to chuckle to himself when members of the company spoke of the Pennsylvania "mountains" in the vicinity of Harrisburg. Mountains, to him, meant the towering, snow-capped Rockies, some of them so high that, probably, no man had yet climbed them. All the same, he had to admit that the Pennsylvania terrain was rugged, and people who'd always lived on flat land had a right to call such high hills mountains.

The air had become balmier, though the nights were still chilly, and the brown grass of winter had vanished almost overnight, to be replaced by a delicate carpet of pale green that grew deeper each day. And the maple, oak and elm trees were in full leaf.

Spring was Sam's favorite season of the year. In spring, the whole world seemed to come alive. Wilderness creatures began to stir, moving swiftly through the underbrush. Fish were running again in swift-flowing streams, and flights of birds appeared overhead each day, heading north.

Sam was somewhat surprised to discover that Claudia Humphries, too, was sensitive to the changing season. He had convinced himself that the "great lady" was too absorbed in herself to be conscious of her surroundings. But that wasn't true. She was proving herself amazingly alert to the wonders of nature. Sam had always assumed that only those thoroughly familiar with the outdoors could appreciate such beauty.

Claudia was so contradictory he couldn't understand her. She was a snob, yet she went out of her way to be kind and genuinely friendly to people who would've been beneath her notice if she'd been living in a city. And it was just possible he was even getting used to her manner of dressing and her use of cosmetics. He had to admit that she was attractive. Secretly, he enjoyed the way she looked.

More important, she was neither flighty nor a flirt. He'd been wrong to conclude that she was like his mother. In all honesty he had to admit that he had only the vaguest recollections of the woman who'd walked out on him and his father.

She certainly had the ability to startle him. What exactly had prompted her sudden desire to learn how to shoot? Though he was still leery of her because her tongue was so sharp, he was willing to grant that she could make a mighty fine mate for the man who tamed her. Not that Sam wanted to be that man. He preferred a quiet, uncomplicated existence.

Having ridden through Harrisburg on his eastward journey he elected to give the place a wide berth now because he knew it was too cramped to allow the wagons easy passage. Avoid complications of all kinds, he told himself.

In mid-afternoon they arrived at an open field, where eight wagons were already camped. Some had been waiting several weeks for the arrival of the company, and the veterans of the train were greeted with cheers.

Sam smiled to himself when he saw the greenhorns' lack of organization. Their wagons were scattered all over the field, facing different directions. He'd teach them new procedures, beginning this very night.

There would now be fourteen wagons in the company, and a number of children, a very respectable train. Hereafter, they'd form a circle at the end of each day's ride, making them more secure in case robbers tried to isolate a single wagon. Later, after the train crossed the Missouri River, the circle would be essential to protect the company from Indian attacks. It was wise to teach the new travelers the right way to do things from the very beginning.

The cooking fires would be built inside the circle every evening. And after nightfall, no one would be permitted to wander beyond its circumference. The safety of each individual had to be the primary concern of the wagonmaster.

The addition of children to the company changed the whole nature of the adventure. Their sense of excitement raised the spirits of the adults. But the children made Sam's job more complicated. Wagon-train living was an experiment in cooperation. Even the children had tasks and responsibilities, and keeping out from underfoot was one of them.

Teaching them, Sam quickly discovered that his own patience was limited. He was, after all, thirty-nine years old. He had spent much of his life alone. But to his surprise, Claudia got along well with the children, teaching them and assigning chores, which they did without complaint.

Eventually, when the company was big enough, the work horses and the few personal mounts would graze only within the circle. That way, no animals would stray.

Now daily life was more complicated. The wagon train stretched in a line several hundred yards long. Sam was unable to both lead the column and ride up and down its length, and until some of the newcomers proved themselves he knew of only one solution.

Because the distances between communities would increase as they moved westward, and because the wagons would have to cross open country in the absence of roads, Sam felt it his duty to form the vanguard and lead the group. Someone else would have to be monitor, and Sam knew of no one except Tonie Mell who was competent. True, she was only a woman, but few men anywhere could equal her skill as a rider. She had a quick eye and in an emergency she was a sure shot. One of the newcomers could drive her wagon while she spent each day on the back of her horse, going up and down the line.

A wagon from Philadelphia had brought him laudanum and other needed medical supplies from the Army Medical Corps warehouse there. He stored these essentials himself in the special wagon, unwilling to entrust anyone else with the task.

Tonie Mell was delighted with her promotion to the post of line monitor, and to an extent her pleasure was genuine. At the same time, however, her burden of guilt became heavier. If Sam had enough faith in her to make her responsible for the safety of the line, she knew she couldn't betray his trust. She'd simply have to find other ways to slow the westward progress of the caravan.

The addition of the newcomers deeply disturbed her. She was still waiting for the British agent to reveal him- or herself. As nearly as she could judge, none of her earlier companions was a foreign spy, but she dreaded the arrival of each new wagon.

Tonie had procrastinated repeatedly, performing no

acts of sabotage. Because she lacked experience the Russian Legation had agreed not to require written communications from her. As far as the *chargé d'affaires* knew, she was following his orders.

But once the British agent discovered who she was, her situation would change. Then, if she failed to do what was expected of her, he'd complain to his superiors, and when that information was forwarded to the Russians, her parents would never be allowed to leave St. Petersburg, unless it was to go to Siberia.

The very idea made Tonie shudder. She tried to picture her mother and father, but she could only see them in broad outline. Her aunt had brought her to the United States when she was four years old, and she found it difficult to fill in her parents' portraits; they always took on the likenesses of her aunt and uncle.

But that didn't prevent her from shedding secret tears for the mother and father she scarcely knew. It was enough for her that they were eager to come to America. Their future was in her hands, and if she failed to do the bidding of the vicious *Cheka,* they might end their days instead in the frozen wastelands of Siberia. The thought tormented her constantly.

But the arrival of the newcomers had a far different effect on Henry St. Clair. Until now he'd been biding his time; it would have been too dangerous to act within such a tiny company. Now he had more room to maneuver. Soon he planned that the train would be beset by seemingly natural "accidents." Soon his real work could begin.

Henry hoped to discover his Russian colleague among the newcomers. After discussing Europe and the world with Claudia Humphries, giving her plenty of possible openings, he'd decided that she wasn't the representative of St. Petersburg. He'd enjoyed her company, to be sure, but he wasn't along for the sake of pleasure. He'd much prefer to be watching a theatrical performance at Drury Lane or sitting in his favorite London tavern, drinking ale with a buxom blonde.

Not that the Russian spy would make any real contribution to his work, Henry thought. But he wanted to keep an eye on whoever it might be. He wasn't allowing himself to forget that the Russian was actually his rival, no matter how many friendly messages were exchanged between the British and Russian foreign ministries. Henry had no intention of doing anything that would help the Russians to gain possession of the Oregon territory. If this mission was successful, he'd be given a secure post at headquarters, and remain in London for the rest of his days.

For their part, Otto and Cathy found it easy enough to meet the newcomers and become acquainted with them. But it was far more difficult for Claudia, a woman on her own, to mingle with unmarried male members of the company. So she stayed in the vicinity of her own wagon without giving them the wrong impression, hoping that Sam Brentwood would find the time to give her another lesson in marksmanship before the day ended.

After awhile, it was obvious that Sam was too busy

to spare any time for her. So she borrowed Henry St. Clair's handsome rifle, accepted the gift of twenty-five rounds of ammunition from his seemingly inexhaustible supply and went off alone to the nearby woods. She had to smile to herself when she saw some of the newcomers watching her. It was bad enough, she thought, that Tonie Mell swaggered around the camp in men's buckskins, a pistol in her belt. The sight of a woman in a silk gown carrying a rifle might convince these people that they were joining a company of Amazons.

Claudia was indifferent to their opinions. She intended to become an expert shot and make Tonie stop smirking at her.

She set up a target, measured off thirty paces and then went to work. It was heartening to see that she was gradually improving, and she was sufficiently encouraged to try all the harder.

When she returned to the camp it was time to fetch water. She was mildly surprised when Terence Malcolm joined her.

"There are too many of us now," he said, "for one person to do it alone, so I'll be helping you regularly. Sam Brentwood gave us a choice and that's what I chose to do. I'm stronger than you think. You'll see."

That evening several of the new women helped Cathy prepare supper for the enlarged company. After eating, others helped clean the dishes and cutlery in pots of hot water. For the first time the company seemed like a caravan bound for far places.

The next morning, fourteen hooped canvas tops bulged. The special wagon was located in the center of the column for security. The owners of each wagon made final checks to make certain nothing was left behind.

Tonie Mell, beginning her new duties as monitor, rode her gelding slowly from the front of the line to the rear. She could tell at a glance whether harnesses were secure, and whether the canvas side flaps were properly held down to keep out the dust. She also made sure there were no obstacles on the road beneath wagons that might break axles or damage wheels.

When she reached the end of the line, assured that all was well, she drew her pistol and fired it into the air. That was the signal that Sam Brentwood was waiting for. His stallion started off at a slow walk on the road that led west across the Appalachian Mountains. Then, one by one the wagons behind him began to move. The dust in their wake was enough to make both women and men tie bandanas around their heads.

Sam Brentwood heard the reassuring cacophony behind him. Harnesses jingled, the steady plodding of horses' hooves made a pleasant sound, and into it were blended the rattle of wheels and the creaking of boards. He grinned. Each wagon seemed to whisper, "Oregon, Oregon, Oregon." He had waited a long time for this train to form, and the frustrations of the early part of the journey were forgotten. He was glad he'd accepted the assignment.

Tonie rode up to report that all was well, before doubling back on her rounds.

The wagon train was under way. The weather was

ideal. The temperature in the mountains was cool, but during the morning the sun grew hot. Men rolled up their shirtsleeves, women discarded their shawls and the entire company enjoyed the warmth of the sun.

Nature had been cooperative, rain falling only at night. Sam was glad to hear it as he slept, because it laid the dust. But he knew the day was coming when the weather wouldn't be so considerate.

They headed across Pennsylvania toward Pittsburgh, at the western end of the state. There were fewer farms here, and more large tracts of forests and uninhabited land. The isolation and grandeur of the wilderness was visible for the first time, even though they were still traveling through parts of the United States considered civilized.

It took time to sort out the personalities of the newcomers, but one family in particular drew Claudia's attention. James Caldwell was a burly, middle-aged farmer who had sold his property and gathered together the last of his possessions to make this long journey. Dressed in worn linsey-woolsey, he was taciturn and withdrawn, not taking part in general conversations. All day he sat silently behind his team and as soon as he ate his evening meal he withdrew inside his wagon.

Lena Caldwell, however, was all that he was not. The contrast between them was startling. Slender and tiny, with stringy, dark hair, she would have been attractive had she looked less pallid. But she was always cheerful and always willing to help, even though she carried a small baby on her hip. She appeared to be no more than eighteen or nineteen, and the difference between her age and her husband's reminded Claudia of her own sister's sad situation.

One day, after she and Terence had returned to camp with the water—a task that required each of them to make four trips to the bank of the river—Claudia saw Cathy and Lena Caldwell chatting together as they cleaned the fish and placed them into frying pans. The two women had become increasingly friendly.

On an impulse she joined them, stopping to admire Lena's baby, who was wrapped in a blanket and sleeping soundly on the grass. "The fishermen are having good luck today," she said. "Whatever the hunters bring in can be saved for tomorrow."

"Otto won't like that," Cathy said. "You know how he hates fish."

"It's the same in our family," Lena said.

"Then your husbands will have to be less particular," Claudia said. "As the train grows we'll have to eat whatever we get."

The younger girls exchanged glances.

"It's all right to tell her," Cathy said. "She's my sister. You can trust her."

Lena sighed. "Well, it won't be long before everybody knows. I don't have a husband."

Claudia was startled.

"James Caldwell is my father," the girl said. "The reason we're making this trip is to get away from home and go where nobody knows us. Pa says that I—I disgraced our family name."

"Now, don't you start that again, Lena," Cathy said, patting her new friend on the shoulder. "You're not an abandoned woman. I don't care what your father says." She turned to her sister. "Lena was in love with a boy who got scared and ran off when he learned she was pregnant."

"Having Lenore is wonderful, no matter what Pa says." Lena raised her head defiantly.

"Of course it is," Claudia said, though she privately thought the girl had been foolish. "It's just as well you've come with us. You can make a fresh start for yourself in the Oregon country."

Terence had come up behind her. "I brought some extra water," he said, placing two buckets on the ground.

Claudia wondered if he'd overheard the conversation. Oh, well, there was no real harm done. As Lena herself had said, everyone on the wagon train would soon know that she was the mother of an illegitimate child.

At the end of each day's journey, Tonie Mell continued to ride off alone, after finishing her monitoring duties, sometimes to allow her gelding to canter, sometimes to hunt for game. So when the newcomers saw her go off by herself one day about a week after they joined the caravan, they thought no more of it than did the others.

But today Tonie's purpose was different. She'd taken the precaution of tightening her breastband under her buckskins, and borrowing Terence Malcolm's broadbrimmed hat—without his knowledge. After taking the road to the west, she put the hat on. She had finally made up her mind to follow the instructions given her by the Imperial Russian *chargé d'affaires* in Washington. She had no choice.

According to Sam Brentwood's map, a small town lay four or five miles ahead, and the caravan should reach it the following day. Tonie rode into the town at dusk and found the place she sought, a small tavern. After steeling herself she sauntered inside. Several local farmers and a couple of merchants in black suits were drinking at the bar. She took a place at the end near the farmers, then lowered her voice as best she could in order to disguise it. She ordered a mug of beer.

The men glanced at her as they chatted, apparently accepting her as a boy. Her ruse was successful—so far.

As she sipped her beer, a drink she loathed, one of the farmers struck up a conversation with her, which she'd hoped would happen. "You come from around here, sonny?"

Tonie shook her head. "I'm goin' t' visit the Applebys, this side of Harrisburg," she said, speaking as roughly as she could in order to conceal her soprano voice.

The man had not heard of the Applebys, which was understandable, because no such people existed, but his curiosity was satisfied.

"Are the roads clear thataway?" Tonie asked.

"Far as I know," the man said. "I ain't heard of no rockslides."

"Then I ought to be all right. Less'n I come across that wagon train."

"What wagon train?"

"The one that's aimin' t' reach Oregon," Tonie said, her heart pounding. "Ain't you read about it?"

The farmer nodded. "How come you don't want to see 'em?"

Tonie pretended amazement. "Jeez, I thought everybody knew." She had the drinkers' complete attention now. She lowered her voice to a near-whisper, feeling as though she might be sick to her stomach, and said, "I figgered everybody in Pennsylvania knew about that wagon train. They got the smallpox. Three or four cases."

Tonie paid for her beer, took another token swallow and then hurried away, her legs unsteady. She made a wide detour around the town before heading back to camp. She had succeeded in doing precisely as she had planned, but her perfidy made her feel ill and feverish. She went straight to her own wagon. She certainly couldn't eat a bite of food tonight.

Only when the others went to the campfire for supper did Tonie remember she still had Terence Malcolm's hat. She made her way to his wagon, making sure not to be seen, and returned it. Then she sneaked back to her own wagon, threw herself down on the mattress and wished she were dead.

Cathy van Ayl, the first to notice her absence from the campfire, went off to investigate. She returned with the news that Tonie felt sick.

Henry St. Clair volunteered to take her place as monitor, and Cathy duly informed the invalid.

For Tonie, the night was interminable. Sleep was impossible. She tossed fitfully on her mattress, wide awake and miserable.

When she appeared the next morning for a token breakfast of bread and tea, the others couldn't help staring. For the first time since joining the caravan, she was wearing a dress, put on because she wanted to take no chances that anyone in the town ahead might recognize her.

Sam Brentwood seemed especially struck by the girl's appearance, Claudia noted. And she admitted to herself, grudgingly, that a dress showed off Tonie's slender figure to very good advantage. Her waist was so tiny a man could span it with his two hands, and Claudia was annoyed because Sam looked as though he'd enjoy being that man. It was absurd the way men who should have known better went sniffing around girls with supple figures. Well, Sam's lack of judgment indicated to Claudia that his taste was poor, and he was welcome to Tonie Mell.

Henry St. Clair decided to use one of his own horses for his monitor duty, so after breakfast Tonie returned to her wagon. As she'd done early on in the journey, she held her gelding on a long lead after climbing onto her board.

Before the train got under way, Hester Browne, a little girl of eleven, raced up to Tonie from her family's wagon farther back in line. The sight of the child cheered Tonie somewhat. Hester was wearing a pair of breeches.

"Please, ma'am," the child said, "seeing as how you aren't riding your horse today, I wonder if I could ride him."

Tonie weighed the request. "Do you know how to ride?"

Hester nodded. "I do it pretty good."

"Well, all right—provided I keep hold of this lead, so he and you don't take off across the country on your own."

At that moment Henry came along, monitoring the line. He dismounted and lifted Hester into the gelding's saddle.

Tonie placed a large scarf over her head, then used a smaller one as a mask. In spite of her precautions to disguise herself, she still felt heartsick. She had committed an act of treason against the United States. Even if nothing untoward happened as a result of the lie she'd told, nothing could erase that stain from her conscience.

When the vanguard reached the crest of a heavily wooded hill, Sam could see the town in a valley ahead. Suddenly, a large party of men appeared out of the woods, blocking the road. Their attire indicated that most were farmers. All of them were armed, some with rifles and pitchforks, while a few carried flintlocks that appeared to be relics of the War of Independence.

Their aggressive hostility and display of weapons caused Sam to lay his rifle quietly across his saddle and loosen the pistols he carried in his belt.

The caravan was forced to halt, and Henry St. Clair rode up to the head of the column. Other men joined Sam Brentwood, too. Several had the presence of mind to bring their weapons.

Tonie wondered if it would be possible to avoid bloodshed.

"You folks ain't goin' through this town," the leader of the townspeople shouted. "Find yourselves another route."

Sam remained calm, as he always did in a time of crisis. "Why can't we go through?"

"You know damn well, mister!"

"Not unless you tell us," Sam said reasonably.

"Because of the smallpox you got in them wagons!" The leader was angry, and several of the men brandished their rifles and flintlocks.

Sam Brentwood's smile was placating. "I don't know where you heard such rubbish. No one in this company has smallpox."

"We knew you'd lie about it!"

"Inspect the wagons for yourselves," Sam suggested.

Several of the locals laughed harshly.

"Not us!" the leader shouted. "Now go back where you came from!"

The closest alternate road was fifty miles away. In order to reach it across the mountains, Sam knew, he'd be forced to double back for several days. In all, he'd lose at least a week and a half.

Sam knew he had no choice. He had to lead the caravan through the town.

"Friends," he said, his manner still amiable but with the ring of metal in his voice, "I told you the truth just now, no matter what you choose to believe. Now I'll tell you something else. We're going to use this road and pass through your town. We won't tarry there, you can depend on that, but we're going through."

"The hell you are!" the leader shouted.

One man became excited and accidentally discharged his flintlock, shooting it into the air.

Tonie's gelding, already skittish because of the unfamiliar rider, reared high. Hester Browne, who was unprepared for the horse's sudden move, was thrown to the ground. She screamed.

Several people raced toward the fallen girl, but Claudia Humphries was the first to get there. "Don't touch her," she said. "She seems to have broken her arm. Somebody fetch her some brandywine, quickly. And bring me some cloth and some strong, straight sticks."

Hester was still crying. Even the appearance of her frightened mother, who tried to soothe her, didn't silence the injured child.

James Caldwell appeared with a flask, and Claudia forced the child to swallow from it. Then, as Tonie tore strips from a cotton petticoat she had hastily removed, someone handed Claudia the sticks.

Taking a deep breath, Claudia straightened Hester's broken arm, and with Tonie's help she bound it, the splints holding it straight and firm.

Hester's mother fed her more brandywine and then, as the girl's screams subsided, her father carried her back to their wagon.

Hester's mother tried to thank Claudia, who shrugged off the expressions of gratitude. She had become expert in setting broken limbs when her late husband had fallen during his drinking bouts.

Tonie Mell felt sick. She alone was responsible for the accident, and she knew she'd hear the little girl's screams of pain as long as she lived.

Someone hurried to report what had happened to Sam Brentwood.

"A little girl was thrown from a horse as a result of that shot," Sam told the men in front of him, when the excitement died down. "Her arm is broken. But I don't aim to allow any more injuries. To anyone. Henry," he directed, "ride over yonder."

Henry St. Clair obediently moved off toward the woods, halting at Sam's gesture after going about twenty paces.

"Do you have a penny, Henry?" Sam asked. "Good. Throw it into the air, high as you can."

Henry St. Clair, thoroughly mystified, obeyed Sam's instructions without question.

In a smooth, effortless motion, Sam plucked a pistol from his belt and, scarcely seeming to take aim, fired it as the coin reached its apex in the air.

The penny was deflected in the direction of the locals, and one of them picked it up. He showed it to his neighbors in astonished silence. The coin was bent double. No one there had ever seen such marksmanship.

"We've lost enough time today," Sam said casually, reloading his pistol. "I reckon we'll be on our way before we lose any more." Slowly, he began to ride forward, replacing the pistol in his belt and gripping his rifle. The other members of the company raced back to their wagons, as Henry monitored the line. The column began to move.

The sullen townspeople continued to block the road, eyeing each other uneasily. Sam's smile fading, he raised his rifle. Before he could point it, however, the ranks of the locals broke, and they scattered into the woods on both sides of the road.

The train rolled on in a silence broken only by the familiar sounds of horses' hooves, creaking leather and rattling wheels.

Tonie Mell was exhausted. Thanks to Sam's courage, skill and knowledge of men, no one had been killed. Yet she was responsible for little Hester's accident, and she would never forgive herself. But at least her attempt to sabotage the wagon train had ended in failure, and for that she was grateful. If the *chargé d'affaires* of the Russian Legation ever learned of the incident, he would know that at least she had tried.

V

As the wagon train made its way across the mountains to Pittsburgh, a series of accidents took place, severely slowing the progress of the expedition. First a wheel fell off a wagon. By the time it was repaired and put back into place a half-day was lost. Then two work horses went lame, and a halt had to be called for thirty-six hours before the animals recovered sufficiently to travel.

The following day, during a sudden, unexpected rain squall, a second wagon lost a wheel. Soon thereafter another broke its rear axle. This vehicle, which the owner had constructed himself, was of an unconventional size, so none of the spares in the special wagon fit it, making it necessary for several men to go to the nearest town, twenty miles away, to purchase the part.

Sam Brentwood was heard to express the belief that the company was suffering from a streak of exceptionally bad luck, and most people agreed with him. Tonie

113

Mell suspected that the "accidents" were being produced by deliberate sabotage. If she was right, the British agent must now be a member of the group. Still deeply depressed by the incident that had resulted in Hester Browne's broken arm, Tonie played a guessing game, trying to determine the unknown spy's identity.

The task proved impossible, and she soon realized its futility. Certainly no member of the expedition could know that she'd been forced into the service of the Imperial Russian government. And even if someone learned she had been born in St. Petersburg, there was only a remote possibility that a link could be established between her and the *Cheka*, which was putting pressure on her. Why should the British saboteur be any easier to recognize?

All she could do, Tonie decided, was keep her eyes open and hope she might see the British spy at work. What she would do if she recognized him, she didn't yet know. The idea of joining forces revolted her, yet she couldn't expose him to Sam Brentwood without compromising herself.

Nevertheless she made up her mind to remain close to the camp, and refused an invitation to join a hunting party while the caravan waited for the crippled wagon to be repaired.

Ordinarily Sam Brentwood would have gone hunting on his own, a function he continued to perform regularly. But he was so disgusted that he was willing to let others do the job for him, staying behind to take charge of repairing the damaged wagon. He was finding the repeated delays intolerable.

Claudia was delighted to find him at liberty. She

wanted to show him how much her marksmanship was improving. "I'm not quite ready for a contest with you," she said, "but I think you'll be surprised by how well I can handle a rifle now."

Sam had nothing better to occupy his time at the moment so he agreed to watch her shoot, but his mind was elsewhere as they walked to a stand of trees some distance from the train. "If I believed in supersitions," he said, "I'd begin to suspect a jinx has been laid on us."

"When this many people are traveling together," she replied, "accidents are bound to happen."

"Then I hate to think what will happen in Ohio, Indiana and Illinois when we pick up new people. We'll be a year behind schedule just getting to the Missouri River."

She had to admit he was conscientious. "We didn't have any problems until recently," she said. "They'll soon clear up."

"I hope you're right." He handed her his rifle, powder horn and bullet pouch. "Do you think you're good enough to hit any part of that tree branch that's almost touching the ground?"

"We'll soon see." She loaded the weapon, reminding herself that it was heavier than Henry's and had a stronger recoil. Bracing herself, she took aim and fired. The branch, some five inches in diameter, cracked and sagged to the ground.

Sam was pleased. "Not half bad," he said, "for a woman."

Claudia was furious. She stalked back to her wagon without saying another word.

He couldn't understand why she was annoyed. But

soon he had other troubles on his mind. He discovered a leak in the roof of the supply wagon, which had been added to the train at the stop near Harrisburg. The previous night's rain had ruined two hundred pounds of flour. The company would have to do without bread until they reached Pittsburgh where more flour could be purchased.

That evening, Claudia was more receptive than usual to Henry St. Clair's attentions. After supper they sat together near the fire. He chuckled as he pointed to a pair of shadows on the far side of the dying flames. "Young Terence and the Caldwell girl seem to have discovered each other."

Claudia had also become aware of the growing friendship between the young couple. She nodded.

"On a journey like this there's bound to be romance in the air," Henry said. "I'm surprised you haven't been swept off your feet."

"I don't sweep all that easily," she replied, her tone dry.

"I'm delighted, my dear, but also puzzled. The more I see of you the more I believe that you'll never be happy scratching for an existence on the Oregon frontier."

"Oh?" She hadn't flirted with anyone for a long time. "What do you think would make me happy?"

"The best way I could answer that question would be to show you London. The theaters, the excitement, the inns and taverns where they serve most elegant suppers. You'd love relaxing in a boat on the Serpentine and riding in a carriage down Pall Mall—gorgeously gowned, of course, as befits your beauty."

Had a less sophisticated man been speaking, Claudia would have assumed he was proposing marriage, or leading up to it. But she couldn't decide whether Henry was just being complimentary or if he meant his remarks in a personal way.

"Then there's Paris," he said, gazing dreamily into the fire. "The monarchy under that middle-class buffoon, King Louis Philippe, is a wretched piece of business, but the city is quite lively. Do you happen to speak French?"

"I've never had the opportunity to learn."

"A tutor could remedy that defect in a very short time," he said. "You're so clever you could master any language."

Although Claudia enjoyed his flattery, she knew she had to call a halt before their relationship became too complicated. "For the present," she said, "I have no need for French lessons. I wager not many people in Pittsburgh speak French these days."

When the axle was repaired the journey was resumed. Terence Malcolm surprised Lena Caldwell by asking her and her baby to ride with him that day. She was too apprehensive to accept, but her father, who'd overheard the invitation, drew her aside.

"Do it," he said emphatically.

"You don't mind, Pa?" Lena was wide-eyed.

"Mind? There aren't many respectable men who'd as much as spit at a harlot who's saddled with a bastard brat."

Lena told Terence she'd changed her mind.

After making her baby comfortable on a nest of blankets inside the wagon, Terence gravely helped

Lena to a place beside him on the boards. For more than an hour they rode in silence, unmindful of the dust kicked up by the wagons in the line ahead of them. He seemed preoccupied and nervous, frequently pushing back the lock of sandy hair that fell forward over his eyes. Finally, he spoke.

"I guess you've heard," he said, "that I don't expect to live very long."

"Cathy told me. I'm sorry, Terence."

"You needn't be. I don't feel sick, and I've been having the best time I ever had. By the time the train reaches Oregon, I won't be around, but that can't be helped. I'd sure like to see the country out there. Failing that, I'd like to do what I can to help other people."

"That's a wonderful attitude."

He flushed beneath his tan. "I don't mean to sound noble, Lena. I'm much too practical for that. Anyway, I've been thinking about you and Lenore."

"What about us?" she said.

"Don't get riled up now. Just hear me out before you put up any objections. I've had this notion, see? Suppose—just suppose—you and I got married and I got the preacher to make out adoption papers for Lenore, too. That way, when I'm gone, you'd be a genuine widow, and the baby would have a proper last name."

Tears came to Lena's eyes. "I think you're crazy."

"I told you not to interrupt." Terence was stern. "I don't want you to get the wrong notion. There's nothing personal in my suggestion."

Lena laughed through her tears. "Nothing personal . . . in a marriage proposal?"

"I just don't want you to think I'm making you this

offer because I—I want to fool around with you." He swallowed. "Things would be just like they are right now."

"You mean . . . we wouldn't really be married?"

"Not that way," Terence said. "It would be legal because the preacher would see to that, but that's where we'd stop. And when I die, you'd just be a widow in name, not in fact."

The girl was silent for a long time. "Why are you offering me this?"

"I've already told you." He sounded cross. "It won't hurt me any, and I'll be doing something for somebody who has a problem, a problem I can solve easier than falling off this wagon."

Lena took a handkerchief from the belt of her homespun dress and blew her nose hard. "You're sweet, Terry," she said, "and so generous I can believe again that there are good people in this world."

"It just makes sense, that's all," he said, embarrassed by her praise.

"But I can't accept." Lena was firm.

"Blamed if I can see why not. One of these days I'll be in a roadside grave. So somebody may as well get some good out of my life while I'm still here."

"It wouldn't be fair to you."

"Different folks have different ideas about fairness," Terence said. "Let me know if you change your mind."

They spent the rest of the day companionably, exchanging only occasional, casual comments. Lena was overwhelmed by his offer, but she had no intention of mentioning it to anyone. There was already too much gossip about her on the wagon train.

When a halt was called that afternoon she attended to her baby, then went off to join the women, as though nothing unusual had happened. Terence, at peace within himself for having spoken his mind, went off with Claudia to fetch water, then helped gather wood to make the fire.

After supper, when the dishes were done, Lena went to her father's wagon, carrying the sleeping Lenore. She was surprised to find James Caldwell still awake, waiting up for her.

"You've been avoiding me tonight," he said. She knew from his tone that he had been drinking. He kept his whiskey hidden in his tool kit.

"There's no difference between tonight and any other night, Pa." She tucked the baby into her makeshift crib.

"Damnation girl! What did Terence Malcolm want to talk to you about?"

Almost without thinking, Lena told her father the story of the strange proposal.

"The Lord be praised," Caldwell said.

"I thanked him, Pa, but I couldn't accept. It wouldn't be right."

Her father stared at her for only a moment. Then he slapped her so hard across the face that she staggered and fell to the floor of the wagon. Slowly, deliberately, he removed his leather belt and stood over her. "I ain't whipped you since the day you came home and told me you was having that little bastard," he said. "If you forgot the feel of leather on your hide, I'll remind you."

The girl was terrified. "Please don't beat me, Pa! Please!"

He drew back his arm, then struck her with all his might across the shoulders.

Lena knew better than to cry out. If she screamed, arousing the people in nearby wagons, her father might well kill her before anyone could come to her assistance. He was a demon when aroused, unable to control his emotions. Cowering and trying to crawl beyond his reach, her one thought was to protect her baby, no matter how badly he whipped her.

Caldwell raised his arm to strike her again, then thought better of it. If she looked too battered in the morning other members of the company might take notice of her condition, and he, of course, would be blamed. "You goddamn harlot," he said. "He offers you the chance of a lifetime and you muff it. That young idiot asks you to marry him, and you refuse. He's crazy, so his reasons don't matter. He's a puny little son of a bitch, but that ain't important, either. You finally got a chance to be respectable—and you're going to take it. If I have to beat you within an inch of your life, you're going to do what I say."

In her fear, Lena was willing to give in. "Leave me alone, Pa. I'll talk to Terry tomorrow—unless you hit me one more time."

He dropped his belt, took another drink from his bottle and then retired to his bed.

After a sleepless night, Lena was waiting for Terence in the morning when he emerged from his own cramped wagon to help Claudia fetch water.

121

He stopped in surprise when he saw her strained face.

"I—I didn't get much rest last night," she said, "thinking over our talk. If it's still agreeable with you, Terry, I—I accept your offer."

"I'm glad to hear it," he said, smiling broadly. "Now you're being sensible."

"I'm—very much obliged to you," Lena said.

They announced their news at breakfast, to the great delight of the entire company. It would be the train's first wedding. Sam told them they'd have no trouble finding a clergyman when they reached Pittsburgh, where they'd be joined by another group.

Only Claudia, who had seen their remote, impersonal encounter outside Terence's wagon, suspected the real reason for the marriage, but she kept her thoughts to herself. It was enough that Lena would become an honest woman and give her baby a proper name.

The Allegheny River, some fifty miles northeast of Pittsburgh, had been swollen by heavy spring rains when they reached it. And although the floods had subsided somewhat, the river was still too wide to be forded. So the caravan traveled south along the banks of the river until they came to a ferry.

They made a deal with the ferry owner. Sam and several other men would swim the horses across the river, and the wagons would be carried two at a time on the ferry. The owner agreed. Such transactions weren't unusual, and he charged them a reasonable fee.

The horses crossed without incident under the expert

supervision of Sam, who remained in the water astride his stallion, calming the more skittish animals and keeping them in line. Quincy swam tirelessly alongside, barking furiously whenever one of the horses was inclined to turn back or drift downstream.

Then it was the turn of the wagons. Family groups went first. The wagons were hauled onto the ferry two at a time and as they reached the west bank, they were moved into place. The whole operation would take several hours.

When the two bachelors, Henry St. Clair and Terence Malcolm, made the crossing, St. Clair's large wagon took up the better part of the ferry, crowding Malcolm's near the broad stern. Suddenly Malcolm shouted. As the horrified onlookers watched, his wagon slid slowly into the water and disappeared from sight.

In an effort not to lose the other wagon too, the boatmen poled the ferry to the west bank and unloaded it before returning to the middle of the river with Terence and several volunteers, Sam among them.

"I don't believe there's any way to fish it out," the ferry owner said.

"I'm afraid you're right," Sam replied. They looked down at the water, where some of the wagon's contents were already being forced to the surface and propelled downstream. "I'm sorry, Terry. The river is just too deep."

Terence shrugged. "Except for my gun, what I own isn't worth very much."

When Terence reached the west bank again, almost the entire company rallied to him. He was besieged with offers of spare clothing, food, cooking utensils and other supplies. James Caldwell, somewhat ungraciously, said his future son-in-law could move into his wagon after the wedding, and several others offered him shelter until that time. Lena was mute, and very disturbed by the tragedy.

Now only the special wagon remained on the east bank of the river, held until last because its bulk would completely fill the ferry. Henry St. Clair volunteered to recross the river in order to help Abe Ellis with the bulky last wagon. The assistance of one more person was needed, and Tonie Mell volunteered.

They reached the far side without incident. The boatmen rigged a pulley to haul the big wagon onto the ferry. As Ellis and Henry pushed from behind, Tonie guided the vehicle. Even the boatmen had to strain in order to move the ungainly wagon into place. At last, when the supply wagon was finally aboard, the raft sank lower into the water, but stayed afloat.

Blocks were placed at all eight wheels to prevent them from slipping during the rough crossing, and Abe Ellis helped the boatmen pole. The ferry began to make its way slowly across the swollen, swirling river.

Tonie had remained near the prow, watching the progress of the raft. Suddenly it occurred to her that if the contents of the big wagon shifted position, the ferry's own balance might be disturbed. She went quickly aft, intending to look inside the unlocked vehicle to insure that all was well within.

Henry St. Clair didn't see her. He was crouched beside a rear wheel, the bulk of the wagon concealing him from the eyes of those who were waiting on the

124

west bank. He had already removed the blocks from one wheel, and was carefully at work on another, when Tonie Mell rounded a corner and saw him. What on earth was he doing?

Suddenly, in that instant, Tonie knew that St. Clair was the British agent.

Something inside her exploded. The outrage that Henry was perpetrating made her ignore her own troubles. She knew that if she stopped him, she'd be severing the ties that bound her to the Russians. She'd have to abandon hope that her parents would ever be given visas to leave Russia, and she knew that they might be sent to Siberia. But she knew that she had to perform her duty, regardless of the consequences, and no matter what might happen to her. If the special wagon was lost in the river, the train would be held up for months in Pittsburgh before it could be replaced. If that happened, the expedition, for all practical purposes, would have to be abandoned.

She was furious! Quietly, Tonie Mell made a detour. She crept up behind Henry St. Clair, withdrawing her knife from her belt.

"You bastard!" she said in a low, intense voice, pressing the knife point hard against his back.

The interfering bitch! St. Clair knew he could probably disarm the girl, but he also knew that she could fight—and scream. The boatmen and Abe Ellis would be bound to hear the scuffle. Short of killing her, there was no way he could silence the girl before she cried out, and if she did, his perfidy would be discovered.

Silently he cursed this headstrong young woman

125

from the frontier country for blundering into him at the worst possible time, arousing her bloody patriotism.

"Are you trying to wreck the whole wagon train?" Tonie said.

"You don't understand," Henry said, trying frantically to find a plausible excuse for what he was doing.

"I understand, all right," Tonie said, applying more pressure with the knife. "Now put those blocks back where they belong, and do it mighty quick. Otherwise I'll kill you."

He knew she had the strength, the will and the courage to carry out her threat. The point of the knife was increasingly persuasive. He replaced the first block.

"Now the other wheel," Tonie said, the knife at his back.

Again he obeyed. He cursed his bad luck.

The perfect opportunity to dump the special wagon overboard had been lost. Now he'd have to content himself with minor sabotage until he got another chance to deliver a crippling blow.

By the time the second set of blocks was moved back into position, the ferry was drawing close to shore. Tonie removed the knife from St. Clair's back.

"I want to have a private talk with you tonight," Henry said, standing up. He knew he had to silence her before she could reveal what she'd learned about him. And if he had to, he was even prepared to murder her.

Tonie saw the death threat in his eyes, and knew she had to proceed carefully. "All right," she said.

"I wasn't doing what you thought I was doing," he said. "I was just moving the blocks to make them secure. They had slipped. I'll tell you all about it to-night." Maybe she'd buy his story.

Tonie Mell was cagey. "Fair enough," she said. She hoped she sounded convincing.

When the ferry reached land on the west bank, lines were thrown ashore and the raft was made fast. Willing hands dragged the special wagon ashore.

As though he didn't have a care in the world, Henry St. Clair went ashore and sauntered off to his own wagon with cool aplomb.

Angrily Tonie watched him, forced to admire his play-acting. Then she went ashore to search for Sam Brentwood. It no longer mattered that her parents would never be able to come to America. She would grieve later, she knew, but she couldn't worry about that now. And she worried even less that she'd be forced to expose her own treason.

"Sam," she said, when she'd found him, "I've got to talk to you."

"Can't it wait?" He was trying to get the train once again underway.

"No," she said. "I need to talk to you right away. Privately."

Something in her expression told Sam Brentwood that her demand was not mere feminine whim. Tonie knew enough not to needlessly interfere. Whatever was troubling her had to be important. Gesturing toward the woods, he started toward them.

Tonie almost had to run in order to keep up with his long-legged pace.

Claudia, watching them go off together, was irritated. She hadn't realized that the redhead was so brazen. Obviously Sam Brentwood wasn't aware of it, either. He was becoming mighty thick with her. Well, Claudia thought, if he was going to make a fool of himself over the girl, she had no intention of stopping him.

A short distance into the woods, Sam halted and turned to face Tonie Mell, his thumbs hooked under his belt. "All right," he said, "what's the problem?"

She took a deep breath. "I'll have to start at the beginning," she said. "My real name is Antoinette Melichev, not Tonie Mell, though that's what I've been called since I was a baby. And I'm not a missus. I've never been married to anybody."

Tonie told him in detail about her meeting with the *chargé d'affaires* at the Imperial Russian Legation in Washington, holding back nothing.

Sam listened in silence. Not until she revealed her smallpox hoax did he try to speak.

"Wait till I'm done," she said. "I've found out who the British agent is. You blame near lost the special wagon in the river just now."

Then she told him what had happened on the ferry.

"And there you have it," Tonie said. "If you want to send me off to jail for being a traitor, I won't blame you. I'll even make a full confession in writing to make it easier for you."

"You're going to keep your mouth shut," Sam said, his voice firm and calm. "You're not going to repeat one word of this to anybody, not ever."

Tonie looked at him in astonishment.

"You've more than repaid your debt to your country and to the wagon train," Sam said. "Andy Jackson would kiss you if he knew what you've done, and President Van Buren would give you a medal—if they gave medals to ladies."

To Tonie Mell, Sam's words sounded miraculous. Her relief was so great she had to lean against the nearest tree to support herself, fighting back the tears she considered alien to her nature. "You're not going to send me to jail?" she asked, her voice unexpectedly timid.

"I'm happy and proud that I know you," he said. "And I hope you'll go all the way to the Pacific with the wagon train. With women like you, no country in the world is going to take the Oregon territory away from us."

The tears came freely now, but Tonie was ashamed of what she regarded as a display of weakness, and tried to blink them away.

Not wanting to embarrass her, Sam turned away abruptly and started back to the clearing.

Tonie followed him and touched his arm. "What are you going to do about Henry St. Clair?"

Sam squinted up at the sun. It was too late to get the caravan restarted today, so he gave up the idea. There were more important matters to be settled. "I'm going to have me a little talk with Mr. Henry St. Clair," he said.

"I'll come with you." Her reaction was spontaneous.

"You've done enough, Tonie." Sam was firm, tolerating no argument. "You head back to your wagon, and stay there till I say it's all right to come out again." If the coming confrontation turned nasty, he didn't want it complicated by the presence of Tonie Mell, no matter how resourceful she was.

Although she wanted to be present when he settled accounts with Henry, Tonie Mell knew better than to argue. Not even the roughest and most contrary of mountain men would seek a showdown with Sam Brentwood. She started off toward her wagon.

"Thank you," he called softly.

And once again Tonie felt like weeping.

Sam watched her for a moment, and then the compassion in his eyes vanished. Hitching up his buckskin trousers, he looked around at the scene spread out before him. Some of the horses had already been hitched to wagons, and were being urged into line by their owners. There were worse places to spend the night, but he wouldn't yet pass the word that they were staying right here beside the river bank. A far more urgent matter required his attention.

Sam started toward St. Clair's luxurious wagon at the far side of the clearing, his gait deceptively casual. As he walked, he loosened the pistols in his belt. Quincy, appearing out of nowhere, wagged his tail furiously. Sam bent down to pat the animal, as the dog trotted beside him.

St. Clair's horses were still untethered and browsing on the far side of his wagon. He himself was leaning against the front of his vehicle, writing something down in his journal.

At the sound of footsteps, Henry looked up, then smiled when he saw the wagonmaster. "We did well today," he said. "The river crossing could have been unpleasant."

"I want a word with you about the crossing." Sam's tone was blandly conversational.

"Of course." Henry snapped his fingers and Quincy came to him. He began to stroke the dog.

"You and I have been friends, or so I thought." Sam's manner had changed. There was now a hint of menace in his voice. "And if there's one thing I hate, it's the betrayal of a friendship."

Henry knew then that Tonie Mell had given him away and that he could no longer serve Queen Victoria as a member of this wagon train. Thinking quickly but methodically, he weighed his options, searching for the best means of escape. Eventually, he'd get his vengeance from the interfering Tonie Mell, but he couldn't permit himself to think about her right now. He had to concentrate on saving his own skin.

"If you're accusing me of anything," he said, stalling for time, "I have a right to know what it is."

"Glad to oblige you," Sam said. "Why did you try to dump the special wagon into the river?"

"Who says I did?" Henry retorted, working to perfect his escape plan.

Sam had no taste for a quarrel. "It's possible," he said, "that you're on the payroll of London." Not waiting for a reply, he reached for his pistols.

Henry responded instantly, hurling his journal into the wagonmaster's face.

Instinctively, Sam ducked.

Trained for a type of combat that no American frontier guide or mountain man knew, Henry struck swiftly. Before Sam could recover, Henry tripped him. Sam fell to the ground.

As he fell, Henry hurried to the other side of his wagon and leaped on a horse. Quincy, playing a game, ran beside him, barking joyfully.

Furious because he'd allowed himself to be tricked, Sam got up to give chase. But by this time Henry was galloping toward the safety of the woods beyond the clearing, the dog keeping pace with his horse.

Sam raised a pistol, took aim and then lowered it again. Granted that he was a superb marksman; at this distance, shooting at a fast-moving target, he was afraid he would hit the dog.

Claudia, breathless and distraught, ran up to him, concerned for the safety of Quincy. She called his name repeatedly.

By the time the dog turned back, Henry St. Clair was just inside the woods. Sam raised his pistol a second time, then lowered it again. Henry St. Clair had vanished.

Quincy raced up to his mistress.

"What happened?" Claudia said. "I saw you and Henry talking, then all of a sudden you were on the ground."

Grimly, Sam nodded. Rarely had any man fooled or beaten him, and he looked forward to his next encounter with the British agent. That meeting would be a fight to the finish—and he intended to win it.

His expression was so forbidding that Claudia asked no more questions. Not until now had she realized what furies dwelt behind Sam Brentwood's placid front. He could be a ruthless man, she decided, quite capable of killing.

Sam was reluctant to satisfy her curiosity, and

would have preferred to keep silent. But she'd seen enough to whet her appetite for more information, and he felt he had to tell her something, if only to keep her silent. The morale of the entire company would suffer if people learned that a foreign agent had been living in their midst—and trying to prevent Americans from occupying the Oregon country.

"Claudia," he said, addressing her by her given name for the first time, "I hope I can rely on you to keep your mouth shut."

"Of course you can," she said.

"Only one other person knows what you're about to find out. Come along." He entered Henry's sumptuously furnished wagon, with Quincy at his heels, as Claudia followed.

A small chest of drawers, made of carved mahogany, stood at one side. A jar of ink and the pile of papers on top indicated that it had also been used as a desk. The drawers were locked, but Sam used the blade of his knife to depress the lock tongues to open them, and began to examine the contents. Soon he handed her a box filled with money.

"Count this," he said, continuing his search.

Claudia was shocked. There was more than one thousand dollars in paper money inside the box, and another four hundred in gold coins. Obviously Henry St. Clair hadn't lacked for funds.

Sam unfolded a sheet of parchment. A coat of arms was engraved at the top, and Claudia thought she recognized it. "That looks suspiciously like the official insignia of the British government," she said in surprise. Frozen-faced, Sam nodded. The message, written in the neat hand of a professional copyist, was brief:

> Upon the recent accession of Her Majesty to the throne, she received the assurances of Lord Melbourne that her government would make every effort to expand the boundaries of her Empire. Queen Victoria graciously consented to this course of action.
>
> The first objective in North America is the territory of Oregon, which will be incorporated into Canada.
>
> All concerned will conduct themselves in such a manner that these goals will be obtained.

The signature was a scribble that couldn't be deciphered.

"Who in blazes is Lord Melbourne?" Sam demanded.

"The British Prime Minister," Claudia said, shocked anew by the implications of the document.

"Henry St. Clair," Sam said, "is a British spy."

Claudia was dumbfounded.

"No wonder we've had so many accidents," Sam said. "It was Henry's job to prevent this wagon train from ever reaching the Oregon country." Clearly Tonie had told him the truth.

"All his stories must have been lies," Claudia said.

"When we get to Pittsburgh," Sam said, "I'll send this document to President Van Buren. Somebody in Washington City will recognize the signature. And I'll also write to Andy Jackson. Old Hickory never trusted the British—and, by God, he was right."

"What will you do with this wagon?" Claudia was already thinking in immediate, practical terms.

Sam thought briefly. Then he grinned at her. "Terry Malcolm. I'm going to turn over St. Clair's property to him, including the money. On my own authority. He'll need to buy another horse in Pittsburgh, and I reckon he'll also want a rifle to replace the one that went overboard. Beyond that, he'll have a tidy home and a nest egg to start life as a married man."

Claudia clapped her hands in approval.

Sam sobered. "We're lucky we found out about St. Clair this early. But you can wager a stack of beaver hides that the British will try again."

"Perhaps when he hears about the spying, the President will want to call the expedition off," Claudia said.

Sam's laugh was harsh. "There's no more chance of that than there is of my giving up! This wagon train is going to Oregon, come hell or high water!"

VI

Almost a century had passed since a retreating French force had burned Fort Duquesne at the "Forks of the Ohio," but the new Pittsburgh—built at the confluence of the Monongahela and Allegheny rivers, where they formed the mighty Ohio—still had a frontier mentality. Long the gateway to the West, it supported a large population of boatmen familiar with the wilderness. Coal and iron had been found in the nearby hills, encouraging industry, and the residents of Pittsburgh believed that no other city in the United States held greater promise for the future.

Pittsburgh was hurting, all the same, as was the rest of the nation. Because of the Panic of 1837, banks were closing, businesses were going bankrupt and the ranks of the unemployed were increasing.

To many people, the promise of free land on the frontier was the greatest hope of salvation. The disillusioned and the jobless were moving to Illinois, Missouri and the Iowa country by the thousands, where they hoped to create new lives for themselves.

So the presence of the wagon train created an unusual stir in Pittsburgh. Five families had already gathered in their wagons to await the arrival of Sam Brentwood. And by the time the train departed, its ranks were swollen by the addition of seventeen new wagons. In spite of the many hazards to be faced on the long trail, the lure of rich farm lands was overpowering.

The day before the caravan was to depart, Lena Caldwell and Terence Malcolm were married in a modest church ceremony. Cathy van Ayl was matron of honor, and Sam Brentwood stood up with the groom. James Caldwell showed up drunk, and later became even more intoxicated. The bride and groom exchanged a light, token kiss, and Claudia noted that both were flustered.

Lena and her baby moved at once into the luxurious wagon that had belonged to Henry St. Clair. Terence, whose wardrobe had been enhanced by his windfall from Henry St. Clair, surprised his wife by spending some of Henry's money on several new dresses for her, a warm coat for winter and a new pair of shoes.

When they entered the wagon that night, Lena was overwhelmed. "I never expected to live in any place this pretty," she said.

"It belongs to us now," Terence said. "Sam Brentwood said so."

Stroking the expensive furniture, she gazed in awe at the sturdy closets built into the sides. She almost wept at the iron skillets and pots, the chinaware, mugs and eating utensils in the cupboard. "I never dreamed I would be so rich," she murmured.

"Neither did I." Terence was embarrassed, and quickly changed the subject. "Yonder is the crib I bought for Lenore, and there's your bed." He pointed to a thick mattress that boasted two pillows at the top and was covered by blankets of the finest wool.

Lena hesitated. "It's a grand bed," she said, "plenty big enough for two."

"The baby can sleep with you, if you like," he said.

"Where will you sleep, Terry?"

"I'll show you what I've rigged up." He had attached wooden pulleys to the center ceiling strut, the main support of the canvas cover, and when he pulled a rope, a length of thick, bleached linen was lowered, dividing the interior into two compartments. "I'll roll up in my blanket on this side," he said.

"That doesn't . . . seem . . . fair to you," Lena said.

He shrugged. "It's a heap better than what I had in my old wagon, I can tell you. Besides, it doesn't much matter. It didn't seem right to buy another mattress when I won't be around long enough to get much use out of it."

Lena tried to express her gratitude for all he was doing for her.

"Daytimes," he said, tugging at the rope and raising the curtain, "we'll keep the inside open. That way nobody else will guess about our . . . private agreement. It's nobody else's business, anyway."

"Oh, Terry," Lena said. "I'll mend your clothes and

cook your food and wash your dishes. And if you'll teach me how to control the horses, I'll relieve you driving when you get too tired."

"Oh, I can go near all day without feeling an ache in my bones," Terence said. "But I'll be glad for your company any time you want to ride the boards with me. Sometimes it gets a mite lonely out there and I sure would enjoy your companionship, if you don't mind too much."

"I give you my word I won't mind," Lena said. He was the most extraordinary, self-effacing person she'd ever known.

Although Pittsburgh had regarded itself as the first city of the West, for the better part of a half-century, times were changing. Few men in buckskin wandered around by the waterfront nowadays and only rarely was an Indian seen. But there were thousands who remembered the old days, and young men still went into the hills to search for herds of wild horses, although none had been reported in the vicinity for more than a decade.

The caravan bound for Oregon was a reminder of Pittsburgh's past. Senior citizens remarked solemnly that they had never seen its equal. Twenty-six wagons comprised the train that passed slowly through the streets, and those who'd been members of the expedition from its earliest days knew that the reception being accorded them was unique.

Citizens by the thousands lined the route to cheer and wish the pioneers godspeed. Young men on horseback appointed themselves escorts. In some places the crowds were so thick that fathers had to hold young children on their shoulders so the boys and girls could watch the extraordinary sight. The fife and drum corps of a Veterans of the War of 1812 post turned the ride through the city into an impromptu parade by forming a vanguard, playing medleys of patriotic airs.

Here and there women came forward to give the pioneers cakes, smoked hams and loaves of freshly baked bread. Several men from a tavern dumped a cask of ale on the tailgate of a wagon, as the crowd roared in approval.

Tonie Mell, resuming her duties as monitor, moved up and down the line on her gelding. The object of considerable attention, she responded cheerfully, waving and smiling even when some of the men shouted raucous comments.

Claudia Humphries, driving the lead wagon, drew her share of comments, too. And by now she was able to laugh at remarks that would have insulted her earlier. She knew her clothes were too fancy, and she'd purchased several lengths of cloth for new dresses. She had learned that a ladylike appearance took second place to practical comfort.

Even the usually sober Sam Brentwood enjoyed the spectacle that he and his charges were providing. Spectators broke into applause when they saw him appear, and he grinned until his jaws ached, now and again raising his rifle in salute.

To the spectators, the long, impressive wagon train meant far more than a brief thrill. Farmers and housewives, bankers and merchants, river traders and industrialists realized that if the pioneers actually reached

Oregon and managed to settle there, the dream of extending the boundaries of the United States from the Atlantic to the Pacific would at last come true. Other settlers by the tens of thousands would follow in the wagon tracks of these pioneers. A vast new area would be opened to trade, and the raw materials of the West would enrich the nation's economy. To the farsighted this caravan was a symbol of America's future. She would become one of the greatest powers on earth, as Martin Van Buren had said in his inaugural address.

When the fife and drum corps played "Columbia, the Gem of the Ocean," fresh applause broke out. Then gradually the crowds thinned, the musicians departed after a final salute of ruffles and flourishes, and the mounted escorts returned to the city. But the excitement that Pittsburgh's rousing farewell generated heartened everyone in the wagon train for a long time to come.

The next few days on the trail were confusing. The many newcomers, like those who had joined the caravan earlier, had to learn what Sam liked to call "the manners of the trail." Skill and practice were needed to move a wagon into a circle at the end of the day. Those who were unfamiliar with outdoor living had to learn to distinguish between green and seasoned wood for the making of the nightly fire. And women who'd grown accustomed to using all the water they could draw from their own wells were forced, overnight, to make do with much less.

By far the most valuable addition to the party was Dr. Robert Martin, an energetic and personable physician of about forty. He told Sam that his wife had died recently, and in his heartbreak he wanted to go west to start a new life.

His first patient was little Hester Browne. He examined her mending arm thoroughly. Then he congratulated Claudia on the job she had done and asked her to assist him in any future surgery.

"With more than sixty of us now," Claudia said to Sam, "we're fortunate to have a doctor along."

"Especially this one," he replied. "He not only knows his profession, but he's a good, solid man—somebody we can trust."

She asked him how he could know so soon.

"Hellfire," Sam said, "nine times out of ten you can tell what a man is by looking into his eyes."

Claudia was revising her opinion of Sam Brentwood. She had thought him a boor, a crude frontiersman who knew nothing about the world or its people. Little by little, however, she was beginning to appreciate the depth of his judgment.

Obviously he had been fooled by Henry St. Clair, but so had everyone else in the wagon train. He couldn't be faulted for his failure to recognize a shrewd operator as a foreign spy. Claudia couldn't understand what he saw in Tonie Mell, but she realized she might be biased. He was entitled to seek the company of any woman who appealed to him.

What impressed her most was his quiet ability to bring people with disparate backgrounds together, and make them into a homogeneous whole. Never raising his voice, never losing his temper, he encouraged and prodded new arrivals into working and living together for the common good. To the best of her knowledge, no one in the caravan actively disliked him.

She should have known, because of his closeness to Andrew Jackson, that he was no ordinary man. She herself had never been one of Old Hickory's enthusiastic supporters, but she had always admitted that he was a man of stature. Such a man wouldn't have chosen an incompetent as his friend.

It might be a problem to lower the barrier that stood between them, and she wasn't even sure that she wanted it lowered. Not that he was likely to develop a personal interest in her, of course, yet she couldn't help wondering what she would do if he actively paid court to her. Then she was irritated with herself for thinking such things. Not only was Sam very proper in all of his dealings with her, he spent much of his free time chatting with Tonie Mell. They spoke the same language and obviously had a great deal in common. It was only natural to assume that they had ignited a mutual spark.

Tonie was welcome to Sam if she wanted him. The only reason she herself even wondered about him, Claudia told herself, was because Sam Brentwood was the only unmarried man in the wagon train with any kind of magnetism.

Sam might insist that they were making good time, but it was tiresome and it was slow. The changing scenery had little appeal for Claudia. Too, she had very little in common with most people in the train, and she was often bored. It was that state of mind, she told herself firmly—but without conviction—that was basically responsible for her increasing concern with Sam Brentwood.

The train rolled on, and each day the weather grew warmer as summer approached. Duties were redistributed. The new arrivals were assigned to chores, and the veterans who had been on the road for many weeks were given supervisory positions. Cathy van Ayl and a woman who had joined the company in Harrisburg were placed in charge of the cooking. Terence Malcolm had proved so useful and so eager to help that Sam made him a special assistant, assigning him any critical job that arose. Claudia was in charge of the water brigade.

One of her new helpers became an admirer. Chet Harris was fourteen, a rawboned boy who watched her constantly, his eyes adoring. He forced his three younger brothers to do their share of the work. She appreciated his help and was amused by his infatuation.

But she felt sorry for the mother of the boys. Emily Harris was a widow, poverty-stricken, driven by desperation to make the long journey across the continent with her brood. Only because Chet assumed some of the responsibilities of a man was she able to keep her other sons under control.

"If I had my life to live again," she told Claudia one evening after supper, "I'd marry a capon who couldn't give me any young'uns. There was a time I didn't have a care in the world, but that was so long ago I don't rightly remember how it felt."

Sam was in undisputed command of the caravan, but as the group moved westward along the Ohio River he began to rely for assistance on an informal council. Dr. Martin, always grave and courteous, became his closest advisor, and to Claudia's surprise she found that Sam frequently came to her for help, too.

"I don't know much about women," he told her, "so you understand better than I do how the ladies feel. Take last night, for instance. Why were they ready to spit at me for stopping near those falls?"

"Because they couldn't wash their clothes there without getting soaked in the spray, of course. If we'd made camp a half-mile farther downstream, it would have been much more convenient."

"You're right, Doc," Sam said to the doctor. "After this I'd better listen to her."

Another newcomer, also friendly with Sam, caused Claudia some uneasiness. Baron Ernst von Thalman was an Austrian nobleman in his early fifties—by far the most colorful member of the party. His wagon, pulled by a matched team of four magnificent horses, was the only vehicle with hard sides and a hard top. It more nearly resembled a traveling home on wheels than a wagon. Always impeccably attired, wearing polished boots and crisp linen, the Baron was attended by a personal manservant named Schultz, who slept in a corner of the wagon and seemed to live for no purpose other than that of doing his master's bidding.

The Baron's manners were extravagant. He not only clicked his heels and bowed to everyone, but he irritated Claudia immensely by kissing her hand whenever they met. Although he said little, he spoke perfect English with only a trace of an accent and was always smiling. It was obvious that he regarded the adventure as a lark.

Claudia's unsettled anxieties about the Baron grew. One evening, she decided to speak to Sam Brentwood. He was eating with Dr. Martin some distance from the fire, so she carried her plate of fish, beans and freshly baked bread to the rock on which they were sitting.

"I hope you don't mind if I join you," she said.

It was obvious that neither man did.

"Mr. Brentwood," she said, "I believe you're making a mistake with a certain man on the train and it bothers me."

Sam's smile was ironic. "I reckon I'll have to mend my ways, Mrs. Humphries."

"Don't laugh. We may have another spy in our midst. Baron von Thalman."

To her astonishment both the wagonmaster and the physician whooped with laughter.

"You're mistaken, Mrs. Humphries," Dr. Martin said. "Ernst von Thalman has a distinguished record as a cavalry officer in the Imperial Austrian Army. He commanded a brigade for years."

"That doesn't prove he's not a spy, Doctor!"

"It so happens that he fought beside the British at Waterloo, and he dislikes them intensely. He believes they've wrongly claimed all the credit for beating Napoleon Bonaparte."

Sam mopped up the gravy on his plate with a chunk of bread. "Put your mind at rest, Mrs. Humphries. The Baron is a friend of Andy Jackson and visited him at the Hermitage a few weeks ago. In fact, he came straight to Pittsburgh from Tennessee—at Old Hickory's suggestion. And he brought me a letter from Andy, saying he thought we'd enjoy having the Baron travel with us. Ernst von Thalman may be a strange bird, but he's no spy!"

"I'm relieved to hear it." Claudia's manner was frigid.

Dr. Martin, at least, understood her feeling of humiliation. "I'm sure Mr. Brentwood appreciates your caution," he told her. But Sam was nonplussed when she glared at him.

Claudia had to concede thereafter that perhaps her fears had been exaggerated. The Baron seemed to make himself helpful in many different ways. When the men went fishing after the caravan halted each day, the Baron accompanied the Harris boys. He also made certain that they did their chores for their mother. He went out of his way to be kind to Lena Malcolm. And one night, when Terence was tending the fire and Lena was cooking, Claudia found the Baron quietly entertaining the baby, cooing at Lenore and making faces.

The following Sunday she saw another side of the good Baron's nature.

The caravan had halted for a day of rest on the Sabbath. The wagons were grouped in a semi-circle near the banks of the Ohio, and the horses were grazing on the lush grass in the enclosure. That morning Dr. Martin had read from the Bible for all who wanted to attend services, and the company was relaxing on a lazy afternoon. Men were mending harnesses and repairing the canvas roofs of their wagons and women were sewing. Those of the children who hadn't gone fishing were playing a game of tag outside the circle of the wagons.

Terence Malcolm, who seemed incapable of remaining idle, was gathering firewood. Claudia, with nothing better to occupy her time, sat on the upper of a pair of boards that served as the back steps of the Malcolm wagon, idly chatting with Lena and Cathy. The baby was in her crib, napping, and Lena was in a talkative mood.

"Is it true that the berries in Oregon are big as melons?" she asked.

"I very much doubt it," Claudia said.

"That's what the Baron told me."

Claudia refrained from remarking that the Baron knew no more about Oregon than anyone else, and had been teasing her. Lena was much more attractive these days: she was gaining weight, and her face no longer looked strained. Though she and Terence behaved in an oddly formal way toward each other, the marriage seemed good for her.

Then, all at once, the Sunday afternoon peace was shattered. Eight roughly attired men, several of them bearded and all armed with braces of long-barreled pistols, rode into the enclosure. A single glance was enough to confirm that their visit wasn't friendly, even before they drew their pistols.

"Stay where you are, folks, and nobody'll get hurt." The spokesman wore a high-crowned, broad-brimmed hat that shaded his face. "Money and jewelry won't do you any good where you're going, so we'll do you the favor of taking them. Just rest easy while the boys here go from wagon to wagon. Anybody who acts up will regret it!"

Claudia was outraged. "Lena," she whispered, "sneak into your wagon and bring me Terry's rifle. Quickly. His powder horn and ammunition, too."

Startled, Lena hesitated.

"Do as I say!"

Lena crept inside, unnoticed by the intruders.

Three of the thieves dismounted and began to ransack the nearest wagon.

Claudia had never fired Terence's new rifle. But there was no opportunity to test it now. Thanking the Almighty that it was already loaded, she raised it to her shoulder, aimed at the leader on horseback and fired.

The bullet passed through his hat, knocking it to the ground. That brief diversion was all Sam Brentwood and Baron von Thalman needed. At opposite ends of the circle, they opened a murderous crossfire. The Baron used two rifles. His manservant reloaded one for him while he used the other. But Sam needed no one's help, and reloaded his long rifle with amazing speed.

Before the robbers knew what was happening, two of their number went down.

Claudia too, had managed to reload, and as she raised the rifle to fire again she saw that the leader was aiming his pistol at her. But she was too angry to be frightened. She squeezed the trigger as he fired at her.

His horse, unnerved by the explosions, side-stepped, and the man's bullet passed over Claudia's head. But her own aim was true, and she had the satisfaction of seeing the leader clutch his shoulder. She watched the spreading patch of blood on his shirt, horrified by what she'd done.

Meantime Sam and the Baron were giving far better than they received. Coolly ignoring the bullets that whistled past their bodies, they kept up a steady fire until six of the intruders were either dead or injured and the last two raised their hands up over their heads.

"Terry!" Sam called. "Take the Harris boy with you and go get the sheriff. Tell him we've got some customers for him."

Terence and Chet Harris galloped off.

Two of the intruders were dead and four others had been wounded. The members of the wagon train had suffered no casualties.

Lenore, awakened by the commotion, began to wail.

"Soothe your baby, Lena, and tell her everything's all right," Claudia said. Then she began to feel sick.

After the sheriff and his deputies arrived, to remove the dead thieves in a cart and take the others off to jail, the Baron came up to Claudia, bowed low over her hand and invited her back to his wagon for what he called "a little celebration."

Not wanting to be alone with him, she tried to say no.

"I insist," Ernst von Thalman said, and offered her his arm.

Because they had worked in tandem to overcome the robbers, Claudia felt she couldn't refuse again.

Sam was seated at a small teakwood table in the ornately furnished wagon, drinking tea. He smiled as he raised his cup to her. "You won't need many more lessons in marksmanship," he said. "But your reloading is sloppy and far too slow. You should've gotten off your second shot before the robber had a chance to take aim at you."

Claudia's indignation was heightened by the knowledge that what he said was true.

As she sat, the Baron held her chair, bowing again before he took his own seat. His manservant brought her a tiny silver cup filled with a clear, strong-smelling liquid.

"Schnapps," the Baron told her. "A true warrior's drink."

"I believe it's too strong," she said.

"Sip it or drink it down, as you will," he replied. "But I assure you, Madame, that after what I've seen today, no liquor on earth is too strong for you." He raised his own cup.

Claudia took an experimental sip. She felt she had to be polite.

Von Thalman applauded. "Bravo, Madame! If you can ride as well as you shoot, I'd give you command of a troop of my elite cavalry with no questions asked."

His compliment was obviously sincere. Accepting it as he meant it, she glowed.

"Sam," the Baron continued, "when we come to wilder country we must take her hunting with us."

"Maybe," Sam said. "But her shooting today could be a fluke. So maybe we'd better put her through her paces on the practice range first."

Claudia had to exert all her will power to keep from hurling the schnapps in his face. She was furious. Sam Brentwood lost no opportunity to denigrate her, mock

her, hold her up to ridicule. She kept her peace, however, partly because she didn't want to lose her temper
in the presence of the Baron, who was still a stranger.
Even more important, she refused to give Brentwood
the satisfaction of knowing how he could infuriate her.

Sam, however, was far more sensitive to her changing moods than she knew. He could almost feel her
stiffen, although he had no idea what had upset her,
and when he glanced in her direction she deliberately
averted her gaze. Then, shrugging almost imperceptibly,
he looked at the Baron.

Ernst von Thalman knew exactly why the young
lady was suddenly out of sorts. At first he wanted to
wait until later to explain to Sam. But on second
thought he decided to see what amends he could offer
right now, in the spirit of celebration.

"I'm sure Sam didn't intend his remark the way you
took it, Mrs. Humphries," he said.

There, the matter was in the open now, thought
Claudia. And she wasn't responsible. "Are you trying to
say that Mr. Brentwood was flattering me?" she said
coldly. "Mr. Brentwood makes it a practice never,
never to say anything pleasant to a lady if he can pos-
sibly make an unkind remark."

"I do?" Sam was astonished.

Claudia continued to address the other man. "I'll
tell you a secret, Baron. Mr. Brentwood can show great
courage in dangerous situations. But I believe he feels
compelled to tear down women for a very simple reason. He's afraid of us."

Ernst von Thalman roared with laughter. There was
just enough truth to the comment to give it a valid sting.

Sam felt the bite of her verbal lash, and color rose to his face.

Claudia knew she had scored, and was satisfied. Taking a token sip of her drink, which was too strong for her, she rose demurely, and said she had to return.

"I'll walk you back," Sam said. He had no intention of allowing their dispute to remain unresolved.

"That won't be necessary," she replied sweetly. "I know the way, and I'm sure no harm will come to me."

His temper soaring, Sam surprised himself by shouting. "Damnation, woman, if I have a mind to walk a few yards with you, that's blame well what I'm going to do!"

Ernst von Thalman almost choked on his drink, averting his face in an effort to hide his laughter.

The Baron's amusement made Claudia smug. "Really, Mr. Brentwood," she said, "I don't care to make an issue of it. You're bigger and stronger than I am, so there's no way I can prevent you, is there?"

Now Sam was even angrier. Muttering something to the Baron about returning in due time, he stomped out behind the young woman.

The sun had been shining earlier, but now a late spring rain was falling, which spoiled Claudia's chance to confuse the man even more—by taking his arm. Instead she walked rapidly in order not to be soaked by the heavy downpour.

"You've got me all wrong," Sam said.

Claudia was pleased. She continued to hold the upper hand. She shrugged, the rise and fall of her shoulders indicating that nothing could have meant less to her.

Limping along beside her, his arthritic hip aching afresh, Sam fought the urge to grab her shoulders and shake some sense into her.

When they reached Claudia's wagon, she decided to be generous. "If you wish," she said, "you may come in with me."

He grunted, aware that she was placing him at a disadvantage. At the same time, it was foolish to stand in the rain, arguing.

Instead of lighting the lamp or a candle, Claudia rolled up the canvas on one side of the wagon, just enough to let a little light in but keep the rain out. Sam did the same on the other side of the wagon.

Claudia seated herself on a leather clothing box, her manner as regal as though she was entertaining in a grand New Haven parlor. She gestured at the opposite box.

Sam, however, preferred to remain standing. He knew he was on the defensive. "I didn't mean to hurt your feelings," he said.

"You didn't," she lied.

"Or insult you."

Claudia noted how rigid he had become. She knew how difficult it must be for such a proud, stubborn man to offer her an apology. All at once the game she was playing lost its savor, and she softened. "It seems to me," she said, "that when people spend so much of their time together they become much more intense than if they lived in a city and only met occasionally."

Sam knew nothing about city living, but he understood what she meant, and nodded.

"Maybe both of us are guilty of making too much

155

out of nothing," Claudia said and then hesitated. It was very difficult for her to back down, too, but she refused to let him make the more generous gesture. "Perhaps I've been looking for slights where none were intended."

"Believe me, they weren't." Her gentleness disarmed him.

"Apparently you and I grate on each other, Mr. Brentwood. But since we're going to be traveling together all the way to Independence, Missouri, unless I can find some way to leave the train before then, we really should try to be friends."

"You bet, ma'am." He found himself hoping she wouldn't give up the journey, astonished by his own reaction.

Impulsively she held out her hand to him. Never before had a woman offered Sam the hand of friendship, and he responded quickly, without even thinking.

As their hands touched Claudia felt herself weaken. She thought for a moment that he was going to kiss her. Then he gained control of himself, and her relief was mingled with a strange sense of lingering regret that he hadn't lifted her to her feet and taken her in his arms.

Sam felt the same magnetic current, and was stunned by it. Claudia's smile was unexpectedly tremulous.

As he left the wagon, Sam discovered it was cold sweat, not rain, that soaked his buckskin shirt.

Otto van Ayl had been in a foul mood for days, and his wife had borne the brunt of his displeasure. The money under the false flooring of his wagon had become an obsession. Afraid that some of the newer arrivals might be trying to rob him, he had conceived an intense dislike for virtually all of them. Retreating more and more into his shell, he had as little intercourse as possible with the rest of the company.

He freely criticized the others to Cathy, however, and one evening, shortly after supper, he approached her as she sat near the campfire, chatting with Lena Malcolm. "Come back to the wagon," he said, glaring at her. "I want words with you."

Cathy knew he was angry, but she had no idea what had upset him. But she didn't want to create a scene in public, so she said nothing as they walked to the wagon. There she lighted three candles and waited for what he would say.

Otto promptly blew out two of the candles. "There's no need to light up this place like a Christmas tree," he said. "One candle gives plenty of light. You don't seem to care how you waste my money."

His excessive frugality had almost driven Cathy to distraction. But she knew from bitter experience that she'd be subjected to a more severe lecture if she had the temerity to oppose him. So she contented herself with a quiet, "Yes, Otto."

The wagon was so crowded there was scarcely room for their mattress at one side. Pointing an accusing finger at her, he said "You're becoming too friendly with that Malcolm woman. Why?"

"I like her very much," she said. The charge was absurd.

"Answer my question!"

157

"But I did," she said. "There's no special reason. You can get along all right by yourself, but I can't. I need to talk with other people. What don't you like about Lena?"

"She and that boy she married are paupers. She's getting friendly with you so they can find some way to steal my money."

"That's absurd." His accusation was so ridiculous Cathy forgot her resolve to avoid a dispute with him. "In the first place Lena and Terry are fine people, and I enjoy them very much. In the second place, they're anything but poor. When Mr. Brentwood gave them the wagon they got the contents, too, including a lot of money. They probably have more money than anyone else in the caravan."

"Then they're greedy for more. I notice the way they fawn on you."

"They do no such thing." Cathy's patience was exhausted.

"Are you calling me a liar?"

"All I'm saying," she replied, "is that your imagination must be playing tricks on you."

Otto drew himself up to his full height. "You know nothing of the world because you're just a child. I forbid you to associate with Lena and Terence Malcolm!"

Cathy suddenly felt rebellious. His order was unfair and unrealistic, and she was sick of giving in to his commands. "Otto," she said, "I'm your wife, not your daughter. You didn't consult me before you decided to make this trip to the ends of the earth, but when you told me you were going, I agreed to go with you, because I believed it was a wife's place to obey her husband."

"It is," he said.

She paid no attention to the interruption. "I gave up my nice, snug home for a life that even the gypsies would hate. I've never complained about the hardships on this wagon train, not once. And if I choose to talk with a decent and honorable girl, that's my right. You have no proof that Terence and Lena are intending to rob—"

"Must I wait until my money vanishes?" Otto demanded.

"You have no evidence against them. You have no evidence against anyone else in the company. I've never disputed your word and I've never disobeyed your orders. But this time you've gone too far. I'll see as much of Lena Malcolm as I please!"

Now he looked apoplectic—a dangerous condition in a man of his age. "I won't tolerate such conduct."

"Do as you please," Cathy said recklessly. "I refuse to consult you on everything I do. I realize I'm committed to go all the way to Oregon with this train, and I'll honor my obligations, although there are things I'd rather do. But I won't tolerate your bullying. My sister will gladly take me into her wagon, and so will Lena and Terry, crowded though they are."

Otto was incredulous. "You would dare to leave your husband's bed and board? That's cause for annulment."

"Then have our marriage annulled, and be damned to you!" Never before had Cathy been so defiant. "If you behave sensibly, I'll stay with you. But if you don't, I'll go my own way. Sam Brentwood says I'm earning my keep, so I'm no longer beholden to you, Otto van Ayl."

Giving him no chance to reply, she stalked out of the wagon and disappeared in the darkness.

Otto was tempted to call her back, but he was afraid she wouldn't come. It was inconceivable that she could show such gumption. He no longer knew how to handle her. When she had said he treated her like a daughter instead of a wife, she had spoken the truth. But that didn't matter. What worried him the most was the fact that he'd lost his moral authority over her. He felt almost paralyzed.

Cathy wanted to see no one. She stayed away from the campfire, wandering aimlessly around outside the circle, staying in the shadows near the wagons. Now that she'd spoken her mind to Otto, she felt sick. She was afraid she'd gone too far. It was too late to undo the damage, however. If he refused to take her back in their wagon, she'd have to bear the consequences.

Pride made it difficult for her to ask Claudia or Lena for refuge, and she would prefer not to. Maybe she could simply wait until Otto went to sleep, then creep into the wagon and go to bed. Otto's pride was fierce. If his young wife left him, he'd expect the entire company to laugh at him. Rather than suffer that humiliation, he'd more likely have her back and try to pretend that nothing had happened.

The sound of laughter and conversation within the circle disturbed Cathy. Eager to be alone, she felt a sudden urge to wander into the woods beyond the perimeter of the camp. There, in the solitude, she might be able to think more clearly and plot a sensible future.

Suddenly, Whip Holt entered her mind, the memory of his presence so strong it was like a physical blow. For weeks she had fought her own feelings. Now she knew that the struggle had been a waste of time. She was in love with Whip, she had to admit it. And although he hadn't expressed his innermost feelings to her, instinct told her that he loved her, too.

But Cathy realized that she had to put Whip out of her mind. As a decent, self-respecting wife, she couldn't tolerate such feelings for any man not her husband. Though her marriage had been unsatisfactory from the beginning, and grown worse during the expedition, there was nothing she could do to change it. When she had been too young to know better, her father had married her to the wrong man. He had meant to provide her with lifelong security, but Papa had been mistaken, and she had to suffer the consequences.

As she walked toward the woods, someone called out to her. It was the voice of a young woman. "Hello, wait! Please stop!"

Cathy halted, feeling almost like a little girl caught in a naughty act.

Tonie Mell materialized beside her in the dark. "I saw you slipping away just now, so I followed," she said. "Where you headed?"

"No place in particular," Cathy replied, feeling somewhat guilty. "I felt like a stroll through the woods, that's all."

"I reckon you weren't listening when Sam said he didn't want anybody wandering away from camp after dark. River pirates and other scum make their headquarters in these parts, and they've been known to kidnap unwary travelers and hold them for ransom."

"I remember now, and I'm sorry," Cathy said. "I certainly don't want to cause trouble." They turned back toward the wagons.

Tonie allowed Cathy to go first through the opening between two wagons, then touched her arm. "I'm feeling a mite restless tonight myself. Come along to my wagon for a chat."

Cathy neither liked nor disliked Tonie Mell. She hesitated only for a moment before agreeing.

They walked in silence to the wagon, where Tonie produced a jar of crushed raspberries she'd mixed with water, sugar and wild mint leaves. "This is a drink I learned how to make in Missouri," she said. "It tastes like lemonade, but I like it better."

"So do I," Cathy said, after taking a sip.

They sat side by side on the lowered back steps of the wagon. "To tell you the truth," Tonie said, "I saw you leaving your wagon. I could tell from your walk that if you were a yellow jacket or a hornet you'd be buzzing."

Cathy laughed.

"I was very young when my aunt and uncle took me out to Missouri," Tonie said, "but I can remember plain as day that they never stopped bickering. Most settlers who've gone out there aren't on speaking terms with each other by the time they set up a homestead.

It stands to reason that two people get to feeling ornery after sharing living quarters the size of a cupboard."

"Did it show all that much?" Cathy was aghast.

Tonie grinned. "Talking to your husband just now, you weren't exactly keeping your feelings a secret."

"Oh, dear!"

"Don't let it bother you. I just happened to be walking past your wagon at the time. Nobody else heard you, just me." Tonie patted her on the shoulder.

"Please let me apologize."

"Like hell! You'll do fine on this march, and after you get out to Oregon, too, if you keep saying what you feel right out. You'll do better than your stuck-up sister, that's for sure. I just spent a little time in the East, and I didn't like it. Everybody's polite, everybody hides what he really feels, and that's what makes trouble. Trouble in families, trouble between neighbors. Look at New York and Philadelphia. They don't even like each other. Out west folks are honest. We say what we mean. We get our grudges off our chests and everybody feels the better for it."

"Suppose a neighbor doesn't like something you say?"

Tonie patted the butt of the pistol she carried in her belt and laughed. "There are ways of handling arguments like that."

"I'm not sure I'll like the West."

"Sure you will, Cathy. You try not to take offense when somebody shoots off at the mouth, because you know there'll be a real feud if you do. Then they're nice and easy with you when you get to talking, so it all works out."

Cathy sipped her raspberry drink. "Perhaps it'll be all right," she said. "But I'll never be able to ride and hunt and fish the way you do."

"There's no need. That's just the way I was brought up. My uncle had nobody else to help him on the ranch. You know how to cook and sew and take care of a house, and every man appreciates those things."

Every man except Otto, Cathy told herself, who took them for granted.

"Sometimes," Tonie said, "I envy you."

"Really?" Cathy blinked in surprise.

"The men in this train treat you like a woman. Not because you wear pretty clothes and go around with your nose in the air, either, the way your sister does. Just because you're a woman."

"So are you, Tonie."

"Nobody would ever know it. Not around here. Sam treats me like I was his younger brother, and now the Baron is doing the same thing. Even . . . even Dr. Martin doesn't seem to think I'm a female, so I have me a hunch he's no great shakes as a doctor."

Her tone, even more than her actual words, gave Cathy the idea that she was developing a personal interest in Dr. Martin. If so, Claudia was mistaken in believing that Tonie had set her cap for Sam Brentwood. Though Cathy didn't want to embarrass the girl, perhaps she could offer some friendly guidance.

"Do you mind a little advice?" she said.

"Fire away!"

"If the men seem to think of you as a man, maybe it's because you act and dress like one. Instead of hunting, why not help with the cooking, or fetch water, or wash dishes."

"I can do all those things," Tonie said. "I do them at home. But hunting's more fun."

"Then go hunting, but not every day. And stop acting as line monitor. There are plenty of men who can handle that job now. The Baron is as well qualified as you are," Cathy said.

"What in the world would I do instead?" Tonie looked at her blankly.

"Exactly what the rest of us do. Start wearing dresses and drive your wagon every day. Then the men will know you're a woman, even if you change into buckskins to go hunting every night."

For a long time Tonie was silent. "I only own two dresses," she said. "I bought them back East."

"Can you sew?"

"Tolerably. My aunt saw to that."

"Then the next time we come to a town, buy yourself some pretty material. And make yourself some dresses. They'll do wonders for your femininity."

"It could be."

"If you like," Cathy said, "I'll lend you some lip rouge and cosmetics."

"I don't want to look like your sister!" The redhead was alarmed.

"No fear of that," Cathy said with a laugh. "Nobody else looks like Claudia—or ever will."

"I'm willing to try," Tonie said. "Would you come

with me to buy some of that paint I can smear on my face? I never thought the time would come when I'd start daubing myself up like an Indian. But I sure do get my dander up when I see the way men make a fuss over girls who wear it."

"Of course." Cathy decided that this "untamed" westerner might actually be more feminine than anyone had realized.

"There's just one more favor I'd like. I hate to ask it of you, seeing as how you're the sister of that high and mighty one. So I won't mind if you turn me down."

"I'll gladly do whatever I can," Cathy said.

Tonie hesitated, then blushed. "Don't tell anyone we had this talk."

"I won't say a word to anyone, including Claudia." Cathy vowed to keep her promise.

"I'm much obliged to you," Tonie said. "I wouldn't want any woman to laugh at me. 'Specially your sister."

It was strange, Cathy thought, how much Claudia and Tonie envied each other, how much each wanted to cast herself in the other's image.

VII

A gentle rain started to fall as the caravan approached the town of Wheeling, in western Virginia, and gradually the weather got worse. Because no one was planning to join the expedition there, as far as Sam knew, he preferred to move through the town without stopping, then make camp in the open country beyond.

But the fame of the wagon train had preceded it, and in spite of the rain the citizens of Wheeling turned out in force to see the pioneers. Hundreds lined the muddy streets. Those whose houses boasted glass window panes peered out of them, while others stared from open front doors.

Sam and Tonie, mounted and wearing their buckskins, seemed impervious to the weather, and so did the mounted Baron von Thalman. He was wearing a water-repellent coat and headgear of wool that had been treated chemically. But the drivers of the wagons were as miserable as they looked. Soaked to the skin,

167

they clung to their wagon perches, watching water run off the backs of their horses. Occasionally they took off their own sopping hats to wipe the water from their faces.

From inside their wagons, other members of the expedition peered out. Perhaps, they thought, their unusual reception was due to their bedraggled appearance.

The residents of Wheeling watched them in virtual silence. Few people waved, few cheered, and only a handful of children ran for short distances alongside. But the townspeople of Wheeling weren't hostile. On the contrary, they showed a sense of kinship and understanding that had been lacking in many towns.

Residents of Wheeling regarded it as a frontier town. They were aware of many of the hardships the company faced. Just beginning to flourish as a coal-mining and manufacturing center, Wheeling had been forced to struggle for existence. Settlers from Virginia, Maryland and the Carolinas had cut down trees, built their homes and fought starvation on land that resisted their efforts at cultivation. They clung to the hope of founding a major river port that could supply factories elsewhere with vitally needed coal. Now their dream was being realized.

They and their fathers had come to this town on the Ohio River in wagons, some of them covered, some of them open carts dragged by hand when horses were lacking. Unlike the residents of many communities, they saw little romance in the long line of covered wagons slushing along through the mud. There would be days, they knew, when everyone in the company would be cold and tired and hungry. There would be periods when disease would sweep through their ranks, but disease wouldn't stop them.

Of the company, Sam Brentwood alone realized the extent of the danger. The waters of the Ohio were already rising, swollen by the rains. Then would come the Mississippi and the Missouri, and after them the great rivers of the West, the Platte and the Colorado. Ahead, too, lay the endless plains and prairies, the towering peaks of the Rocky Mountains and the equally rugged ranges west of the Great Divide. Indian tribes, resenting the incursion of strangers into their territories, would be a constant menace. Sam knew that many who were huddled in their wagons wouldn't survive the arduous journey, the longest ever made by American men and women.

As they left Wheeling behind to move south along the Ohio, the rain worsened, coming down in torrents. Claudia was reminded of what was called a "nor'easter" in New England. The storm was merciless and unrelenting. The ground became so soggy that the wagons often had to keep in constant motion to avoid bogging down in the mud.

The downpour continued for three days. The river rose so high that Sam directed the wagons to move farther inland. Eventually he was forced to call a halt at a makeshift campsite. It was the pioneers' first major confrontation with the elements, and new problems were waiting to greet them.

With Sam's help, Abe Ellis covered the special wagon with a second layer of canvas to protect its precious cargo. Under no circumstances could water be allowed to dampen the gunpowder or cause the emergency supplies of food to spoil. Men and women had to protect their own property as best they could. Some buried flour, sugar and salt beneath clothing. A crude, temporary stockade fence was erected in the forest to contain the horses, huddling beneath dripping oaks and elms in a vain attempt to keep dry.

Trees were felled in the heavy rain. Then logs were split, the rails placed beneath the wheels of the wagons so they wouldn't sink in the mud. But at least drinking water was no longer a problem. Empty barrels were filled within hours, and the water-gathering detail was relieved of its responsibilities.

Some salt was spoiled, but that loss didn't concern Sam unduly. He knew they would come to salt licks, where supplies could be replenished.

When the sun came out after four days of rain, everyone cheered. But Sam insisted that they remain at their campsite for an additional twenty-four hours. Clothes and blankets were hung out to dry on lines stretched between wagons. Canvases were removed to allow the sun to reach the insides of the wagons, and perishables were placed in the sunlight.

Sam rode ahead to determine the amount of damage. When he returned, late in the day, he assembled the entire camp.

"I have bad news," he said. "The road on this side of the river has been washed away. The west bank, over in Ohio, wasn't hurt as much because the road there is wider and built on higher ground. That means we'll have to cross the river in the morning."

Otto van Ayl was alarmed. "How can we cross a river that's raging like an ocean?"

"The water is already going down," Sam replied. By tomorrow it should be safe. All we need do is find the best place for our crossing."

Otto wasn't satisfied. "Should be safe?"

"That's what I said. If you were unwilling to take chances, Mr. van Ayl, you should have stayed at home."

Otto subsided. Cathy felt mortified.

Before sundown, Sam went ahead on foot, taking several men with him, to explore the river banks. After a careful exploration of the better part of a mile, Sam found the place he was seeking. He pointed toward the distance. "Look yonder," he said. "There are two little islands in the river, like stepping stones. Even now the water between them is fairly shallow. By morning it will be even lower."

"How will we make the crossing?" Dr. Martin asked.

"The horses ought to be able to walk most of the way, hauling the wagons behind them. But if they have to swim, the wagons will float for short distances. I've seen it done that way many times on the Tennessee and the Missouri. There's no real danger, if folks keep their heads."

"Did you say the wagons will *float?*" Ernst von Thalman looked dubious.

"Hellfire, Ernie, you've told me how you floated cannon across the Rhine!"

"True, but we used pontoons."

"The weight of a wagon is more evenly distributed across a greater area," Sam said. "Of course floorboards might get a mite damp, so folks will have to keep their food and valuables off the floor. Everything depends on whether the good weather holds."

The caravan took most of the day to detour to the crossing site. There they formed a line, ready for the new adventure. The weather held, the morning dawned bright and clear and the level of the river was still lower.

First, Sam crossed alone on his stallion. The beast walked slowly through the water from island to island, swimming only a short distance on the final part of the journey. From the far shore, Sam raised an arm and beckoned.

Baron von Thalman was the next to cross, knowing more about horses than anyone else in the train. He held the reins himself, talking constantly to his horses, reassuring them. His manservant sat rigidly beside him. When they reached the other side, the entire company applauded.

At her own insistence, Claudia went next. "I want to set an example for the women and children," she explained. "They'll be much calmer if they see I'm all right."

Her team needed only gentle urging to step into the water. And with Quincy beside her on the boards she felt the wagon move into the Ohio. The river flooring of pebbles was smooth, which reassured her, and she reached the first grassy island without difficulty, then went on to the second.

Only at that moment, when she looked down the

length of river, did she feel any qualms. Less than a half-mile away, on the Ohio side, there were jagged rocks in the stream, with white-water frothing around them. It certainly wouldn't pay to be carried downstream and smash her wagon on those rocks.

Sam cupped his hands. "Easy now! When the horses start to swim, keep a firm hold on the reins, but don't haul them in too tight!"

Claudia nodded. Then she began the final crossing. When the team began to swim, she caught her breath. She could feel the buoyancy of the floating wagon beneath her. But Sam Brentwood had been right. Almost before she knew it her team dragged the wagon onto dry ground. She could hear the company applauding on the far shore.

Dr. Martin made the crossing with ease, as did Tonie. They were followed by Otto and Cathy van Ayl. Cathy smiled in relief when they reached the shore. Next came Terence and Lena Malcolm, whose eager young faces showed their pleasure in the experience.

One by one the others crossed. There was one early mishap. When his horses began to swim, a Pennsylvania farmer lost his courage. But Sam was prepared and rode his horse to a place alongside the endangered wagon, took the reins from the farmer and guided the team ashore.

Emily Harris held the next to last place in line because her youngest son, a boy of six, had been sick earlier in the day. But she was undaunted by the obstacles ahead, and with Chet sitting beside her and the other boys peering out from the rear, she began the crossing.

The last in line was James Caldwell, who was suffering from a hangover. It had been impossible to arouse him in time to award him an earlier place. Bored by the long wait, he had started drinking again and decided to try the crossing two at a time, though Sam had expressly forbade it.

His pace was reckless, and he was almost directly behind Mrs. Harris as her team moved into the final phase of the crossing.

"Hold back, there!" Sam shouted to Caldwell. "The goddamn fool," he muttered.

Caldwell paid no attention, and actually seemed to be racing as his team moved abreast of the Harris team.

Sensing the danger, Sam rode into the water, closely followed by Ernst von Thalman.

The inevitable happened. A Caldwell horse kicked a Harris horse, and both reacted violently. As the animals thrashed about in the water, the two wagons locked together.

Emily Harris tried valiantly to draw her team free. But it required all Sam's and the Baron's skill to pry the wagons apart. Then Caldwell became so impatient to reach the shore that he tried to move ahead, almost capsizing his wagon. Terence Malcolm showed his resourcefulness by rigging an emergency pulley, attaching a strong rope to one of the sturdy, rear wheels of his wagon.

A teenaged boy took the loose end, quickly tied a rock to it and heaved it with all his might toward Sam.

Sam managed to catch it and swam his horse into position beside the Harris wagon. Leaning over as far as he could, he passed it to Chet, and gave the boy crisp instructions. "If you can, climb forward on your mare's back. Move gently so you don't upset her more than she is already. Then tie this rope to the yoke—double knots, triple knots, as many as you can—so it'll hold."

White-faced, Chet nodded. He stood and balanced himself on the careening wagon, the cries of his frightened younger brothers echoing in his ears.

"Hold the reins firm, Mrs. Harris!" Sam ordered.

The terrified woman did her best.

Chet inched forward. He reached the wet, slippery back of the mare. He knew he'd be done for if he fell into the water, where thrashing hooves would kill him. Finally, he made his way forward to the yoke and did his best to tie it.

"It's secure now!" he cried at last, gasping for breath, and praying that it was.

Terence tugged at the spokes of his pulley, using all of his strength. He was quickly joined by a number of volunteers, who worked in unison. Little by little they drew the frightened team and the Harris wagon closer, using the hub as a spindle.

Meantime the Caldwell horses were out of control. Baron von Thalman risked his own life to ride close enough to cut them loose. "Jump overboard and swim!" he shouted to Caldwell. But the advice was in vain.

The man was crazed, and stayed on his wagon as his horses made their way ashore, where strong men began to soothe them.

The wagon, partly submerged now, was picked up by the current that became stronger below the islands.

Bobbing and jolting, it was carried faster and faster toward the jumble of rocks and white water that appeared at the bend.

A dozen people urged the man to jump overboard and swim, but he seemed not to hear them. Clinging to the wreckage of his wagon, he was being carried to certain doom. Other men followed downstream along the bank, in a futile effort to do something.

Meanwhile, inch by precious inch, the Harris wagon was moving toward safety, but the danger was far from ended. Mrs. Harris clung doggedly to her reins, using all of her strength to hold the team in line. Chet, both arms around the mare's neck, did his best to calm her and the gelding with a steady flow of quiet words.

Never had Terence Malcolm labored so hard. He was the anchor man in the team turning the wheel, and he strained with all his might, grasping a spoke and hauling it toward him, then grabbing the next and doing it again, and yet again. Breathing hard, blinded with sweat, he didn't even look at the horses and wagon he was trying to save. His mind was a blank. All he knew was that he had to succeed. Five lives were at stake. Five lives were dependent on him.

Lena stood alone near the river bank. After watching her father lose control of his wagon she had to turn away. At that moment she knew she had hated him all of her life. His browbeating had killed her mother when she was a little girl. And in his drunken rages he'd come close to murdering her, too. When an observer let loose a bloodcurdling scream, Lena didn't even look.

Some day, perhaps, she might feel sorry for him. But

there was no pity within her now. Even her hatred had drained away, and she felt nothing for him, not even regret that he might have been different had he not abused himself and those closest to him.

She heard it happen. The remains of his wagon smashed on the rocks. Odd bits and pieces of cargo bobbed up and down in the water before drifting on downstream. James Caldwell vanished from sight, and though one man ventured as close to the rocks as he dared in an attempt to locate it, his body was never recovered.

The Harris horses had at last found their footing. As they did, Sam and the Baron closed in on either side, making it impossible for the gelding and the mare to break away. They climbed up onto the river bank, where other men grasped their bits and held them firmly. Soon the horses became completely docile, their nightmare behind them.

Mrs. Harris managed a weary smile. "I'm much obliged to all you folks," she said, then turned to her younger sons behind her. "Boys, everybody has worked up an appetite for supper, so get jumping and collect some wood for the fire."

Chet was hailed as a hero of the occasion, and Sam Brentwood awarded him his highest acclaim. "I like your style," he said.

Terence Malcolm slumped to the ground in exhaustion, barely nodding when he was told that Caldwell had drowned. When he got up, he was so wobbly he had to be helped back to his wagon. Everyone was concerned for his health. An anxious Lena arrived a few moments later with Dr. Martin, having left her baby in the care of Cathy. She lighted a lamp, then waited outside while the doctor examined her husband.

"I reckon this is the end of me, Doc," Terence said gloomily, stripping to his small-clothes.

"What makes you think so?" Dr. Martin observed the man's deep torso, rippling shoulders and muscled arms.

"My consumption. The doctor gave me no more than a year to live."

The physician made no comment. He thumped Terence's chest and back repeatedly, had him breathe deeply and ordered him to cough. His examination lasted forty-five minutes.

Finally he put away his instrument bag. "When was the diagnosis made, Malcolm?"

"Six months ago. Not long before I joined the wagon train."

"And you've been on the trail several months?"

"That's right."

"Well, young man, the fresh air and exercise must have had a healing effect on your body. I can find only minor traces of consumption. Keep living a healthy life, and in a few more months you'll be cured."

Terence was incredulous, unable to believe the good news. "You mean I'm not dying?"

"You'll probably outlive all of us." Dr. Martin slapped him on the shoulder and left, pausing for a word with Lena, who was waiting on the back steps. "Don't make yourself a widow's dress just yet," he told her. "You'll have no use for it."

Terence was still dazed when a radiant Lena entered

the wagon, carefully lowering the rear flap behind her and making it secure.

"I can't believe it," Terence said.

"I can. I've seen you getting stronger every day, and I watched you haul in the Harris wagon. A sick man couldn't have done that."

"Now what are we going to do?" he said.

"What do you mean?"

"I made you a promise, marrying you and adopting Lenore. Now, since I'm not going to die, I don't know what to do."

"I know." She ran a hand across his bare chest.

Terence gaped at her.

Slowly, she removed her dress. "We've been married for quite a spell now," she said. "I think the time has come for me to start being your wife."

"But—"

Lena placed a finger over his mouth, curling an arm around his neck. "I always thought the husband made the advances. But I guess a woman does what she must in this world."

He grinned. "I'm sometimes a mite slow to catch on. You . . . you're sure you want me, Lena?"

"I've been wanting you too long, Terry. I wish you'd realize there are times when a man has to learn to act instead of just talk."

Terence took her in his arms. His exhaustion was forgotten as they kissed, then stretched out together on the bed and began to make love in earnest.

That evening Terence did no chores, neither fetching wood nor helping to build the fire, and Lena did no cooking. But those who noted their absence and assumed that the girl was grieving for her father realized they were mistaken when the young couple finally appeared for supper, walking hand in hand. The doctor had spread the good news.

And the radiance on their faces told its own story.

Henry St. Clair's dream of spending the rest of his life in his beloved London was still ever-present in his mind. He could almost taste the food and ale and feel the warmth of the wench he coveted, in the atmosphere of the world's most civilized city.

But the reality he faced was far different. He was now a fugitive from American justice. Once Sam Brentwood notified the authorities that a British spy was roaming through the Pennsylvania countryside, U.S. Army troops would be on the lookout for him. He might well be caught and sent to prison. If that happened, his dreams would come to nothing.

But Henry St. Clair had no intention of being caught. Ruthless and hard-bitten, he was determined not only to survive, but to carry out his mission, no matter how great the odds.

Lesser men might have regarded those odds as overwhelming, but not Henry St. Clair. He only exerted greater effort. His situation was far from hopeless, and a number of factors could tip the balance in his favor. He had ample funds, thanks to his habit of carrying money in his belt. He had been forced to leave a portion of his operating capital behind, but most of what he'd been given to do the job was still safe on his person.

His biggest problems were immediate—and solvable. He needed a stallion or a gelding to replace the work horse he'd made his escape on. He had eaten nothing for three days, and he was ravenously hungry. His clothes were soiled from three nights in the woods, and he required a new wardrobe, preferably inconspicuous, to make himself presentable. Thanks to his hurried departure, he hadn't even brought a razor with him, and he had a three-day growth of beard. Always fastidious, he wouldn't feel clean until he shaved.

All of these difficulties, however, were minor. During the next week or so, before the United States Government learned what had happened and initiated a manhunt, he'd have ample opportunity to alter his appearance. He was determined to complete his assigned task. One way or another, he had to destroy the wagon train bound for the Oregon territory. Not until the Union Jack flew unopposed there would he be content. The London post would be a fitting reward.

Others might regard his predicament as desperate, but he was filled with self-confidence. True, he had to be careful. He couldn't stay overnight at inns, trade his horse, or buy clothes and weapons, for fear that people might remember him if they were questioned by pursuing soldiers. But he could travel faster than the wagon train, and it would be easy enough to discover some way to wreck it completely.

His mission had become more than a mere assignment to win a coveted promotion. Now he had a personal score to settle with Tonie Mell. Now his goal had become a crusade.

Experience had taught him the value of patience. Biding his time, he followed in the wake of the wagon train, awaiting the right time to strike a crippling blow. It was far better to create major incidents than to leave a long, identifiable trail of minor acts of sabotage behind him. It was almost irrelevant that he was famished, his growling stomach protesting. He had subsisted in the Caribbean jungles for two whole weeks on water and edible roots. He thought it unlikely he'd be forced to suffer that much again.

Late on his third afternoon as a fugitive Henry's resilience paid off. Riding across open country not far from the caravan route, he was impressed by a homestead in the distance ahead. A neat fence, a barn, storage sheds and a whitewashed farmhouse suggested that he might have found what he was looking for. He slowed his pace to make a closer inspection.

A woman was working in a vegetable garden about a hundred yards from the house. Two children were helping. It was likely, Henry figured, that no one was in the house. Detouring around it, he saw the farmer chopping wood. Through the open door of the barn he could also see a sleek chestnut horse in a stall—a perfect mount for his purposes.

Leaving his horse to graze, well screened behind trees, Henry picked up a heavy piece of wood to use as a club, then discarded it when he saw a hammer with a metal head. When necessary he could move with the stealth of a mountain lion, and he made no sound as he crept closer to the unsuspecting farmer, now sawing a log four feet thick. With his future at stake, the Englishman drove all unnecessary considerations from his mind. There was no room in him now for compassion.

When he had crept up sufficiently close to the farmer, he raised the hammer and smashed it into the man's head, cracking it open. The farmer dropped dead, and pitching forward across the log, blood and brains oozed from his head.

Henry wasted neither time nor pity over the fate of his victim. He hurried to the stable and saddled the gelding. Then he went quickly to the house, found the master bedroom, and helped himself to shirts, trousers, stockings, underwear, and a jacket.

Luck still running with him, he found a pistol in a drawer, along with a length of lead, a bullet mold and a pouch of gunpowder. Packing his booty into a sheet, he went to the kitchen. He took two loaves of bread and a cold ham, from which only a few slices had been cut.

Then he heard the sound of a woman's scream, soon joined by the cries of her children.

After tying a handkerchief around his face to hide his features, Henry carried his booty across his left shoulder, leaving his right hand free. Now he had to finish the job.

The woman stopped screaming when she saw him. The two children clinging to her skirt, she looked at him in silent terror.

Henry knew that there was little chance she could identify him as the killer of her husband, but he didn't want her stirring up the neighbors. It wouldn't take more than an hour to organize a posse, and then his problems would be multiplied. He had to stop her somehow.

Eyes icy, he went up to her and put all of his weight behind a punch that caught her full in the face and sent her sprawling to the ground on her back. He thought he heard a bone snap and figured that he might have broken her nose.

Not bothering to assess the damage, he ran to the barn, mounted the gelding and galloped off toward the west, the wails of the two little children following him until he could no longer hear them.

Congratulating himself, Henry felt no remorse. The end justified the means. Opposing armies on the field of battle might still obey the ancient laws of chivalry, but a spy knew no rules. It was his duty to carry out his mission, no matter what stood between him and his goal. He put the death of the man and the injury to the woman out of his mind, along with their children. He'd scored a capital success; nothing else was important.

Spurring the gelding, he galloped until the animal began to lather, then reduced his pace somewhat. He rode until long after nightfall, avoiding towns and villages and resisting the temptation to eat. Rigid self-discipline was the key to success for any espionage agent worthy of the name.

Making his way through a heavily wooded area, Henry was pleased when a thunder shower obliterated his tracks. Even the elements were cooperating with him. Finally, at midnight, he dismounted in a small clearing beside a brook, where his exhausted horse could drink and graze. Not even then did he eat, however. Other things had to be done first.

He changed into the farmer's clothes, which fitted him reasonably well, and enjoyed an immediate feeling of relief. Now he'd be indistinguishable from the Pennsylvania farmers. He could appear in the open without fear. Packing his belongings in the sheet, which would do until he got a pair of saddlebags, he made some bullets, loaded the pistol and stuck it in his belt. He was armed and ready for any contingency.

Only then did he tear off a chunk of ham and a piece of bread and eat. Although he was very hungry, he held on to his sense of caution. Realizing that he might get sick if he ate too fast, he took small bites, careful to leave the second loaf of bread and a portion of the ham for the next day. He'd wait another thirty-six hours before buying food and whatever else he needed. Surely then he'd be safe, some fifty miles from the home of the dead farmer.

Henry drank deeply from the brook, then stretched out under a tree for a few hours of sleep. He'd resume his journey well before dawn, but it was best to rest for a time. His progress then would be more rapid.

Perhaps, he thought, it was just as well that he'd been forced to leave the wagon train. Now he could function more freely, bedeviling the train until he found a way to disrupt it permanently.

Dozing on the hard ground of the forest that stretched across North America for hundreds of miles on end, Henry St. Clair finally allowed himself the luxury of dreaming about London again. He was almost four thousand miles from home, but he could still picture himself sitting in his favorite tavern, eating a savory meat pie, drinking several mugs of the finest ale brewed anywhere on earth and then going upstairs to a snug private room for the night with a compliant barmaid.

Nothing would stand between him and the realization of that dream.

VIII

Summer was at hand. The heat during the days was intense, and even showers provided only temporary relief. The nights were balmy, too, and sometimes muggy along the Ohio River. Many of the travelers slept with the canvas sides of their wagons rolled part-way up to enjoy any breeze that might be blowing. Horses and oxen tired more quickly in the heat, so the halts at noon were extended to give the animals longer periods of rest.

But as Sam well knew, the coming season had its advantages. Wild berries were beginning to ripen, and he showed the teen-aged boys where to find the edible roots in the forest. Sometimes, too, they bought grains and fresh vegetables from local farmers.

Meat remained the staple of their diet, however, and there were so many mouths to feed that the need for fresh game never ceased.

"I want to save our pickled beef and salt fish for emergencies," Sam explained to Claudia, when she asked him why hunting trips were so important. "We're lucky there's game in such settled territory. And I'm talking about real game."

"Real game?" Claudia looked at him blankly.

She continued to astonish him. "Ma'am," he said, "if you brought back a brace of rabbits, you and some friend could have yourselves a cozy supper, maybe. But that's what I call luxury eating. Look at all those wagons. We've got dozens of people to feed. We haven't come to buffalo country yet, and bear meat can be as tough as boot leather if you don't cook it just right. So real meat means venison. Enough for a big barbecue that will give us one hot supper and a lot of cold ones."

She wasn't particularly fond of the strong taste of venison, but she could understand his point. No wonder Europeans were intrigued by the ability of Americans to utilize nature to their advantage. Nowhere in the crowded countries of the Old World would it be possible for such a caravan to live off the land. Even without the beef, the fish, the bacon and flour in the special wagon, the company could survive.

When the wagon train reached the southern tip of Ohio, adjacent to Kentucky and Virginia, a halt was called for a day. This country was sparsely settled. Several hunting parties were organized, each assigned to a different section of the forest.

Sam and Baron von Thalman went off together, returning with the best fortune of the day, a buck and a doe. Others brought smaller game, so supplies were replenished, and the meat that wasn't eaten at once was salted for later use.

After supper Sam prepared the skins of the buck and doe, a task most of the women found too disgusting to watch, but one that attracted the children. First he removed all hair from the outside with his razor-sharp knife, then he scraped every trace of meat and fat from the inside.

Next he broke off a chunk of soft limestone from the side of the hill overlooking the river, then pulverized it with the butt of a pistol. He mixed it thoroughly with coarse salt, and added the brains and intestines of the slaughtered animals to the salt and limestone dust.

Chet Harris was given the privilege of mixing this concoction, and he performed the duty with vigor. Then, as Sam showed the boys how to proceed, the mixture was rubbed by hand into the skins.

"This is the important part," he told the youngsters. "One winter in the Rockies it was so cold I needed an extra coat to keep me from freezing. I was in such an all-fired hurry that I took a shortcut and didn't rub the skin as hard and long as I should have. Three days later that buckskin shrank to about half its size. It was hard as the rocks it was laid on."

"Did you freeze?" Chet asked, kidding.

Sam shook his head and grinned. "Next day I shot me an elk. That time I did a proper job of curing the skin, and I had me a real fine cape that kept me warm the rest of the winter. I might well have died, however, so I want you lads to remember one thing. When you're doing a job, do it right!"

Next day the skins were stretched and spread on

top of the Baron's wagon, where they remained for more than a week. When they were ready to be used Sam presented them to Claudia. "I promised you these," he said. "Now maybe you can get your sister or somebody to sew them for you."

"I do my own sewing, thank you," she replied.

"I wasn't sure," he said. "I know you can't cook."

Claudia was exasperated.

"It so happens I'm a very good cook. I just don't enjoy it, that's all." She took the skins from him and flounced off.

Sam told himself that she was the most contrary woman he'd ever known.

The next few evenings Claudia was busy with needle and thread. She wouldn't let anyone help her. Then, one morning, she appeared at breakfast in a fringed buckskin shirt, enlivened with doeskin fringe, and a long buckskin skirt decorated the same way. She wore her high, laced boots and she went straight to Sam. He was devouring pancakes with wild honey taken from a complex of hives by boys who had smoked out the bees.

That task, carried out under Sam's supervision, had been surprisingly safe and simple. First the boys gathered firewood, mostly small tree trunks that hadn't been seasoned for more than a few months. The fire had been laid with these trunks, split and chopped into pieces no more than two feet long, on top of a bed of kindling.

As soon as the fire had caught, the boys were told to walk twenty feet away. When the top wood began to smoke, the bees came into the open, and the boys saw the reason for Sam's precautions.

The smoke poured upward, enveloping the hive. The bees, unable to breathe, swarmed into fresh air, searching furiously for the agent destroying their home. The fire continued to burn for hours, making it impossible for the bees to return to the hive, which never caught fire.

Eventually the smoke drove the bees away. When they tried to return after the flames had died down and the smoke had lessened, the odor of the smoke still clung to the hive, making it uninhabitable. During the early hours of the morning, the bees had gone elsewhere to make a new home.

The boys weren't permitted to approach the smoked-out hive until breakfast-time. By then all the bees were gone, and no one was stung. The boys had to agree with Sam that the wild honey was delicious, and worth all of their effort.

Claudia watched Sam enjoy his breakfast.

"I'm ready now," she said. "The next time you go hunting I'm coming with you."

Sam nodded reluctantly, afraid he'd bitten off more than he could chew or digest.

When another halt was called for a day of hunting, fishing and foraging, everybody was given an assignment. The Baron suggested to Sam that they hunt together again.

"Not this time, Ernie," he said. "I've got me a lady partner today."

Ernst von Thalman chuckled. "Good luck," he replied.

Claudia borrowed Terence Malcolm's rifle. He was spending the day on a fishing expedition and picnic with Lena and Lenore.

As they entered the forest, Claudia's manner was defensive. She expected criticism, and it wasn't long in coming.

"Don't clomp," Sam told her. "You'll scare off every animal within earshot."

"Show me how to walk!"

"Always lift your feet," he said, "like this. Never slide or stamp on underbrush, and avoid exposed roots, they'll grab you every time. Animals depend mostly on their hearing, and even the best hunter can give himself away."

Claudia watched him carefully, then did her best to follow his example.

She continued to surprise him. In spite of her hot temper and naturally cantankerous nature, she had a genuine desire to learn. No one was forcing her to become a hunter, and no one would have blamed her if she'd stayed behind at the camp with the rest of the women. But here she was, exposing herself to discomfort because she'd made up her mind to broaden her education.

Compelled to admire her spirit, Sam turned and grinned at her.

Claudia immediately bristled. "I'm glad you find me amusing, sir," she said, her voice tart.

She'd misunderstood him, as usual, but he was damned if he was going to explain his feelings.

"If you prefer," she said, "I'll hunt by myself."

"You'll do no such thing, ma'am."

"Why? Do you think I can't?"

"Mrs. Humphries," Sam said curtly, "you're talking so much that every animal within earshot will take cover. Do me a favor. Do yourself a favor. Just this once, see if you can't keep quiet."

Claudia flushed. She knew the rebuke was deserved. She didn't speak again, but followed him doggedly. Her rapid progress pleased him, but he wanted to make certain she knew what she was doing. So he moved more rapidly, testing her. When she kept up his pace without complaint, he realized he was being unfair to her and walked more slowly. Occasionally he paused in little clearings or beside brooks to study the ground. Sometimes he dropped to one knee in order to examine the earth more closely.

Once Claudia put her lips close to his ear. "What are you looking for?"

"Paw prints or hoof prints," he replied. "Bent or parted grass. Any sign that will show me an animal has recently passed this way."

Claudia began to look at the ground, too. And she was the first to notice that a stretch of almost knee-high grass leading from a small pond was parted slightly, indicating that a large animal had cut a path there after drinking from it. She touched Sam on the shoulder and pointed.

His nod told her she was right, but that was his only sign of approval.

Suddenly Claudia froze. A hundred yards ahead in a hillside hollow, a pair of sleek wolves were sleeping, their fur a dark gray. She immediately raised her rifle to her shoulder.

Sam, who had heard her movement, astonished her by pushing the barrel skyward.

Perhaps his motion awakened the wolves. Whatever

the reason, they leaped to their feet and were gone, disappearing into the woods on the far side of the hill.

"Why did you spoil my shot?" Claudia was too angry to keep silent any longer.

"Wolf meat isn't much good unless you're starving," he said. "I don't believe in killing just for sport, and they're friendly beasts. Except when they're hungry, and then—watch out!"

"Friendly?" Was he joking at her expense?

"They'll fight if they're cornered," he said. "Even a rabbit will do that. Otherwise they're as harmless as Quincy. Anybody who thinks a wolf is dangerous is dead wrong."

Claudia couldn't argue with him, and her annoyance subsided. The outing was proving instructive, though game was scarce. She was beginning to tire, though she had no intention of admitting it, and she was relieved when Sam called a halt at noon.

They sat on rocks at the edge of a brook. Sam offered her a strip of meat.

Claudia hesitated. "What is it?"

"Venison," Sam replied. "From the buck and doe we shot to make your new clothes. Slice it thin as you can, dry it in the sun and it lasts a long time."

She tasted it. She found the meat tough and stringy, and had to chew each bite thoroughly before she could swallow it.

Sam relished his meal, however, eating one strip after another. "You don't seem to like it much," he said amiably.

"Not particularly," Claudia admitted. "It's a taste that takes time to appreciate, I imagine."

"Maybe so. But I'd rather eat jerked venison than a beefsteak."

Again she wondered if he was joking.

"There's a reason, of course," Sam said. "About five or six years ago, near the Great Divide, some Cheyenne warriors asked my help in the dead of winter to run down a band of renegade Apache who were looting and killing. We ran out of food in a week and blame near starved. Then I shot two bucks. We were above the timber line, so there was no wood handy to make a fire, and we had to cut the meat in strips and dry it out with salt and sun. Nothing I'd ever eaten in my life tasted as good as that jerked venison. It was even better than the ten-course banquet when Andy Jackson invited me to the White House."

How could he speak so lightly of the tribulations he must have suffered, she wondered, almost starving to death in mid-winter. It was remarkable. Surely it wasn't accidental, either, that he brought down those two bucks, but he was so casual he made it sound commonplace.

They resumed the hunt after finishing their light meal, and came to another break in the forest. Ahead lay rock-strewn hills where tall grass and tangled bushes were the only vegetation. Sam studied the hills at length, then indicated in pantomime that he'd make a circle around the hills in one direction while Claudia went in the other.

She had no idea why he wanted them to separate, but she obediently climbed onto higher ground, moving to her right. She was able to make out here and there what appeared to be caves. She took care to move silently and cautiously. The sun was warm, the breeze was gentle and she was reminded of similar weather at picnics on Long Island Sound.

Well, she was far from home now. This wilderness near the Ohio River didn't appeal to her. She was hunting because boredom had forced her to challenge Sam Brentwood, and for no other reason. Even her buckskin clothes were ludicrous. She wasn't cut out for a life in the wilderness. She'd much rather be stretched out on a hammock in New Haven, reading poetry. The printed word was far more romantic than pioneering.

Suddenly she heard a low, deep growl. The next thing she knew she was staring at a bear, emerging from a clump of bushes. Six feet in length, he must have weighed three hundred pounds. The beast's fur was black, and his yellowed teeth resembled fangs. The baleful expression in his small, beady eyes told her that she was his enemy.

The bear lumbered forward, moving with remarkable speed, until he rose onto his hind legs and towered above her. He was only a short distance from her, drawing back his front paws in a manner that resembled a boxer at a county fair.

Claudia was petrified. She couldn't move. She knew that one blow from his giant paws could kill her.

The bear took a step toward her, then another.

She was afraid she would faint. Then a shot rang out, and the bear halted abruptly. When a second shot sounded, the beast toppled backward onto the ground.

Sam arrived on the run, making certain the bear was dead before turning to Claudia to shout:

"Why in thunderation didn't you shoot him?"

Claudia was trembling violently. She couldn't reply.

Sam began to cut long, supple branches from the bushes and plaited them together. "If you aren't totally helpless," he said, "give me a hand."

His words stung her into action, and she followed his example, not even knowing his purpose. She tried to thank him for saving her life.

"Firearms," he said caustically, "were invented so folks could defend themselves."

Claudia was too mortified to reply.

Sam made what looked like a crude mat. Then, acting with the smooth efficiency that came from long experience as a hunter, he lopped off the animal's head, removed the paws and, after gutting the body, kept only the carcass.

"Why butcher it here?" Claudia said.

He shook his head. The reason seemed obvious. "Try picking up that much dead weight," he said. "It's three hundred pounds, maybe more. We'd have hell's own time hauling the whole thing back to camp, so I'm just keeping the parts we can use for food."

She was beginning to understand that there was far more to hunting than shooting animals.

"There are two rules," Sam said. "If you follow them you won't ever go wrong. The most important is, always hunt for need, never for pleasure. The next is, don't bring down more game than you can reasonably handle."

"In this case," Claudia replied with spirit, "we had no choice. That bear would have finished me if you hadn't killed him."

"True enough. But now we have all this good meat,

and I'm not going to let it be wasted. Not with all those hungry people back there waiting for us. Ordinarily I wouldn't shoot a beast of this size, but I'm not going to leave the carcass for the buzzards and the ants to feast on."

For the first time she was conscious of the inner spirit that motivated a man of the frontier. He killed when he was hungry, not because he enjoyed hunting for its own sake. Above all, he was practical in his approach to life. Newspapers and magazines might picture him as a romantic figure, but he was actually a hard-headed realist who scoffed at romanticism.

Sam shoved the bear's carcass onto his crude stretcher and Claudia realized that he meant to use it as a sled. He made a harness for himself out of vines, and began to pull his burden, slinging his rifle over his shoulder. "We'll take a short cut to the wagon train," he said. "It's no more than a couple of miles."

Claudia had no idea where they were, but his sense of direction was uncanny, and soon she caught a glimpse of the Ohio River through the trees. Even if she disliked him, she had to admire his knowledge of the wilderness.

In spite of his limp Sam was tireless as he hauled the bear back to the train. Not until they approached the campsite did he address her again. "This wasn't too bad a day's outing. I'm not partial to bear stew, but it's all right with parsnips and the like. Bear steaks are fine, provided they're pounded first. The bacon is the best part."

"I'll cook a bear steak for you tonight, if you like,"

Claudia said in a small voice, "and start smoking the bacon."

He knew she was doing her best to thank him, and he recognized how much the gesture had cost a proud woman. "I'll look forward to that," he said, and grinned.

More recruits were expected to join the caravan in Cincinnati, and a majority of the party were anticipating a sojourn in the river town, after spending many days on the road. Shoes could be repaired, notions could be purchased and those with sufficient funds could buy such delicacies as raisins and sugar.

Cathy van Ayl had her own reasons for wanting to visit Cincinnati, but she dreaded to tell Otto what they were. Since leaving home, they'd grown even farther apart. He was now so uncommunicative, Cathy spent most of her evenings with Claudia and Lena Malcolm. Otto went straight to bed after supper. He didn't care when she joined him, he told her, provided she didn't disturb his sleep.

The night before they were scheduled to reach Cincinnati, she hurried to their wagon when she saw him leave the campfire. When he reached it, she was waiting. "Otto," she said, "I need to talk to you."

"Let it wait till morning," he said. "We drove a long ways today, and I need my rest."

"It's important." Cathy was blocking the entrance to the wagon.

Otto sighed.

"I need three dollars, maybe four, when we get to Cincinnati," she said.

"That's a lot of money," he countered.

"Look at my dress. It's nothing but a rag, just like my other two. Travel is hard on dresses, and I need to buy some strong material to make new ones."

"I don't see anything wrong with what you're wearing."

"Please, Otto. I've never asked you for a penny I haven't needed."

He had to concede the point. Still, he hated to throw good money away. "Make yourself a dress out of skins, like your sister did."

"I'll be glad to, Otto. Just shoot a buck for me, and cure the skin."

Otto was annoyed. He was a dirt farmer who'd never in his life gone hunting. She knew that. "I demand the respect due a husband," he said.

Cathy felt pushed beyond endurance. "And I demand the rights due a wife!" she said. "How would you like it if I disgraced you by going naked in front of the whole wagon train. That's what's going to happen when my clothes fall apart."

Otto tried not to show his alarm. Ordinarily Cathy was a good, obedient woman. She cost him a lot less than a servant. But he suspected her head had been turned by the attentions of Whip Holt and that snippet who'd married young Malcolm. If he had to give in, he could still make it plain that he was the head of the family. "We'll finish this talk inside."

Inside the wagon she lighted two candles, using an old-fashioned flint and tinderbox that had belonged to her mother.

"You're wasting tallow again," Otto said. "There's no call for more than one light."

Cathy snuffed out one of the candles.

Otto took the precaution of closing the flap and making it secure. Then he went to a box containing most of their cooking utensils. Digging out an old teapot from the bottom, he rummaged through the pile of old rags it was stuffed with and pulled out a roll of tattered, yellowing one-dollar bills. They had been printed during the administration of President Thomas Jefferson a quarter of a century earlier.

Turning his back to Cathy, he counted out the money carefully once and then again, before he was satisfied. Finally he handed her two dollars, sighing heavily. "Here," he said, "this is all I can afford to give you."

Cathy hid her elation. She understood him better than he knew. By asking for four dollars, she'd been able to obtain half that sum, enough for her purposes. For a dollar she could buy enough stout, durable corduroy to make two dresses and a spare skirt. That would still leave a dollar for more feminine material to make two other dresses, but she wouldn't wear them till they reached Independence.

Suddenly she was brought up short. Why Independence? She knew the answer, of course, even before asking herself the question. Whip Holt would be rejoining the wagon train there, and she wanted to look her best when she saw him again. Not, of course, that anything could come of their friendship. She was still Otto's wife and an honorable woman, just as Whip was an honorable man.

Even so, they'd be harming no one when they met again. And she was looking forward to watching the glow of pleasure in his eyes when he saw her. No one was hurt if she enjoyed the admiration of a man whose expression told her he thought she was lovely. She couldn't ever remember when anyone else had looked at her that way. Claudia told her she was pretty. So did Lena. And both of them kept saying she was foolish to feel inferior to other women.

Well, she sure didn't feel inferior when Whip Holt looked at her!

By the time Cathy had pinned the dollar bills inside her dress and quietly left the wagon, Otto was sound asleep, his snores rattling against the canvas.

When they reached Cincinnati the next morning, Cathy went shopping with Claudia and Lena. Because Sam warned them that it was dangerous to wander around the city without escorts, hinting they might be taken for loose women, they went straight to the small general store only a few minutes' walk from the campsite.

Cathy knew exactly what she wanted and made her purchases at once.

Claudia, who hadn't intended to buy anything of consequence, changed her mind when she saw several lengths of sturdy cloth in attractive patterns. It would be wise to enlarge her wardrobe, she reasoned, since she'd stopped wearing her silk gowns on the road. She couldn't be like those women who didn't care how they looked. Even if clothes got dusty and soiled on the road, there was no reason why a woman shouldn't try to look her best.

Lena Malcolm needed help. Not until the two sisters began to advise her did they discover that this was the first time in her life she'd ever bought material for clothes. Her father had always bought the cheapest cloth he could find, so the new experience was delightful.

As she hesitated, holding swatch after swatch up to the light to study them critically, a new customer entered the shop.

It was Tonie Mell. Claudia exchanged a cool nod with her. Tonie was brusque, as always, and selected a length from the first bolt at hand. It happened to be a bright red that would clash with her hair, and even though Claudia still disliked the tomboy intensely she felt compelled to intervene.

"Don't buy *that*," she said.

Tonie bristled. "Why not?"

Claudia led Tonie to the only mirror in the store, which was hanging on a wall, and held the material up to her hair. "See? The color combination is terrible."

Tonie had to concede that Claudia was right. "Gee," she said, "I never thought of that."

"Obviously," Claudia said. Her good deed accomplished, she rejoined Cathy and Lena, who was beginning to narrow down her selections. But Tonie Mell wasn't on firm ground yet. Looking thoroughly confused, she tapped Claudia on the shoulder. "If you aren't too busy," she said, "maybe you'd do me a favor."

"Of course," Claudia replied.

"When it comes to riding and shooting I know what I'm doing. I'm not so bad at branding cattle, either." Tonie swallowed. "But the only time I ever wore a dress back home was when I went to church or when the pastor came calling. I can cut out patterns and sew. My aunt taught me that. But I don't know what looks bad on me and what looks good."

No lady could refuse such an earnest appeal for help. Claudia sighed and led Tonie Mell to a counter on which many bolts of cloth were piled.

"First of all," she said, "decide on what style you want."

"Something simple." Tonie looked hopeful.

"We'll decide on the cloth first, then match it to a pattern in the book over there." Claudia examined the bolts and picked up a soft, mossy green wool. "This would be pretty with your hair and coloring," she said.

"Pretty?" Tonie was dubious. "That's not likely."

It was something of a shock to realize that the girl didn't think of herself as attractive. "Take my word for it, Tonie. You'll look good in this."

"Whatever you say." Tonie didn't know how to express her gratitude.

Claudia picked out two other bolts, a deep yellow broadcloth and a dusty blue corduroy.

"How much of each should I get?"

The poor girl was helpless, Claudia thought. She led Tonie Mell to the pattern book. "Choose styles that will show off your figure," she said. "Your tiny waist. Your high bustline. Your long body."

Frowning as she concentrated, Tonie pored over the pattern book.

When the other three women completed their purchases and left the shop, she was still choosing patterns.

Claudia had been far more generous than she'd

meant to be. Maybe she should have let Tonie buy the red material. Now, thanks to her help, Tonie would look her best, and Sam Brentwood would think her even more attractive than he obviously did already. There was a limit to charity, Claudia reflected, and wanted to kick herself.

Many of the pioneers saw their first Indians on the Cincinnati waterfront. One of the Harris boys expressed a common disappointment when he said, "Golly! They look just like everybody else." And indeed the braves, who worked as longshoremen, wore the shirts and trousers of white men, cut their hair in the same styles and even spoke a tolerable English. When Claudia had accompanied Cathy and Lena on their shopping expedition, she had hurried the two women past a doorway in which a heavily made-up Indian girl was loitering.

"Just wait," Sam Brentwood told the Harris boys. "These Indians have been exposed to the white man's civilization for more than fifty years. You'll see a different breed on the other side of the Missouri River, and more often than not you'll wish you hadn't. But even here you've got to be careful. Don't stare too hard at them. There's no telling what an Indian will do if he thinks you're being rude. And stay away from any redskin who's been drinking. Then they're as ornery as I used to be."

Claudia had read that Cincinnati was the only city in the United States where North, South, East and West met and lived together in harmony, and the description was accurate. Settlers had come to Cincinnati from every state on the Eastern seaboard, and in recent years they had been joined by thousands of immigrants, most from the German states and Ireland. Slavery was prohibited in Ohio, so many free blacks lived there, working in peace and security. But numerous slaves from across the river in Kentucky also came to town with their masters, and the Southern influence was strong.

It was the steamboat traffic on the Ohio, recently expanded with canals and extending all the way to the river's conjunction with the great Mississippi at Cairo, Illinois, that gave Cincinnati its character. Fur traders in buckskins were everywhere, together with farmers from the West, trappers and even mountain men who treated themselves to the delights of the bordellos on the low-lying plateau near the waterfront.

The more elegant homes were located in the hills behind the plateau, and industry was thriving. There were fur-processing plants, heavy industries and a number of factories making consumer goods. The pioneers were astonished by the prevalence of pigs. There seemed to be several in every back yard, and it wasn't uncommon to see stray pigs wandering down the streets. Even the well-informed Baron von Thalman hadn't known that Cincinnati had become the meat-packing capital of America. More sausages were made there than in all the rest of the country.

With all its frontier location, Cincinnati hadn't neglected its culture. Music groups and art societies flourished, there were three thriving theaters where plays were produced and lectures given, and Claudia, after visiting several bookshops, returned to her wagon with armloads of books that would keep her busy on the long journey that still lay ahead.

Fourteen wagons joined the train in Cincinnati, making a total of forty, including the special wagon. Now the phenomenon was unique. Never before in all human history had any people used such an extraordinary means of transportation for a migration covering thousands of miles. It didn't occur to these colonists, however, that they were doing anything unusual. Practical men and women, they had chosen the method best suited to their needs.

No one who saw the procession could fail to be impressed. Scores of settlers had left their homes and families to travel to the distant Oregon country, where they hoped to make new lives for themselves. They were motivated, in the main, by blind faith. Two hundred acres was available to every settler, a tract far larger than most would ever be able to acquire elsewhere, even after a lifetime of hard labor.

An enterprising family could make a living on two hundred acres of fertile land. Unknown to the pioneers, however, unscrupulous men were scheming to deprive them of their heritage. Land speculators eager to profit themselves were already doing what their predecessors had done in the Ohio Valley and elsewhere—offering cash for titles to the land. Unaware of the true value of real estate, many would-be settlers gave in to temptation and sold their futures for a small fraction of what the speculators would charge in a few years' time.

The system the speculators employed was simple.

The early settlers would struggle to build new homes and forge a civilization in the wilderness. All a shrewd speculator need do was sit tight while the pioneers did his hard work for him. After travel became safer and living conditions less primitive, he could easily resell the tracts to those who could afford them. The more the pioneers accomplished, the more attractive the country became to those who followed, men who didn't mind paying substantial sums for land that would continue to increase in value.

Sometimes, to be sure, the plans of the speculators misfired. Sometimes they invested too much, leaving nothing in reserve, and when it took longer for a territory to be developed than they had planned, they went bankrupt. Then the government stepped in, reclaimed the land and offered it again to homesteaders.

So far the blight of speculation had not infested the Oregon venture. When the company reached Independence, Missouri, the take-off point into the wilderness, the head of each family would be given a deed for two hundred acres of his own choice within a large, prescribed area. Those deeds promised solid homes, enough food to eat and a chance to walk with dignity. That was all the poor and the ambitious wanted, as their large numbers testified.

If the East was in the grip of an economic depression, there would be no fear in the Far West, where a man would grow his own crops and raise his own livestock. Here in America something was being born, a new country. Men, women and children were marching toward this unknown land, confident of survival and prosperity.

In effect the pioneers were conducting an experiment in communal living. Each woman and man held a measure of responsibility for the safety of all. And Sam saw to it that there were no shirkers. Old-timers helped to train newcomers in their duties. The morale of the company depended on the knowledge that people were working together for the common good, each individual doing his or her share.

"Eventually," Dr. Martin said, "this kind of cooperation should create a truly unifying spirit."

"It happened when settlers first went to Tennessee," Sam said. "And I saw for myself that it worked in Texas, too. The lazy and the shiftless can't stand the pace and turn back, so only the strong stay in the wagon train. They're the ones who learn to handle any kind of situation and face any emergency. Together. That's the spirit I'm hoping to build."

When the caravan left Cincinnati, its length was more than a quarter of a mile. The couple in the tail wagon were the most noticeable of the newcomers. Nat Drummond, who had sold his failing farm across the Ohio from Cincinnati in Covington, Kentucky, was a slender, nervous man in his mid-forties who always wore a timid look on his face. The reason was obvious: his wife, Grace, was as tall as Nat and outweighed him by at least twenty-five pounds. And Nat couldn't call his soul his own. Everyone in earshot could hear Grace's early-morning command, issued in a resounding contralto: "Nat, stow away the dishes and hitch up the team!" At night she was equally brusque: "Don't just sit there, Nat. Stir yourself for firewood, then peel the potatoes. After that you can knead the dough.

You know I have only two hands. I can't do everything."

Soon Drummond was known to one and all as "poor Nat." But he remained good-natured, always eager to please everyone, and appeared to take his wife's bullying in stride. Grace, on the other hand, became friendly with only one person, Otto van Ayl. This friendship bloomed with the discovery that each believed in planting green beans, squash and cucumbers as soon as possible after the ground thawed in the spring. They discussed crop-tending together at supper every evening, stopping only when Otto got sleepy or Grace directed Nat to help wash the dishes.

Another new arrival seemed drawn to Claudia. Arthur Elwood was a former member of the Ohio legislature who surprised most of his listeners by announcing that he knew nothing about farming. Dapper, in his late thirties, with sleek, black hair and a mustache, he wore city clothes even on the road, confessing to Claudia that he had no wish to look like a common laborer.

He seemed interested in her without trying to pay court, and gradually Claudia began to express her own opinions to him, telling him how much she missed the life she'd known before joining the expedition. He proved to be a good listener.

"I've been thinking about your situation," he said one morning, "and I sympathize with you. I don't know you all that well, of course, but I can tell you'd be more at home at a lecture than planting a two-hundred-acre farm."

Claudia laughed. "It would take me a lifetime to plant two hundred acres."

"That's what you'll be awarded, you know. So will every settler who signs the letter of agreement."

She didn't know what he meant.

"Every member of this wagon train," Elwood explained, "will be presented with a document drawn up by John Jacob Astor and his associates. In return for your pledge of your intent to settle in the Oregon country you'll be given a deed for two hundred acres of land. The exchange of papers will take place in Independence, before the caravan moves into the wilderness."

"I hadn't been told," Claudia said, "and I'm not sure it very much matters, according to what I read in the newspapers back home. Since the United States hasn't established sovereignty over the Oregon territory, I don't see how Astor or anyone else has the right to hand out property deeds."

"You're mistaken," Elwood said forcefully. "The deeds are based on the assumption that the United States will establish its sovereignty there, and then the deed will be binding—and valuable."

"You must be joking," Claudia said.

"On the contrary, I've never been more serious. Suppose you become so disillusioned that you decide to turn back in Independence—"

"How I wish I could!"

"Hear me out, Mrs. Humphries. You simply sign the letter of intent, as they call it, but you're not obligated to go to the Oregon territory in person. You can dispose of your deed to someone else. I've looked into it carefully, and you'd be within your legal rights."

"But why would I do a thing like that, Mr. Elwood? Why would I accept a deed for land I wasn't going to use?"

"Because it's worth cash to you," he said with a smile. "I myself would be happy to pay you a dollar per acre for an otherwise worthless scrap of paper. Two hundred dollars in all."

It dawned on Claudia that he was more clever than she had realized. If he could persuade a number of the would-be settlers to sell him their deeds he could acquire large tracts of property. Then he could easily double his money by selling the property for two dollars per acre, and if the land was as fertile as the sponsors claimed, he could get far more. Only recently, she had read, homesteaders who had obtained free land in Illinois a decade earlier had been selling their property for as much as five dollars per acre.

She had no desire to make a firm commitment to Elwood, however, so she hedged. "Thank you for the lesson in real estate," she said. "I'll think about what you've told me."

She mentioned their conversation to no one, but she noted that Elwood, although still friendly toward her, began to devote more of his attention to others. He appeared to be ingratiating himself with the occupants of one wagon after another. It dawned on her eventually that he was making cash offers to them, too.

Claudia neither approved of what he was doing nor disapproved. Newspapers for years had been filled with complaints from the citizens of the new states and territories in the West, who called land speculators vultures. But in her opinion a businessman was entitled to earn money in any legal way he saw fit. George Washington had invested heavily in the Ohio Valley land many years earlier, and through no fault of his the venture had failed. Washington had lost a fortune, but no one had ever called the first President of the nation a vulture.

Sam Brentwood, as usual, disagreed with her. Watching the former legislator engaging in an animated private conversation with Emily Harris at the campfire one evening, he muttered to Claudia, "That man is asking for a punch in the nose."

"Why?"

"Maybe you don't know what he's up to, offering folks money for the deeds they'll be issued when we reach the Missouri River."

"I do know," Claudia said, "but I don't see what's wrong."

It wasn't easy for Sam to explain, but he tried to. "Take Mrs. Harris. Everything she owns in the world is in her wagon, and she has four boys to support. The Oregon country offers her the chance to make a new life for herself and her family. Two hundred dollars is a heap of money to a poor lady. But she can't buy a farm or a business or blame near anything else in the settled parts of the country for that kind of money, and once she spends it, she and her boys could starve to death."

Claudia began to understand.

"That's why people like Elwood are leeches. If I had my way I'd boot him out of this wagon train. But

I can't. I'm under orders to accept every last person who joins us, and I'm not allowed to judge."

Sam was exaggerating somewhat. Certainly he had the authority to reject strays, but it became apparent one morning when the caravan was moving through the hill country of southern Indiana that he sometimes chose not to exercise that power.

The women had just cooked breakfast, and were handing out chunks of bread and bowls of steaming fish chowder. They had used corn, which was plentiful, in the chowder rather than potatoes, which were scarce. A bedraggled figure emerged from the woods. Barefooted, dressed in a patched shirt and worn linsey-woolsey pants, he appeared at first glance to be a boy. When he spoke in a soprano voice that turned to a baritone, however, people realized he was in his early teens.

"I don't reckon you got any vittles to spare," he said, approaching the fire.

Emily Harris looked at Lena Malcolm, who was helping her serve, then handed the boy a bowl. He ate quickly and it was obvious that he was ravenous. Emily refilled his bowl.

"You folks got any odd jobs you want done?" he asked, wiping his mouth on his sleeve.

The women directed him to Sam Brentwood, who was organizing the day's march.

The boy spoke to Sam, adding, "I can do anything, mister. I can chop wood and curry horses and gather hay and mend harnesses and wash clothes and drive a wagon. I can do anything that needs being done."

Sorry for him, Sam studied the scrawny youth. "Who are you and how old are you?"

"I'm called Danny. I ain't got no other name. I figure I'm thirteen, or thereabouts."

"Where's your family?"

"I never had any." The boy's slender shoulders rose and fell.

"Well," Sam said, "I reckon we can give you a try. Let's see you make yourself useful."

Danny's energy was astonishing. He hitched horses to wagons, put out the breakfast fires and even helped the women wash the dishes, a task he accomplished with demonic fury. He accepted Claudia's invitation to ride with her and Quincy, but sitting on the boards beside her he seemed to lose his powers of speech.

She made a number of attempts to draw him out, but he answered in monosyllables or merely nodded, so she decided to wait until he thawed before trying to learn more about him. During a brief pause at noon he was the first to race down to the river, then ranged up and down the line, offering water to the company. Later, Claudia unwrapped one of the redolent sausages she had bought in Cincinnati, and the boy devoured all of it.

That afternoon, he gathered more wood for the fire than anyone else, and when Chet Harris invited him for a quick swim in the river he insisted on getting Sam's permission before he accepted. The boys stripped to their smallclothes, then plunged into the river, where Danny's talents as a swimmer indicated that he had lived near some body of water.

215

When she saw his back, Claudia gasped. Many others noticed it, too. From his shoulders to his waist, a mass of crisscrossed scars covered the skin, many old and healed, some still livid and swollen. Anyone looking could tell that the boy had been beaten often and severely.

Danny made himself so useful before and after supper that the entire company became aware of his presence. His desire to be helpful was genuine, his energy seemed inexhaustible—and his appetite was enormous, no matter how much he ate. Claudia supplied him with a blanket, and Emily Harris offered him a place to sleep in her wagon with her sons. So did Grace Drummond, who said, "You can sleep with Nat on his mattress."

The boy refused, however, and insisted on sleeping in the open, near Sam. He was the first to awaken in the morning, and not only had the fire built but had most of the water fetched by the time others began their chores. Before his second day with the company came to an end, he was accepted without reservation by virtually everyone, although many were curious about his background.

That mystery was partially solved the following morning. As camp was being broken before the day's journey, a tall, thick-shouldered man in rusty black rode into the encampment on a gelding, a long rifle laid across the pommel. He halted, pushed his battered hat to the back of his head and demanded, of no one in particular, "Who's in charge of this lot?"

He was directed to Sam Brentwood, who had already noted his presence and loosened the pistols in his belt.

"Name's Homer," the man said to Sam. "Lookin' for my bound boy. He run away a coupl'a days ago, when you was campin' near my property. And if you got him here with you, you'll damn well regret it."

Sam's pale eyes became flint-like. "I don't take kindly to threats, Mr. Homer," he said. "I'm courteous to anybody who is polite and reasonable with me. So state your business like a gentleman, or be on your way before I run you off."

Homer heard Sam's cold voice, saw his expression and became a shade less belligerent. "Here's the papers provin' he belongs t' me," he said, taking a tattered document from his belt. "Five years I've had him, and he ain't been worth the food he eats."

A large crowd was gathering around them, and people were listening but saying nothing, their faces blank.

"You seen the kid?" Homer demanded. "I warn you, I'm huntin' through every wagon for him if I have to, and if I find him I'll have the law on your heads."

Arthur Elwood stepped forward. "I assume you carry a properly executed search warrant?"

"I don't need none," the man declared. "I already told you, he's my bound boy."

"I'll allow no one to go through these wagons except a sheriff who carries a warrant signed by the judge of the local county court," Sam said.

Claudia was seething with resentment at this boy-beating man, but her smile was sweet. "Forgive me for interrupting, Mr. Brentwood," she said, "but we're not hiding anyone. So I suggest there's no need to stand on formality with this—ah, gentleman. By all means let's allow him to go through the wagons."

No one knew where Danny was hiding, and there was a stir in the crowd.

Sam grinned, instantly approving Claudia's strategy. If they seemed to satisfy the man, he'd leave in peace. Otherwise he'd be certain to return with a sheriff and a duly executed warrant, and then real trouble would develop. "Mrs. Humphries," he said, "for once I agree with you. All right, Homer, you can search the whole blamed train. But leave your horse and your rifle right here."

"I never go anywhere unarmed!"

"Those are my conditions." Sam stood his ground quietly.

The man dismounted, placing his rifle in a sling. He was badly outnumbered, so he had no choice.

Chet Harris started to inch away, intending to find Danny and warn him, but he stopped short when his mother glowered at him, her expression indicating that this was a situation adults had to handle.

"Folks," Sam Brentwood said in a voice loud enough to carry far beyond the edge of the crowd. "I've given Mr. Homer permission to search the train for his run-away bound boy." Then he added, strictly for Danny's benefit, "He'll start at the front and work toward the back. Now, then. Your wagons are your private property, your homes. So if any of you don't want to let him into your wagons, that's your right. Speak up now."

No one responded. Only Homer looked pleased.

"Fair enough," Sam said. "Now I want each wagon owner to be on hand when we come to your property, so I suggest you go there right now."

People looked surreptitiously for Danny as they scattered, but he was nowhere to be seen.

Chet and one of his brothers picked up pails, ostensibly for the purpose of going down to the Ohio River for water, but their mother stopped them, afraid they might give away Danny's hiding place.

"Mr. van Ayl," Sam said, "we'll start with your wagon."

"This is tomfoolery," Otto said. "We're being delayed when we could be on the road."

Cathy peered inside their wagon before she opened the flap wide for Homer's inspection.

When the man approached Claudia's wagon, closely attended by Sam, Quincy's low, deep growl forced his mistress to hold him. And the dog's hostility was echoed by the occupants of wagon after wagon. Some pretended Homer didn't exist, others glowered at him, and even the meek Nat Drummond indicated his opinion of the man by spitting on the ground.

Unmindful of their attitude, Homer conducted a careful, slow search, scrutinizing the interior of every wagon.

Still no one spoke, but members of the group exchanged quick, worried glances. Some were afraid that Danny was doing a self-appointed chore and would wander unawares into the compound. Others were equally afraid that he'd become privy to the danger and run away again.

After the last wagon had been inspected, Sam escorted Homer back to his waiting horse. "I hope you're satisfied," he said.

"I guess I got to be," the man replied. "If the brat shows up, just notify the sheriff of any county in this part of the state. I'm offerin' a reward of ten dollars in gold for his live skin, and half will go to anybody who turns him in."

Sam didn't deign to reply, and waited until Homer rode off before cupping his hands and giving the signal for the start of the day's journey. "Wagons, ho!"

People stood on their boards now, looking openly for Danny, while Chet Harris and two of his brothers spread out, one hurrying down to the river and the others dashing into the woods. Danny was still nowhere to be seen.

As the wagons began to move off one by one, Claudia felt heavy-hearted. She couldn't blame Danny for fleeing, but she'd miss him, as would all the others. In trying to help him, the whole company had banded together for a single purpose.

As she flapped her reins and her wagon started to move, a small figure darted out of the woods and climbed up onto the boards beside her. "I was lucky," Danny said, trying to sound nonchalant. "I was off at a little pond, gettin' you a special present, when that Homer showed up, or he'd have nabbed me for sure."

Her relief was so great she wanted to hug him. "What was the special present?"

He opened a grubby fist. Nestled in his palm were three tiny, fragile duck eggs. "They're a rare treat when you scramble them up," he said.

The only way she could prevent herself from weeping was to stand for a moment and shout to the occupants of other wagons, "Danny's here!"

The word passed up and down the line, and suddenly, spontaneously, people began to sing one of the most popular songs of the day, "Illinois," and seemed to be of one mind when they substituted Oregon for the name of the older territory.

> Way down upon the Wabash,
> Such land was never known,
> If Adam had passed over it,
> The soil he'd surely own;
> He'd think it was the garden
> He'd played in when a boy,
> And straight pronounce it Eden
> In the state of Oregon.
> Then move your family westward
> Good health will you enjoy,
> And rise to wealth and honor
> In the state of O-re-gon!

They bellowed verse after chorus, indifferent to the fact that many lines ended with words that rhymed with Illinois rather than Oregon. Only after they'd grown quiet again did Danny speak.

"Folks hereabouts is sure good t' me."

"They think you deserve it, Danny," she told him.

He became ruminative. "I got me only one trouble now."

She knew him well enough by now not to question him, knowing he'd offer an explanation in his own way when he was ready.

Danny remained silent for a time, and seemed reluctant to express what was on his mind, but finally he felt compelled to speak. "I was waitin' t' get my chores done before I ate anythin', but with hidin' in the woods and all, I plumb missed breakfast."

"You know where I keep the Cincinnati sausages. Help yourself." Having seen Homer, she felt sure the boy had been deliberately starved.

He climbed back into the wagon and returned with a whole sausage, which he proceeded to eat. In spite of his hunger, however, he took care to break off several generous chunks for Quincy, which cemented their friendship.

When the caravan halted for the day Danny was surrounded by well-wishers, the entire company congratulating him on the escape in which all of them had played a role. The atmosphere at the campfire that night was festive. Those who had been reserved became more talkative, and people from the East went out of their way to be friendlier to more recent arrivals.

As the meal ended someone began to sing. Nat Drummond went off to his wagon for a fiddle, which he played with surprising skill and feeling. Even though they'd be making an early start the next morning, people lingered at the fire, and the singing went on and on. Jugs of wine materialized and were passed, and even Otto van Ayl stayed awake long past his usual bedtime.

The Baron chatted with Emily Harris, and in spite of the disparity of their backgrounds they engaged in a lively conversation. Grace Drummond presented Danny with a shirt and a pair of trousers, saying, "Nat doesn't need these." Even Arthur Elwood relaxed and refrained from trying to persuade anyone to sell him a property deed.

Sam Brentwood stayed somewhat apart from his charges, smiling steadily, and Claudia realized why he was so pleased. By banding together in an illegal act for the protection of an abused child, the company had been infused with a new spirit. They had become united. They were no longer strangers, and Danny's presence was the symbol of their determination to work together for the common good.

Oregon no longer seemed a distant, impossible dream, but a practical reality.

IX

Henry St. Clair was bored and frustrated. It took little effort to follow the wagon train, which was moving even more slowly since the company had grown to more than two hundred people. Sometimes, in his eagerness to push ahead, he became a trifle careless, and on several occasions he had not only come within sight of the tail end of the caravan, but had actually seen Tonie Mell riding on her monitor rounds.

A map he'd purchased at a country store near the Ohio-Indiana border proved helpful, and eased his situation. A study of the map convinced him that Sam Brentwood would be forced to continue using the road that ran parallel to the Ohio River. There was literally no other trail big enough.

So Henry sometimes dawdled for a day or two, setting animal traps in order to test his skill, then feasting on roasted meat. It was no problem to give the caravan a head start of two days, then catch up again within a few hours.

Sometimes Henry augmented his stolen wardrobe with new purchases made at small general stores. Chief among them were a pair of sturdy boots and a marvelously sharp double-edged knife. His stolen gelding was ordinary, and he wanted a more spirited mount, but he knew better than to resort to theft again. Men in this semi-wilderness were utterly dependent on their horses, and the robber who dared to take a man's horse was hunted down by a determined posse and hanged without benefit of a trial.

It was far preferable to buy a new mount. Wandering away from the river one day while killing a few hours, Henry came to a farm where horses were sold. Eagerly seizing his opportunity, he traded his gelding and a sum of cash for a strong, two-year-old stallion. His mental state improved, but his new horse covered ground so quickly that he had to find additional ways to fritter away his time.

He was almost sorry that circumstances had caused him to flee the wagon train. Had he remained a member of the company he could have found ways to slow the journey. But he reminded himself that patience was still his greatest virtue. One of these days luck would turn in his favor, and he would have the opportunity to destroy the train completely. Certainly he'd recognize his chance when it came his way.

In the meantime he needed a better weapon than his stolen pistol, which was cumbersome and unreliable. The few muskets he'd seen for sale were second-hand firearms that didn't interest him. What he

wanted was a modern, accurate rifle of the type manu-
factured in England for the Royal Army. Even the
new American guns being made in Connecticut were
inadequate. Sooner or later he'd have a direct confrontation with Sam Brentwood, and when that time
came he'd need a gun that would shoot true.

Henry's wishes soon were fulfilled. One day, allowing
the wagon train to gain a good start, Henry meandered
north into the hill country on the Ohio-Indiana border. After an aimless ride of an hour or two he came
to a farm. A hand-lettered sign on the gate advertised
poultry and smoked bacon for sale. Bacon would be
useful, Henry decided, so he opened the gate and rode
up to the unpainted one-story farmhouse.

He met the proprietor and his wife, a young, attractive couple, and told them his mission. They welcomed him and invited him into their combined living
room-dining room.

"You got here just in time, mister," the farmer said.
"I'm heading into town to buy some pigs, that's how
good business has been lately. How much bacon can
you use?"

Henry scarcely heard him. Resting on the mantel
was a superb rifle, obviously made in the English
Midlands within the past five years. How, he wondered, could a man in this remote part of the American hinterlands have come into possession of such a
fine weapon?

"Uh—ten pounds of bacon, please," Henry said,
his mind racing. Somehow he had to obtain possession
of that rifle.

"Do you come from these parts?" the wife asked as

227

her husband went off to the smokehouse to fetch the meat.

She was young, pretty and blonde. Henry would have enjoyed a mild flirtation with her had his mind not been otherwise occupied. "I'm from Cincinnati," he said. "I'm making a surveying trip for a land company."

"That so?" she said. Surveyors were everywhere these days.

When the husband returned with the slab of bacon, wrapped in burlap, Henry paid him the seventy-five cents he asked for. He wondered whether to make an offer for the rifle. No, the risk was too great. Even an ignorant American peasant was certain to realize the value of such a fine weapon. If the man refused to part with it, which seemed likely, it would be difficult to steal the rifle without placing himself under suspicion.

Henry thanked the couple, walked back to his horse, placed the bacon in one of his new saddlebags and rode off, after closing the front gate behind him.

When he was out of sight of the house, he doubled back through the woods behind it, halting at a vantage point from which he could see the path leading to the gate. He didn't have long to wait. Soon he saw the farmer hitch a team of horses to a large cart and drive off, just as he'd said he would do.

Waiting a quarter of an hour to be on the safe side, Henry dismounted, cocked his pistol and approached the house on foot. Just before he reached the front door it opened and the pretty housewife emerged.

She recognized the intruder and started to speak, but something in his expression frightened her. She took a single step backward.

Henry would have preferred to negotiate with her, if possible, or at least to leave her unharmed. As he'd remarked to Sir Edwin at their last meeting, his reputation didn't do him justice. He never enjoyed bloodshed for its own sake.

But the young woman left him no choice: She'd be able to describe him in detail to the authorities if he simply bound and gagged her.

He raised the pistol at short range and put a bullet into the center of her forehead.

He was already in motion before she crumpled to the ground. He leaped over her body, went inside the house, snatched the rifle from its place on the mantel and looked around for the ammunition. Aware of the Americans' habits, he soon found a box of bullets in the hutch.

Returning the way he'd come, Henry stepped over the woman's body without looking down, hurried to his waiting stallion and headed west. He rode hard for the better part of the day, avoiding roads when he could. He was certain he had crossed into Indiana, and that was all to the good. There were different sheriffs here, and little coordination between law enforcement authorities of one state and another.

Still, it was best to take no chances, so he rode on until almost midnight. He had left the wagon train far behind now, but that would enable him to rest for several days until the caravan caught up with him. It was far more important to elude an Ohio sheriff and his deputies. In fact, Henry decided, he'd move on again as soon as he and his stallion had rested.

His own supplies of gunpowder were ample. As he loaded the rifle he felt a sense of elation. The weapon, known as the needle gun, had been invented eight years earlier by Johann von Dreyse of Berlin. The British had been the first to recognize its efficacy. Manufacturing their own version of it, they had already equipped most English regiments, while the Prussians had only recently become aware of its accuracy.

Henry St. Clair would have chosen it over any other rifle on earth. He felt certain now that his luck had changed. He doubted that there could be more than a dozen or two such guns in the whole United States and, miraculously, he had possession of one. With such a gun tucked under his arm, he believed himself invincible.

Shortly after the wagon train halted for the night, Sam Brentwood found recent deer tracks at a nearby salt lick, so a larger than usual number of men went hunting with him. Ordinarily Tonie Mell would have been eager to join them, but today she had other plans.

She was covered with a film of dust, so she went to a small stream that flowed into the Ohio. There, in an area the women had reserved for themselves, she bathed and washed her hair. Then she returned to her wagon and changed into the new moss-green dress she'd finally completed. It fitted her perfectly, hugging her supple body. She reflected that her aunt would be proud of her accomplishments.

All at once a thought occurred to her: it should have been obvious. For all practical purposes her aunt and uncle were her parents. The mother and father in St. Petersburg whom she could scarcely remember had brought her into the world, to be sure, but she'd discharged her obligation to them when she had attempted to follow the orders of the *chargé d'affaires* of the Imperial Russian Legation in Washington.

Although Russian by birth she was as much an American as any other member of the wagon train. She felt no regrets that her conscience had forced her to rebel against the Imperial Russian government and come to the aid of her fellow pioneers. The simple act of changing from her buckskins into a dress gave her a different perspective on herself and her situation. She might be able to ride and shoot like a man, but she was still a woman, and an American woman, who owed her loyalties to her aunt and uncle and to the United States.

The oppressive feeling of guilt that had burdened her for weeks was lifted from her. She had sacrificed more for her natural mother and father than they had ever done for her, and now she owed them nothing. The time had come to think of herself, and of her own future.

This journey had been good for her, because circumstances had forced her to dwell on her own situation. Now, for the first time ever, she was willing to admit, if only to herself, that she hoped to marry some day, settle down in a home of her own and raise a family. Doing a man's work on her uncle's ranch, she had concealed the truth behind a screen.

"May I come in?" Cathy van Ayl called from the far side of the wagon.

Tonie raised the flap, then self-consciously took several backward steps.

"Don't you look nice!" Cathy's admiration was spontaneous.

"I—I feel a little strange," Tonie confessed.

"That's because a few things are still missing. Here, try these."

Although Tonie's ears had been pierced, she'd rarely bothered with jewelry, but she obediently slipped on the earrings—green stones that seemed to bring out the rich highlights of her red hair.

"That's better." Cathy gestured toward the leather clothing box that was the wagon's closest equivalent to a chair.

Tonie sat.

The other girl put rouge on her mouth, with touches on her cheeks, then placed a thin coating of kohl on her eyelids.

"Not too much, now," Tonie said, her apprehension increasing. "I don't want to look like a harlot."

"You won't, I promise you," Cathy told her. "You are a woman, and it's no crime to look like one."

Tonie's laugh was shaky as she picked up the square of burnished metal that was her only mirror. She stared at her reflection in silence, then thrust the square of metal aside.

"Don't you like yourself?"

"I don't know. I don't look like me."

"Ah, but you do," Cathy said. "That's the whole point. Just watch the fuss the men make over you when they come back from their hunting trip."

Tonie felt terrified. "I don't aim to budge. I'm going to stay right here in my wagon."

"You'll do no such thing," Cathy said firmly. "You're coming with me right now so you can judge for yourself."

Tonie allowed the other girl to take her arm and half drag her outside. Inside the circle, however, no one paid the slightest attention to Tonie. The women, the children and the men who had stayed behind were staring in open-mouthed astonishment at an Indian, mounted on a small but spirited horse, who had just entered the circle.

In his late twenties, he was tall, broad-shouldered and sinewy. He carried himself with great dignity, though wearing only a breechcloth of leather, with a blanket over one shoulder. Certainly he had never spent years in the cities and towns of the white men. His head was shaved on both sides of his long scalp lock, in the manner utilized by many tribes, and there were streaks of green and yellow paint on each side of his face. At his waist was a long knife with a bone handle, and on his back was a container filled with arrows, his long bow resting on his pommel.

The members of the company were gaping. They had been told that they might eventually encounter hostile tribes. But here was a savage on the Ohio-Indiana border, and they didn't know what to do.

Abe Ellis reacted first. He reached for his rifle.

As she saw him raise it to his shoulder, Tonie remembered that he hated all Indians, never tiring of calling them lazy, shiftless and untrustworthy.

The warrior had raised his right arm, the palm of his hand extending upward.

Tonie forgot she was dressed like a lady. She threw herself at Ellis, hoping to knock him off balance before he could fire the shot. "Are you crazy?" she shouted. "He's made the sign of peace!"

Ellis staggered as the rifle discharged. The shot went wild.

Aware of the attempt on his life, the Indian continued to sit on his horse, his arm upraised, his expression unchanged.

Tonie approached him on foot and addressed him in the language of the Kiowa, which virtually all of the Plains Indians understood, regardless of their tribes. People who lived in Independence necessarily learned a number of Indian dialects.

The warrior replied in the even more commonly used tongue of the Cherokee. "Stalking Horse," he said, slowly lowering his arm, "owes his life to the squaw."

"You are Stalking Horse." Tonie hadn't spoken Cherokee for a long time, but the language came back to her in a rush.

"The son of Roaring Thunder, sachem of the Cherokee of the West." He deigned to address a mere woman not only because she had saved his life but also because only she, of all these people, could understand what he said.

"I am Mell," Tonie said. "Why does Stalking Horse, the son of Roaring Thunder, come to this place?"

Some of the children were regaining their courage, though they couldn't understand what was being said. Danny and Chet Harris inched closer.

"Stalking Horse always keeps his promise. Many moons ago he promised his brother, Brentwood, that they would meet again."

Tonie laughed, then turned to the others. "He's Sam Brentwood's friend."

Everyone began to talk at once. Only Abe Ellis looked disgruntled.

Tonie raised her arm in a gesture similar to the warrior's. "Welcome to the brother of Brentwood," she intoned, then muttered to Danny. "Quick. Bring something to eat and drink. No matter what it is."

The best the boy could manage in a hurry was a cup of water and a chunk of bread. Tonie took them from him and held them out to the Indian in a traditional offering of hospitality.

Claudia, who had witnessed the scene, was relieved that the Indian had escaped death, but she resented the role Tonie was playing. Above all, she was startled by the girl's appearance, and realized she had never done her justice. Claudia had to admit, grudgingly, that Tonie was actually pretty.

The warrior had dismounted slowly, then started forward to accept the bread and water, when the hunters returned, carrying two bucks and a doe they had already butchered to make the meat easier to carry.

Sam, who was in the lead, took one look at the brave and emitted a loud, sustained war whoop, as he jumped to the ground.

Stalking Horse let out a similar whoop, an expression of joy lighting up his grave face.

The two men embraced, pounding each other joyously on the back.

At first they addressed each other in Cherokee, then Sam switched to English. "Folks," he shouted, "this is Stalking Horse, my blood brother for the past ten years. We've fought side by side, we've explored together, we've lived together. He swore he was going to join me on this march, but I'd just about given him up for lost."

"I come," Stalking Horse said. "I am here." Reverting to Cherokee, he told his friend of his arrival. Then he drank the water and ate the bread that Tonie had continued to hold.

Sam stared at Tonie as though he barely recognized her, causing her heart to sink.

"Thank you, Tonie," he said, and with something far more pressing on his mind he walked slowly toward Abe Ellis.

The hired driver of the special wagon shrank as Sam approached.

"Ellis," he said, "you're lucky that Tonie Mell spoiled your aim. When Stalking Horse and I put the knife to each other and mixed each other's blood, we took an oath to avenge the death of either of us. If you had shot him, I'd be obligated by my word to put a bullet through you."

"How was I to know?" Ellis whined.

Still looking at the man, Sam called, "Is it true, Tonie, as Stalking Horse says, that he gave the sign of peace when he rode into the circle?"

"That's exactly what he did," the girl replied.

"Ellis," Sam said, "you're no greenhorn. You've been dealing with Indians for years, so you recognized the peace sign. Yet you'd have killed him in cold blood anyway."

"I've yet to see the Indian worth saving," Abe Ellis muttered, trying to show bravado.

"You've been saying for a long time that you want to get back to Albany," Sam said. "Well, early tomorrow morning you'll be on your way. I'll give you a letter to Mr. Astor, in New York, so you'll be paid in full." He turned on his heel and walked away.

The entire company was embarrassed. The women busied themselves roasting the meat while the men gathered in small groups to talk.

The warrior addressed Tonie in his own tongue. "Stalking Horse will remember what the squaw has done for him."

"So will I," Sam added in English. He still had made no mention of the radical alteration in her appearance. Instead he conferred briefly with Ernst von Thalman and Dr. Martin, whom he was treating as his lieutenants. "I'm going to offer the job of driving the special wagon to Nat Drummond," he told them. When they gaped at him, he said, "It makes sense. His wife drives their wagon, so he has nothing much to keep him occupied. But in spite of her bad opinion of him, he knows horses, and he's handled a lot of carts over the years. What's more, I'm sure he can use the wages that Astor will pay him."

"He'll accept," the Baron said, "but not because of

the money. In the special wagon, he won't have to listen to his wife all day."

Sam went off to join Stalking Horse, and Von Thalman began to supervise the preparation of the venison, which needed to be cooked more slowly than other kinds of meat.

Tonie Mell stood alone, nursing her rebuff and wondering whether she should go to her wagon and change back into her buckskins. Her attempt to emerge from her cocoon had been a failure, in spite of Cathy van Ayl's encouragement, and only her pride kept her from crying. Perhaps the dramatic arrival of Stalking Horse had diverted attention from her transformation, but she couldn't use that as an excuse. Men simply didn't think of her as a woman, and that was that.

Tonie began to make her way unobtrusively around the edge of the crowd. But someone blocked her path. It was Dr. Martin. He looked her up and down slowly, his eyes showing his appreciation. "You look lovely," he said.

Tonie felt as though liquid fire had been injected into her veins. Rooted to the spot, her face burning, she didn't know what to say. One thing was certain: she'd get to work on the other dresses. Hereafter, she'd wear women's clothes every evening.

Abe Ellis left the camp before sunrise, riding a spare horse he'd purchased from an Ohio farmer. An hour later the caravan was on the move in the opposite direction, a proud Nat Drummond driving the special wagon, a task he performed with flawless ease. Stalking Horse joined Sam in the vanguard, and

Tonie returned to her regular duties as monitor of the line. She was deluged with complaints. Claudia reported that she couldn't locate a gold locket containing a miniature portrait of her late mother. Grace Drummond said that her best carving knife was missing. Emily Harris was disturbed because a large smoked ham had vanished from her meager larder. Even Baron von Thalman was upset. He couldn't find his finest gold cufflinks. Others had suffered losses, too.

At noon, when the wagon train halted to eat and rest, Tonie went to Sam Brentwood with the complaints. "I hate to make accusations," she said, "but there must be a thief in the company. If just a couple of people misplaced things, it could be accidental. But with so many on the same day, it becomes suspicious."

Sam wasted no time. He questioned each of the people who'd lost property, then returned to the head of the line and summoned Tonie, Dr. Martin and the Baron. "I want you to go on without me," he said. "I should rejoin you no later than tomorrow night. Meantime, Ernie, you'll be acting wagonmaster. Keep Stalking Horse beside you, and know you can rely on him as you'd rely on me. Tonie can translate if you need his help."

"I assume," Dr. Martin said, "that you're heading back to search for Abe Ellis."

Sam nodded. "I can't prove he's a thief, at least not yet. But I find it mighty odd that a dozen people in the train are missing property just after he's left us."

"Why not let us hunt for him and you go on with the train?" the Baron asked.

"This is a task for a man who can cover ground in a hurry, and I'm that man," Sam said.

He filled one pocket of his buckskin shirt with ammunition and the other with jerked venison. Then, even before the caravan resumed its march, he rode off toward the East.

His sense of urgency was communicated to his stallion. The great beast thundered down the river road at a gallop. In an hour they reached the site of the previous night's camp, and a short time later Sam picked up the trail of a lone horseman. It had to be Ellis. The hoofprints in the dirt were plain, thanks to a light rain that had fallen during the night, so Sam was forced to reduce his pace only slightly.

Late in the afternoon the tracks multiplied. He dismounted to study them, and soon he figured out what had happened. The rider had met two other horsemen, and all three had headed toward the East. There were no clues to the identities of the newcomers, but at least Sam knew that he was outnumbered.

Shortly before sundown the tracks vanished from the road. The three men had ridden away from the river through knee-high grass. It was more difficult to follow their trail now, since dusk had fallen, but the task offered him no serious challenge, and Sam reflected that it was easier to follow these white men than it had been to pursue renegade Apache above the timberline in the Rockies.

He had to slow his pace considerably, however, and occasionally he was forced to dismount to examine flattened grass and broken twigs. Night came, a partial moon rose and the trail led into deep woods of pine, elm and maple. The stallion advanced very slowly now, the occasional touch of his master's hand on his flank cautioning him, and his hoofs made no sound on the soft, mossy turf.

Sam automatically checked his rifle and pistols to make certain that all were loaded and ready for immediate use. He smelled the campfire long before he saw it, and dismounted. His horse followed obediently as he made his way forward on foot. Sam heard voices, and soon he could make out three men sitting at a small fire in a clearing. One was Abe Ellis. The other two were strangers.

The contents of a saddlebag were spread on the ground beside Ellis, who was talking earnestly. "I ain't greedy," he said, "but I got my own reasons for wanting to get out of this part of the country fast. That's why fifty dollars will buy you everything in this bag."

One of the men took a swig from a bottle. Then he handed the bottle to his companion, who followed his example and passed it to Ellis.

"I want to look at the cufflinks again," the older stranger said.

"Them and the gold locket are worth at least fifty dollars, all by themselves," Ellis said, handing the man two objects. "You gents are getting a bargain."

"How do we know we won't be arrested for dealin' in stolen property?" one man demanded.

Sam had heard enough. Positive now that Ellis had stolen the wares he was trying to peddle, he decided the time had come to intervene.

Stepping out of the shadows into the clearing, he said, "You would be dealing in stolen goods. And I'm sure none of you men want to go to prison. Including you, Ellis. So I'll just take these things that don't belong to any of you, and we won't bother to prosecute —mostly because it would take too long to go all the way to the Cincinnati courthouse."

Abe Ellis' hand moved toward the pistol he carried in his belt.

"None of that!" Sam said. "Hold still!"

Ellis ignored the order.

The sound of a shot from Sam's rifle echoed through the woods, and Ellis was thrown backward onto the ground, a bullet in his shoulder. He screamed, then moaned, but no one paid any attention to him.

"I suggest," Sam told the strangers, "that you gather up the stolen articles, one at a time, nice and slow and easy, and drop them into the saddlebag. That way nobody else will get hurt."

"Sure," the older man said, his hand creeping toward an object half-hidden in the grass.

Almost too late, Sam saw the blade of a knife gleaming in the light of the fire. Before the man could pick up the knife and throw it, Sam wielded his rifle like a club, grasping it by the barrel, and brought the butt down on the stranger's hand with all his strength.

The man shrieked in pain. "My God! You broke my hand!"

"You're lucky I haven't broken your neck," Sam said. "Yet. You lads don't appear to be too bright. Two of you are hurting because you didn't do what you were told. When I give an order I expect it to be obeyed."

Ellis was still moaning, and the older man was whimpering.

"You!" Sam said, looking at the other man and drawing a pistol from his belt. "Stand up!"

The younger man rose sullenly to his feet.

Sam plucked a pistol and a knife from the man's belt and threw them into the woods. "I'm keeping you covered, and don't you forget it. Put those belongings back into the saddlebag yonder. One at a time. And don't try any tricks or you'll get a bullet in your head."

The silent man followed instructions to the letter.

Sam placed the saddlebag over his shoulder, keeping the man covered with his pistol. "Vermin like the three of you should be in prison," he said, "but I can't place two hundred people in jeopardy while I haul you all the way to Cincinnati." He snatched the pistol from Ellis' belt and sent it sailing off into the woods. "Abe, I'm blamed if I know how you'll get your shoulder fixed, and I'm blamed if I care. It'll serve you right to rot before you ever get back to Albany. As for you two buzzards, anything bad that happens will be too good for you. Just heed this warning. May the Almighty have mercy on your souls if I ever set eyes on you again!"

Disappearing from the clearing, he leaped onto the back of his stallion and rode off through the woods, leaving havoc behind him.

At sunrise, members of the wagon train were eating breakfast when Sam quietly rode into their midst. Handing Tonie the saddlebag, he asked her to distribute the property to those who'd been robbed.

Then, offering no explanation, he shaved, doused his head in cold water and ate some ham and bread before leading the group on the day's march. He had not rested since he had arisen the previous morning, but he was cheerful, energetic and untiring all day.

X

Indiana was one of the older states of the West, having been admitted to the Union twenty-one years earlier in 1816. Citizens of Indiana had enjoyed prosperity through the years, but now the Panic of 1837 was hitting them hard. With the shortage of money, and limited funds available for the agricultural products on which the economy of the state was based, silos and barns were glutted. No one was starving, but farmers who couldn't pay their bills were becoming increasingly disenchanted.

The grass in far-off fields looked greener than the grass at home, and twenty-three wagons joined Sam Brentwood's caravan in the state of Indiana. Most of the new arrivals, like those who'd joined earlier, had made their living from the earth.

Now, when Sam Brentwood and Stalking Horse mounted their horses at the head of the line, they sometimes couldn't see the wagons bringing up the rear. Snaking along roads that curved first in one direction, then another, they followed the course of the Ohio River. The great wagon train inspired awe in the few other travelers who saw it. Occupants of passing river boats stared in wonder, fog horns blowing in salute.

One monitor could no longer control the whole column. Reorganizing his command, Sam appointed two front and two rear monitors, thus splitting the line down the middle. Tonie continued to ride tirelessly up and down the whole line, and the monitors were ordered to report directly to her. It was her duty to notify Sam when it was necessary to call a halt.

The familiar music of the wagon train—the creaking harnesses, the thud of horses' hooves, the clatter of turning wheels—was louder now, a symphony that could be heard for miles around.

Hunters and fishermen could no longer supply enough food. For the first time since the start of the journey, it became necessary to start spending the money that John Jacob Astor and his associates had provided for the purpose. Dr. Martin and the Baron frequently went to nearby towns, villages and isolated stores to buy flour and bacon, corn and rice, dried beans and occasional sides of beef.

According to Stalking Horse, they would be coming to buffalo country soon, and Sam was relieved. He made it his business to identify the best marksmen in the company. When they encountered a large enough herd of buffalo, they would shoot enough to supply meat for many days.

The newest arrivals, including the children, were

given the simpler duties, and were coached by the veterans. No one took advantage of his or her authority. Cathy van Ayl commanded a cooking detail of thirty women. They worked together harmoniously, and none appeared to resent Cathy, though she was one of the youngest in the group.

The word of the wagonmaster remained final in all matters. Dr. Martin was respected because of his profession, and people listened to the Baron, too, but because of his skills instead of his wealth. All pioneers were equal.

The faith of Andrew Jackson and the men who had financed this expedition was being justified. A small army was on the march, its members optimistic, looking forward to the day when new homesteads could be built in Oregon.

A few wouldn't go that far. Sam Brentwood planned to stop in Independence, where he would set up a supply depot. Tonie Mell had planned to go only as far as her uncle's ranch, although she found herself wondering if she shouldn't go all the way. Claudia Humphries still dreamed of returning to New Haven. And Arthur Elwood complained about the hardships. And hardships there were aplenty, for all of them.

Of the newcomers, one was a man of some mystery. Ted Woods was a blacksmith by trade. Endowed with a powerful torso and arms, he was a welcome and useful addition. Now, when horses needed to be shod, Ted Woods did it. Taciturn and withdrawn, he refused to discuss his background. It was enough, he said, that he was going to the Oregon country.

It was obvious, however, that he was very poor. His

wagon was ramshackle and his horses were painfully thin. He appeared to be carrying few personal possessions and little food. He always refused cash for his services, and asked for payment in flour, bacon and coffee. His complexion was so pale that many wondered if he had been ill, but he answered few questions.

Danny, who worked as hard for the newcomers as the veterans, was the first to penetrate the mystery. Riding beside Claudia one morning, he announced casually, "I think I got me that Woods figured out. Some of the Indiana folks got a suspicion about him, but he's so ornery they don't like t' talk about it out loud."

"Perhaps you shouldn't, either," Claudia said.

"Oh, I ain't spreadin' no tales, Miss Claudia! Not me. What I got t' say is b'twixt us, and you can decide if you want t' tell Mr. Sam." The boy took a deep breath. "One o' them farmers from northern Indiana let on that he read in a newspaper about a murderer bein' let out o' prison after servin' ten years. He don't rightly remember the feller's name, but he swears the man was a blacksmith afore he got sent t' jail."

Claudia felt uneasy. A long term in prison would certainly account for Ted Woods' pasty skin. "Did you find out who he killed, or why?"

"No, Miss Claudia. The farmer was so busy packin' up for this here trip that he didn't pay much mind t' the piece in the newspaper. He wishes now he'd read it better, but he's keepin' his mouth shut and I don't blame him. That Woods looks like he could tear a man apart with his two bare hands if he got riled up."

"Don't mention this to anyone, Danny," Claudia said, and extracted a solemn promise from him.

She thought about Danny's information all day, and that evening she went privately to Sam. "I don't know what you might want to do about this," she said, "but you have the right to know."

He nodded, looking off into space, then bent down and plucked a blade of tall grass, which he tasted experimentally as she told the story. "You're sure Danny has no intention of spreading this tale?"

"I'm positive!"

"Obviously you don't intend to talk about it, either."

"Hardly."

"Then I won't do anything. We'll see how Woods works out. If he made a mistake, he's paid for it and deserves a chance to begin a new life, free and clear."

"I quite agree," Claudia said, "though I must confess that the thought of having a murderer in the company makes me uneasy."

"It all depends on how you use words," Sam replied. "I've killed more than a few men in my day, but I haven't been branded a murderer. There are different rules in the wilderness than in civilized places, and I wouldn't want to condemn a man without knowing what he did and his reasons for doing it. In this case, even if Woods killed somebody, it's none of my business—provided he behaves himself as a member of the wagon train."

Claudia had to admit that Sam was being fair, but thereafter she couldn't help watching Ted Woods surreptitiously. He sat alone at meals, eating quickly and then retiring to his wagon. He had rebuffed so many friendly overtures that the other pioneers gave him a wide berth, which he appeared to prefer. He worked quickly and expertly when someone needed a horse shod, and he proved himself equally proficient when the metal rim of a wagon broke or had to be rejoined or replaced.

Danny, who was friendly with everyone, made it his business to gather extra fodder for Woods' team. "Them horses is too skinny," he told Claudia. "I got t' put some meat on their bones."

Woods was aware of Danny's efforts but ignored him.

Claudia decided that Woods was too surly and ungrateful to deserve Danny's gestures, but she refrained from expressing her opinion to the boy. It would be wrong to curb his generous nature, she decided, but she was prepared to intervene if Danny seemed threatened in any way.

One hot, sultry day, when Sam called an early halt because the air was so humid that the horses were suffering, Danny, the Harris boys and several other youngsters went for a swim in a nearby lake, as the adults relaxed on the grass, enjoying the unexpected respite.

Soon, high clouds formed overhead, gradually becoming darker. Thunder sounded in the distance. A heavy rain was coming, the farmers told each other, and after it passed the air would be less sultry. The men bestirred themselves, tethering their horses, making certain the canvas tops of their wagons were secure.

Only the boys cavorting in the lake ignored the gathering storm.

When Cathy van Ayl screamed, the company was electrified. But Cathy was so frightened she could only point.

A long, dark shape had emerged from the clouds.

"A twister!" a man cried out in a thunderstruck voice.

Enormous at the top and slimming to a narrow tail at the bottom, it vaguely resembled a mammoth carrot. Ripping up trees, sucking in dust and debris as it whirled, it became ever more ominous and threatening as it moved at lightning speed toward the campsite. Its power was enormous, and the whole company was paralyzed. No defense against the swift, brutal power of a cyclone had ever been devised, and Sam Brentwood could only shout, "Hug the ground!"

Only a few had the presence of mind to drop to the ground. Others remained sitting or standing, and could only gape as the black funnel swept toward them. A handful began to pray, but the others were too stunned by the evil, howling wind mass that raced toward them. The boys in the lake managed to scramble to safety— all except Danny.

A large maple tree on the bank of the Ohio was sucked up into the vortex and vanished from sight. Horses neighed. Quincy, crouching beside Claudia, whimpered and shook.

Then all at once the tornado changed directions and swerved cross-country, missing people, wagons and horses by no more than a hundred yards.

Before anyone quite realized what was happening the funnel was gone. The tornado had vanished, leaving a path of pure devastation in its wake several hundred feet wide. The grove of cedars and ailanthus trees that stood at the shore of the lake was gone. Some trees were toppled, others had disappeared into the cyclone. A few were scattered across the surface of the water like kindling.

Thunder roared and a pelting rain began to fall in sheets. Suddenly a burly man ran at full speed toward the lake. For a man of his bulk Ted Woods moved with remarkable speed. Throwing himself into the water, he swam a short distance, plunged under the surface and came up with a body in his arms.

Only when he returned to shore, carrying a limp burden, did the pioneers see that he was carrying Danny. Neither then nor later did anyone ever know whether the boy had been struck by a tree limb or knocked off balance by the ferocious power of the cyclone.

Ted Woods carried the boy to his own wagon, and the first to join him there was Dr. Martin, who sprinted across the compound. Within moments others gathered outside, unsure if Danny was dead or alive.

Dr. Martin checked the boy's pulse, listened to his breathing and held a phial of smelling salts under his nose. Danny stirred, sat upright and began to cough. He looked at the physician, then at his rescuer, and grinned. "I ain't fond o' twisters," he said. "Thanks, Mr. Woods."

The blacksmith grunted in an effort to reassure the boy.

"I think you'll be all right, Danny," Dr. Martin said. "I'll check later to be sure. Meantime stay where you are, and don't move."

"But I got chores—"

"You heard what the doc said." Ted Woods' voice was almost as deep as the thunder that rumbled overhead. "You'll stay where you are if I have to tie weights to your ankles!"

Danny subsided, and the physician departed.

The blacksmith went to the rear of his wagon to inform the group still standing in the rain. "Go on about your business," he said, sounding angry. "The boy needs to rest."

The crowd dispersed. The storm lasted another half-hour, then cleared away. Soon the sun came out again. Only the path cut into the landscape as though by a giant scythe was left as a reminder of the cyclone.

Supper was delayed. It took time for the firewood to dry, and a number of people wandered back to Ted Woods' wagon, but he shooed them away with curt, threatening gestures. Danny was asleep, and the blacksmith sat near him, keeping a silent vigil, allowing no one but the doctor to enter.

When supper was ready and the blacksmith didn't join the company, several of the women took food to his wagon. Woods glowered at them. "When I'm hungry," he said, "I'll eat. The doc says the kid needs rest, so leave him be."

Later, when the last embers of the fire died away, Ted Woods was still sitting, keeping watch.

The next morning, after Dr. Martin gave his reluctant consent, Danny resumed his chores. Displaying his customary energy, he seemed no worse for his experience. He didn't know what had happened, he told his many well-wishers. His only memory was seeing the cyclone move toward him.

Ted Woods ate his breakfast alone.

When camp was broken and the wagons began to form for the new day's journey, Danny came up to Claudia, already seated on her boards. "If you don't mind, Miss Claudia," he said, "I'm goin' t' hitch me a ride with that Woods feller today. I figure maybe he needs some comp'ny." Claudia's quick smile sent him on his way.

As the boy climbed up beside him, Ted Woods paid no attention. Danny waited until the wagon was moving before he broke the silence. "Your team is gettin' fatter."

"I've noticed," the man said.

They rode for a time before Danny spoke again. "You saved my life."

Ted shrugged.

Although the day was warm the boy broke into a cold sweat. "You was in jail."

Ted Woods nodded.

"How come?"

"You're too young to understand."

"I been around. Try me."

"I shot my wife. And my brother. I thought I had good cause. The judge said he was sorry, but he sent me to prison for ten years anyway."

Danny digested this information. "I won't tell nobody. What my friends say t' me is private."

The man ran a brawny hand through his thick,

black hair, and for the first time since he joined the expedition he smiled, relaxing his facial muscles. "We're friends, are we?"

"You bet!" Danny replied. His enthusiasm would not be denied.

They exchanged no additional words that day.

When they halted in the afternoon Danny went off to his chores with his usual gusto. A wagon owner came to Ted, needing a new shoe for one of his horses. The blacksmith lighted a fire in his portable burner, accepted the metal shoe the man handed him and soon had the task done.

"I reckon I owe you some flour and bacon," the man said.

Ted shook his head. "You don't owe me anything," he said, and turned away quickly, ending the conversation.

That evening, at supper, he took his place alone in the shadows at the outer edge of the campfire. Although a number of people wanted to invite him to join them, they decided it was best to respect his privacy. Danny, however, felt no inhibitions. Carrying a chunk of dripping meat and a slab of bread, he made a place for himself beside the blacksmith.

Neither spoke, but they seemed to enjoy each other's companionship, with no need for words. No one was surprised, that night, when Danny rolled up in his blanket in a corner of Ted Woods' wagon. Thereafter they were inseparable.

Ted Woods remained aloof from the company, consistently refusing to accept money for his services. And when he sometimes chopped down a dead tree for firewood he worked so quickly that no one was able to help him.

Cindy struck the wagon train with a force almost as great as the tornado. She was a member of a party of forty, traveling in her own sturdy wagon, who had crossed the river in flatboats from Louisville, and traveled upriver to meet the wagon train. There were three hundred and fifty people in the wagon train now, and from the moment of her arrival Cindy was one of the more conspicuous.

In her early twenties, she had waist-long red hair that glowed when the sun fell on it, and the green of her deep eyes was enhanced by a liberal use of cosmetics. Her skin-tight green satin dress was cut to reveal every line of her ripe body, and created a sensation. She had a way of wriggling her hips that caused every man in the company to stare at her.

The girl's mere presence outraged many of the women, and both Cathy van Ayl and Lena Malcolm thought she should be sent on her way. But some of the older women were more tolerant. "Leave her be," Grace Drummond said. "I've got no call against her, unless she makes eyes at Nat."

Emily Harris was equally philosophical. "We've got to give her a chance," she said. Tonie Mell calmly agreed.

Claudia instinctively disliked the new arrival. From the moment Cindy joined the caravan, she secretly agreed with her sister that a disruptive force had been added. She took care to keep her opinion to herself, however, principally because she didn't want Sam

Brentwood to think she was jealous of a trollop. He made Cindy welcome, as he did everyone else who joined. Claudia knew he believed every newcomer had a right to a fair trial.

Cindy did her best to become friendly with the women, but was prepared for their rebuffs and didn't seem hurt when they shunned her. She was more cautious in her dealings with men, which won her the grudging respect of some members of her sex, but the task she had assigned herself was overwhelming. She was a natural flirt who couldn't help rolling her eyes when she spoke to a man. And Claudia noted that Sam, like every other male, watched her swaying hips when Cindy walked away from the fire.

She made no secret of her background, and it soon became common knowledge. She had gone to work in a New Orleans bordello at a very early age. More recently she had been the star resident of a house in Louisville. Tiring of the life, she had invested her considerable savings in a comfortable wagon and a team of horses.

She put on no airs. Claudia had to admit that. She volunteered for duty with the women, though she cheerfully admitted that she had never cooked a meal in her life. Cathy and Lena took an adamant position, however, so Claudia added Cindy to the water-gathering detail. Danny was delighted, as was Chet Harris. Both boys would have carried her share of the load had Cindy permitted it. But she insisted on doing her share, though she was totally unfamiliar with the outdoors.

A few days after Cindy joined the company, Claudia realized that the newcomer was watching her surreptitiously. The scrutiny made her uncomfortable, so she became even more remote. That Sunday, however, while the train enjoyed its customary day of rest, Claudia was sitting on the back steps of her wagon, mending a skirt, when Cindy approached her.

"Could I have a little chat with you?" Cindy spoke in the thick drawl of the Deep South.

There was no escape. "Of course," Claudia replied stiffly, busying herself with her sewing.

The girl sat on the bottom step. "You don't like me," she said.

It was pointless to deny the obvious. "I don't see what possible difference my feelings could make."

"They make a difference to me, because you're a lady. I've seen the way everybody looks up to you, even Sam."

Her easy use of Brentwood's first name caused Claudia to stiffen. She didn't know what to reply.

"You don't really know me," Cindy said, "so your only reason is because I was a whore."

A lady, Claudia thought, didn't even use that word. "I suppose you're right," she admitted.

"It's plain that a lot of the others feel the same way. So I thought with you I ought to bring it into the open. Sam says it'll be two years or more before we get to the Oregon country. I'll die if we stay on bad terms for that long a time."

Claudia saw that she was sincere, and couldn't help melting a little. "I don't mean to be unkind. I suppose it's just the way I grew up."

"Oh, I don't blame you." Cindy remained cheerful.

"When I walked down the streets of Louisville, ladies swept their skirts out of my way. You'd think they were afraid of contamination by a Jezebel." She giggled, then sobered. "If I had wanted the kind of life I was living, I'd have stayed in Louisville. But I didn't. Tell me what I need to do to make all these she-cats stop hissing at me."

Her appeal seemed genuine. Claudia realized with a shock that the girl, in spite of her experience with men, was almost a child. "For one thing," she said, "you might try using a little less rouge. And less of that black stuff around your eyes."

"I'd feel naked," Cindy said, and laughed.

"Just a suggestion," Claudia replied.

"But I'll do it. You sound strict, like the madam of the first place I worked in New Orleans."

Claudia had to avert her face to hide her smile. "You might try dressing more appropriately, too."

The girl ran her hands down her sleek, low-cut gown of yellow silk. "You don't like this dress?"

"It might be just right for the parlor of a house in Louisville, but on a wagon train it makes you too conspicuous in the wrong way."

"But all my clothes are like this!" Cindy wailed. "Besides, they cost me a fortune."

"They'll be in rags before we get as far as St. Louis," Claudia told her. "Surely you can understand that such gowns entice the men and cause the women to resent you."

"What should I do?"

"Buy some material—sensible, strong material—the

first time we come to a town. Then make yourself a new wardrobe. Eventually, you can make pillow cases and curtains out of your present gowns."

The girl swallowed. "I'll do it," she said, "if you'll teach me how to sew."

Claudia had no choice. She had allowed herself to be maneuvered into a corner, and couldn't deny the candid request for help. "Very well," she said, "I'll do what I can."

Cindy's quick smile was radiant.

She made no secret of her pending transformation. And Sam and the Baron returned from an all-day hunting trip with two bucks and presented her with the skins, after treating them for her. Cindy asked Claudia to help her cut, fit and sew the leather. They spent a whole Sunday together, working on the project, much to Claudia's annoyance, but she knew of no way she could back out.

To her surprise Claudia found that Cindy, although inept at first, was eager to learn. Her enthusiasm at least partly compensated for her lack of ability. She acted like someone in her teens. It was proving easy, she said, to forget her former profession. She had toned down her use of cosmetics, and she was sufficiently conscious of her appearance to appear in public with a shawl draped around her shoulders, partly nullifying the effect of her provocative dresses.

Only her occasional comments about male members of the caravan revealed her expert knowledge on the subject. "I'd like to shake some sense into poor little Nat Drummond," she said. "All he has to do to make his wife behave is clout her a couple of times."

She also proved illuminating on the subject of the Baron: "Would you believe he's a very lonely person? He hides behind all that heel-clicking and hand-kissing, but he'd make a wonderful husband for a woman who showed him a little sympathy."

She was emphatic about Ted Woods: "There's a real man. He has a bad hurt bottled up inside him, but he'll be someone pretty special if he ever gets rid of it."

When Cindy remarked about Sam Brentwood, Claudia was resentful. "He's the best there is in this wagon train," Cindy said. "You don't find many men of his class anywhere. The only trouble with him is he's been a bachelor so long. He's set in his ways. But I bet I could tame him if I had the chance." She winked, then exploded in a long fit of giggling.

Claudia knew it was absurd to feel jealous. She and Sam Brentwood had developed no personal relationship, in spite of their constant association, but she disliked the way Cindy airily assumed that he was fair game for any woman who wanted to win his affections. What she particularly resented, she decided, was the girl's easy use of his first name. She herself continued to be formal in her dealings with him, and it irritated her that a newcomer could establish such friendly terms with him so easily.

But that, she told herself, was none of her business. If the wagonmaster allowed himself to become a victim to Cindy's obvious charms, he would just have to pay the consequences. She had always believed that most men preferred virtuous women, and she clung to that conviction. If Sam Brentwood proved foolish and vulnerable, that was none of her concern.

Certainly she couldn't blame Cindy for sparking to him, and vowed that she wouldn't permit the girl's feelings to stand in the way of their own association. She still regarded the long journey as difficult and dreary. It was. But it would be even more unpleasant if she allowed herself to be on bad terms with someone who was actively seeking her friendship.

Being nice to Cindy, however, didn't mean she had to go out of her way for Sam Brentwood. That very Sunday, with work on Cindy's new buckskin outfit about half completed, Claudia was cool to Sam, returning his customary, cordial greeting with a stiff nod.

Cindy appeared to have no idea that she was creating any new tensions. Bubbling with enthusiasm, she showed Sam and the Baron her handiwork on what she called "their" leather dress.

"I told you that you were silly to do her a favor," Cathy murmured to her sister, as they watched Cindy laughing and chatting with Sam and the Baron at the far side of the fire. "I knew you'd regret it."

Claudia shrugged. "I don't know what you mean, and I don't really care."

Her sister stared hard at her. "I've never known you to be so stupid," she said, before going off to her wagon.

The entire company retired early on Sunday nights so they could make an early start on Monday. If the roads were good, they might travel as far as ten miles. There was conjecture tonight that they might reach the first major goal, the meeting place of the Missouri and Mississippi rivers at the little town of Independence by late in the following fall.

Cindy had long been accustomed to sleeping by day and working by night, and she was trying to acclimate herself to her new life. When the teenaged boys began to bank the fire for the night, she followed the example of others and drifted off to her own snug wagon after first bidding Sam Brentwood a warm good night.

Men's eyes were fastened on her as she walked, but she had known such tributes for so long that she paid scant attention to them. She disliked being the center of attention, and she could only hope that people soon would accept her for what she was trying to be, rather than for what she had been. The advice Claudia Humphries had given her was sound, and she was doing her best to make her appearance less flamboyant. A change of heart was more important than dress or cosmetics, she felt, and she was satisfied with the progress she was making.

It was still difficult to go to sleep so soon after sunset, however, so she lighted two large candles and decided to sew together the front and back panels of her new buckskin shirt. Claudia had told her that practice would improve her skill with a needle, and she knew her mentor was right. After only one day of work she was already less clumsy.

Leaving the rear flap of her wagon open to catch any breeze that might blow in on a sultry night, Cindy discarded her shawl and began to sew with a vengeance. Sam had told her she would find a general store at Cairo, if not before. She would not only buy enough cloth there for several new outfits, but make them herself, stitch by stitch.

It was odd, Cindy thought, that the prospect of becoming a talented seamstress could intrigue her. As recently as a year ago, she would have laughed at the idea. She still had no concrete notion of what had soured her on the life of a trollop. Perhaps the profession had lost its savor; she had grown tired of playing the same, inevitable scenes with man after man, allowing them to do what they pleased with her body, pretending they were arousing her when she was actually bored.

Perhaps she had changed because she'd seen what happened to girls who stayed in the profession too long. Some of them aged prematurely, yet seemed incapable of becoming honest women. Many drank to excess, and a number took the risk of stealing from their clients, a sure road to disaster. She was proud of having shown enough common sense to get out before it was too late, and her conviction that she was doing the right thing was unshaken. The rough life on the road, which lacked almost every convenience she was used to, didn't appeal to her. But unlike Claudia Humphries, who loathed the pioneer life, Cindy believed that in time she'd grow sufficiently experienced to take it for granted. Her ease in dealing with men had been one of her principal assets. Now that same ease, directed into other channels, would continue to serve her well.

Footsteps sounded on the wagon stairs. Cindy looked up to see a man standing in the wagon entrance.

"Good evening," Arthur Elwood said. "I hope I'm not intruding."

The familiar expression in his eyes made her uneasy,

but she wanted to be polite. "That's all right," she said.

"May I come in?"

"I guess so."

He took care to lower the flap behind him, and her nervousness increased.

Neither of them knew it, but a burly figure from a nearby wagon approached stealthily, remaining hidden in the shadows. There, he could hear what went on inside without being seen.

Elwood stared at the cleavage revealed by Cindy's low-cut gown. He moistened his lips. "I've been looking forward to paying you a visit ever since you joined the wagon train," he said.

His meaning was all too clear, but Cindy preferred to avoid an open controversy if she could. "I'm always happy to chat with people at mealtime."

"I'm sure you'll agree there are occasions when a private meeting can be much better." Elwood's smile was ingratiating.

"That depends," Cindy said.

"I don't like to hem and haw," he said, "so I'll come right out with it. You're the best thing that's ever happened to this wagon train, and I'm prepared to show my appreciation."

The girl compressed her full lips. "No, thank you."

"How much did your customers in Louisville pay you? A dollar?"

She didn't deign to reply.

He thought she was teasing him into paying a higher fee. "See here, I'm no stranger to the best houses in

Louisville, and I've never paid any girl more than two dollars, usually for the whole night."

"Please leave," Cindy said. "You don't understand."

"I realize that in a group like this, where you're the only one, you can set any figure you want, and I'm willing to go along with that. After all, I'm in business, too, and I believe in getting a top price. So I'll pay you three dollars, which is more than fair."

Cindy felt weary. "You could offer me ten. Or even twenty. But I wouldn't take it."

Elwood laughed, sidling toward her. "Maybe you need a little persuasion."

"Don't come near me, Mr. Elwood. Don't touch me!" She replied softly, but there was a note of alarm in her voice.

"I don't know what kind of game you think you're playing," he said, "but it won't work with me. You flaunt yourself all over the caravan. The way you bounce up and down and wriggle your rear is enough to drive a man crazy. So stop all this damn-fool pretending."

"I've done nothing deliberately to attract anyone, and I'm sorry if that's what I did to you," Cindy said. "You'll have to take my word that I didn't mean it the way you think."

He laughed and reached for her. "You're clever as they come," he said.

She dreaded a scene. It would be the talk of the caravan for days and further damage her already tarnished image. Still hoping to persuade him to behave sensibly, she allowed him to fondle her breasts while she spoke to him earnestly. "I'm not in a Louisville house any more. I'm heading out to the Oregon country to make a new life for myself, just like the rest of you. All I ask is that you leave me alone."

His hands became busier.

The girl knew from experience that the time for words was past. He was becoming excited, and not listening to a word she was saying. "That's enough! Take your hands off me!"

Elwood grasped her buttocks and hauled her close.

Cindy was no weakling, but she realized that he was stronger, so she had to resort to drastic means. Struggling hard in an effort to free herself from his grasp, she managed to bend down sufficiently to snatch her sewing scissors from the table beside her. Pressing the point of the closed blades against his chest, she raised her voice for the first time.

"Mister," she said, "I'm not fooling. Stop right now or you're going to get hurt. I'll scream, too, and when people come running I'll tell them you tried to rape me!"

The point of the scissors cut through his shirt and broke his skin. It was the pain rather than her words that penetrated his consciousness. His hands fell to his sides. As he saw a smear of blood spreading across the front of his shirt, he gaped in disbelief.

Cindy was ready to strike again. "Get out!" she said. "Don't come back, that's all. There's no hard feelings!"

"You goddamn bitch!" Elwood's chest was still stinging and he was furious.

"Call me any names you like, mister. Just keep your distance, and we'll get along fine."

He stamped out, cursing under his breath.

Cindy fastened the flap behind him, making it secure. Not until his fading footsteps could no longer be heard did she begin to weep. Claudia Humphries was right: the way she dressed still gave some men the wrong idea. She knew she would have no real peace until she put together a new wardrobe.

It was tempting to blame Elwood and all the others like him for what had just happened, but she had to accept part of the responsibility. To hell with men like that; she'd show all of them. She threw herself onto her mattress, still fully clad, and after a time she slept.

Danny was still awake when Ted Woods returned to the ramshackle wagon, his movements remarkably quiet for a man of his bulk. Woods wrapped himself in his blanket, and a chuckle rumbled up from within him.

It was the first time Danny had heard him laugh, but there was no joy in the sound. The boy couldn't quite analyze what he had heard. All he knew was that Ted seemed to be experiencing a sense of grim satisfaction.

XI

The addition of the Indiana newcomers to the caravan changed the nature of the expedition. Most of them used oxen rather than work horses to draw their wagons. These patient, gentle animals foraged on the high grass, as did the horses, but they lumbered along the trail at a much slower speed, and now Sam Brentwood was satisfied if they covered as much as eight or ten miles in a day. In spite of their strength the oxen needed more rest than the horses, so a longer halt was called at midday. This pause became known as "nooning," and most of the pioneers welcomed the respite.

Most drivers, not wanting to inhale the dust kicked up by the iron-rimmed wheels in front of them, instinctively fell back and allowed gaps of up to a hundred feet to develop between wagons. This, in turn, made the entire procession less manageable, and at times the line stretched out on the river road for a distance of two miles. Tonie Mell and her assistants worked hard to keep a more compact formation, and hoarse shouts of "Close those holes! Move smartly, now!" were heard all day.

A majority of the vehicles were the bulbous-topped prairie schooners used by others on shorter journeys for the last quarter of a century. But there was a scattering of lighter wagons in the line, and their presence caused problems. Known as "Dearborns," they were hard-topped, with canvas sides, and held only a fraction of the household goods and other belongings that could be jammed into the larger vehicles. Named for former Secretary of War Henry Dearborn, who was said to have designed the first of them, they were much cheaper than the prairie schooners. But they lost wheels more frequently, sometimes broke their wooden axles on ruts in the road and jolted their occupants unmercifully as they bounced along the trail.

The Dearborns were barely large enough to house childless couples; a number were occupied by men or women traveling alone. Even their owners soon regarded them as a nuisance, but there was no practical way to exchange them for heavier wagons. As Sam said, "We're stuck, so we'll have to make do with what we've got."

The very size of the train created difficulties. Stalking Horse took over the role of scout and ranged as far as two to four miles ahead of the caravan. Sam remained the undisputed head of the expedition, but there were so many people in the company now that families began to bicker with their neighbors over inconsequential matters. "We need some sort of self-government, so folks will keep the peace," Sam said.

An election was held. Ernst von Thalman became president and Dr. Martin vice president. It was their duty to adjudicate arguments and insure that every member of the expedition carried a fair share of the work load. Their task was thankless, but they took their new responsibilities seriously and made no complaint.

No one worked harder than Tonie Mell. She moved untiringly from the front of the line to the back, goading the laggards, closing gaps, exhorting, cajoling and, when necessary, issuing crisp instructions. She was the one person every member of the company came to know, and she estimated that she rode at least forty miles each day.

By the time evening came she was exhausted, but she insisted on changing from buckskins into her feminine attire. Sam saw to it that she did no evening work, and she sat at the campfire, eating and relaxing with people at whom she had bellowed earlier in the day.

Late one sultry afternoon, camp was made opposite the city of Louisville, and Sam announced that the party would remain there for thirty-six hours. Those who wished could cross the river by ferry the following day and purchase any goods they might be lacking. Louisville, he emphasized, was the last major metropolitan center they would be able to visit on their long trek across the continent.

There was nothing Tonie wanted in town, so she slept late, an unaccustomed luxury. Cathy van Ayl had saved some bacon and biscuits from breakfast for her, and Tonie heated them over the fire. While she was eating, perching on a rock, she was joined by Cindy, who had good reasons of her own for wanting to avoid Louisville.

Never had Tonie known such a person. As they chatted aimlessly it occurred to her that Cindy, in spite of her experience in dealing with men, was naive, almost childlike. Certainly her daydreams of what lay ahead were false.

"I'll bet the scenery in the West is beautiful," Cindy said.

"I only know it as far as Independence, where it's about the same as it is here. A big river and lots of trees. It gets cold in the winter, and in the autumn and spring there's more rain than most people want to see."

"I was thinking about the mountains."

"I don't envy those of you who're going all the way to Oregon," Tonie said. "I've met a lot of trappers and hunters who've spent time in the Rockies, and I don't for the life of me see how a whole wagon train can get across those peaks."

"It should be exciting."

"It'll be dangerous." Tonie, afraid she'd sounded curt, softened her attitude. "Whip Holt will be in charge after Sam sets up his supply depot in Independence, and from what I've heard about Whip, there's no better guide anywhere."

"I don't know how those mountain men can go for months at a time without women," Cindy said. "It doesn't seem natural."

Tonie didn't know anything about the physical

needs of men, but felt she had to offer some sort of explanation. "People who live close to nature aren't like city folks."

"They're not all that different. Look at you. Every day you ride up and down the line until I get dizzy just watching you. But at the end of each day you put on a pretty dress. So you know there are men on this train. Or maybe there's one in particular you want to impress."

Tonie felt her face burn. The girl was being a little too perspicacious, and she didn't know what to reply. Before she could speak, however, a man wearing a black suit, a clean white shirt and well-shined shoes strolled toward them. Apparently, he'd been a passenger on the ferry from Louisville.

Cindy instantly jumped to her feet, smoothed her skirt and turned away. "I'm not sure if he's somebody I once knew in Louisville," she muttered, "and I don't want to take the chance that he might be." She hurried off to her own wagon.

Tonie continued to eat as the man approached her.

He bowed, his manner a trifle formal. "I was told that you're Mrs. Mell," he said.

Tonie stiffened. She had dropped the fiction that she was a widow since confessing the truth to Sam, and everyone in the train knew her by her first name. "My name is Mell," she replied guardedly.

"I'm eager to have a private discussion with you," he said, not introducing himself. "Is it possible for us to talk here?"

"I'm listening," she said. "Who are you?"

"My identity doesn't matter all that much."

Studying him, she decided he was nondescript, a short, graying man who'd be lost in a crowd.

"We have some mutual friends in Washington City," he said, and smiled.

Tonie remained grave. "I have no friends there."

"At a certain legation."

Her guess had been correct. The Russian *chargé d'affaires* had sent an emissary to check up on her. She looked around. They were alone at the fire. A few children were playing about a hundred feet away, but there were no adults within earshot.

The man misinterpreted her look. "Perhaps we'd be wiser to walk into the woods where no one will over-hear us."

"I'm staying right here," she said, a strong hint of belligerence in her voice.

He coughed nervously, then spoke in a lowered voice. "Our mutual acquaintance is eager to receive a report from you to send on to his superiors. You needn't make it in writing. He understands the deli-cacy of your situation. Just tell me whatever it is you've been doing, and I'll pass along the word."

"I have nothing to report." Tonie was seething.

The man raised a gray eyebrow. "Surely you're joking, Mrs. Mell."

"I don't work for your employers. They mean noth-ing to me, and I want no part of them!" She realized her self-control was slipping, but she no longer cared.

He stared at her in disbelief. Anyone familiar with the *Cheka* knew that these highly favored representa-tives of the Czar regarded a defection as the most serious of offenses. People who defied the organization, even if they lived far from Russia, had been known to die of mysterious causes.

Tonie guessed from his expression what was going through his mind. "I was blackmailed," she said, "and at first I was frightened into accepting an assignment. Since then I've changed my mind. The Czar and everybody who works for him can go to the devil."

"Would you deliberately cause your parents suffering?" He sounded incredulous.

"The people I consider my parents live in Missouri, and I can promise you my uncle would put a bullet into the head of any *Cheka* snooper who trespassed on his property. As for the man and woman in St. Petersburg who brought me into the world, I haven't seen them since I was a baby, and I've never corresponded with them. If they're abused and mistreated after doing no wrong and no harm to anyone, then the Imperial Russian Government is even more despotic and rotten than anyone in the United States knows. But they'll find out. I'll tell this whole country the story of what was done to me." She had no idea how to carry out her threat, but she was too angry to care.

"Is this your final word?"

"You just bet it is. Tell that slimy worm in Washington not to bother me again!"

The man bowed again, his eyes glittering. "As you wish, madam," he said. "I'm glad that you, not I, will pay the consequences of such insubordination." He turned away, then stalked back down to the ferry landing, his back stiff.

He would report the incident to the Imperial Russian

Legation in Washington immediately, and he had no doubt that his superiors would deal with this girl appropriately. Nobody could treat Mother Russia this way. God help Tonie Mell in the months to come.

Tonie watched him leave, her rage giving way to a sense of despair. It was true that she owed her real parents nothing, but at the same time she hated to cause them needless anguish. The cloud that had almost dissipated had formed over her head again, and it did no good to tell herself that she was an innocent pawn in a struggle being waged by the great powers of the world for territorial gain.

Feeling sorry for herself, she made no attempt to stem the tears she'd held back for so long.

"Are you in distress, Tonie? Perhaps I can give you a powder to relieve you."

She looked up in horror to see Robert Martin, of all people, smiling down at her. She didn't want him to see her cry, but the tears continued to fall.

His smile faded and he handed her a bandana handkerchief.

She accepted it from him, averting her face as she dabbed at her eyes. "Thank you," she muttered, "but please go away."

Dr. Martin made no move. "It's my job to help people when they're in trouble. That's why I went into Louisville early this morning, to buy various medicines I wasn't carrying in my kit."

"There isn't a medicine or a powder made that will cure my problem."

"Tell me the symptoms and let me decide." Aware

of her need to talk, a need she hadn't yet recognized, the physician drew Tonie to her feet.

Following his lead, she walked beside him to the riverside. They could see the warehouses of Louisville opposite, the church spires towering above the lower buildings.

Dr. Martin had mastered the art of keeping silent. He strolled beside the girl on the bank as though this were a social occasion.

All at once Tonie felt compelled to tell the truth to this man, whom she admired and respected above all others. He was thinking of her as a patient, she knew, and not as a woman, but her conscience would bother her unless she confessed everything to him.

"I'm going to tell you something that only Sam Brentwood knows," she said. "You're going to despise me for it, but that can't be helped."

He listened without comment as she told him her story, including the meeting with the representative that had just ended. When she was through, she was breathless, and stood with downcast eyes.

"I congratulate you on the stand you've taken," Dr. Martin said, "and I'm sure Sam feels as I do."

"You're forgetting that poor couple in St. Petersburg who'll be made to suffer for my sins!"

"You've committed no sins. Czar Nicholas may be a tyrant, but he's trying to convince the world he's the ruler of a modern, enlightened state. I remember what you told me, but I think it unlikely he'll ship your parents off to Siberia without cause. That sort of thing isn't done any more."

Tonie didn't know whether he was speaking the truth or just trying to raise her spirits, but she was beginning to feel better. "You don't look down on me for deserting my mother and father when they need me?"

"I'm proud of your loyalty to the United States, and to the aunt and uncle who reared you as their own child."

Her skin tingled.

"My only regret is that we didn't have a chance to talk with the man who came to see you just now. You say he's gone back over to Louisville?"

"I saw him get on the ferry."

"Then he'll be gone by the time we could form a posse to go after him. It's just as well, perhaps. Put him and the Russian Legation out of your mind."

"I—I'll try." She wished she weren't so self-conscious in his presence.

"Maybe I can be of help there, too. Why are you all dressed up today?"

"I'm not, really." She felt like squirming. "I get tired of buckskins, and I like to wear dresses."

"That's natural enough. But you have no plans for the day?"

Tonie shook her head.

"Then now you have," Dr. Martin said. "I saw what looked like a splendid inn near the medical supply house I visited this morning. You and I will go over to Louisville and eat dinner there. We won't have many meals served to us on pewter platters in the next year or two."

She desperately wanted to go with him, but didn't want him taking her out on a false premise. "I'm not planning to go to Oregon," she said. "I'm aiming to go back to my uncle's ranch in Missouri."

"So I've heard. That's something I want to discuss with you. I wish you'd open your mind to the possibility of going all the way with the wagon train. You hold a very special place in this expedition. We need you."

Had he said that he himself needed her, the matter would have been settled then and there. "I'll be glad to have dinner with you," Tonie said demurely, "and thank you for asking me."

It was odd, Robert Martin thought, that this girl who could ride and shoot like a man, who was a hellion in her duties as monitor of the march, could be so shy and withdrawn in a personal relationship. She intrigued him, and he wanted to become better acquainted with her.

Several more wagons, all drawn by oxen, crossed the Ohio from Louisville to join the train. Sightseers came, too, and gaped at the pioneers. Because many members of the company were absent for the day, those who remained in camp pitched in to fetch water, collect firewood and cook, whatever their regular assignments.

No one was busier than Nat Drummond. He had stayed behind while his wife went to the city for blankets and a pair of scissors. Stronger than his frail physique indicated, he carried two buckets of water at a time without tiring, then brought armloads of wood to the fire.

Cindy had volunteered to work as a cook. She had

never cooked before and Nat noted the clumsy way she held a large skillet. Sensing that the preparation of food was alien to her, he offered to help.

The girl was delighted. He was one of a very few men in the company who accepted her for her own sake, never sized her up and down with his eyes and never appeared to be on the verge of making advances.

"Cooking," he said, placing her skillet on a metal tripod over the flames, "is like anything else. Just do what your common sense tells you, and you won't go wrong—most of the time. The worst that can happen is you'll burn up this mess of potatoes you're fryin'. Then you'd have hell's own time scrubbin' the skillet."

Cindy laughed. "You make it sound easy."

"Most jobs are easy. There are women who like to make them sound complicated so's to puff themselves up, but don't pay them no heed." He refrained from mentioning his wife by name.

As Cindy observed him, then took a long-handled spoon to stir the potatoes, she saw Ted Woods watching her. He was carrying an enormous load of kindling and logs to the fire. She didn't quite know what to make of the blacksmith, who always seemed to be looking at her. He stared without flirtatiousness; in fact he just kept his eyes on her, his face expressionless.

Here on the expedition, he was the only man she couldn't categorize. Danny idolized him, and Ted Woods treated the boy with gentle kindness. She found it hard to believe that he was mean or dangerous, though she'd heard rumors that he'd murdered his wife. Wanting to be accepted without prejudice herself, she gladly extended the same courtesy to others. Since she'd never spoken to Woods, except to wish him a good morning, she had no basis for judgment. But she knew for certain that she wasn't afraid of him, though he looked strong enough to tear her apart with his bare hands.

Nat sliced more potatoes. After setting the cooked batch out to drain, she refilled the skillet. The camp was quiet; there weren't more than twenty people in it. And as Ted Woods moved around, bringing more water, building up the fire and otherwise making himself useful, Cindy could feel his eyes fastened on her.

Whenever she glanced in his direction, however, he hastily looked away.

A number of sightseers still lingered outside the large circle of wagons. Cindy realized that she was attracting more than her share of attention from a pair of young men in their early twenties. She found it easy to ignore their comments on her physical assets. She had heard them all before.

Bored, intent on causing mischief, the young men began to throw stones at some of the grazing horses. One of them heaved a rock at Sam's stallion, left behind while Sam spent the day in Louisville. The rock struck the animal between the eyes, startling him and causing him a measure of pain. He reared, neighed a trumpeting call, plunged forward and reared again.

Suddenly Cindy realized that she was standing directly in the angered stallion's path, almost within reach of his flashing hooves as he reared in the air. The girl was so terrified she was unable to move, though she knew she might well be trampled to death unless she could escape to the far side of the fire.

The stallion seemed to be drawn to her as though to a magnet, moving ever nearer. Other members of the company had scattered.

All at once the great beast was towering directly above her, his front legs pawing the air. When he crashed down, she knew it would be the end of her, but she was still too petrified to move.

Suddenly she felt herself being lifted into the air.

An instant later the stallion plunged forward again, landing exactly where she had been standing.

Ted Woods was holding the girl in his arms as effortlessly as though she were a small child. Then he put her down. "Take her to one of the wagons, out of harm's way," he told Nat Drummond.

Ted walked alone toward the raging stallion, speaking in a voice that only the animal could hear. A blacksmith respected a flailing hoof, but wasn't afraid of it, and a blacksmith knew horses, too. Yet Cindy and the other pioneers were astonished by the giant's calm. The stallion continued to buck.

Staying on the animal's left side, Woods circled the open area beside the horse, still speaking in a soft voice as he inched ever closer.

Cindy could scarcely breathe. Ted Woods was obviously courageous, but even a man of his size was no match for an enraged stallion.

Woods made his move so swiftly that the frightened onlookers weren't aware of what he was doing until he had done it. Displaying remarkable agility and grace for someone so big, he leaped up onto the stallion's bare back.

Outraged, the great beast reared and plunged repeatedly in an attempt to throw his rider.

But Woods seemed glued to his back. Curling his arms around the stallion's neck he continued to talk, simultaneously stroking the animal. And at last the stallion recognized his rider as a friend. Subsiding abruptly, the huge creature stood still, breathing hard and whinnying.

"Danny," Ted called, "bring some of them apples we bought at the orchard this morning."

The former bound boy walked across the open space, apples cupped in his hands. He showed no fear.

Ted dismounted, held an apple in the palm of his hand and offered it to the animal that had been his antagonist only moments earlier. The stallion, completely docile now, took the apple, then ate another and yet another.

Ted patted him again. "You'll be all right now, boy," he said, and walked toward the edge of the circle.

The two young men from Louisville suddenly realized that this bear of a man was moving toward them, though he didn't once glance in their direction. They took to their heels and raced toward the riverbank.

Woods ran after the two men. In spite of his awkward gait he gained on them, and finally caught them some two hundred yards away.

No one could hear what he said to them as he held each youth in the grip of a huge hand, but his remarks were brief. When he finished talking, he cracked their heads together, dropping them to the ground. Then, seemingly unconcerned, he strolled back to the circle of wagons.

Cindy hurried forward to meet him, still finding it difficult to breathe. He would have brushed past her, pretending not to see her, but she halted directly in front of him, blocking his path.

"Mr. Woods," she said tremulously, "you saved my life."

Ted was so embarrassed he looked down at the ground and shuffled his feet. "That's all right," he muttered.

"It's more than all right," she insisted.

He had picked up color on the trail, but was still pale enough for his face to show a flaming scarlet.

Cindy had no desire to embarrass him, but wanted to make sure he realized she was eternally grateful to him. "I'm in your debt," she said. "I just hope that some day I can do a favor for you."

When she had first joined the company, others would have laughed at what they would have regarded as an obvious invitation. But the company was learning to reassess Cindy. They knew she was sincere, and no one smiled.

"Hellfire, ma'am," Ted said, half under his breath as he continued to fidget, "I'd have done it for anybody."

"Well, you did it for me, so I thank you." Cindy reached up impulsively to touch his brawny arm, then quickly returned to the cooking fire.

Ted walked to his wagon, looking at nobody, one

hand clutching the spot on his arm that the girl had touched.

The potatoes were ruined, so the skillet had to be scoured. No matter. Ted Woods was strange, Cindy reflected. He'd been remarkably cool during the crisis, knowing precisely what to do, but now he was behaving like a small boy. She couldn't understand him at all. What confused her most was her inability to make an impression on him. No other man had ever reacted to her as Ted Woods did.

Henry St. Clair saw the three horses tethered at the edge of the little clearing, and then he heard a man moaning. No, there were *two* men in pain, the second grunting and gasping for breath. Something out of the ordinary was afoot, so he unlimbered his new rifle and rode into the clearing.

Two men were stretched out on the ground, as a third was saying in a whining voice. "Tell me where to find a doctor who won't ask too many questions, and I'll do it," he said.

"Maybe I can help," Henry said, and at that moment he and Abe Ellis recognized each other.

Ellis pointed to the bloodstained shoulder of his shirt. "Sam Brentwood," he said, gasping, making the name sound like a curse. "He shot me. And he dislocated the fingers of Digby's hand. We've had hell's own time here the last few hours."

Always clear-headed in an emergency, Henry examined Ellis' wound, then looked at the hand of the trampled man. "I may be able to offer assistance, gentlemen," he said, paying little attention to the third member of the party, who appeared to be useless. "But I'll want something in return."

"We don't have much money," Digby said between moans, "but we'll give you all we've got."

"I've no need for money." Henry was crisp. "Ellis, do I gather you're no longer employed by the wagon train?"

"Brentwood threw me out and sent me home to Albany." The reply was surly, and the man continued to clasp his injured shoulder. "I was doing a little business with these fellows when he rode after me and blame near killed all of us."

There was no need for Henry to ask why Sam Brentwood had resorted to violence. Obviously Ellis had stolen something, or engaged in some kind of chicanery, which was all to the good. If he handled these people correctly, he stood to benefit. But one thing puzzled him: none of the trio was armed. "What happened to your guns?"

"They're in the brush someplace, where that demon threw them," the third man said.

Henry wondered if the man was capable of speaking in any voice other than a whine. Digby's moans became louder.

"Lads," Henry said, "I'm willing to make a deal with you. I'll take care of your physical ailments and get you back on your feet. In return, I want you to work for me—"

"Doing what?" the third man interrupted.

"I'll explain in good time, at my own convenience."

Henry St. Clair was terse. "I'll buy your food, and pay each of you fifty cents a day for the next month or two, while I organize my operation. Carry it off at the appropriate time, and I'll give each of you a bonus of ten dollars. The one thing I won't supply is your liquor."

"Your pay is as good as the wagon train's," Ellis said, between gritted teeth. "Just get this damn bullet out of me and I'll do anything you want."

Digby, moaning again, could only nod his acceptance of the terms. The third man, whose name proved to be Lemon, quickly assented.

"Very well." Henry dismounted and went to work.

Taking a bottle of brandywine from his saddlebag, he cleaned off a knife with it, then gave Ellis a small swallow. "Hold him down so he doesn't thrash around," he told Lemon. "And Abe, try not to jerk. This won't take long, but it won't be pleasant."

He began to probe with the sharp point of the double-edged blade, his hand as steady and his touch as deft as a surgeon's.

Ellis screamed, and perspiration covered his face as he made a supreme effort to hold still.

"There it is." Henry brought the bullet to the surface, then threw it away. Still acting swiftly, and deliberately not warning his patient, he poured brandywine into the wound, which was now bleeding freely.

Ellis screamed again, tears in his eyes.

"Tear up a clean shirt," Henry told Lemon, and when the man obeyed he bandaged the wound.

Ellis' pain began to subside somewhat.

287

"You'll be sore for a few days, but you'll soon be all right again, Abe," Henry told him. "You're lucky you just suffered a flesh wound."

Now it was Digby's turn, and he shrank from the Englishman. Henry lacked the patience and tact of a professional physician. "Either you'll let me help you, or you can go straight to the devil. Which shall it be?"

Curbing his fears, Digby extended his hand.

Henry gave him a swallow of brandywine, then made a careful examination. Telling Lemon to hold the patient, he saw that three fingers had been dislocated. "Lean away from me," he ordered, "and exert steady pressure."

Grasping Digby's wrist with one hand, he pulled hard at one finger, then at a second, and both snapped back into place. The injured man jerked his hand away and doubled up with pain.

"Once more," Henry said, "and that'll be the end of it."

With great reluctance the patient extended his hand again, then leaned away from his tormentor. Henry snapped the third finger into place.

The improvement in Digby's condition was so rapid it seemed miraculous. He managed a broad grin. "I don't know what you did," he said, "but my fingers are straight again and the pain is almost gone."

"In a couple of days the soreness in your joints will disappear, and you won't even know there was anything the matter with you." Henry allowed himself the luxury of a small swallow of brandywine before carefully replacing the bottle in his saddlebag.

He was in no hurry to resume his march in the wake of the wagon train, and he decided to stay in this clearing until the following morning so both injured men could enjoy a longer rest. In the meantime there was work to be done.

"Search for your guns in the underbrush," he told Lemon. "After you find them, gather wood for a fire. Then locate a brook and bring back some water." Lemon hastened to obey.

Abe Ellis, enjoying a measure of relief, found it difficult to hide his curiosity. "I heard all kinds of stories about you after you left the wagon train, Henry," he said.

"Oh?" Henry trusted no one, least of all a discredited man, so he feigned little interest.

"There was talk that you were working for some foreign government, that don't want this country to settle in Oregon," Ellis persisted.

"Would it bother you if I were?" Henry demanded.

The former driver of the special wagon shrugged. "It ain't no skin off my nose, one way or t'other. I got me a house in Albany, and I don't care what happens across a continent."

Henry concealed his pleasure. At least one of the trio might well make a valuable subordinate. "I presume," he said, "that you wouldn't mind getting even with Sam Brentwood."

"There's nothing I'd like better."

"You shall have your chance," Henry said.

XII

Rather than follow the Ohio River to Cairo, Illinois, where it joined the mightiest of American rivers, the Mississippi, and then move north again to the bustling trading post, St. Louis, Sam Brentwood decided to take a shortcut that would save at least two hundred miles of travel. The one advantage of following the rivers was that well-defined roads had been built on their banks. Now he'd be marching across open country where there were only a few dirt roads used by local farmers.

But the saving was well worth the inconvenience, so the caravan headed northwest from the Ohio River and came to the flatlands of the Illinois prairie. There were no hills anywhere in this endless valley. By consulting detailed maps Sam was able to avoid most towns and settled farmlands. He quickly discovered one advantage to the route he had chosen. Instead of moving in a single, long line, he formed his wagons into three short, parallel columns that made up in width what they lacked in depth.

It was far easier to control these shorter lines, and Tonie Mell needed the help of only three assistant monitors, one assigned to each of the lines. Experience was teaching the wagonmaster other tricks. Since the horses were inclined to outpace the more cumbersome oxen, he put a wagon drawn by oxen at the head of each line, and let these heavy creatures set the pace.

No member of the expedition had ever seen land like the Illinois prairie, where the midsummer grass was knee-high and there were few trees to be seen, only patches of woods here and there. When wood was sighted, a special detail gathered firewood there, then caught up with the rest of the company. Ted Woods, whose strength was so prodigious that he could fell a tree with a few blows of an ax, volunteered to be a member of this group and turned his wagon over to Danny.

Most of the company were farmers. They marveled at the black earth, the marvelously rich soil that was almost completely free of rocks, much less the roots of trees and bushes. It retained moisture for days after a thunderstorm, or even a shower. "I reckon just about any crop could be grown here," Nat Drummond said one evening, sifting a handful of earth through his fingers after supper. "Think of it. You don't have to plow up rocks and roots. Just loosen the topsoil a little and plant your seeds. Nature will do the rest."

Otto van Ayl said nothing. He still retired early, according to the habit he'd formed, and Cathy was surprised to find him still awake when she returned to their wagon.

"I've been thinking," he said. "I'm of half a mind to drop out of this train and buy some land here in Illinois. There's no law says I'm obliged to travel all the way to the Pacific. I never knew there was soil like this anywhere."

Cathy felt a quick pang of regret. The first thought that crossed her mind was disloyal to Otto and deeply disturbing. If they dropped out of the wagon train to settle in Illinois she would never see Whip Holt again. The certainty of their meeting again at Independence had bolstered her during many difficult hours of the long, tiresome journey, and the realization that their paths might not cross again dismayed her.

She had no right to dwell on Whip. Not under any circumstances, even though she knew he was drawn to her every bit as much as she felt drawn to him. She was an honorable, respectable, married woman, and she couldn't allow herself to forget it, not for a moment. Granted she was Otto's wife in name only. They never had intimate relations, never shared their hopes and troubles. But in the eyes of God and man, she was a married woman, and that was that.

She couldn't control her dreams, of course, and they nagged at her. Night after night she found herself dreaming that Whip would ride up to her on a great stallion, scoop her into his arms and make off with her. These images were so vivid they almost seemed real, even after she awakened. She knew, of course, that Whip was too honorable to make advances to another man's wife, just as she wouldn't accept them if he did.

All the same, the prospect of seeing Whip Holt had been the highlight of her future, and Otto's words were so jarring, so disconcerting that Cathy silently cried herself to sleep. In her heart she was an abandoned woman, but she lacked the strength of character to put the lean, handsome guide out of her mind.

The next day, while the caravan was nooning, a party went off to a farmhouse in the distance to purchase any produce the proprietor might be willing to sell. Sam, who was leading the group, was surprised when Otto van Ayl offered his services. It was the first time the dour Long Islander had volunteered to do more than was required of him.

The farmer proved willing to dispose of large quantities of green beans, peas, onions and cartloads of corn, which would be cooked for human consumption and used for animal fodder. Three substantial barns located behind the house were full, and the pioneers were impressed by such evidence of plenty.

Otto remained silent during the negotiations, but became more animated while the farmer's sons were loading the grain and vegetables on carts for delivery to the train. He drew the farmer aside, then said, "Your yields are the biggest I've ever seen."

The man nodded complacently. "I grow double what I raised back in Maryland," he said. "My boys and me, we work plenty hard, but not near as hard as we did in the East."

Otto lowered his voice. "What kind of prices are folks asking for farmland hereabouts?"

"You aiming to buy?" The man looked at him sharply.

Otto became noncommittal. "Maybe, maybe not. It's a long haul to the Oregon country."

"A farm of five hundred acres—and you can't show a cash profit every year on less—goes for ten dollars an acre in today's market."

Otto was shocked. "Ten per acre! That's three or four more than anybody ever paid on Long Island."

The farmer's smile was superior. "Look at the difference in what we grow."

Otto couldn't argue with him, and fell silent until the party was returning to the nooning site. "They want an arm and a leg for Illinois land," he said. "But blamed if it may not be worth every penny they're asking."

Sam was aware of Otto's greedy nature, but wasn't impressed by his reasoning. "I'm no farmer, mind you, and I've never in my life grown a crop. But I still know good land when I see it, and the soil in Oregon is as black and heavy as this land here."

Otto found that difficult to believe. He shook his head.

"If you're thinking of leaving the train and getting yourself some property in Illinois," Sam said, "don't do it. I'd hate to see you make a mistake, Otto, so I'll let you in on a secret I've been directed to announce after we get to Independence. Every householder and head of family who goes all the way to Oregon will be given a deed to six hundred acres there."

"Six hundred acres? Free?"

"President Van Buren will announce the expanded policy at the end of the year. Nothing has been said until now because the government didn't want too many volunteers signing up at the start. This first wagon train would have been too big. Once we establish the route, settlers by the thousands will follow."

"Six hundred free acres!" Otto was still stunned, and the issue was settled. Even if Sam was exaggerating and the land in Oregon proved less fertile, he couldn't resist the bargain. He dismissed the black soil of the Illinois prairie from his mind.

When he told Cathy his decision she was so relieved she was speechless. But her sense of guilt almost overwhelmed her. She was almost sorry Otto hadn't bought land here, and she wondered how she could ever face Whip Holt again.

As soon as the corn and vegetables were distributed the afternoon march began. Stalking Horse, having found an adequate campsite for the night, returned and rode at the head of the caravan beside Sam. Jumping to the ground from Claudia's wagon, Quincy followed his usual practice and happily trotted between them. The late summer sun was warm, the sky was cloudless and even the most critical of travelers, Grace Drummond included, could find no fault with the weather.

Suddenly the shepherd dog raced ahead, halted in the tall grass and began to bark furiously. Sam and Stalking Horse, who could see nothing amiss, exchanged glances and then spurred forward.

The Cherokee was the first to reach the spot. He grinned. "Quincy," he said solemnly, "meets a friend."

When he saw a prairie dog a tenth of Quincy's size crouching in a nest below the surface of the ground, Sam laughed aloud. Smooth-haired, his short fur a pale tan, the animal's oversized paws and long legs indicated that he was a puppy. He wagged his tail tentatively, but was terrified by the shepherd.

For the sake of the children in the company Sam called a halt. He summoned the youngsters, who were joined by a number of adults. "It looks to Stalking Horse and me as though this pup is on his own. Something must have happened to his mother."

Several children, including the younger Harris boys, clamored for the right to adopt the puppy. Cindy, who said nothing, was enraptured, too.

Sam shook his head. "Prairie dogs don't make good pets," he said. "They're accustomed to wild ways from the time they're born, and they're hard to train. We'll let the little one be."

Claudia had to call Quincy several times before he'd return to her wagon. Then Sam raised his hand, blew his whistle and the journey across the flat countryside was resumed.

A half hour later, as Tonie was making her rounds, she noted that Ted Woods' wagon, bringing up the rear of the center column, had fallen far behind, although he seemed to be trying to keep pace. She rode back to him, calling, "Any trouble?"

"No, ma'am," Ted replied politely. "We're doing just fine."

In spite of his reassuring words, she noted that the blacksmith looked strangely guilty, as did Danny, seated beside him. She peered at them more closely, realizing that Ted was using his body to shield the former bound boy from her view. Then she saw that Danny was cradling the young prairie dog in his arms. "Oh-oh," she said. "Sam won't like this."

"To hell with Sam Brentwood and to hell with you, too." Ted's anger suddenly flared. "If I want to pick up a stray puppy that's my right!"

Tonie shrugged and spurred forward again. She thought it strange that Ted Woods had stopped to pick up the little dog, but his private life was his affair. She had no intention of earning the powerful man's ill will by reporting the matter to Sam. A wise woman took care not to be caught in the middle of a dispute between two strong men.

The instant the day's march ended Ted jumped to the ground, carrying the puppy and leaving Danny to maneuver the ramshackle wagon into its place in the circle. He headed straight for Cindy's wagon, reaching her side as she finished unhitching her team.

"I've got a present for you if you want him," he said, thrusting the prairie dog at her. "Here."

Cindy clapped her hands together in delight. "Oh, how wonderful! But Sam Brentwood said—"

"I don't give a hang what he said. He ain't the final authority on everything in this world. It so happens I know more about prairie dogs than he does. If you don't want the pup I'll keep him myself. He's been taken too far from his nest to survive all by himself."

"Don't put words in my mouth," the girl replied tartly. "I certainly didn't say I don't want him." She paused, softening somewhat. "You truly do know about dogs like this?"

"If you knew me better, ma'am, you'd realize I never lie to anybody. About anything."

"Oh, I take your word," Cindy assured him. "I just wondered how you—"

"I spent ten years in prison," Ted said harshly, interrupting her. "For more than half that time I was considered so dangerous they kept me in solitary confinement. But the warden wasn't all that mean. He had four children, and four different times he brought me prairie dogs to train for them. He figured I had a way with dogs, and he was right. Those dogs were the only friends I had for many years."

"I—I'll be very happy and pleased to accept this puppy as a gift. Thank you."

"If you want, I'll break him in for you, and he'll be the friendliest, most obedient pet you ever did see." An invisible chip then settled on the blacksmith's shoulder. "Unless you don't want anything to do with a convict."

Cindy looked at him, her gaze level. "You aren't a convict, Mr. Woods," she said, "any more than I'm a harlot. Your past is behind you. I, for one, don't care in the least that you were in prison, and I really have no interest in why you were sent there."

"If you want to know," Ted replied, wide-eyed, "I'll be glad to tell—"

"Don't bother. Some other time, maybe. Every last man and woman in this wagon train has done something stupid sometime. It's just more obvious with you and me, that's all. And I don't care to hear another word on the subject."

He swallowed hard.

"Let's start breaking in the puppy right now," Cindy said. "You must help me give him a name."

Claudia, who happened to be walking past the wagon on her water-gathering detail, had never seen such a gentle, sweet smile on any man's face.

When a steer was purchased from a nearby farmer, making it unnecessary for the hunters to leave camp, Ernst von Thalman was at loose ends. His air of jaunty self-confidence was an accurate reflection of his personality, but he was also lonely, though he took pains to conceal it.

He had joined the wagon train for adventure and excitement, never intending to settle in Oregon with his American companions. Now, however, he had no idea how he would spend the rest of his life after the long journey finally came to an end. He had no intention of returning to Austria. Life at the Imperial court in Vienna was dull and boring, and his hunting lodge in the Alps above Innsbruck was equally unappealing. Fortunately he had the means to do as he pleased.

Perhaps he was spoiled by his life as a bachelor, with too much money, too many homes and servants, too many lovely ladies clamoring and conniving for the privilege of becoming the Baroness von Thalman. These Americans were unique, unlike any people he'd ever known, and he enjoyed their company immensely.

They not only paid lip service to a democratic, egalitarian way of life, they practiced what they preached. Those whose ancestors had come to America in the seventeenth century were no better than recently arrived immigrants. And their ability to assimilate was miraculous. He had heard inflections in Tonie Mell's speech patterns that told him she was of Imperial Russian descent, and perhaps had even been born in the Old World, but there was no one in the company more completely American. Claudia Humphries was obviously a lady of background, breeding and wealth, but Cindy, until a few weeks ago a prostitute in a Louisville bordello, was regarded by most members of the company as Claudia's equal. Stalking Horse was an Indian, and if everything the Baron had read in Europe about redmen was true, he was the enemy of the whites. Yet everyone on the expedition liked, trusted and respected him. Nowhere else on earth was there such a harmonious blend of peoples.

Ernst had no idea whether he would even like Oregon, the supposed land of milk and honey. He had many private doubts. But he had to wait till he saw the region for himself before he formed any final conclusions. In the meantime, having broken the bonds of convention that had tied him down for more than four decades, he was free to live as he pleased and do what he wanted. He knew of no greater luxury.

These Americans, born in freedom, at liberty to do what they wished with their lives, had no idea what it meant to be a member of an ancient, aristocratic family in one of Europe's oldest and most powerful empires. For as long as Hapsburgs had sat on the throne in Vienna there had been von Thalmans on hand to advise them, help them, fight for them.

As the second son of a duke, a baron in his own right, Ernst had been destined for a military life from birth. Sent to a special academy at seven, he had enlisted as an ordinary trooper at eleven, and been made an officer-cadet at fourteen. Winning his commission on the Turkish frontier, he had risen to the rank of colonel, with his own cavalry regiment to command. Had he stayed in Austria he would have been promoted to general, and ultimately made a member of the Imperial General Staff.

But an assignment as military attaché of the Austrian Legation in Washington City had been his undoing, and his friendship with President Andrew Jackson had given him an insight into a way of life previously unknown. He was still a subject of the Emperor, to be sure, but he had resigned his commission rather than return home. Now he was tasting the freedom that Americans took for granted, and he was inclined to suspect, if he liked the Oregon territory, he just might settle there permanently and become an American citizen. There were other Von Thalmans to carry on the family traditions in Austria, which gave him the privilege of becoming a member of this new breed that would conquer the New World wilderness, establishing their civilization in the far reaches of the West. In no hurry to make any final decisions, he was having the time of his life.

Wandering aimlessly around the inside of the circle, Ernst exchanged greetings with almost everyone, but paused for conversation with none. He was restless, perhaps seeking something that even he couldn't identify.

He saw Emily Harris sitting on the rear steps of her wagon, sewing as usual. She was such a skilled needlewoman that she had been placed in charge of a special detail to repair clothes and make shirts and dresses of old sheets.

As he walked slowly toward her Ernst smiled to himself. Even he, an aristocrat who could trace his noble ancestry back to the early days of the Holy Roman Empire, was becoming Americanized. If Emily Harris lived in Vienna, she'd belong to the upper portion of the serving class, but as an impoverished seamstress she could never rise above her position as a servant. In this American group, however, no one ranked above her, himself included. It didn't matter to her that he was a baron, a title that had no significance in her world, and she called him by his first name.

"Well, Ernie," she said, "I see you're loafing this evening."

Ernst found her good nature contagious, and grinned at her. "Loafing? Never. I've come to persuade you to put aside that infernal needle and walk out into the prairie with me. You need the exercise, Emily."

"Are you telling me I'm getting fat?"

She was the only woman of his generation he knew who wasn't overweight. As a matter of fact, her waist was small, her breasts almost as high and firm as a girl's, and her thighs under her dress of soft cotton were lean. A remarkable figure for a woman who had brought a whole brood of children into the world.

"You are not fat, Emily," he said in a chiding tone. "You work so hard you'll soon lose weight—unless you get some exercise to improve your appetite."

She sighed, putting away the trousers she was mending. "You're a bad influence on me, Ernie. Sitting here and smelling that side of beef barbecuing reminds me of how long it's been since I tasted beef. If I stay here much longer I'll start feeling sorry for myself, so I will take a walk with you."

They meandered together toward the far side of the circle. Ernst, still in a reflective mood, laughed inwardly. How the princes, dukes and his fellow barons of the Austrian court—and their grand ladies—would snicker if they could see him strolling with this unpretentious American widow. Not so long ago he would have snickered, too, but he was learning a lesson taught only in the United States, that of accepting people for what they were.

Everything in the encampment appeared to be normal. Horses and oxen were grazing. Firewood gathered during the day was being stacked in neat piles. The water-gathering detail was finishing its work, and several women were ladling a sauce they had made over the side of roasting meat. Others were pouring water into vats for boiling corn. Tonight Ernst had been promised a treat he couldn't envision, an Illinois delicacy called corn-on-the-cob.

Off in one corner Dr. Martin, aided by Claudia, was lancing boils on the back of a middle-aged man who was drowsy from laudanum, a liquid opiate that eased his pain. Sam was studying a detailed map with Stalking Horse and Tonie, plotting the next day's march, and because it was easier for the Indian all three were speaking in Cherokee, their voices a blend of what sounded like deep grunts and high, liquid nasal sounds. Just outside the circle, Ted Woods was trying to give the prairie puppy a lesson in obedience, but the creature was in a playful mood, encouraged by a laughing Cindy. Ted didn't seem to mind too much.

Emily and Ernst made their way into the open, where the flat prairie stretched toward the horizon in every direction. The woman shook her head. "I could never live in this part of the country," she said. "I have almost no sense of direction, and every place looks so much like every other place that I'd soon get lost."

"The countryside isn't that much alike," he told her, and pointed out subtle differences. The grass toward the south was coarser, that on the east grew longer and there were bare patches of ground to the north. Had he been born an American, Emily thought, he might have become as competent a guide and scout as Sam Brentwood, and she could pay him no higher compliment.

In the distance they heard the shouts of young voices, mixed with loud laughter, so they walked in that direction.

"I can recognize the noise each one of my sons makes," Emily said, shaking her head. "Would you believe I can even distinguish between their footsteps? But I wouldn't admit it to them. All of them hate being babied, except Billy, the youngest."

"They don't really hate it. Quite the contrary, provided you pet and kiss each one privately. Boys are so eager to prove they're men they'll go to any extreme to avoid being thought weak. What *they* regard as weak, that is." Ernst smiled.

Drawing closer, they saw that the boys of the expedition had been swimming in a small, spring-fed pond. Now they were racing back and forth through the tall grass, throwing a ball of yarn in a game they had devised, with Chet as the head of one team and Danny as captain of the other. The sport made no sense to the adults, but the boys seemed to know what they were doing.

Only little Billy Harris seemed to have been left out. His legs were too short to match the strides of the bigger boys. Ignored by both teams, he moved up and down the side of the field, his short legs pumping. "Throw it to me!" he implored, but they failed to hear him.

Emily became indignant. "They should find a place for him. This is cruel." She was about to intervene, but Ernst stopped her.

"No," he said. "Don't interfere. If you force them to include Billy they'll resent him, and you'll do more harm than good. It isn't easy for Billy, but let him make his own place. Eventually they'll accept him. Boys are thoughtless, but no one is ever too young to learn to stand on his own two feet."

He was right, Emily realized, and thought—as she had so often in the past—how difficult it was for her to rear her sons alone. They needed a father, someone who knew instinctively what was right and wrong in situations that confused her. Too often she made the wrong decision, she knew, and although her boys were surviving, they needed firm, sympathetic guidance from an adult male.

Suddenly Billy screamed, in a voice of pure terror. Rooted to the spot where he was standing, he pointed with a stubby forefinger at something in the half-trampled grass only a couple of feet away.

It was a rattlesnake, coiled to strike. The serpent had been disturbed, and there could be no doubt that it meant to retaliate.

"Dear God," Emily murmured.

Ernst took charge. "Billy," he called sharply, "don't move a muscle. Stand very still! Boys, keep your distance!"

Billy did his best to obey. He wanted to show great courage. He didn't know why he'd been given the order, but sensed that running would be the wrong thing to do, so he obeyed the command.

Ernst took his pistol from his belt, cocked it and took careful aim. He had to hit his target with one shot. If he missed, he might strike the already endangered child. Beads of sweat appeared on his forehead, and he wiped them away with his free hand so they wouldn't run into his eyes and blind him.

Emily caught and held her breath. Billy's legs trembled, but he didn't budge.

The snake's rattle sounded ominously, a warning that it was about to strike, and it raised its head, fork-like fangs showing.

Ernst had only a fraction of a second to zero in on his target. If he missed the small child would surely die of poisoning. He squeezed the trigger.

The bullet struck as the snake began its attack. The rattler's head suddenly disintegrated.

Someone else had witnessed the narrow escape. Stalking Horse had dashed out of the compound when he had heard the child's scream. Now, racing forward, he snatched Billy up into the air, then handed him to his mother.

Emily clasped her son tightly, but even now Billy didn't weep. He was pale, still trembling, but he knew he'd been saved, and that was what counted.

The snake, although dead, continued to thrash violently.

"Baron shoot good," the Cherokee said.

Ernst could only nod. He was so relieved he felt weak. Nevertheless, he reloaded his pistol before placing it in his belt.

The older boys were staring at the still-writhing rattler.

The Indian drew a knife, moved forward and picked up the serpent. Examining it, he nodded in satisfaction, then cut out the double sacs of venom still attached to the corpse. "Stalking Horse make belt for boy," he told Billy, then said something else to Ernst under his breath.

"Listen, all of you," Ernst called. "Stalking Horse says that rattlesnakes almost always travel in pairs, so there's sure to be another one in this tall grass. Form quietly in a single file. No noise, no pushing or shoving. Stalking Horse will lead us back to the wagons. Follow exactly in his footsteps." He took Billy from Emily and sat the boy on his shoulder.

Apparently the Cherokee had no need to cut the grass with his knife or beat it with a stick. Carrying the dead snake, he walked slowly but confidently, picking a path.

Emily came behind him, followed by the silent boys and Ernst, with Billy still perched on his shoulder, bringing up the rear. They reached the campsite without further incident.

Promising to cure the snakeskin and make it into a belt for Billy, the Indian dipped the tips of his arrows into the rattler's venom. The group of youngsters watched him in awe.

Suddenly he grinned. "Make bow and arrows for boy, too," he said. "Then Stalking Horse show him how to shoot."

All at once little Billy was the hero of the moment. His courage had been genuine, and the boys respected him for it. But now, in addition, he was going to be given a belt made of rattlesnake skin and a genuine Indian bow and arrows. His envious elders surrounded him, clamoring for his attention.

As Ernst von Thalman walked her back to her wagon, Emily Harris was still thinking of the terrible danger. "I keep wondering what would have happened if you had missed," she said.

Like the boys, the Baron preferred to dismiss the matter from his mind. "I couldn't afford to miss," he said with a shrug.

Emily was struck by the similar attitudes displayed by men and boys. "Well, I'm grateful to you," she said.

"I'm glad I was there . . . at the right time," Ernst said.

Western Illinois was sparsely populated, in part because the fertile land was so expensive. The relatively few established farms were large, some as big as ten thousand acres, but there were those who said the wilderness began here. That view was something of an exaggeration since Missouri, which lay to the West, had already been admitted to statehood, and the adjoining Iowa territory was rapidly approaching the time when it, too, would apply for admission to the Union.

All the same, those who believed the West began in Illinois were not entirely mistaken. Sam Brentwood deliberately chose a route that avoided towns, villages and even farms, so for three days the members of the expedition saw no signs of civilization. As they made their way across the vast expanses of unoccupied prairie they began to realize that the United States was an enormous country, with enough territory to support millions of settlers.

Until now the nooning halt had been informal, the wagons remaining in line, the teams unhitched so oxen and horses could browse where they pleased. But Sam increased discipline in western Illinois, insisting that the wagons be moved into a circle at noon, too, with animals confined inside it. The maneuver was not easy to perform even once a day, so many travelers grumbled, complaining that they were wasting their time. Certainly there were no hostile Indians or other marauders in these parts. The precautions appeared unnecessary.

When asked to relax the rule, Sam didn't explain his reasons for enforcing it. "I've got to use my own judgment," he said, "and in my opinion we'll be safer if we make our night circle in the middle of the day, too."

Not until the third day of the trek across western Illinois did some members of the expedition understand.

The day was quiet, the prairie baking in the stifling, breezeless, late summer sun. The water-gathering detail had returned from a nearby brook; oxen and horses were grazing inside the circle. As usual at noon, families provided their own food, usually eating leftovers from the communal breakfast. Remembering Billy Harris' near mishap, few people wandered far from the confines of the circle.

Billy himself was one of the exceptions. Stalking Horse had made him a bow small enough for the boy to handle, along with a half-dozen arrows. Both had finished eating quickly, and the child was being given a lesson in how to shoot.

The target was a corncob the Indian had placed on top of a forked stick about twenty yards from where he and Billy were standing. The Cherokee's instructions were succinct. "Boy hold bow steady. Aim. Pull bow hard."

Billy tried to follow orders, but his arrow followed a wobbly course and fell short of the target.

Stalking Horse was patient. "Boy pull bow harder. Aim better. Never look away from target."

The next arrow flew on a straighter course, almost reaching the target before it dropped to the ground. Billy whooped in glee.

As he ran forward to retrieve his arrows, Stalking Horse became distracted. He stood erect, apparently listening to sounds the boy couldn't hear.

Billy returned to his side and started to speak. The Cherokee silenced him with a sharp gesture, then astonished him by bending low and placing one ear to the ground, pressing it against the black earth. Then he jumped to his feet. He seemed to be in a hurry. "No more shoot today," he said. "Come."

Billy had to trot beside him in order to keep pace. Stalking Horse went straight to Sam, and conferred with him in a low tone. Then the Baron was summoned, and all three spoke briefly. They scattered momentarily to mount horses. All three were armed as usual—Sam and Ernst with rifles, the Indian with his bow and a full quiver of arrows.

Sam summoned Tonie Mell. "Pass the word," he said. "I want nobody to leave the circle, and that's an order. People and animals will stay inside where they'll be safe."

Something out of the ordinary was obviously in the offing, but Tonie asked no questions. She hurried from wagon to wagon, repeating the instructions.

The trio started toward the western end of the circle, intending to ride into the open.

Quincy, who had been sharing Claudia Humphries' light meal, jumped to the ground, his tail wagging, and fell in beside Sam.

"Go back, boy!" Sam said firmly. "Join your mistress and stay with her."

He had never before addressed the dog so sharply, and Quincy was bewildered.

"Put a leash on your dog and keep it on him," Sam called to Claudia. "Hold him beside you and don't let him get away, or that'll be the end of him."

Claudia wondered why Sam spoke so curtly when a gentler tone would have sufficed. Nevertheless she called repeatedly to Quincy, then had to descend to the ground and hold him before the three men could ride out of the circle.

Danny approached with a length of rope, and Claudia formed it into a makeshift leash, then returned to the seat of her wagon with the recalcitrant shepherd in tow. Quincy was growling. His feelings were hurt.

Suddenly he raised his ears, his body became tense and his growl died away. Although Claudia could hear nothing, Quincy continued to listen, then began to quiver. Moving close to his mistress, he leaned against her and whined. Never had Claudia known him to demonstrate such fright.

Sam, Ernst and the Indian had taken up a position about a hundred feet beyond her place in the circle. All were facing the West, and although their mounts were becoming skittish the men themselves were calm. Sam checked his rifle, then the powder he carried in the horn slung from his neck.

Aware that someone was watching him, he turned and grinned at Claudia.

His expression reminded her of the Harris boys when they were waiting for fresh fruit pies to bake. Whatever might be developing, Sam Brentwood was looking forward to the experience. But that realization failed to soothe her. As nearly as she could judge, Sam remained complacent no matter what danger threatened. Perhaps that was the quality that most annoyed her; she had yet to see him flustered, or unable to make the right decision in an emergency. The man's ability to function competently under stress was downright irritating.

A rumble of thunder sounded in the distance. This was odd, because the sky was pure blue and almost cloudless, as far as Claudia could see. Others heard it, too, and the strange phenomenon made them uneasy.

Off to the West, on the horizon, Claudia was able to make out a small, dark cloud. As the cloud grew larger and the rumble of thunder louder, it occurred to her that the cloud was made of dust. No rain had fallen for more than a week, so the surface ground under the prairie grass was relatively dry.

Something was moving closer, then closer still.

Stalking Horse raised a hand to his forehead to shield his eyes. Claudia followed his example, and was startled when she realized that what she saw was not one moving object, but many.

Other members of the company peered out through the openings between the wagons, jostling and nudging each other to obtain a better view.

"Buffalo!" someone shouted.

Of course. Claudia wondered how she could have been so stupid. A herd of buffalo was approaching, and appeared to be headed straight for the wagon train. Their ranks were so tightly packed, they looked like a single object.

As they drew ever closer, Claudia was able to make out individual buffaloes. In the lead were several horned bulls, shaggy beasts as large as the oxen. Their gait was clumsy, but they moved with great speed.

Other bulls spread out behind the leaders, and then came the cows, accompanied by their offspring. Other bulls were galloping on the flanks. Without lessening

314

their speed, they were able to turn straying cows and calves back toward the center. Their discipline was impressive.

The lead bulls were ugly monsters, so large they appeared able to trample and destroy anything in their path. Unless they changed their course it looked as though they'd crash through the wagon train.

The work horses were now upset, neighing and pawing the ground, and even the placid oxen were disturbed.

Quincy nestled closer to Claudia, and buried his face in her lap. Stalking Horse and Ernst von Thalman were holding their horses on short rein, and finding it difficult to prevent their mounts from bolting. But Sam continued to slouch comfortably in his saddle, an occasional, quiet word enough to keep his great stallion quiet. He was actually enjoying the challenge, Claudia decided, and so was his horse.

Some members of the company were growing nervous, and several frightened women were no longer able to watch the rapidly approaching avalanche. There were more buffalo than anyone could count. If they continued on their course, every living being in their path would be crushed, and the wagons reduced to splinters.

Quincy's whimpers became louder, but were barely audible. The steady, increasing roar of pounding hooves drowned out all other sounds.

Claudia too, became apprehensive. She had read about buffalo stampeding wildly, racing in unison over open spaces for no apparent reason, and she concluded that these animals were engaging in such a mindless stampede. Several lead buffalo were frothing at the mouth, and the whole herd had given in to panic.

Lena Malcolm, standing inside the circle, screamed in fright, clutching her baby. Terence tried to comfort her, but failed.

With the slight breeze blowing from the West, the stench of the herd became almost unbearable. It was a smell that would never be forgotten. Although Claudia felt like retching, her fear was so intense she couldn't remove her gaze from the herd.

The three waiting men held their places as the herd drew closer. Claudia wondered if they were mad. What were they waiting for? The buffalo were within rifle range, but neither Sam nor Ernst fired a shot. The trio would be the first to die.

The ground trembled. The contents of the wagons rattled ominously. Now the buffalo were close enough for Claudia to see the tiny red eyes of the leaders. The animals seemed unaware of the wagons blocking their path. Within moments the train would be inundated by a tidal wave of charging animals.

Calmly, Stalking Horse notched an arrow in his bow and shot. The shaft landed between the eyes of one of the bulls in the front rank. The beast stumbled, but his momentum was so great he continued to move forward, and it took a second swift arrow, then a third, to bring him down.

The rifles of Sam and Ernst spoke more or less simultaneously. Both men reloaded with a speed that Claudia envied. After they fired again two more buffalo fell and rolled on the ground.

The work horses and oxen, now panicky, had to be calmed by owners who expected to die momentarily. Some people were calm. Nat Drummond appeared to enjoy the spectacle, and so did Ted Woods, whose frequent nods indicated his approval of the tactics being employed by the three men sitting on their horses.

Suddenly, miraculously, the herd split, half passing the caravan on one side and the rest sweeping by on the other. Many animals were so close to the wagons that Claudia could have reached out and touched them.

The cloud of dust was suffocating now, so thick that it clouded vision. Coughing could be heard from one wagon to the next. The herd thundered on, a number of the young bulls recklessly grazing the wagons.

Then the rifles spoke again, and this time two calves were felled. The herd paid no attention, both columns still racing eastward.

When she saw Sam and Ernst grinning, Claudia was outraged. Even the stone-faced Stalking Horse was smiling broadly. She wondered how they had the temerity to enjoy themselves when the whole expedition had been in such danger.

She realized that the last of the herd was gone, running east at full speed. She didn't understand what the three men had done to prevent the wagon train from suffering harm, but not one wagon was damaged, not one human or animal was injured. The herd of buffalo was disappearing from sight. It was no accident that the entire company was safe, and Claudia's anger turned to admiration.

Three bulls and two calves had been killed, and Sam called for the help of experienced hands to butcher the carcasses. It was questionable now whether the march could be resumed before the next morning, but no one cared. For days to come, people could eat their fill of meat.

Before joining Stalking Horse to supervise the butchering, Sam rode to Claudia's wagon, leaned out of his saddle and stroked the reviving Quincy. "Sorry I had to be mean to you, boy," he said. "I figured the herd would part at the last minute like the waters of the Red Sea if we brought down a few of them. It's a trick that usually works. But buffalo are such stupid, ignorant critters that you never can tell. So if anything had happened to me, you had to be around to look after the lady."

Not glancing at Claudia, he turned away abruptly.

She looked after him in wonder, scarcely able to believe her ears. His compliment was oblique, to be sure, but its implications hinted at an intimacy that had never yet been present in their stormy relationship.

XIII

The Illinois prairies seemed endless, but suddenly, when the company least expected it, the wagon train reached the banks of the great Mississippi River. Its waters swollen by early autumn rains, it had spread to a width of almost a mile directly below its junction with the Missouri, its major western tributary.

The Mississippi more nearly resembled a large lake, and Claudia realized why it was called the lifeline of the West. From the eastern bank she could see a steady stream of barges. They were laden with furs, agricultural produce and lumber heading downstream to New Orleans, where the cargo would be transferred to the holds of merchant ships and carried to the Eastern Seaboard in a fraction of the time that overland transportation would take. It was the Mississippi, together with the Ohio and the Missouri, that provided the basic, unifying economic force in America, and it was thanks to this network of rivers that the nation continued to grow.

Only now did Claudia realize how completely the West was cut off from the rest of the United States. The Rockies and two other mountain ranges stood between the Pacific and the eastward-flowing rivers. Some western products would have to be carried by sea to the Isthmus of Panama, transported overland through the Panamanian jungles to the Atlantic and then reshipped for sale to the East. Now the prospect of traveling to Oregon appealed to her even less than it had, but she no longer had a choice. She had destroyed her bridges; she had lost her options. She had to make the best of her lot.

She found it vastly comforting that Sam Brentwood was in charge of the wagon train. She had seen enough of him in action to know that he had the ability, the resilience and the courage to deal with any crisis, whether natural or man-made.

She was willing to admit to herself, if not to him, that she had misjudged him in thinking him crude and primitive. He lacked her sophistication, to be sure. He was in no way like the worldly men she had known in New Haven and New York, but that was all to the good. His strength of character lay in his uncanny, natural ability to cast aside surface elements that confused other people. When a problem arose he grasped it instinctively, and he knew what to do. She would never forget his calm in the path of the buffalo herd.

Now she was dismayed at the thought that he would leave the wagon train in Independence. It did no good to tell herself that her sense of loss was unreasonable and illogical. Whip Holt, who would replace him as wagon master, was certainly competent, and able to deal with any situation.

But Whip Holt wasn't Sam Brentwood. And it was difficult for Claudia to imagine crossing the Great Plains, the Rocky Mountains and the so-called Second Chain, the mountains of the far West, without him. The very idea depressed her, and she had to struggle to prevent herself from dwelling on it.

More than once she was tempted to speak to Sam, but it was impossible. They were separated by barriers they themselves had built, and Claudia was convinced there was no way to remove or even lower them. She had to live one day at a time. That's what she was learning to do on this weary, interminable journey.

Crossing the Mississippi was difficult and time-consuming. The owners of barges and ferries on the St. Louis waterfront, located on the west bank, were attracted by the army of covered wagons, and large numbers of river craft came in search of business. But most of the boatmen were unscrupulous, long accustomed to fleecing Easterners, and the prices they demanded were so high that Sam Brentwood simply waved them away without bothering to bargain.

"I don't rightly know what he has in mind," Nat Drummond muttered, "but we can't swim horses and oxen across a river this wide. And the special wagon will sink for sure."

Sam waited patiently for any boatman to make him a reasonable offer. It became evident, however, that the owners of barges and ferries were in league with each other. They demanded outrageously high fees because they believed the travelers would be compelled in time to weaken.

But they failed to take into account Sam Brentwood's temper. Standing beside his stallion at the river's edge, he listened without comment to the bids made by a half-dozen boatmen, and then he exploded. "Out at Fort Laramie a few years ago," he said, "we hanged a couple of scoundrels who tried to charge us too much for flour and bacon when we were hungry."

"You can't do that here," a boatman said.

"Can't I?" Sam's savage laugh astonished Claudia, who was standing within earshot. She thought she knew him fairly well, but she saw, better than ever, his hard, primitive core. "I know St. Louis as well as I know any town in the West," he said. "I know every street, every tavern. The only law here is the law a man makes for himself."

Several boatmen began to sidle away.

Sam drew and cocked his pistols in one swift, smooth motion. "Don't leave just when our chat is becoming interesting," he said.

The boatmen returned.

"It so happens," he said, "that I carry letters from President Van Buren and former President Jackson officially requesting every U.S. Army garrison to cooperate with me. Well, I could hang a couple of you to teach the rest manners, but I'm peaceable by nature. So I'll just have the troops at Fort Jefferson build me some barges. A whole fleet of barges, which three or four hundred men can do in a day. I'll not only carry my wagon train across the river, but I'll be the owner of the biggest fleet in St. Louis. I'll even go into the ferry business myself. And no matter what prices you no-good, money-grubbing bastards charge, I'll carry passengers and cargo across the river for half. It won't take me long to drive every last one of you out of business!"

Claudia knew he wasn't bluffing. He was angry enough to carry out his threat.

The boatmen realized it, too. They were unprepared for the unyielding attitude of a tough mountain man, and they dreaded the competition that a large fleet of twenty or thirty new barges would offer them.

Sam moved away from the boatmen, but spoke loudly enough for them to hear him. "Ernie," he said to Baron von Thalman, "form the wagons in a circle. Make sure every man in the company carries his firearms. I'm going to swim my horse across the river to Fort Jefferson, so you're in command until I get back. Don't allow any outsiders into the compound, and shoot to kill if anyone tries. I'll return with our own barges, manned by members of the garrison. As we say out in my country, there's more than one way to get the last laugh on a hyena."

Two ferrymen had heard enough. One of them called out, "Mister, you name a reasonable price."

"Fifty cents a wagon and a dollar for my special wagon," Sam replied promptly. "Fifty cents for each ferry load of horses and oxen. No bargaining. That's my fee, and you can either take it or go to hell. Which you'll do if you get into a fight with me."

The man took a deep breath. "We accept," he said.

The others immediately began to clamor for their share of the business. The price Sam had quoted was the current, fair rate, as they well knew. His firm stand had completely altered the picture.

His good humor restored, Sam accepted the offers. Soon the wagons were unhitched, then hauled onto barges for the crossing.

What made the incident memorable, Claudia decided, was that Sam behaved as though nothing untoward had happened. He refrained from gloating or rubbing salt in the wounds of the boatmen; it was enough that he had beaten them at their own game. He had achieved his goal, so he was satisfied.

Riding on the decks of the ferries transporting them across the Mississippi, the pioneers looked at the ramshackle, one-story buildings of St. Louis. Those who were aware of the town's romantic, exciting past were disappointed. The city looked drab.

Founded in 1764 by French fur traders from New Orleans, more than one thousand miles away, St. Louis was at first a village clustered beneath a high, protective bluff, but soon it spread to the adjoining prairie-land. Controlled successively by France, Spain and the United States, St. Louis, inspired by Great Britain during the War of Independence, had fought off a vicious attack by the Sioux nation.

As the original starting point for western explorers, beginning with the Lewis and Clark expedition of 1804-1806, the town had become familiar to every Rocky Mountain man, every trader and trapper and guide who had ventured to the Pacific. Striving for a respectability it hadn't yet achieved, it was now the principal headquarters of John Jacob Astor's fur company and a number of other major business enterprises.

The respectable citizens lived in one neighborhood, which was guarded by private, armed sentries. And no one of stature ever ventured beyond the confines of this enclave after dark. There were some parts of town which only the foolhardy dared to visit even in broad daylight. The roughest was the waterfront area, where French, Spanish and English were spoken. Indians daubed with paint brought furs here to sell, and escaped slaves from the South holed up in riverfront shanties en route to safety in the North. Mountain men came to the town in search of pleasure after living in isolation for months at a time. Farmers congregated here as they arranged to ship their produce to New Orleans and beyond. Adventurers preyed on the unwary, and any newcomer was regarded as fair game.

After the crossing, the wagon train reassembled on the waterfront, watched by a crowd of loafers, and then moved away from the town to a spot about a mile and a half from the river. There the usual circle of wagons was formed, and Sam assembled the entire company.

"Folks," he said, "we're going to spend about a week in this town. It's the last place we can buy all sorts of things you'll need in the wilderness. I've been authorized to give fifty dollars to the head of every family for spare iron-rimmed wheels, harnesses and other items you can't get elsewhere. If you need new winter clothes, get them here. However, don't, under any circumstances, buy food here." He spoke with slow emphasis. "A warehouse filled with basic foods has already been established and stocked at Independence. Once I set up my depot there, we'll have many other things we can send to you on the trail. There are honest food dealers in St. Louis, but you'll have to search mighty hard to find them."

Many people laughed.

"Now," he said, "I have some special rules for you to follow while we're here. Ernie and I have set up a sentry schedule that includes every last man in the company. We'll be standing watch twenty-four hours a day. At no time will you admit outsiders to the compound. *Any* outsiders! If a visitor tries to sneak in, challenge him, and if he doesn't stop, shoot him. Always shoot to kill!"

Otto van Ayl was shocked by the drastic order. "I think you go too far, Mr. Brentwood," he said. "People in the United States don't engage in such lawless acts. We could be prosecuted and hanged for killing people."

"You'll be very dead yourself if you let in a visitor who sticks a knife in your ribs!" Sam retorted. "You're on the frontier now, Mr. van Ayl. If the St. Louis constabulary was multiplied by ten it still wouldn't be big enough or strong enough to do the job of protecting decent citizens. River pirates make their headquarters here. So do sneak thieves, confidence men, card sharks and pickpockets. The riffraff from the prisons of a dozen states come here. There are mountain men who've had a lean year and aren't above robbing the innocent. Then there are the bad Indians. Tell them, Stalking Horse."

The Cherokee faced the company, his arms folded across his chest. "Many Indians bad, same as many white man bad," he said. "Some Indians drink white man's liquor. Not good. Make loco in head. Make crazy. Bad Indians kill. Steal."

"He's telling you the truth," Sam said. "These braves have been disowned by their own nations. They stay here because they have nowhere else to go, and the more they drink, the worse they get. Steer clear of them, and stay away from the longshoremen on the river, too. If you're smart, you'll avoid the waterfront district like the plague. Never leave the campsite alone. Always go in groups, buy what you must and come back here as quickly as you can. Just remember that the most lawless town in America is no place for sightseeing or loitering. If any of you want to eat at inns, I can give you the names of some relatively safe places. But even there—count your change!"

The pioneers took the warnings to heart. In the next few days no problems developed. Only Sam and Stalking Horse went off on missions by themselves, and they encountered no difficulties because of their familiarity with the pitfalls that could trap the unwary in a frontier community. Even the resilient Ernst von Thalman and the quietly efficient Dr. Martin, who had decided to buy several new surgical instruments, made certain they were accompanied by others when they ventured into town.

327

Some of the company, like Terence and Lena Malcolm, felt no need to visit any of the stores or shops and were content to remain at the campsite until the journey was resumed. Nat Drummond, who was responsible for buying flat strips of iron that could be used as replacements on the rims of the special wagon's wheels, was accompanied on his visit to a drygoods store only by his indomitable wife. And when they returned Grace reported that no one had dared to molest them.

Claudia Humphries decided she'd be wise to purchase a heavy sheepskin coat for the coming winter, since her city attire had proved so unsuitable for the road. Cathy wanted a new coat, too, so they planned to go into town together. But Cathy was near tears the morning they planned to go.

"I can't go with you," she said. "Otto refuses to give me the four dollars I need for the coat. He's in such a bad mood he won't even talk about it."

"I'll loan you the money," Claudia said.

Cathy shook her head. "Thank you, but I have no way of repaying you except through Otto. He'd be so angry if I defied him he'd never give me another penny. And I don't want to be in debt." Afraid of crying, she moved off quickly to supervise the cooking detail.

Tonie Mell, squatting and resting on her heels as she ate a slab of cheese with a chunk of hot bread, spoke up. "I wasn't eavesdropping," she said, "but I couldn't help overhearing you. Your brother-in-law is really a stingy bastard."

Claudia wouldn't have used such strong language, but she had to agree.

"If you still want to buy a coat for yourself, I'll be

glad to go with you. I want to buy some little presents I can take home to my aunt and uncle."

Claudia was uneasy, but was somewhat reassured by the appearance of the girl, who was wearing her worn buckskins.

Tonie was aware of her hesitation. "You're probably right. I've come to St. Louis a half-dozen times with my uncle, so I know my way around town. But with just two of us we might run into complications. We ought to find somebody else to go with us."

Claudia approved of her thinking.

"Anybody interested in going shopping this morning?" she called.

The only person to respond was Cindy.

Claudia still felt somewhat ill at ease in the company of the former bordello inmate, but didn't want to be rude.

Tonie was blunt. "Come along if you want," she said, "but wear something with a higher neckline and wash that paint off your face. Or you'll be back in your old business before you know it. You heard Sam say last night that a party of mountain men just got here yesterday with a big load of furs. By this morning they'll have sold their bundles, and all that cash will weigh down their saddlebags. I've seen men like that at my uncle's ranch on their way back to civilization. Nobody ever pestered me there, but I'd hate to meet one of them on a narrow street in this town."

Cindy hurried off to her wagon to scrub her face and change into more modest attire.

When she returned, the three young women left camp without delay. Tonie carried a short knife, as she always did when she wore her buckskins, but neither she nor the others were anticipating any trouble. After all, there was safety in numbers.

They made their way down a dirt road past a residential district made up of log cabins, interspersed with a few slightly larger dwellings of whitewashed clapboard. The men of the district had gone off to work, and there were none to be seen. A few toil-worn women were hanging washing to dry in their small backyards, and some grubby children were playing a game of tag, their shouts echoing down the unpretentious street.

Claudia reflected that, of all the places she had ever seen, this would be the worst to live in. She couldn't understand why the residents were willing to condemn themselves to a miserable, marginal existence for the rest of their days. How much better it would be for them to pull up stakes, go west and accept a grant of land from the government, even if Oregon deeds were of questionable legality since the United States had not established its sovereignty over the territory.

She had to smile at the change in her own thinking. The last thing on earth she herself had wanted was such a move, but now it began to make sense. There was something to be said for an outdoor life that she hadn't been able to imagine or appreciate in New Haven.

Their first stop was a drygoods store, where Tonie made a purchase of some material which she would make into a shirt for her uncle. It was something he could always use, and it would be an opportunity for her to show off her needlework.

When they emerged from the store they were vaguely conscious of a stocky Indian with shaggy hair leaning against a building across the street. He was attired in buckskin trousers, worn moccasins and, in a futile attempt to appear dignified, had wrapped a tattered blanket around his shoulders. It appeared that he had been drinking.

The young women paid no attention to him until Tonie glanced over her shoulder. "We're being followed," she murmured.

Cindy shrugged and dismissed the problem from her mind. She could scarcely remember a time when men hadn't followed her.

Claudia, however, tried to suppress a feeling of alarm. She remembered Sam's warning, as well as that of Stalking Horse, and St. Louis certainly wasn't a civilized community.

Tonie wasn't too concerned. "He looks like a renegade Kiowa," she said. "Most of them are good people, but when they drink they turn sour. And from the looks of this one, he's been drinking. If we pay no attention he'll go away."

Tall Oak had ideas of his own on the matter. He had earned money on the docks the previous day, and spent just enough on whiskey this morning to feel a sense of rare exhilaration. The willowy girl with long red hair had attracted his immediate notice, and he wanted her. His judgment clouded by liquor, he assumed she and her companions worked at one of the brothels in the waterfront area. These trollops ordinarily disdained Indians, but weren't above taking their money, and Tall Oak had enough cash to pay for the redhead's favors. Knowing how these white women could be touchy, he decided to wait until an appropriate moment to make his approach.

Neither Tall Oak nor the three women realized it, but someone else was following them. Ted Woods had left the campsite in the wake of the girls, and was staying far enough behind them, so they wouldn't know he was keeping watch. Tonie and Claudia might be annoyed, but he didn't really care what they thought of him. But he was worried that Cindy might laugh and tell him she didn't need a guardian.

Realizing that his temper was explosive, Ted had taken care not to carry firearms. Even if an altercation of some kind developed, he didn't want to be sent back to prison. He had armed himself only with one of his blacksmith's tools, a long-handled hammer with a flat, iron head. It was an ugly weapon, particularly when wielded by someone endowed with his strength, and he warned himself repeatedly not to use it. If that mangy Indian was following Cindy, as he appeared to be, a single punch in the face would be sufficient to discourage him.

The next shopping stop was a store that specialized in clothing and leather goods. There Tonie found a length of fine wool to take to her aunt, and Cindy was overjoyed to discover a pair of heavy boots, precisely what she'd been seeking. Her dainty city shoes not only wore out too quickly, they were too impractical for wagon-train travel.

Armed with their purchases, the girls emerged into the street again, and Claudia was relieved when she didn't see the Kiowa.

"All we need to buy now is your coat," Tonie told her. "The only trouble is that the stores that sell such coats aren't far from the river."

"If you think it's safe," Claudia replied, "I'm willing."

Never one to admit defeat, Tonie shrugged. "Why not? We can look after ourselves."

Not until they had walked another block did they realize that the Indian was following them again. Tall Oak was growing more excited. Just as he'd thought, the women were walking toward the riverfront bordello where they worked. He fell in behind them again, deciding to wait until he discovered which of the houses employed them before he made his approach. The girl with the long red hair soon would be his, so he was in no hurry to make his move.

There was no longer any doubt in Ted Woods' mind. The Indian was up to no good, so he walked more rapidly to close the gap between them.

The coat store was a trading post that bought direct from trappers and ranchers. Although Claudia could buy skins of beaver, lynx or fox and then sew them together, the hides were thick and she had no experience in trimming furs. She decided to get a ready-made coat of sheepskin.

The proprietor asked ten dollars for it, but she engaged in spirited bargaining and was able to buy it for seven. Feeling pleased with herself, she left the store with the other two women, carrying it over her arm.

Tall Oak had decided to wait no longer. The waterfront brothels were close to the store, and he was afraid the women might duck into one of them before he could make his desires known. So he approached them boldly, pointing a grubby finger at Cindy. "Tall Oak want," he said. "Pay plenty."

All three girls were startled, and Cindy was outraged. "Go away!" she said.

The Kiowa was offended. "Have plenty money. Pay as much as white man."

Several passersby were watching, and the embarrassed Claudia wanted no scene. "Let's just ignore him," she said, and began to move away. But she paid no attention to where she was going, and Tonie, flanking Cindy on the other side in order to protect her, made the same mistake. Before they realized it they had reached the wharves that faced the Mississippi River.

Tall Oak felt that the redhead believed she was too good for him. He persisted in badgering her, following close on her heels and repeating his offer in a loud voice that caused everyone within earshot to stare.

Ted Woods began to close in. But he was forced to halt when a cart loaded with merchandise from a river barge came between him and his quarry. The driver arrogantly assumed he had the right of way, and his horses would have run Ted down if the blacksmith hadn't stopped.

There seemed to be no escape as the girls retreated onto a wharf that jutted out into the Mississippi.

By now Tall Oak was convinced that the red-haired girl was teasing him in order to get more money, so he shouted, "Pay silver dollar! Go bed all day!"

A number of the ferrymen and boat owners were loitering in the vicinity. Realizing that the girls must be from the wagon train, they gathered at the foot of the wharf to watch the fun.

Arriving at the foot of the wharf, Ted Woods pushed through their ranks and instantly antagonized them. A burly ferry operator shoved him back in return, causing Ted to stagger and lose his balance. When he pulled himself to his feet, he was angry and it appeared that a fight would develop.

The ferryman saw the long-handled hammer in the blacksmith's hand and drew a knife. Ordinarily Ted would have plunged into a fight without hesitation, but now it was more important to him to protect Cindy than to teach this lout a lesson. First he would dispose of the Indian, and then he'd attend to the ferry operator.

But the other rivermen were not to be denied their sport. They closed ranks in front of him as he tried to move onto the wharf to gain access to the girls.

"Let the Kiowa have the wench!" one man called. "We'll take the other two!"

A large crowd had begun to gather, and Ted was blocked. He was tempted to clear a path for himself with his hammer, but realized he'd be cut down by a score of men armed with knives and pistols.

Meanwhile the girls knew they were trapped. They went all the way to the far end of the wharf, where they were forced to halt. A grinning Tall Oak pursued them, groping for Cindy.

Reverting to the habits of her Louisville days, she cursed him. Tall Oak was too drunk to pay any attention to what she said. But the rivermen heard her, too.

Only harlots used that kind of language, as they well knew, and they were encouraged.

"Maybe we'll take all three of them!" one of the group shouted. "And to hell with the Kiowa!"

Claudia and Tonie tried to appear calm, but both were badly frightened. Neither knew how to cope with the ugly situation that was developing, and Cindy was too busy fending off the Indian to offer any suggestions.

Ted knew he'd have to act before things got out of control, regardless of the consequences.

Then two men, moving shoulder to shoulder, made their way through the crowd. "Clear a path here!" Sam Brentwood ordered, and the ring of authority in his voice, combined with the sight of his rifle, caused the other men to stand aside.

Stalking Horse, Sam's companion, was holding his bone-handled knife in his hand, ready to slash any riverman who continued to block their path.

Everyone in the waterfront crowd was familiar with Indians, and none of them wanted to tangle with this sober, grim Cherokee whose attitude was unyielding.

Sam and Stalking Horse reached the wharf, then turned.

Claudia was so relieved to see them she felt weak. She exchanged a wan smile with Tonie.

Cindy was still fending off Tall Oak, who was paying no attention to the commotion at the land end of the wharf.

"Ted Woods!" Sam called. "Join me!"

Now the rivermen made no attempt to block Ted as he moved onto the wharf.

Sam handed him a pistol, then raised his voice.

"People who enjoy molesting ladies get what they deserve. I reckon I'll have to teach some manners to any man who doesn't go about his own business. Now!" He continued to face the crowd and calmly raised his rifle to his shoulder.

A number of men found it convenient to take themselves elsewhere, and the mob began to melt away.

"Ted," Sam said, "hold the line here with Stalking Horse. If any man tries to set foot on this pier, shoot him, and shoot to kill!"

Ted Woods' lips parted in a humorless smile as he and the Cherokee faced the diehards in the crowd.

Sam wasted no time. Moving quickly to the far end of the wharf, holding his rifle in his left hand, he lashed out at Tall Oak with his right, striking so swiftly and with such power that the Kiowa had no chance to duck or protect himself.

The blow caught him full in the face, and he sagged. Then Sam reached out with a foot and contemptuously shoved him off the wharf. Tall Oak fell into the muddy waters of the Mississippi, where he floundered before finding firm ground and staggering toward the near bank.

"Stay close behind me," Sam told the girls, wasting no words and heading back toward the shore end of the wharf.

They followed him, huddling together and clutching their purchases.

"Stalking Horse," he ordered, speaking in English for the benefit of the remaining rivermen, "bring up the rear. And don't hesitate to cut the hand off any man who even touches one of these ladies! Ted, stay beside me and blow the head off anybody who doesn't move out of our way in one almighty hurry." He emphasized his orders by raising his rifle to his shoulder again.

The ferry operators and boatmen didn't want another confrontation with this mountain man, who had ice water running in his veins. They scattered, leaving the end of the wharf free.

But Sam took no chances. Ted beside him, he marched slowly back from the river, Stalking Horse bringing up the rear behind the three young women. Not until they had walked the equivalent of two full blocks did Sam somewhat relax his vigilance.

"We're not staying in this part of town," he said. "Keep walking. Fast, but not too fast, and we'll soon be out of trouble."

As they headed toward the wagon train on the outskirts of the town, no one had the temerity to follow them, and the crisis ended as abruptly as it had started.

Sam took no chances, however, and doubled the guards on sentry duty. It was possible, he explained, that the disgruntled ferry owners and boatmen might try to obtain revenge by creating mischief, and he didn't want to be caught unprepared.

He had another reason, too, which he confided only to Dr. Martin and Ernst von Thalman. While in town he had visited old friends at nearby Fort Jefferson, commonly called Jefferson Barracks by residents of Missouri. There he learned that a "cage convoy," wagons with bars on all sides that were used to transport criminals, had encountered a serious mishap on the road.

Forty military prisoners, most of them deserters who had been recaptured and were regarded as dangerous, had managed to escape from their cages. They had killed or wounded most of the troops in the platoon that had been escorting the convoy to St. Louis.

"I don't want to alarm folks unnecessarily," Sam said. "I don't think the deserters would be stupid enough to attack a wagon train of this size. All the same, those men must want horses and food and weapons, so we might be a tempting target. I've already told Stalking Horse that when we start out again I want him to keep his eyes open for the prisoners on his scouting trips."

"Is there much chance the Army will pick them up soon?" Ernst asked.

"Well, a number of cavalry patrols have been sent out of Jefferson on search missions," Sam replied. "I have a lot of confidence in them. They know they've got to pick up that gang before more people are killed and hurt. Just keep what I've told you to yourselves for now. I don't want to make our people jittery without good reason."

The others agreed to say nothing.

Sam left them and went in search of Claudia. He found her emerging from her wagon after putting away her new sheepskin coat.

She came to him at once. "I haven't thanked you properly for your help on that pier just now," she said. "I don't know what would have happened to us if you hadn't shown up when you did."

"I don't want your thanks." Sam sounded curt. "All I ask is that you stay out of trouble."

Claudia became indignant. "We didn't deliberately get into difficulty, you know! Tonie and I had no idea that mob would form, and neither did Cindy, I'm sure. All we knew was that we were being followed by that drunken Indian."

"You're on the frontier now," he said, "and it's easy to get yourself killed by making just one little mistake."

"May I ask what we might have done to avoid an unpleasantness that none of us enjoyed?" She couldn't keep the sarcasm out of her voice.

Sam shrugged. "Anybody can give advice after something nasty has happened," he said. "The trick is learning how to avoid trouble in the first place."

Apparently, she felt, he was still blaming her for something beyond her control. "All three of us were in the same spot," she said, feeling aggrieved. "Why do you single me out for your little lecture?"

Sam looked at her. There was an expression in his eyes that she had never before seen. "Maybe," he said, finding it difficult to get the words out, "you mean more to me than those others."

Before the astonished Claudia could reply, he moved away, not glancing at her again.

As she watched him cross the compound, his limp more pronounced than usual, she was stunned. Under no circumstances had she expected him to express a personal interest in her. It was impossible for her to guess how long he had harbored such feelings. All she knew for certain was that his brief declaration changed the nature of their relationship.

She was unsure how she felt toward him, but she

knew she was flattered. Her self-discipline was so great that she had not allowed herself to dwell on the possibility of becoming involved in a romance with Sam, but she realized that she had been suppressing her own natural desires.

It had been a long time—far too long—since she had permitted herself to think of marrying again. But in spite of the differences in her background and Sam's, she had to admit that the idea neither alarmed nor upset her.

The day was warm, but Claudia felt a sudden chill move slowly up her spine, and she rubbed her arms vigorously, then retreated to her wagon so no one could see the color that suffused her face.

Sam, meantime, was startled by his unexpected brashness. He was rarely impulsive, but the words had popped out before he could halt them, before he could even think about them or weigh their impact. He had been badly shaken by Claudia's narrow escape from an ugly situation that could have had serious consequences for her.

But he needn't have gone so far. Good Lord! He had virtually proposed marriage to her. Now she had every right to expect such a proposal. Remembering how her eyes had widened, how her lips had parted in surprise and how the color had risen to her face, he knew she'd have every right to be hurt and deeply insulted if he just let the whole matter drop.

He was afraid of no man on earth, but he sure didn't want Claudia Humphries to laugh at him. Not that she'd looked as though she felt like laughing, he had to grant that.

But the very idea of marrying her—marrying anyone, for that matter—stunned him. In a few weeks,
he'd be forty years old. He couldn't imagine why a
beautiful woman would want to spend the rest of her
life with a crusty old bachelor. Or why he'd want to be
tied down to any female that headstrong and opinion-
ated.

One thing was certain. He'd never be able to tame
her. But he'd be damned if he'd let her lead him
around by the nose, either.

Well, his choice was simple: either propose, or avoid
the woman as he would the plague. It annoyed Sam
that he was too confused to think straight. That almost
never happened to him. Thank the lord, he still had
time to find his way through this unfamiliar forest.
Before the wagon train reached Independence he'd
have to try to figure out where he stood. The worst of
it was, he had no way of knowing whether she'd accept
or reject him. Life had been a lot less complicated
when he lived alone in the mountains.

XIV

The wagon train left St. Louis and started toward the Missouri River, intending to follow it across the state to Independence, on the final leg of the journey across the settled portion of America. In another month the pioneers would arrive at this outpost of civilization, before going on into the wilderness.

Even as the last of the wagons were bumping down the rutted dirt road that led to the river, Henry St. Clair and his companions arrived in St. Louis after making their camp nearby, absenting themselves from the town as long as the pioneers stayed there. Henry owed himself a few good meals, and he knew that his unreliable subordinates required a day or two of diversion before they picked up the trail of the caravan again.

Abe Ellis was the best of the sorry lot. Buying the former driver of the special wagon a drink of whiskey in a riverfront tavern, Henry reflected that the man would function willingly enough after he saturated himself with liquor and visited one of the neighborhood brothels. Ellis had one asset: he was thoroughly familiar with the wagon train. Ultimately that knowledge could be used to good advantage.

Digby and Lemon, in the British agent's opinion, were virtually useless. The former was inept and the latter was a whiner, always sorry for himself. Perhaps it would be wise to pay them a few dollars and be rid of them, but Henry was reluctant to part company until he figured out a plan of action to cripple the wagon train beyond repair. He knew he needed helpers, and it was better to have Digby and Lemon than no one.

Contenting himself with a small mug of ale, as Ellis made inroads on a bottle of whiskey, Henry paid scant attention to a scruffy Kiowa brave who shuffled into the place. But a half-dozen men standing at the bar immediately took note of the Indian's presence. "Well," one of them boomed, "if it isn't the great lover! Are you following any more women from the Oregon train around town, Tall Oak?"

Tall Oak didn't reply. But Henry's interest was sparked. To Ellis's surprise he called the Indian to the table and offered him some whiskey. Tall Oak eagerly accepted.

Questioning him gently, Henry learned the whole story of the incident that had disrupted the waterfront and almost caused a riot. The British agent didn't know Ted Woods, but he realized that he was making progress when Tall Oak expressed his burning hatred for Sam Brentwood. This opportunity was too great to be missed.

"The man-with-the-rifle," Henry said, "hit you and kicked you into the river. Now everyone laughs at Tall Oak. So Tall Oak wants to prove he's a man. He'll do this when everyone laughs at the man-with-a-rifle."

The Kiowa nodded gravely.

"It will be done." Henry spoke slowly, so the Kiowa would comprehend every word. "Also there will be whiskey for Tall Oak to drink and food for him to eat."

Abe Ellis, who hated all Indians, poured himself a stiff shot and downed it. Henry St. Clair ignored him. If necessary he would sever his ties with Ellis in order to gain the services of this sorry warrior. Ellis' usefulness was limited, and an officer of the Crown who sought advancement took advantage of every break.

Tall Oak, delighted with his good fortune, reached for the whiskey bottle. Henry deftly moved it to the far side of the table. In the days ahead he had to maintain a difficult balance, that of satisfying the pathetic brave's craving for alcohol while simultaneously keeping him sober enough to destroy the wagon train. Such a challenge was worthy of the talents of a man who hoped to give up field work for all time in order to spend the rest of his career lolling behind a comfortable desk in London.

The wharf incident influenced Tonie Mell more than she realized. She had thought of herself as a resilient woman of the frontier, almost impervious to the fears suffered by ordinary members of her sex. But she'd been as frightened as Claudia and Cindy, though she'd been prepared to fight for her honor. It was a shock to discover that she was as vulnerable as other women to the threat of abuse and rape.

Hating herself for what she regarded as weakness, Tonie tried to compensate by becoming more efficient in her duties. As the wagon train moved slowly out of the prairie flatlands and into the rolling hill country that covered much of Missouri, she took her duties as monitor so seriously that many members of the caravan became annoyed.

The road that ran parallel to the Missouri River on the south bank was little more than a trail, forcing the wagons into a long, single line again. Most of the travelers were weary, others were careless. The train stretched out interminably behind Sam Brentwood in the vanguard. In some areas forests of cedar, elm and ash, sycamore, linden and hickory grew close to the road, making it difficult for monitors to ride up and down the line, which further irritated Tonie.

From the time the march started out early in the morning, until a clearing large enough to accommodate the wagons was found in the afternoon, Tonie pounded mercilessly at the drivers, shouting at them until she grew hoarse. Some abused her in return, others ignored her, and she rapidly lost much of the good will she had accumulated.

At least it was no problem to obtain fresh meat for the company. Buffalo by the thousands roamed through the fertile valleys of Missouri. Every day or two a small party of hunters went out at the end of the march, some under Sam's leadership, others led by

Ernst von Thalman. These groups almost always returned with buffalo meat. Unfortunately for Tonie, she was not asked to join the hunting expeditions, which further contributed to her sour mood. One day she decided to accompany the hunters, no matter what their wishes.

Ernst, who was in charge, was more brusque than he intended. "We needed you when game was scarce," he said. "But there are so many buffalo around here that we're trying to train the amateurs in the art of hunting. We don't need you, so stay behind."

Tonie was so insulted she went to the bank of the Missouri, perched on a boulder and stared at the churning waters of the mighty river. It was there that Dr. Martin found her a short time later. "Are you ill?" he asked.

"I don't see what difference it makes." Tonie didn't bother to speak civilly.

"I was asking for information in a professional capacity," Robert Martin said, tempering his comment with a smile.

Tonie didn't want to become embroiled in a dispute with this charming, solicitous man whose grin made her dizzy. "I beg your pardon," she said. "There's nothing wrong with me except a foul temper, so I urge you to leave me alone."

He sat beside her on the boulder, and took his time stuffing his pipe. "Tonie," he said, "you're suffering from a malady that can be cured."

Uncertain whether he was patronizing her, she made no reply.

"You're planning to leave the wagon train soon," the physician said, "and that's your problem. You don't want to leave."

"Rubbish! No one really likes the discomforts on the trail, so why wouldn't I want to leave?"

"As Sam well knows—and as you told me yourself in confidence—you made a great personal sacrifice for the sake of this company's success. So you don't want to quit when the most difficult parts of the journey still lie ahead."

He understood her too well, she thought. She had to concede that he made sense. "Maybe so," she admitted.

"There's another reason, too. You're afraid that life on your uncle's ranch will be dull, and you don't want to miss the excitement when the wagon train gets to Oregon."

He was mistaken, Tonie told herself, in triumph. His guess was shrewd, but he was wide of the mark. But at least he had opened her eyes to something she should have recognized, something she couldn't tell him: Robert Martin himself was the basic cause of her unhappiness. She hated the prospect of being separated from him, knowing they'd never meet again, but she couldn't admit the truth to someone who thought of her as a tomboy. At least the St. Louis rivermen had been aware of her as a woman.

Dr. Martin could feel her bristling, though he couldn't imagine what he might have said to antagonize her. Obviously he hadn't improved her mood, so perhaps it was best to leave her to her own devices. He stood, then climbed down the boulder to the ground.

"Don't stay here by yourself too long," he said. "It may not be safe."

She felt a sharp stab of disappointment. "This is my home state. I can't imagine any harm coming to me in Missouri."

He waved cheerfully but without comment as he made his way back up to the circle of wagons.

Tonie was in despair. It was horrid to fall in love with a man who treated you like a younger brother. If she were endowed with Claudia Humphries' beauty, or Cindy's blatant sex appeal, she might be able to attract him. But she was wasting her substance on wishes that would never come true.

It was easy now to give in to tears, and she wept silently, facing the river so no one looking at her from the camp would realize she was unhappy. Her emotional outburst solved nothing, failed to improve her spirits and only succeeded in causing her to feel greater contempt for herself because of her temporary weakness.

She was as lacking in feminine wiles as she was in grace, condemned, she guessed, to spending the rest of her days alone.

Henry St. Clair and his motley group of subordinates remained a half day's journey behind the wagon train, riding on trails that led through thick forests near the Missouri River. Henry knew time was growing short—if he hoped to strike an effective blow before the caravan reached Independence. Thereafter, it would move for hundreds of miles across the Great Plains, where there were few trees. Such lack of cover would make it far more difficult for him to operate.

He made plan after plan as he rode, rejecting each in turn because the odds were too great. The truth of the matter was simple: he could depend only on himself. Abe Ellis would do well enough if cornered. And Tall Oak, if he remained sober, might be capable of performing some simple function, provided a suitable scheme could be devised. But Lemon and Digby, for all their glib talk, were small-time criminals who would take no risks that might endanger their lives.

Sam Brentwood was a resourceful opponent, and Henry knew he must hold the element of surprise in his favor. Otherwise, Brentwood would hold the advantage, particularly since there were so many men in the wagon train now. The only way an assault could be effective would be to find some way to neutralize all that manpower.

Henry was lost in thought, ignoring the low hum of his companions' conversation as they rode in single file behind him. His cleverness had won him three decorations in the past, and the greatest prize of all, a permanent return to London, awaited him after one more display of ingenuity. It was all a matter of utilizing the personnel at his command in the best way.

Suddenly a disreputable man in a filthy blue suit, hatless, a heavy stubble of beard on his face, appeared on the trail directly ahead. He was brandishing a knife.

Henry halted and cocked his rifle. If this was an attempted robbery, he would be merciless.

"If you're a-comin' after us," the man said, "there's no way you'll leave this forest alive. The Lynx will see to that. Ain't nobody goin' to arrest us!"

From this gibberish, Henry gleaned that the man was a fugitive of some sort. "Who is the Lynx?" he asked, playing for time and hoping to learn more.

"You'll find out!" There was bravado behind the man's shrill words.

Abe Ellis leaned forward in his saddle and spoke softly. "That there looks like a U.S. Army uniform without the brass buttons," he muttered.

All at once the pieces of the puzzle fell into place. Of course! Before leaving St. Louis Henry had heard a rumor that a band of Army deserters had murdered their convoy guards and were being hunted. Henry was quick to seize the opportunity.

"We have no intention of arresting anyone, and no authority for that purpose. I'd like to speak to the Lynx."

The disreputable man pointed through the forest. "Follow that line of maples," he said. "I'll be right behind you, so no tricks."

Ellis drew his pistol as he followed Henry, but Digby and Lemon hesitated. Tall Oak, who had been given no arms, merely shrugged.

Henry rode into a clearing where a number of men were roasting sides of lamb, obviously stolen from a nearby farm, over an open fire. Other men were repairing lean-to shelters at the side of the clearing, and still others sprawled on the ground, doing nothing.

The appearance of the strangers galvanized the entire group. They moved forward slowly in twos and threes, surrounding the new arrivals. A few carried rifles, and several were armed with pistols, but the majority had no weapons except knives or clubs. All wore tattered blue from which the insignia had been removed.

None spoke, and it was apparent the deserters were seeking the easiest way to unseat these riders and kill them.

A massive man who stood a head taller than the others came to the forefront, his hair and beard streaked with silver, a dead officer's sword in his hand.

Henry sought an advantage by speaking first. "You're the Lynx," he said.

"Who told you?" The man was taken by surprise.

"Your sentry. As I told him, we're not constables. We have no authority to arrest anyone—and no interest in making arrests."

Several of the deserters inched closer.

"Be good enough to stand back," Henry said coolly, "or I'll be obliged to shoot you. Now, then." He addressed himself exclusively to the Lynx; if his estimate was right, this giant could control the others. "You outnumber us rather heavily, and I have no doubt you could dispose of us, though I assure you I'd take some of you with me. Be reasonable. Five horses and a few guns will do you no good when there are at least thirty of you."

"Thirty-four, accordin' t' this mornin's muster," one deserter said.

Henry nodded. "Suppose I provide you with clothes that will make you less noticeable. Suppose I also obtain horses and weapons for all of you—"

"Why the hell would you do that?" the leader interrupted.

His gleaming eyes resembled those of a wild animal,

Henry thought. "I have my own private reasons. I'm willing to provide you with the means to get away from the Army patrols that are combing the whole area. I'm also willing to provide you with an opportunity to acquire a vast quantity of loot. Yes, and there'll be pretty women who'll be yours for the taking, too."

"I don't like bad jokes," the Lynx growled.

"This is no joke, I assure you," Henry said. "Be good enough to give me a chance to explain. If you won't," he added, his rifle aimed straight at the leader, "I swear I'll take care of you before your men can kill me."

Although the Lynx was a man of limited intellect, he recognized courage when he saw it, and he roared with laughter. "Maybe you're all right. You've got guts, I have to hand you that much. Lads, give these gents breathing room so's we can listen."

The deserters backed away, increasing the space between them.

Henry lowered his rifle, but was ready to use it instantly if the need arose. "Unless I'm mistaken we're partway between the towns of St. Charles and Washington," he said. "We'll buy you civilian pants and shirts in both towns, and we'll pick up horses that local farmers are willing to sell. We'll get you rifles, too, by legitimate means. I don't want the Army patrols and constables breathing down our necks. Our mission is too important."

The Lynx was becoming impatient. "What mission? You talk fancy, but we don't know why you're planning to be so good to us."

"Less than a half day's march from here," Henry said quietly, "there's a wagon train bound for the Oregon country. It is making a journey sponsored by the U.S. Government. Some of the funds are supplied by John Jacob Astor and other rich men. Hundreds of people are in that train. I want it destroyed, so the people will have to turn back."

"How come?" the leader demanded.

"Isn't it enough that I have my own reasons—and that I'm willing to pay you handsomely?" Henry countered. "And that's not all. There's one wagon in the train that has a false bottom. It's filled with gold. You men may take and share every last penny of that money."

"Can you show us which wagon it is?"

"Certainly. And there's another that's crammed with a fortune in supplies. Abe, tell them about the special wagon."

Abe Ellis felt ill at ease, but he described the contents of the special wagon in detail. He had gone too far to back out now.

The deserters were impressed, as well they should have been.

Looking around the circle of hungry, desperate men, Henry struck hard. "You're being offered real freedom," he said. "Clothes, transportation, rifles. The chance to help yourself to gold and precious supplies. When you scatter, you can make new lives for yourselves. What do you say?"

There was a long, tense silence before one of the men called, "If you're buyin' us all those things, mister, you must have plenty of money yourself."

Here, Henry realized, was the greatest personal danger he had yet faced. Not even Abe Ellis and the other members of his little band knew he carried an ample supply of gold and American paper money in a belt he wore under his clothes. If the deserters discovered it, they would almost certainly kill him. "I have my own ways of obtaining funds that I need," he said, and moved rapidly to another point he wanted to make. "Abe, here, can take two of you off to St. Charles," he said. "You can change clothes temporarily with these two." He indicated the unhappy Digby and Lemon, who were finally of some use to him. "I'll stay here myself as a hostage to prove my good faith."

His terms were so fair and generous that even the Lynx was impressed. "All we have to do is attack that wagon train, huh?"

"Under my direction," Henry replied with emphasis. "You'll do it when I tell you and in the way I tell you. I assume that some of you were in the cavalry and that others were infantrymen, right?"

No deserter was willing to discuss his past, and there was another long silence.

"It doesn't matter," Henry said. "Once we're properly organized I'll take the Lynx with me on a scouting trip to find the right spot for an attack. Then I'll plan a diversion. Simple tactics are always the best."

The former soldiers could not help responding to someone who addressed them with the crisp authority of an officer long accustomed to giving commands. The Lynx spoke for the whole group when he said, "The way it looks to me, we got nothing to lose by accepting your bargain, mister. If you cheat us, or go back on your word, that'll be the end of you and your friends —including this Indian."

"He's going to be very valuable to us," Henry said with a smile. "In fact, he's going to provide the diversion."

"Will there be much of a chance of gettin' shot up by the fellers in the wagon train?" one man wanted to know.

"Not the way I'm going to plan this surprise," Henry said. "They have a few marksmen in their ranks, to be sure, but we'll see to it that they're otherwise occupied when we move in."

The deserters seemed to accept his word.

At last, he thought fervently, everything was falling into place. He had a small army of experienced troops at his disposal now, and provided he developed his plans with his usual meticulous attention to detail, the days of the wagon train were numbered.

The outfitting of the para-military expedition proceeded with great caution. Limited quantities of clothing were purchased at each of the shops in nearby towns and country stores, so no merchant would become suspicious. Abe Ellis went out with small groups of deserters to bargain with farmers for one or two horses at a time. Then Digby and Lemon, after their own attire was returned to them, did the same.

Meantime the group continued to move toward the West, keeping pace with the wagon train. Henry was determined to use even greater discretion in purchasing firearms, and he handled this phase of the operation himself, usually accompanied by the Lynx.

There was no lack of muskets, rifles and pistols on sale, particularly at the small crossroads stores frequented by Missouri farmers who kept their weapons handy, both at home and when they worked in the fields.

The Lynx complained about the quality of some of the guns they bought, but Henry explained that they had little choice. When he could find a long rifle like those used by the mountain men, he hastened to buy it, but when he was offered only a forty-year-old flintlock he had to take it too.

Gradually he accumulated stores of gunpowder, supplies of lead and bullet molds. One by one the deserters gained new attire, horses and adequate weapons. Like the members of the wagon train they could shoot buffalo now, so there was no starvation in the ranks. And the Lynx, impressed by Henry's firm arguments, saw to it that none of his men robbed farmers they encountered in the woods, or looted unoccupied houses. The band was safe, Henry emphasized, only as long as they committed no unlawful acts.

There were setbacks, to be sure. Four of the deserters promptly disappeared as soon as they were clothed, mounted and armed. Digby and Lemon, accustomed to dealing in stolen goods on a petty scale, found the prospects of violent action so abhorrent that they, too, vanished into the forest and were not seen again.

Then Abe Ellis created a problem. Since he had been dismissed from the wagon train for dishonesty, and had subsequently been wounded by Sam Brentwood, he had been eager to even the score. But the realization had dawned on him that he was now involved in matters beyond his depth. Not only was Henry St. Clair determined to destroy the train, but his alliance with a gang of desperate, hardened Army deserters caused grave potential difficulties.

The plan to launch a full-scale attack on the train and rob it meant that many people would die, and Ellis had no desire to be hunted by federal and state authorities on charges of murder. Sooner or later, he believed, the Army's search patrols would track down the deserters, and he could be further prosecuted for aiding fugitives from justice.

Stealing the property of others didn't bother his conscience, but serious criminal acts that could send him to prison for years, or even have him hanged, placed him in a different category. He had drifted into a situation beyond his control, and he began to long for the safety of his Albany home, where the presence of his wife and children gave him at least a facade of respectability.

The last straw was the association with Tall Oak that he couldn't avoid. The Kiowa, who was slovenly, lazy and regularly supplied with liquor by Henry in order to keep him in line, represented all that Abe loathed in Indians.

After growing increasingly uneasy and upset, the former driver of the special wagon made up his mind to part company with St. Clair and the deserters. Just the knowledge that they intended to engage in the wanton killing of men and women he knew made him ill. He was reluctant to leave, however, until he received the payment of fifty cents per day that he had been promised. The journey from Missouri to upper New York was long and arduous, and Abe, always greedy for money, was anxious to fatten his purse before he departed.

That desire created complications. He knew he wouldn't receive a penny if St. Clair had any inkling that he intended to pull out before the attack on the wagon train took place. So he decided to resort to a ruse. His normal thinking process was slow and ponderous, and the various schemes that came to his mind were as feeble as they were transparent. He had the good sense to reject them, and finally came to the conclusion that it would be best to demand payment of his wages without offering any explanation at all.

That night, as the deserters were roasting buffalo meat over their cooking fire, Henry sat apart from them, deliberately maintaining the distance that commissioned officers observed in their relations with enlisted men. Abe went to him and sat on the ground beside him.

"Henry," he said, reciting the speech he'd been rehearsing for several days, "I've been thinking. You owe me a lot of money. We've been together a long time now, and you owe me more than twenty dollars."

"I'm good for it," Henry assured him. "You'll also get your bonus, remember, after we put the wagon train out of commission."

"I don't like it when I'm owed money. I want to be paid up to date."

Henry studied him for a moment. "Planning to take off on your own, Abe?"

"Oh, no. No. Nothing like that."

It was obvious to Henry that the man was lying. "I hope not. It would make me very unhappy if you went to Jefferson Barracks and told the colonel in command there where he could find the missing deserters."

"Why would I do a stupid thing like that?"

"Oh, to put yourself in good with the authorities. You might even hope you'd be paid a reward for the information."

"I'm no turncoat!" Abe was indignant.

"I hope not. I can't help wondering, though, if maybe you don't have the stomach for the plan we've been developing."

"You know what I think of Brentwood. I want to put a bullet into him before anybody else has the chance." Abe hoped he sounded convincing.

He didn't. Henry St. Clair, whose career had long depended on nuances in his dealings with others, heard a shallow undertone that convinced him that the man was putting up a front.

"I just want to be paid what's due me, that's all," Abe insisted.

Looking at him again, Henry saw that he was fidgeting with the frayed cuffs of his shirt, his gaze averted. The man reeked of guilt.

There were two ways of handling a matter that could become crucial. Pay Ellis, and he would sneak away at the first opportunity. Refuse to pay him, and he'd hang around for a time, but probably get cold feet and depart before the actual attack on the wagon train took place.

Henry's one consideration was that nothing interfere with his plan to destroy the Oregon-bound caravan. He suffered no illusions about Abe Ellis, certainly: the man was venal. He would do anything to pick up a few dollars. If he could notify the authorities of the intended attack, much less put the Army on the trail of the missing deserters, he'd be in a position to demand a substantial reward, if one wasn't voluntarily offered to him.

So there was only one safe method of dealing with the situation. "I don't want you to be unhappy in this enterprise, Abe," Henry said. "After all, I'm relying on you." He reached into a pocket, drew out two $10 bills and gave them to the man.

Unable to hide his surprise and pleasure, Abe snatched the money.

"Remember, I'm counting on you," Henry said again, and patted him on the shoulder.

Making his way back to the campfire, Abe made a wide detour in order to avoid Tall Oak. In spite of his fears, his quest had been successful. Now he was free to do as he pleased.

Henry watched him and smiled. Then, seemingly lost in a reverie, he stared into the flames until the meal was ready. His own supper could wait, and he allowed the deserters to hack off slabs of meat first. Then he beckoned to the Lynx.

The leader of the band was already wolfing down his meal, tearing a chunk of buffalo meat apart with his bare hands and stuffing the pieces into his mouth. He followed the Englishman to the edge of the woods.

"What would you do," Henry asked blandly, "if you knew someone was going to ride to Jefferson Barracks and tell the colonel where to find you and your friends?"

The man's small, deep-set eyes glittered. He ripped off a piece of meat, held it in front of his face and then snapped at it, cramming it into his mouth in a single bite.

The Lynx was a beast, Henry thought, waiting for a reply to his question.

"I'd cut the throat of the bastard," the Lynx replied.

"Quietly," Henry replied. "After everyone else goes off to sleep. We don't want any of your men picking up dangerous ideas. It would be too bad if one of them tried to win a pardon for himself by turning in the rest of you."

The Lynx nodded, baring his yellow teeth.

"Naturally, you'd want to get something out of it for yourself," Henry said casually. "I happen to know that the traitor is carrying at least twenty dollars in cash on his person."

The leader of the deserters remained silent, but his jaws worked as though he were chewing, and a froth of spittle appeared at the corners of his mouth. Wiping his sticky fingers on the sides of his new trousers, he flexed his long, thick fingers.

It was easy to imagine him curling those fingers around a victim's neck, but Henry refused to allow himself to become emotionally involved in matters that didn't directly concern him. It was his way of keeping his mind free for serious problems that might influence the outcome of his mission.

"Who is he?" the Lynx demanded.

Henry looked slowly around the fire and found Abe, standing alone, gnawing on a piece of meat. He inclined his head slightly in that direction.

"Ellis?"

Henry nodded, then wandered away.

The fate of Abe Ellis was sealed.

His body was found early the next morning in a clump of bushes beyond the edge of the clearing. His throat had been slashed, and his mouth was frozen in a hideous grin. His pockets had been turned inside out, but the deserters didn't think of robbery as a motive because none of them had any money. But they took care to strip the corpse and, before they broke camp, they drew straws for his clothes, his weapons and his horse.

Only at Henry St. Clair's last-minute suggestion did they dig a shallow grave and throw Abe's body in it before they moved on.

Henry knew he couldn't procrastinate. He had to act soon. Most of the deserters were simple-minded men, who thought only in terms of their own profit, as Abe Ellis had done. It was imperative that the attack on the wagon train be launched without delay.

Henry rode ahead rapidly, and came at last to an area where the terrain was perfect for his purposes. A high bluff that extended for miles rose behind the south bank of the Missouri River and the narrow road that ran beside it. The heights were heavily wooded, which would enable him to conceal and shield his force. As nearly as he could judge, there were few settlements in the neighborhood, which would make it difficult for the wagon train to obtain reinforcements. He couldn't have chosen a more appropriate site if he had listed his qualifications in advance.

Rejoining his companions late in the afternoon, Henry knew there was just one more task to be performed prior to his assault. Though the hour was late, he sent the majority of the deserters on a search for a salt lick, instructing them to notify him the moment one was located.

Two of the men returned within an hour to report that they had found a lick on a hillside behind a small pond. Henry issued new orders, and that night he slept well. It wasn't often that he allowed himself to relax in the field, but he had earned the rest. It wasn't often that the details of an operation dovetailed so neatly, but this scheme was foolproof, and he congratulated himself before dropping off to sleep.

This operation would become a classic, he reflected. It would be studied by neophyte espionage and sabotage agents for many years to come.

At dawn the next morning Henry was awake. Before the rest of the band stirred, he went off alone to the salt lick, carrying two empty burlap sacks.

The deserters were eating breakfast when he returned. Tall Oak sat alone, nursing an aching head and awaiting the first swallow of whiskey or brandywine that would ease his suffering. No one seemed to notice that the burlap sacks that Henry carried across his pommel had been filled.

He neither knew nor cared that the deserters' powers of observation were limited. Only one thing mattered to him: the survival of the wagon train was in jeopardy. Within another day and a half, at the outside, it would cease to exist.

XV

Frictions develop within the ranks of any large group traveling together under adverse living conditions, and the wagon train was no exception. Claudia Humphries was annoyed when she found Tonie Mell chatting amiably with Sam Brentwood at the end of a long day's march, and quarreled with the younger girl. Grace Drummond accused Cindy of flirting with her husband when Nat sat beside the girl at supper, and was outraged when other members of the company laughed at her for being jealous. Terence and Lena Malcolm, kept awake nights because the baby was teething, bickered over inconsequentials. A weary Emily Harris reprimanded her lively sons more severely than their conduct warranted, and then was depressed for doing so.

Otto van Ayl lost his temper when Cathy purchased new scissors to replace a pair she lost, and refused to believe that she could do no mending without them.

Ted Woods was kept busy every evening replacing the iron rims of wagons worn out on the rugged Missouri road, and got so little rest that his nerves were frayed. Even Danny, who continued to be helpful to everyone, smiled less frequently.

Stalking Horse, however, was unchanged. Each day he rode ahead to find a new campsite for that night's halt. Perhaps his mood was unaffected because he spent most of his time alone. Sam Brentwood was counting the days until his responsibility for the wagon train came to an end. After spending the better part of his life on wilderness trails by himself, he was tired of shepherding so many people.

But at least he'd found Claudia—for all the good it did him. He knew he had fallen in love with her, though she was hot-tempered and too independent for her own good. She had chosen to ignore his broad hint, however, and behaved as though he hadn't indicated the state of his feelings. Maybe, Sam thought, she was waiting for an outright proposal, but though he had never feared any man, he lacked the courage to ask her in so many words if she'd marry him.

It was a relief to know that in another ten days or so they would reach Independence. There the wagons would be overhauled, new supplies would be forthcoming from the government stores that had been sent ahead. And, hopefully, Whip Holt would be waiting to relieve Sam as wagonmaster and guide.

Forty-eight hours of unrelenting rain did nothing to improve the company's spirits, and then the weather turned cold. Summer had lingered beyond its time, but now it was autumn, and some of the travelers were concerned about the hardships of winter they would be forced to face in the unmarked wilderness that lay ahead.

Shawls and sweaters that hadn't seen service for months were removed from clothing boxes, and children were bundled in scarves. Women put away their cottons and wore their heavier woolens.

Only Sam and Stalking Horse seemed impervious to the cold. Claudia, sleeping under a blanket, wondered how Sam could be comfortable when he stretched out at night with nothing between him and the hard ground.

The animals, too, reacted sharply to the change in the weather, the horses and oxen demonstrating greater stamina, making it possible to shorten the nooning rest period. Quincy became friskier, as did Cindy's puppy.

It occurred to Claudia that schools were reopening for the new term back home. She wondered what arrangements could be made for the wagon-train children to continue their education. Sam was amused by her suggestion that classes be organized, and it quickly developed that her idea simply wasn't practical. The youngsters had too many chores to perform, and their formal schooling therefore couldn't be resumed until the company reached the Oregon Territory and established permanent homes there.

Meanwhile the long journey continued.

At one point, a bluff rose to a height of more than a hundred feet south of the Missouri. The space between the bluff and the bank of the river was so narrow that it was unusually difficult to make the circle each night. But Sam insisted that such a precaution be taken, though they lost an extra half-hour or more of travel time every evening by doing so.

The pioneers could see their breath on the air at breakfast, and some of the women were reluctant to leave the warmth of the campfire when they heard the familiar cry, "Harness your animals! Let's march!"

Tonie Mell, familiar with the countryside, knew better than most that the caravan soon would reach Independence. Because her uncle needed her help on his ranch, she knew there was no way she could continue the journey to Oregon, no way she could prolong her association with Dr. Martin. Her mood unhappy, she was mounted on her gelding every morning even before the breakfast fires were extinguished, so eager to break camp immediately that many people grew angry.

Tonie didn't care what they thought. "Let's go! Hurry!" she called repeatedly. "We don't have the whole day to waste!"

One by one the wagons moved slowly into line, the space so cramped that some wagons had to move out and start off down the road to the west before those at the rear could be maneuvered into position.

Ted Woods, the last in line, half-dozed as he sat on his buckboard, Danny beside him. Gradually he became aware of a rasping sound that grated on his ears. Sitting upright, he listened more intently, and spoke urgently to the boy beside him. "Danny," he said, "run ahead up the line till you find Tonie Mell. Send her ahead to Sam as fast as she can ride, and have her tell him to stop the train. Quick, now!"

The boy asked no questions and sprinted up the road.

It took another ten minutes to halt the lead wagons in the caravan. Sam galloped to the rear, Tonie behind him. They found Ted on his hands and knees in the road, his face pressed between the spokes of a wheel. A moment later they were joined by a silent Stalking Horse, who hadn't yet started out on his day's scouting trip.

Ted didn't look up. "Somebody threw sand into these wheels," he said grimly. "I've examined a half-dozen wagons, and the hubs of all of them are coated with sand. Every last one will break down within a few miles."

"Sand?" Tonie was incredulous. "I know this part of the country pretty well. There's no sand here, not even in the river bed!"

"See for yourself." Ted removed a smear of grease from the inner hub of the wheel. Mixed with it on his finger were many grains of what resembled sand.

Sam was on his hands and knees, too, looking first at the wheels of one wagon, then going on to the next. "This was no accident," he said, his voice sharp. "This is deliberate sabotage. Tonie, tell every wagon owner to look at his wheels."

Almost immediately reports began to filter back down the line. Something had been mixed with the grease in the wheels of at least a dozen wagons.

"Whatever this stuff is," Ted said, "it's got to be removed. The wheels have to be taken off one by one, washed off with water, the axles cleaned with rags, and fresh grease applied. This is going to be an all-day job, even if you give me the help of somebody who knows wheels and axles."

Sam sighed. "Tonie," he said, "turn the wagons at the front of the line around. Have them double back and reform last night's circle."

"That's a waste of time," she protested.

"Not if we're going to be here all day." He returned his attention to the wheels.

Tonie hesitated for a moment, then rode forward, and soon the laborious process of making a new circle was under way.

"Whoever did this job was careless," Ted said. "Look here. There are handfuls of muck covering the axle of this wagon—and none on the next."

The people in the affected wagons clustered nearby, angry and bewildered.

"I believe Tonie is right," Sam said. "You've got to go hundreds of miles west of here to the bed of the South Platte River before you'll find sand."

Stalking Horse, who'd been standing motionless, bent low and scooped up some grease mixed with granular particles. He sniffed experimentally, then tasted the substance on his finger. "Let the brother of Stalking Horse eat, too," he said in Cherokee.

Sam unhesitatingly followed his example. They exchanged a significant glance and spoke to each other in rapid-fire Cherokee. At last Sam turned to Ted and the wagon owners. "This substance," he said, "is a mixture of heavy sand and coarse salt. It can be obtained only at the outer rim of a salt lick. The inner part is usually pure salt, and as you work out toward the edge you find a crust of earth that's been dried by the salt and resembles sand. There are salt licks all over

Missouri, but I'd guess the closest must be at least twenty miles from here."

Nat Drummond was outraged. "Damnation, Sam! That means somebody carried this stuff a long, long way just for the pleasure of throwing it onto our wheels."

"Right." Sam stood, thumbs hooked into his belt and stared into space, frowning. "All I can figure is that somebody was mighty anxious to turn this train into an almighty shambles." He thought of Henry St. Clair, but shook his head. It was unlikely that the British agent had been trailing the caravan for hundreds of miles.

"When we find him," Ted said, "I'd like to string him up. Men, start taking one wheel off of each wagon. Danny, get the water detail busy. I reckon I'll need a few tons of it before this day is over!"

While the messy, painstaking task of cleaning the wheels and greasing them anew was being organized, Stalking Horse wandered off the road to look intently at the side of the bluff. Sam joined him, sensing what he was doing.

"There and there and there," the warrior said in Cherokee, jabbing his finger as he spoke, "only a mountain goat could climb up and down."

"But here and here," Sam replied, also pointing, "a man could make his way to the bottom and then return to the top of the bluff."

With one accord they dropped to their hands and knees and examined the earth with infinite care.

Other company members joined them, as their wagons were returned to the circle and their animals unhitched. Claudia was one of the first. With Quincy beside her, she watched Sam.

Stalking Horse shook his head, then moved on, and soon Sam joined him. The shepherd dog bounded forward, wagging his tail in greeting. Again Sam and Stalking Horse crawled on their hands and knees, studying every blade of grass. Quincy accompanied them, sniffing at the ground.

Claudia wanted to call the dog back to her side, but refrained. Sam would send him away fast enough if he interfered or became a nuisance.

"Look here!" Stalking Horse pointed to a spot a few inches in front of him. Sam leaped to his feet and examined the place.

The witnesses were startled when Quincy uttered a deep, prolonged growl.

"It's a moccasin print, all right," Sam said. "Folks, the damage probably was done by an Indian, whatever his reason."

"Bad Indian," Stalking Horse added.

Quincy continued to smell the place, still growling.

Sam shaded his eyes and peered up at the forests that extended to the edge of the bluff above. Within moments he had made up his mind. "I want every wagon owner to look at his wheels and axles," he said. "Any that have had sand and salt thrown into them will have to be cleaned and greased. Ted Woods needs help from any of you who really know wagons."

Four men volunteered their services.

"Now," Sam said, his voice turning cold, "I want

every man who regards himself as a marksman to step forward."

About fifteen members of the company moved toward him.

He nodded in grim satisfaction. "Fair enough. There are two trails through the forest up yonder. So we're forming two search parties to hunt down that Indian and find out why he played this filthy trick on us. Dr. Martin and I will lead one, and Stalking Horse and Ernie von Thalman will lead the other. If either group finds him, we fire three shots as a signal, and we'll all converge at the one place. Bring plenty of ammunition and powder, boys. I have no idea what we'll find."

Some of the men hurried back to their wagons for bullets, and a few to fetch their rifles. Meanwhile those who were ready joined one party or the other. Tonie pushed forward through the crowd that had formed and stood beside Claudia in the front rank. "I want to come with you," she called.

There was no humor in Sam's pale eyes. "We're not going out for a day's sport. We aim to find out why a deliberate act of sabotage was committed against this wagon train. We don't know what lies ahead, except that no Indian in these parts could be working on his own. So we may run into danger. There's no place for a woman—any woman—on this hunting trip, no matter how well she thinks she can shoot."

Tonie flushed, but there was nothing she could say.

Sam's icy gaze turned from her to Claudia.

"It didn't occur to me to go with you," she said mildly.

His quick smile indicated his appreciation. "If you don't mind," he said, "I'd like to take Quincy with us. Look at the way he's still sniffing around that moccasin print. He could be a big help to us."

"Then take him, by all means," Claudia said. She felt miffed at being excluded, just as Tonie did, but knew that her attitude was absurd.

Sam's attention turned to the tasks at hand. "Ted Woods will be in charge of fixing up the wagons while we're gone, and can call on anybody he needs. Keep your animals inside the circle, and I don't want any children to wander off and play. No one is to leave the circle except members of the water detail to go down to the river. They ought to play it safe, too, by going in groups of three and four."

His orders weren't questioned, but Claudia wondered whether he was anticipating trouble of some sort for those who remained at the wagon-train site.

Sam seemed to read her mind. "Folks who take sensible precautions stay healthy," he told her, before starting up the side of the bluff at the head of his search party.

Members of both departing groups found it difficult to maintain their balance on the steep slope. They had to walk sideways, and even the shepherd dog found it difficult to stay close to Sam, who occasionally slipped, in danger of losing his footing.

"I need plenty of water, all I can get!" Ted Woods called.

Claudia turned her attention to the organization of the water detail. Mindful of Sam's instructions, she sent people down to the river in threes and fours with their buckets. The task of cleaning the gritty sand and coarse salt from the wheel hubs was arduous, and most of those who remained at the campsite offered to help, even the older children. Cathy van Ayl and Cindy took up a collection of rags, and Ted Woods moved methodically from wheel to wheel, demonstrating how the job should be done.

When Claudia looked up at the bluff again the climbing men had disappeared.

There were no clues at the beginning of either trail to indicate which path the guilty Indian had taken, so Sam arbitrarily chose the one that meandered off toward the right for himself and Dr. Martin, assigning the other to Stalking Horse and Ernie von Thalman. "Remember," he said, "three pistol shots will be the signal to get together again."

He limped down the trail at a snail's pace, pausing every few yards to give Quincy an opportunity to sniff the ground. It was possible, of course, that neither party was actually on the track of the Indian who had damaged the wagons. The Indian might have made off through the underbrush, following neither path, but Sam was assuming that he'd been in a hurry, anxious to put as much distance between himself and the caravan as he could. If so, it would have been far more difficult and time-consuming for him to cut his own path or to risk being slowed down by patches of brambles, fallen trees and other impediments.

The odds against finding the Indian were great, but Sam felt it was imperative to conduct this hunt. He found it strange that any one individual would have gone to such lengths to disrupt the operation of the train. It had been necessary to carry the sand and salt a considerable distance from a lick to the banks of the Missouri, and a single man ran the considerable risk of being caught in the act of committing sabotage.

To the best of Sam's knowledge, no Indian was carrying a grudge against the group as a whole or against him personally. And he thought it unlikely that any Indian would have chosen such a sophisticated method of obtaining revenge.

Sam's thoughts returned to Henry St. Clair, who was certainly capable of managing the sneak assault and had reasons enough for wanting to halt the train. It was also possible that the Russians who'd tried to blackmail Tonie Mell were responsible. But the only way of learning the truth was to find the man who had actually performed the deed and then wring a confession from him. Sam disliked the use of violence when it could be avoided, but if and when he caught the Indian he'd utilize any methods at his disposal to unearth the whole story.

Dr. Martin, sometimes falling behind a pace or two and sometimes walking beside Sam, was struck by the stark intensity of the wagonmaster's mood. Never had the physician seen such total concentration. If a second set of moccasin prints had been made, Sam would find them. If a bent blade of grass, a crushed weed or a broken twig indicated that anyone had used this trail recently, Sam would know it.

Dr. Martin shared Sam's indignation, but at the same time he couldn't help feeling sorry for the culprit. Sam Brentwood was a gentle, mild-mannered man, but it was evident that he yearned for vengeance and would show no mercy when he located the perpetrator.

Henry St. Clair was satisfied with the success he was enjoying so far. He watched the wagon train from the top of the bluff, saw it begin the morning journey and then halt. That was all he needed to see before riding off for the better part of two miles, turning away from the river to rejoin the band of deserters who were waiting for him.

Tall Oak had almost muffed his assignment, completing only a portion of the task he'd been given, but Henry had to be satisfied with the results. Instead of pouring the sand and salt mixture onto all of the wagon wheels, the Kiowa had managed to endanger only a third of the vehicles before laziness or fear of discovery had caused him to abandon the job. But at least he had halted the train, and that was what mattered.

Then, instead of returning to the rendezvous deep in the forest, which he could have reached by dawn, Tall Oak had wandered off somewhere by himself. Perhaps it had been a mistake to give him a flask of whiskey to take with him, but the Kiowa had flatly refused to undertake the assignment without it. So it was likely that he'd consumed the liquor and was either drunk or asleep. Well, Henry couldn't worry about him. If he failed to show up again it would be too bad, but the British agent was damned if he'd accept full responsibility for a drunken Indian.

There was only one problem: if apprehended, Tall Oak might be inclined to talk. But there wasn't much he could tell the authorities. He had heard others mention his employer's name, but he probably wouldn't be able to recall that it was Henry St. Clair who had hired him. As for the deserters, their identities were vague, so it was uncertain that he could provide any specific information about them. Even if he could, Henry refused to worry about that detail. Once the deserters had served their purpose, he wanted nothing more to do with them.

After riding an hour and a half, he reached the clearing deep in the forest where the deserters were waiting for him, and quickly brought them up to date. "The wagon train has been halted," he said. "The Indian did that much. As I left, they were organizing a search party, which means their best and most able men will be tramping through the woods. We'll have to avoid them, of course, but that shouldn't be too difficult."

"Where are the wagons with all the loot?" the Lynx demanded.

"The wagon with the gold hidden under false flooring stood third in the line of march. It's one of the few that's painted white, so you can't miss it. As for the special wagon, it stands out, too. It's as large as any two of the others put together."

"There's one thing we ain't talked about," the giant said. "Me and the boys are wondering how big a share you want for yourself."

"None of it," Henry declared. "Keep the gold, and divide the supplies in the special wagon any way you please—along with any other booty you collect."

The military fugitives realized he had his own reasons for wanting to disrupt and destroy the wagon train, but they weren't really interested. It was enough for them that whatever they seized would belong solely to them.

"The side of the bluff is very steep," Henry said. "That means you'll open your attack from the heights, holding your position there until you've silenced any opposition you may encounter. Once you start down that slope you won't be able to stop, so you'll have to conduct a full-scale cavalry charge that'll take you right into the midst of the wagons. Then you'll be on your own."

The Lynx stared hard at him. "You ain't going to join in the battle yourself?"

Henry shook his head. "I can't. They know me, and I don't want any of the survivors to be able to identify me. Since it will be physically impossible for you to ride up that bluff again, we'll arrange—right now—for a place to meet after you've carried off your attack."

"Maybe it's more dangerous than you're letting on. Maybe that's why you don't want to get into the fight."

"I've just told you my reason," Henry said testily. "I'll join you a mile or two down the river, just off the road, before the beginning of the bluff. Where the land is still fairly flat."

"You better be telling us the truth," the Lynx said.

"I am. I have nothing to gain by lying to you," Henry said earnestly. "The wagonmaster is a crack shot, as I've already told you, and we've got to assume that some of the others are, too. But they're neutralized because by now they're already conducting a search for the man who put sand into their wheels. They should be miles from the wagon train when you open your assault. The whole attack shouldn't last more than a few minutes, and you'll be far away by the time the wagonmaster and the others return. As nearly as I can estimate, the plan is foolproof."

"It better be," one deserter declared.

"There's only one thing left to be settled. When do you pay us the cash you promised us?" The Lynx peered suspiciously at the man who had hired them.

These wretches were totally lacking in gratitude, Henry St. Clair thought. He had obtained civilian attire for them, bought firearms for them and provided them with horses. But they still weren't satisfied. "I promised you payment when the job of wrecking the wagon train is done," he said.

"The rules have changed," the Lynx told him. "We want to be paid now, or there won't be any attack, and to hell with you."

"How do I know you'll keep your end of the bargain if I pay you in advance?" Henry demanded.

The giant's harsh, booming laugh echoed through the forest. "We want the gold that's hidden in that farmer's wagon, and we want all the good things that are stored in the special wagon. That's why, mister. Once we have everything we need, we're breaking up. Some of us will go to Texas, and the rest will go where they please. So you'll do this our way. Give us the cash right now, or forget you ever ran into us."

In spite of his reluctance, Henry had anticipated this demand and was prepared to meet it. Unwilling to let the adventurers know of the existence of his money belt, he had already transferred the wages due them to another pocket. He removed a roll of ten-dollar bills, handed two to each and three to the Lynx, thereby insuring the leader's support, at least for the moment.

The potential mutiny was quelled, and with Henry riding at the head of the column, the men made their way to the bluff overlooking the Missouri River. Soon the unsuspecting members of the wagon train would be subjected to a colossal assault that, Henry was convinced, could not fail.

The long trek on foot through the Missouri forest seemed to be producing no results. Leaves were turning red and gold in the crisp autumn air, and there was already a thickening carpet underfoot. As they fell, drifting down silently, the leaves made it increasingly difficult in some places to find any tracks that the fleeing Indian saboteur might have left on the trail.

But Sam Brentwood showed no signs of discouragement or fatigue, even though the men strung out behind him on the path were beginning to be disheartened. He continued to press forward, his limp more pronounced than ever, his face set, his eyes unyielding.

Quincy apparently realized that this was no ordinary outing. Undistracted by the presence of squirrels, rabbits and other small animals nearby, Quincy stayed close behind Sam, his ears raised, his body tense. He seemed to sense that his friend was relying on him for help that mere men couldn't provide. Occasionally he moved ahead a few paces, then waited for the wagonmaster to catch up, but not once did he stray from the path.

Robert Martin was tempted to suggest that the search be abandoned. The attempt to cause permanent damage to the wagon train had failed, and he thought it might be wiser to push on to Independence. He saw little to be gained for the effort and time involved.

But when Quincy halted, sniffed the ground repeatedly and uttered a low, deep growl, a slow chill moved up the physician's spine and he knew that he was mistaken.

Sam remained remarkably calm. "Well, boy," he said, "you've found something. Show me."

Quincy continued to smell the spot, his growls more distinct. All at once he left the trail and moved swiftly but quietly through stands of oak and linden and elm. Ahead stood a tangle of silver birch, saplings and mature trees so close together that it appeared as if no man could force his way through the maze.

Sensing that Sam couldn't follow him, the dog found a way around the birches to an area where hickory trees were growing in profusion. Sam raised a finger to his lips in warning. The men had not been talking, but they walked more carefully to make as little noise as possible.

Then Quincy broke into a run, and Sam had to sprint in order to keep the dog within sight. For a while the dog disappeared, and then Sam saw him again, his teeth bared as he stood over something on the ground.

Sprawled beneath the overlapping branches of two hickory trees was a Kiowa brave, sound asleep. As Sam drew closer he smelled the stench of liquor on the Indian's breath.

Using three pistols, Sam fired three shots into the air in rapid succession. If Stalking Horse was within earshot, it wouldn't take him long to reach the spot.

"Steady, Quincy," Sam said, restraining the dog from attacking the Kiowa. The sleeping man didn't stir. With other members of the party gathering around him, Sam bent down and removed the knife from the Indian's belt.

Then something struck a familiar chord. All at once Sam recognized the Indian. This was the Kiowa who'd made such a nuisance of himself on the St. Louis pier, the brave who'd been pawing Cindy before Sam booted him into the Mississippi. So it was possible that the Indian had been acting on his own initiative, although Sam doubted that he had enough intelligence. In any event, the evidence was incriminating: there were smears of axle grease on his hands and his buckskin loincloth.

Sam nudged him with a foot, but the Kiowa didn't stir.

Dr. Martin knelt beside him, his nose wrinkling in disgust. "This man is dead-drunk," he said. "He couldn't have left the river in this condition because he couldn't have come this far. He's obviously been drinking on the trail."

They spent the better part of a half-hour trying to awaken Tall Oak, but he didn't open his eyes.

Ultimately Stalking Horse and Ernie von Thalman arrived with the rest of the search party. The Cherokee took in the situation at a glance, dropped to one knee and drove the point of his bone-handled knife under the sleeping Kiowa's dirty thumbnail.

The pain awakened Tall Oak with a start.

Sam bent close to him on the other side as Stalking Horse continued to exert pressure with his knife.

"Who paid the brave to throw sand on the wheels of the wagons?" he asked in the language of the Kiowa.

Tall Oak shuddered, but made no reply. Sam had no intention of wasting more time than was necessary. Drawing his own knife, he held the blade close to the warrior's throat. "Speak!" he commanded.

Tall Oak blinked as he tried to focus, and his eyes watered. The whiskey he had consumed still made him dizzy, but he was sober enough to recognize the stern wagonmaster and the Cherokee. The presence of the other men in the circle around him, too, convinced him that his life was in danger. He opened his parched lips, but was so frightened he couldn't utter a sound.

"The heart of the coward will be cut out of his body and fed to the wild boars of the forest," Sam said, pressing the blade closer to the Kiowa's throat.

In his terror Tall Oak panicked, and tried to push away the knife that had already drawn blood from his throat.

Quincy thought the Indian was trying to attack his friend, and a hundred pounds of canine fury were unleashed. Before anyone could halt the dog he launched an assault of his own.

By the time Sam was able to haul Quincy off and quiet him, Tall Oak was bleeding freely from several deep bites. The Kiowa appeared to have lost consciousness again.

Dr. Martin moved Sam and Stalking Horse aside, then quickly conducted another examination. "This man was in a weakened condition due to alcohol," he said at last, "and the fright he suffered from Quincy's bites was too much for him. He's about to pass out again, and there's nothing I can do for him."

Sam dropped to the ground and placed his lips close to the Kiowa's ear. "Why did you put sand on the wheels?" he asked harshly, with no hint of compassion in his voice.

Tall Oak could only whisper, as though he was strangling. "Man pay. Give whiskey, too."

"What man?"

The Kiowa was no longer able to reply. He gasped for breath, made an effort to sit up and then fell back onto the ground.

Dr. Martin took his pulse, then shook his head.

Tall Oak's sightless eyes stared vacantly at the tops of the hickory trees. The secret of the identity of the man who had paid him to sabotage the wagon train had died with him.

Some members of the party were stunned by the scene they had witnessed, but Sam felt no pity for the dead Kiowa, and neither did Stalking Horse. Their one regret was that he had died before telling them what he knew.

The men carried no spades or other tools to dig a grave for the brave, and Sam knew of no reason to bring his body back to the campsite. The best he could manage was a final resting place of sorts beneath the trunk of a huge, fallen maple. The task was accomplished with dispatch, and the abortive mission appeared to be at an end.

Suddenly, the men were electrified by the crackle of rifle fire in the distance. In an instant, Sam knew the reason behind the Indian's seemingly senseless act of sabotage. A clever scheme was being unfolded. The wagon train, unable to move, was being subjected to heavy attack by armed men while the company's best sharpshooters were several miles from the scene.

"We've got to get back—fast!" Sam shouted. His limp forgotten, he ran toward the river. He prayed they would reach the camp in time.

XVI

Earlier it had become obvious that the wagon train would lose the entire day and not be able to advance until the following morning, no matter how hard Ted Woods and his crew worked. So kindling and wood were gathered near the base of the bluff, and another fire was made near the ashes of the last one.

The water detail was at last able to take care of Ted's needs, and with the wheels being cleaned one by one, and the axles greased, Claudia was able to rest for a time. Cathy and Otto were engaging in another of their incessant quarrels nearby, so she avoided them. Instead she headed toward Tonie Mell, who was sitting alone on the steps of her wagon, looking forlorn. Now that Sam had made his personal feelings clear, Claudia no longer disliked the girl, and found herself even sympathetic to someone who looked that woebegone.

As Claudia approached, they heard a sharp, cracking sound that resembled a tree branch breaking, and saw a small puff of dust a short distance away.

Tonie was on her feet immediately. "My God, we're under fire!" she screamed.

Another rifle shot sounded, then another, and soon a fusillade descended on the campsite.

The place became a bedlam. Work horses and oxen roamed inside the circle nervously, women hurried to their wagons, dragging children with them, and many of the men were so bewildered they didn't know what to do.

Tonie Mell was the first to be practical. She dashed into her wagon for her rifle, then scurried for cover behind the inner rim of the circle. Ted Woods followed her example, and within moments a number of other men did the same, Otto van Ayl among them.

Claudia, recovered from her astonishment, looked at Terence and Lena Malcolm, who were standing at the rear of their wagon, staring up at the bluff, where volley after volley of concerted rifle fire was erupting. "Terry," she said, "I'm a better shot than you are, so lend me your rifle. Quickly."

He brought it to her, along with a pouch of bullets and a bag of powder. Emulating the men, Claudia crouched low and ran a zigzag pattern until she reached the inside edge of the circle, where there was greater protection from the rifle fire on the heights. She saw Tonie crouching near the narrow opening between two wagons, and instinctively joined her.

"Judging from the volleys," a tight-lipped Tonie said, "there have to be twenty to thirty men up yonder."

"Indians?"

Tonie shook her head. "No tribe has that many guns. Bandits, maybe."

Could ordinary bandits be launching a concerted attack so soon after the train had been incapacitated? It was too great a coincidence. Claudia thought of Henry St. Clair, wondering if he might be responsible, but there was no time now to dwell on such matters. She was too frightened, too angry.

When she saw some of the men firing indiscriminately at the heights, Tonie was appalled. "Hold your fire till you can actually see your target, you idiots!" she shouted. "They've got to move close to the rim of the bluff before they can look down at us!"

Even as she spoke an attacker drew close to the edge of the bluff. Tonie steadied her rifle, took careful aim and squeezed the trigger. Apparently her shot was a near miss because the man quickly drew back.

Thanks to Tonie's coaching, Claudia knew now what had to be done. She leaned against the axle of the wagon and waited. She had learned to shoot because she had been challenged, and now there would be a need for all the patience Sam had displayed, for the long hours she'd spent alone in target practice.

Soon another rider appeared, and raised his rifle. But Claudia reacted faster than he did. Swinging her borrowed rifle to her shoulder she caught her breath as she peered at her target through the sights, then squeezed the trigger, remembering to hold the butt firmly against her body so the kickback wouldn't knock her down.

The man on the heights clutched his chest, dropping

his rifle, then tumbled to the ground only inches from the edge of the cliff.

Claudia had drawn first blood, and she lost her sense of fear.

"Good shot," Tonie said, a ring in her voice.

Claudia's success heartened the men, and a number of them, including Nat Drummond and Ted Woods, became more selective in their fire. These were men who had occasionally hunted ducks, wild turkeys and perhaps deer in order to put meat on their tables, but none were expert marksmen. None had ever engaged in armed combat with other men.

But they had the good sense to exercise patience. Strung out along the line of wagons, they waited until they could actually see their foes on the bluff before shooting. Even though most missed repeatedly, they forced their enemies to exercise greater care.

A few pioneers refused to learn, however, and the worst was Otto van Ayl. Wishing he'd been sensible enough to buy a farm in Illinois, he was determined that no bandit would steal the gold hidden beneath the floorboards of his wagon. In a fury, he fired indiscriminately at the bluff, reloaded and fired again, then yet again.

The flashes from the same spot beside Otto's wagon attracted the attention of several Army deserters, who already recognized his white wagon as one of their prime targets. Three appeared simultaneously, firing at the same instant. Otto van Ayl fell back onto the ground, his old-fashioned musket dropping beside him.

Claudia knew at once that he was dead and felt

heartsick. But she couldn't allow herself to think of Otto—or of the suddenly widowed Cathy. "Those men up there know how to shoot," she said, between clenched teeth.

"They're marksmen, all right. You and I had best move around and never fire more than once from the same spot. It's too easy to make ourselves attractive targets."

They moved to the other end of the wagon they were using as a shield, and fired together when an attacker showed himself on the bluff. The man crumpled, fell to the ground and then rolled down the bluff, where his body lay at the bottom. Neither girl ever knew which of their shots had killed him.

Gradually it began to dawn on the pioneers that their best available shots were Tonie Mell and Claudia Humphries. It was the two young women who were holding the attackers at bay. They needed help badly, however, and the first to realize it was Ted Woods, who had yet to hit his target.

Casting aside his masculine pride, he acted accordingly. "Danny! Chet Harris!" he shouted to the boys who were grouped at the river side of the circle with the women and younger children. "Join me up here, but don't go into the open. Come round the circle and use the wagons as cover so those bastards up yonder don't take aim on you."

The two boys followed his instructions, and soon reached his side.

"I want each of you to get a rifle, ammunition and powder from somebody who isn't having much luck. Then join Tonie and Claudia as feeders."

In a short time his tactics proved their worth. As soon as Tonie and Claudia fired, they were handed loaded rifles by Danny and Chet, who promptly reloaded the discharged weapons. Thus the girls were able to fire more rapidly, getting off as many as three or four rounds before return enemy fire made it necessary for them and their loaders to scurry to safety behind another wagon.

The men on the top of the cliff were discovering that their assault was far more difficult and dangerous than Henry St. Clair had pictured it. The moment a deserter appeared from behind the trees that screened him, he became a target for the sharpshooters below.

Tonie nicked a horse, and the frightened animal reared, throwing its rider. Then Claudia, narrowly missing her target twice, forced one of the bolder men to draw back.

There was a brief respite, and Tonie, continuing to watch the crest of the bluff, wiped perspiration from her forehead. "So far we're holding our own. We're a good team."

Claudia felt as though she were dreaming. Necessity had transformed her from a soft, civilized lady into a primary defender of the entire wagon train. She had learned to shoot only because she hadn't wanted to be outdone by a member of her own sex, and now the entire company's safety depended on their efforts.

"Even though we've been moving around," she said, "it ought to be plain to the bandits up there that only a couple of us can shoot. If they're smart they'll concentrate on us."

"Then we'll have to be smarter and keep changing our positions," Tonie said. "We'll start moving up and down the line every time we fire a couple of quick rounds."

The idea made sense, and Claudia agreed, but remained fearful. "We can't hang on forever. There seem to be a lot of them up there."

"Sam and Dr. Martin and the others can't be that far off. By now they're sure to have heard the ruckus," Tonie said. "So it shouldn't be too long before we get help."

The deserters adopted a new approach to neutralize the sharpshooters, though it involved a high risk. A dozen attackers appeared simultaneously, strung out along the rim of the bluff, and simultaneously fired a volley before ducking back out of sight.

This gave the defenders only a few seconds to aim and fire, so the odds favored the attackers, who adopted the principle being utilized by Tonie and Claudia, never appearing twice in exactly the same place.

A hail of bullets riddled the wagon train. A work horse was wounded, and had to be put out of its misery by Ted Woods. Then one of the oxen was struck by several bullets and dropped dead.

Again the men on the bluff retreated, then advanced again and fired a fusillade. This time the girls were better prepared. Tonie's bullet grazed the face of one attacker, forcing him to turn away swiftly, and Claudia's shot struck the rifle of another, knocking it to the ground, making it impossible for him to retrieve it as he pulled back.

At almost the same instant a woman inside the circle screamed, then began to sob hysterically.

"That sounds like Ma," Chet Harris said nervously, but stayed at his post, reloading the rifle Claudia had just fired.

Word passed quickly around the circle, and Claudia heard the news from the man stationed behind the adjoining wagon. "Chet," she said softly, wishing she could cushion the blow, but realizing she had to be blunt, "that last volley hit your little brother."

"Billy?"

She nodded.

"Is he—"

"Yes," she murmured.

Tears ran down Chet's face, but he remained at his post. For the moment, others could console his mother; he had a vital task to perform.

Claudia couldn't find it in her heart to grieve for Otto van Ayl, who had compelled her to make this long journey and who had made Cathy's life miserable for years. His death was unfortunate, but at least he had lived a long time. But the killing of a six-year-old child who was incapable of harming anyone was wanton murder, and a cold rage possessed her.

Instead of moving on to the next wagon for cover she held her position and stood with her feet planted apart.

Once again the attackers moved in unison to the lip of the ledge. Claudia instantly raised her rifle, took aim and fired. Even before the man on horseback fell to the ground, she snatched her second rifle from Chet and fired a second shot at another man, unmindful of the bullets that sang past her or bit into the dust around her. Her aim was slightly less than perfect, but she managed to wound the attacker in the shoulder.

"Move on!" Tonie called urgently. "They've spotted our position!"

Claudia crouched low and followed Tonie to a place of cover several wagons farther down the line. Chet stayed close behind her.

"Those two," Claudia told him, "were for Billy."

He nodded, his own face grim as he handed her a loaded rifle.

When the opportunity came to fire again Claudia was overly anxious, and missed with both shots. She had to calm herself, she knew, but it was difficult when the enemy were taking such a toll. A farmer had been killed, and one of the women was wounded; the needless slaughter infuriated Claudia, and her body was shaking.

Tonie was better able to tolerate the situation because she had helped her uncle repulse attacks on his ranch. But she knew the men on the cliff would not be content to repeat their present tactics endlessly. They were suffering casualties, too, thanks to her shooting and Claudia's, but so far they hadn't yielded. Her experience was limited to assaults on the ranch house by outlaw bands of robbers, and she had no idea what the men on the cliff might try next. She didn't know how many there were, but it was obvious that these bandits had considerable strength. Judging from the way they shot volley after volley, they had no lack of ammunition or gunpowder, either.

Tonie told Claudia her fears, speaking succinctly.

The knowledge that the danger could increase steadied Claudia. "We'll just have to do our best," she said.

Twice more, shots were exchanged, and another farmer was wounded. Neither girl was successful in hitting a new target, but at least they managed to drive their opponents away again.

There was a long, ominous lull.

"Danny," Tonie Mell said, "pass the word down the line. I don't know what's going to happen next, but they're going all-out against us. I can feel it."

The silence, broken only by the whimpering of a small child, became oppressive. One of the horses neighed, then all was quiet. The defenders stood behind the wagons in the front semi-circle facing the cliff, nervously bracing themselves for the next attack.

Then it happened. Ten of the deserters, riding with the reckless skill of the cavalrymen they had been, rode forward in unison, spread out in a thin line, their horses plunging down from the heights.

Claudia fired at a rapidly moving target, missed and snatched her other rifle from Chet, who began to reload the first. Again Claudia missed, realizing with dismay that Tonie was doing no better.

The horsemen, holding their fire, loomed larger as they charged down the steep slope. Others appeared behind them on the edge of the bluff, and opened a brisk fire to cover their comrades.

Claudia began to give up hope. There was no way the attackers' new tactics could fail. Even if a few of the riders were killed or wounded, the momentum of the others would carry them into the midst of the defenders as they rode through the openings between wagons. Only superb horsemen endowed with great courage could carry off such a feat.

Chet handed Claudia another loaded rifle. For the third time she missed her target. In despair, she knew the end of the battle was near. Tonie remained calm, but she, too, continued to miss, and the farmers' shots were going wild.

Then, all at once the din of additional fire was heard on the heights, and the riders who had been sitting their mounts at the lip of the bluff began to scatter.

One of the men galloping down the bluff was struck and knocked from his saddle, but the momentum carried the riderless horse down the slope. Then a second was felled, and a third.

The survivors were losing their courage, but the bluff was too steep to change the angle of their descent, and they could only crouch low. A fourth was wounded, then a fifth threw his hands high in the air as he tumbled from his saddle. His body rolled down the slope.

Their comrades, who had maintained a covering fire, had vanished, and in their place stood a line of men on foot.

Claudia didn't comprehend what was happening until yet another descending rider was felled. As he tumbled from his saddle, she was amazed to see an arrow stuck in his back.

Then it dawned on her that the scouting party had returned. She caught a glimpse of the buckskin-clad Sam Brentwood, flanked by Ernie von Thalman and

Stalking Horse, who was sending arrow after arrow down the cliff.

Not one of the attackers reached the wagons alive. Several of their horses were killed, too, or were injured. When they reached the flat land below, the surviving animals veered off in time to avoid colliding with the wagons.

Danny then set an example by racing into the open. Several of the others followed, and the surviving riderless horses were rounded up.

Sam Brentwood led his party down the slope. Claudia moved into the open, not even realizing she was still clutching a rifle. When he saw she was alive and unharmed, the relief in Sam's eyes spoke for him. There was no need for words as he took her in his arms. She clung to him, returning his fervent kiss, not caring if anyone saw them embrace.

The battle had come to an end.

"We disposed of most of them," Ernie von Thalman said. "I regret that a few at the top of the bluff escaped. Since we were on foot, we couldn't follow them."

The bodies of the attackers were examined, but no clues to their identities could be found.

"All I know for sure," Sam said later, "is that this was no ordinary gang of bandits committing robbery."

The beginning of rifle fire in the distance up the river had sounded like a symphony, and Henry St. Clair felt a sense of deep gratification. He sat on his horse in the deep woods beside the bank of the Missouri, listening to the gunfire. Occasionally he glanced in the direction of the gentle slope that rose toward the bluff. Perfect planning, combined with luck, had made it possible to achieve a total victory, even if the execution of his scheme left something to be desired.

He had hoped that Tall Oak would be followed, but it was sheer good fortune that so many men had gone out in the search party. There was no way the weakened defenders could ward off an assault by Army deserters hungry for loot. Ultimately the raiders would be traced and caught, of course. Without his skilled help in covering their tracks, they would be found by the authorities and hanged. And the sooner they were apprehended the better he'd like it. Dead men could tell no stories about the instigator of the plot against the wagon train.

As soon as he knew for certain that the caravan had been utterly demolished, he'd head for Canada, make his way to Quebec as quickly as possible and board the first ship sailing to England. Rather than send a message, he'd carry the good news himself so there would be no need for a delay in claiming the reward he'd been promised. Certainly this mission would rank as one of his greatest achievements. At negligible expense to the Crown, he had delayed the establishment of an American colony in the Oregon country and won time for Great Britain to set up a new chain of forts there. He knew of no other case where a single agent, acting alone, had won such a vast territory.

The rifle fire didn't die out. Instead it became heavier, indicating that the members of the wagon train were putting up a spirited resistance. Somewhat apprehensive, Henry told himself to stop worrying. The deserters would let nothing stand between them and the gold in Otto van Ayl's wagon or the booty in the special wagon. Every rifle shot being fired meant that greater havoc was being wrought.

Henry was tempted to leave now, without waiting to hear a report from the Lynx. Having paid the deserters what he'd promised them, he owed them nothing and had no desire to see them turn on him, which they were capable of doing. But his conscience wouldn't permit him to go until the rifle fire died. That way, he could supply a fact-hungry London with the final, gory details.

Before starting his new position, Henry decided he'd take a holiday—and spend every moment of it in London. He felt no urge to fish on the Cornwall coast or hunt in Scotland. In fact, this long sojourn in rural America had ruined whatever yearning for the outdoors he'd ever had. Once he reached the city he loved, he'd stay there for years, not even going to the country for weekends. After traveling almost half the distance across the North American continent, and with the journey to Quebec still ahead, he'd had his fill of trees, grass and primitive living.

The tempo of rifle fire increased. A wave of nervousness washed over Henry. He listened more intently. He was relieved when he heard the concentrated boom of volleys fired in unison. Only men with military training could fire together with such precision, a feat that the simple farmers and artisans of the wagon train were incapable of. So the operation must be in its final stages.

Chuckling, Henry again felt the urge to leave the area without delay. If he did, however, he'd never know how many people in the caravan had been killed and wounded, how many wagons had been destroyed and how many looted. The Prime Minister would want specific facts to include in his report to Queen Victoria. Men had been knighted, Henry reflected, for successes less solid than the victory he was winning.

A few last, ragged bursts of rifle fire sounded, and then all was quiet. A cricket chirped in the woods. Henry could hear the faint roar of rapids down the river. Sir Henry St. Clair. The name had a pleasant ring.

A single horseman was approaching through the forest, but Henry was not surprised. Most of the deserters, he assumed, were gathering as much loot as they could before scattering, and that was all to the good. The more they stole, the more difficult it would be for the Americans to resume their trip to Oregon.

The Lynx came in view, his rifle resting on his pommel. His savage scowl was not the expression one might expect to see on the face of a conqueror. His shirt was soaked with sweat, which dripped from his beard, too, and there were bramble scratches on the backs of his hands.

Raising an arm in greeting but not yet speaking, the Lynx rode closer. Then, even before he halted, he picked up his rifle by the barrel, swinging it with all of his prodigious might. The butt caught Henry on the side of the head and toppled him to the ground.

The surprise of the assault as well as its violent intensity dazed St. Clair, and he lay on the ground for a moment, trying to collect his wits. Then he reached for the pistol in his belt.

Before he could draw it, however, a huge hand dragged him to his feet, and a fist crashed into his face. Henry staggered backward into a tree, then tried again to draw his pistol. But the Lynx was too quick for him and battered him unmercifully with both fists.

Henry made an attempt to protect himself from the hammer-like blows, but it was impossible to shield himself, and there was no escape. His lower lip was bleeding, he could no longer see out of one eye and he felt certain his nose was broken. Then a crushing blow landed in the pit of his stomach, driving the air from his lungs. He doubled over, swayed and fell to the ground.

But the Lynx was far from done. Methodically, systematically, he kicked his victim, his boots cracking against Henry's head, smashing into his ribs, causing searing agony when they struck him in the groin.

"Why . . . are you doing . . . this?" Henry managed to gasp.

The Lynx' harsh voice seemed to come from a great distance. "You tricked us, you dirty son of a bitch. Their sharpshooters held us off, and then they caught us from behind. Most of my boys are dead. Only a few got away. And you did it to us, you bastard. I don't know why. I don't care why. But you ain't going to do it again. Not to us, not to anybody."

Obviously the attack on the wagon train had failed.

Henry wanted to explain that his plan had been fool-proof, that the deserters must have been at fault in their execution. The deserters had been his allies, not his enemies, and the Lynx was drawing the wrong conclusions. Henry tried to speak, but couldn't form the words he wanted to say. He could only moan.

He was vaguely aware of the rifle butt poised above him, and tried to move out of its path as it descended. But his own movements were feeble, and it had the weight of a demon behind it as it crashed into his face.

The rifle butt descended again and again.

Henry's pain was so great that he could no longer think clearly, but he realized that the Lynx was trying to club him to death.

Then, though the blows continued to rain down on him, the pain began to ease, and he knew he was losing consciousness. No matter how severely this vicious madman beat him, he would not die, and he was grateful for the long years of physical conditioning, the harsh service in the field in so many remote corners of the world.

For reasons he didn't know, the attack on the wagon train had failed. So he'd be obliged to try again—and yet again—until he destroyed it. Nothing could be allowed to interfere with the achievement of his goal.

As he lost consciousness, he was actually smiling.

The Lynx struck him a few more times with the rifle butt for good measure, mounted his horse and picked up the reins of the Englishman's horse, too. The deserter rode off, leaving a bleeding, broken Henry St. Clair stretched out on the ground, more dead than alive.

Volunteers prepared individual graves near the bank of the Missouri River for the wagon-train dead, along with a single mass grave for their unknown assailants. Ted Woods, with the help of three men, fashioned crude coffins.

One attacker's horse had to be shot, but six were rounded up, more than compensating for the pioneers' loss of three horses and an ox. Danny and several other boys collected weapons on the bluff, and these weapons, in good working order, were added to the caravan's arsenal.

Dr. Martin attended the wounded. With the aid of Claudia, struggling to overcome her exhaustion, he removed a bullet from the wounded farmer.

Chet Harris and his brothers tried in vain to console their mother for the loss of Billy. But Emily Harris, who had always shown such strength in adversity, couldn't stop weeping for the loss of her youngest child. She sat on the back steps of her wagon, a bandanna handkerchief pressed to her face as she rocked back and forth.

When she felt a strong hand on her shoulder, she looked up through her tears to see Baron Ernst von Thalman standing beside her. Too sensitive to her plight to offer his condolences in words, Ernie held out a hand.

Emily took it, and felt herself being lifted to her feet.

Ernie led her out of the compound, beckoning the boys to follow. They walked to the mossy bank of the river, where a huge weeping willow stood. It had been discarding whip-like branches in the cold autumn air, and the ground was littered with them.

Ernie put a supporting arm around Emily's shoulders, and together they looked at the moving waters of the river.

It occurred to Emily Harris that this man, until recently a total stranger, was grieving with her for Billy not because of her loss, but because he himself had formed a strong attachment to the child. The ability to share grief steadied her, and the tears on her cheeks dried in the wind that blew from the West. The memory of Billy would accompany them on the long, hard journey that still lay ahead.

Suddenly Emily became aware of her remaining sons, who were pressing close to her. She knew how they felt. Aware of their concern for her, she forced a smile, strictly for their sakes. The still-silent Ernie von Thalman continued to support her, his solid, supple strength as firm as the trunk of the willow tree.

At last Emily broke the spell. She kissed each of her sons, then took Ernie's arm as they made their way back to the campsite. Her grief still burdened her, and she knew she would bear it the rest of her days. But now it had eased a trifle because she was sharing it with others.

Cindy came to Cathy van Ayl, as did Tonie Mell, Grace Drummond and a number of other women. But the dry-eyed Cathy made it plain that she wanted to be alone for a time, so she, too, went down to the river and sat on a boulder overlooking the rain-swollen Missouri.

Otto was gone but she didn't miss him. She told herself that repeatedly, astonished by her lack of feeling. There was a void inside her, an emptiness that wouldn't dissipate.

Logic told her it was impossible to feel deep sorrow: she had never loved Otto. She had been his dutiful daughter, his hard-working servant, but not his wife. Ever since he'd botched his lovemaking in the first days of their marriage, he had never again approached her, and they had shared no intimacies.

She had married him because her father had instructed her to do so "for the sake of a secure future." Well, she had that security now, and it meant nothing to her. In one way or another—and she knew nothing about finances—she would have to find a bank in Independence in which to deposit the gold that lay beneath the false floor of her wagon.

Yes, it was strictly her wagon now. She would give Otto's clothes to any man in the company who wanted them, and she'd distribute his other belongings, too. Her mind whirling, she didn't yet know whether to suggest to Claudia that they return to the East. She had no reason to go back, but Otto—not she—had wanted to settle in Oregon.

Poor Otto. He had never loved her, any more than she had loved him; he had cared about nothing except his money. For all the good it did him now. Cathy had to admit to herself that at times she had hated him, but that hatred was gone now, replaced by a feeling of pity for someone who had never known joy or shared the warmth of a close relationship with any other person.

Perhaps it was wrong to feel only pity, but Cathy had to be honest with herself. She had lost a stern guardian rather than a husband, but that knowledge didn't make her feel guilty. In fact, she was free for the first time in her life, having passed from her father's care to Otto's, and the knowledge was frightening. It was a challenge too, and she was determined to make her own way, as Claudia was doing.

Still dry-eyed, Cathy walked slowly back to her wagon. When she saw sympathy in the expressions of others, she wanted to tell them not to feel sorry for her. She wanted to explain that they could join her in pitying Otto, if they wished, but that she wanted nothing for herself except the chance to stand erect. After a quarter of a century living under the thumbs of others, she wanted an opportunity to guide her own destiny.

She said nothing, to be sure, and she hurried to her wagon to escape from those sympathetic, sorrowing gazes.

Tonie Mell and Claudia Humphries were universally acclaimed as the heroines of the day. Even the monosyllabic Ted Woods became almost eloquent as he sang their praises.

"From the way I heard it," Sam told them, "there'd be no wagon train left if it hadn't been for you two."

Claudia, tired but giddy from the knowledge that she loved him and he loved her, chose to be flippant. "I owe my talents as a sharpshooter to my teacher," she said.

Tonie said nothing, but when she felt Robert Martin looking at her and smiling, she flushed. Damnation, she wanted to be appreciated as a woman, particularly by this one man, not for her talents as a marksman. She turned away abruptly and stalked off.

"She becomes very shy when she's praised," Dr. Martin said.

Claudia could have given him a more accurate explanation, but didn't feel it was her place to interfere. Besides, her whole being was filled with her own unexpected, new-found happiness.

"You and I have some things to settle," Sam said to her, before going off to set up sentry posts for the night. "But I reckon we'd best wait until I've done my duty and taken these folks safely to Independence."

The cooking fire was lighted at dusk, but the preparation of supper was postponed until the dead were buried. Night came, and at last the graves and coffins were ready.

Men stepped forward to volunteer as pallbearers, and the Harris brothers insisted on carrying Billy's coffin, which looked very small. Sam and Dr. Martin led the company to the river and bared their heads, and the other men quickly followed their example.

The flames of the cooking fire leaped high, illuminating the scene, as men, women and children silently filed down to the bank of the Missouri. The night was cold but clear, the sky was filled with stars and a new moon began its slow rise into the heavens.

No one spoke, and the quiet was all-enveloping, with no sounds heard other than the faint shuffling of feet and the whisper of a breeze through the branches of trees that even now were shedding their leaves. Somehow the silent fall of those leaves to the ground symbolized the solemn mood of the sad occasion. The members of the company were mourning their departed. But they realized that others would die, too, before the wagon train reached the promised land of Oregon.

A woman's choking sob seemed to vibrate in the stillness. Someone began to sing, and others joined in, their voices as soft as the night:

> Rock of ages, cleft for me,
> Let me hide myself in thee;
> Let the water and the blood
> From thy side, a healing flood,
> Be of sin the double cure,
> Cleanse me from its guilt and power.

It was not accidental that voices were raised spontaneously in the singing of this hymn. "Rock of Ages" had been written in 1775, the year the War of Independence had broken out. And for more than sixty years Americans had regarded it as their own. Sung in churches of every denomination throughout the United States, it was more than a hymn; it had become a reaffirmation of a people's faith in their own future, in the future of the land of liberty.

By the time they reached the last verse, everyone, including the families of the dead, sang loudly and clearly. Some were weeping, others stood dry-eyed and humble as their voices soared, carrying the tune westward across the forests and up the great river:

> While I draw this fleeting breath,
> When mine eyelids close in death,

When I rise to worlds unknown
And behold thee on thy throne,
Rock of ages, cleft for me,
Let me hide myself in thee.

The silence that followed the singing of the hymn was overpowering. The company had formed in a circle around Dr. Martin, who held a worn Bible in his hands. He opened it, and although it was too dark for him to see the printed page, there was no need for him to read. The Psalm was already engraved on his heart, the memory of his late wife still fresh:

The Lord is my shepherd: I shall not want.

He maketh me to lie down in green pastures:
he leadeth me beside the still waters.

He restoreth my soul: he leadeth me in the
paths of righteousness for his name's sake.

Yea, though I walk through the valley of the
shadow of death, I will fear no evil: for
thou art with me; thy rod and thy staff
they comfort me.

Thou preparest a table before me in the
presence of mine enemies: thou anointest
my head with oil; my cup runneth over.

Surely goodness and mercy shall follow me
all the days of my life; and I will dwell in
the house of the Lord for ever.

The "Amen" spoken by the whole company was soft but fervent. Then the coffins were lowered into the ground and covered with dirt. A stone was placed at the head of each grave, together with a slab of oak onto which the name of the deceased had been burned.

The simple ceremony was ended. Silently, walking singly and in family groups, members of the wagon train went back to their campsite. There was no sound but the quiet shuffling of feet and the whisper of the wind as it blew through the bare branches of the trees.

XVII

In the days that followed, it became clear that most members of the wagon train intended to see the march through to the end. They were bolstered by the rumor that scores of other pilgrims awaited them in Independence, planning to join the caravan there after making their way to the jumping-off place. The company, Ernst von Thalman firmly predicted, would be the largest ever to make a concerted attack on the American wilderness.

There were exceptions, to be sure, and the most prominent of them was Sam Brentwood. He had agreed to lead the train only as far as Independence. He had further given his promise to Andrew Jackson to establish a supply depot there to provide service for the thousands of pioneers who were expected to follow in the wake of the first wave. He fully intended to keep that pledge.

Sam's plans for himself solved Claudia Humphries'

415

problem. "He hasn't formally proposed to me, and being the sort of shy person he is, it may be that he never will," she said to Cathy. "But that doesn't matter. All he's said is that we'll talk after we reach Independence, but I've already decided what we're going to do. We'll be married as soon as possible, and I'll help him set up the supply depot and run it with him. I could never go back to a life of doing nothing, not after coming all this way on the wagon train."

Cathy had smiled infrequently in the days since Otto's death, but a mischievous expression lightened her face, completely altering her appearance. Only the black armband on one sleeve would have told a stranger that she was a widow. "Suppose Sam doesn't ask you to marry him?" she asked with mock innocence. "What then?"

"Why, I'd find a minister, make the arrangements myself and tell Sam we had an appointment."

There was a hint of wistfulness in Cathy's eyes. "I've known for a long time that you and Sam are right for each other," she said, "but I sometimes wondered if you'd ever realize it yourselves. I'm sure you'll have a wonderful life together, although I'd hate to be around when you both get stubborn at the same time."

Claudia laughed, obviously relishing the prospect, and then sobered. "What will you do, Cathy? I haven't wanted to talk about your future too soon, which is why I've waited so long."

"I wish I could make up my mind," the younger girl replied. "I've thought of going back to Long Island—"

"Why on earth would you do that? You always hated living on that farm!"

"I know. So I've at least come to the conclusion that I can't go running back home, because I don't have a home there. Come to think of it, I never did."

"You could stay in Independence with Sam and me. I know he'd be as pleased as I would to have you with us."

"You're sweet and kind, Claudia. But it doesn't seem right to me that a couple just starting out in married life should be burdened with a sister underfoot. Not that I'm rejecting your offer, mind you. On the contrary, I may be forced to accept, like it or not. And with Otto's gold, I could pay my own way. It's possible, you see, that I'll have no real choice."

"What do you mean?"

"It'll be a march of almost two thousand miles from Independence to the Oregon country," Cathy said. "And after what we've seen already, I hate to think of the hardships the wagon train will have to face in the unsettled wilderness. I'm not sure I want to face them by myself. I'm trying to weigh every possibility so I can make up my mind."

"Don't be in a rush," Claudia told her. "Keep thinking. At the right time you'll know what to do."

"I hope so." Cathy was troubled, but knew she had to make her own decision.

The next evening, the next to the last they would spend on the trail before reaching Independence, the company faced the prospect of another defection. Tonie Mell, hailed by Claudia and Sam, who urged her to join them at the campfire for supper, looked unusually woebegone. Claudia and Sam were surprised, but they refrained from commenting.

Tonie was conscious only of Robert Martin, who sat a few feet away. She helped herself to a very small portion of buffalo steak, but refused the dumplings and hot bread that went with it.

Dr. Martin tried to put her in a better humor. "I hope you're not dieting," he said. "If you are, there won't be anything left of you."

Tonie remained glum. "I'm not hungry."

Claudia knew something was bothering her, and tried to sympathize silently. Tonie turned to the young woman with whom she'd formed an unbreakable bond of friendship during the battle with the deserters. "I guess I'm just feeling sad because—after tomorrow—I won't be seeing you folks on the train any more."

"You've definitely decided to go back to your uncle's ranch?" Claudia asked, instantly sympathetic.

Tonie nodded. "I have no real choice. My aunt hasn't been well the past couple of years, and I've got to relieve her of her responsibilities around the house. My uncle is getting on in years, and he needs my help on the ranch. That's the way it will have to be."

"We'll miss you," Robert Martin said quietly.

The girl gave no sign she had heard him. That was preferable to disgracing herself by weeping.

"Well," Sam said, "at least Claudia and I will be nearby, once we find us a place to live."

Males, Claudia thought, including the man she was going to marry, were incredibly obtuse. It was obvious that Tonie was upset because she wouldn't be seeing

Dr. Martin again, and the presence of friends in the neighborhood could offer little consolation.

A heavy rain fell the next morning, slowing the wagon train and destroying any hope of reaching Independence that night. During the nooning the sun came out, however, and a brisk wind off the plains dried the road that ran parallel to the Missouri River.

When they made their last camp, shortly before dusk, Sam predicted they'd reach their destination late the next morning. The entire company was well trained for the journey that lay ahead, and he watched with satisfaction as the wagons were formed into a circle, the animals placed safely inside it to browse. Claudia took charge of the water detail for the last time, wood was gathered and, when the fire was started, Cathy and her many helpers began to prepare the evening meal.

These people, who knew what was expected of them, would form a solid nucleus for the rest of the journey, no matter how many newcomers joined them. They had been hardened, too, by the tribulations they had already endured, so now they were truly ready for the march through the wilderness that lay ahead.

As Sam turned away, he saw Stalking Horse race out of the compound, then lift his hand in greeting as a lone rider approached. It was Whip Holt, slouched in his saddle, looking half-asleep, although he was actually prepared for any emergency. Sam hurried forward to greet his friend, too, his limp pronounced.

Whip returned the Indian's salute and jumped to the ground. They grasped each other's forearms, a gesture indicating to anyone familiar with Indian customs that they were blood brothers. "The sister of Stalking Horse sends him her greetings," Whip said, addressing the Cherokee in his own tongue.

Stalking Horse was delighted. "Whip has seen her?"

"We spent the summer together in the mountains. She has earned much gold from the beaver we trapped. I wanted her to come with me, but you know how much she hates the white man. She will stay with the Cheyenne for the winter."

Stalking Horse nodded happily. There was no need for him to comment. His sister and Whip, his close friend, had lived together for three years, and he regarded their relationship as natural.

Whip turned to Sam, and they shook hands. "I got itchy waiting for you in Independence, so I came out to meet you."

"I'm glad you did." Sam grinned at his bronzed, lean colleague. "You look fit."

"I should be. You know what that mountain air does for a man. How goes it?"

Sam quickly brought him up to date, stressing the defection of Henry St. Clair, the attempts of Imperial Russia to enlist the services of Tonie Mell and the recent battle. "We can talk more later, Whip," he concluded. "In the next couple of days I'll tell you whatever you want to hear about folks in the company. They're all right."

"Well," Whip said as all three strolled toward the compound, the young guide leading his horse, "you don't look as though you've suffered much."

"I haven't," Sam said with a chuckle. "Matter of

fact, I'll be needing you to stand up with me before you pull out and head West."

"You're marrying Miz Humphries," Whip said quietly.

"Who in hell told you?" Sam was astonished.

"Nobody," Whip said, and chuckled. "It was plain as that big nose that spreads across your face. Right from the minute the two of you started spitting at each other in that Long Island kitchen."

Sam was still in a daze as he introduced the new guide to Dr. Martin and Ernie von Thalman.

Whip chatted with them briefly, then went off to greet the few members of the party with whom he was acquainted.

Cathy van Ayl stood over a huge iron kettle, its contents simmering on a low fire. She was using both hands to stir the stew with a large wooden ladle and, flushed from the heat of the fire, she was concentrating on her efforts. She felt, rather than saw, someone staring at her, and glanced up to meet Whip Holt's steady gaze.

She almost dropped the ladle into the kettle.

Removing his hat, Whip came to her immediately. "Ma'am," he said, indicating the black band on her arm, "I didn't know. I'm sorry."

"Thank you," she replied simply. It was wrong, so soon after Otto's death, to be disturbed by the proximity of another man.

"Was it during the battle below the bluff?"

Cathy nodded. She couldn't pretend to be grieving for a man she had never loved, but it would be unseemly to explain to this stranger that she felt sorry for Otto.

"I reckon," Whip said quietly, "that I'll have to keep watch over you myself when we cross the plains."

Before Cathy could reply he turned away abruptly and was gone. She felt shaken, and finally came to the conclusion that what disturbed her was his calm assumption that she intended to make the rest of the march with the wagon train.

Tonie Mell didn't want to prolong the agony of leave-taking, so she said good-bye to the company immediately after breakfast. Now that she was this close to home, she said, she could make better time by going on alone.

She and Claudia hugged each other affectionately, and Sam insisted on kissing her.

"This is no good-bye," Claudia said. "We're going to expect you at our wedding."

The teen-aged boys, led by Danny and Chet, followed Tonie as she went from wagon to wagon. Afraid she would make a spectacle of herself, she limited her farewells to a few, curt words, but she was nevertheless upset when she finally came to Robert Martin's wagon.

"I wish you the very best of everything good, and I'm sure you'll have it," he told her, taking her hand. "You're a very special person."

Tonie was unable to reply. Wrenching away from him, she hurried off and climbed onto her wagon. Danny handed her the reins of her horse and she started off alone, a small, slender figure in buckskins who didn't dare to look back for fear of losing her composure.

She drove her team rapidly over the familiar terrain, taking shortcuts and making her way across open country. Her mind was a blank, her senses were numb. Refusing to let herself think, she hoped she'd remain in this anesthetized state of suspended animation for a long time to come. It was her tragedy that she had fallen in love for the first time in her life, and with a man who didn't know she existed as a woman, a man she would never see again. But that was her situation, and she was forced to accept it.

Her route took her to within a short distance of Independence, and when she reached the top of a little hill she paused to look down at the community. She had left in the autumn and was returning in the autumn. Its growth in the year she had been absent amazed her: it had been a small, sprawling village when she had left, and now it was a real town.

The spires of the two tallest buildings, the Presbyterian and Methodist churches, dominated either end of the main street. The post office had been enlarged, there was a new store that sold hardware and harnesses, a dry-goods shop and a food emporium, a sign suspended above its entrance proclaiming that it specialized in smoked and pickled meats, sugar, flour and cooked vegetables preserved in jars. The old general store was still in its former location, and next to it was what had been the only saloon in Independence. Now there was another, directly across the street, and on its second floor an oil lamp with a bright red shade was burning in front of a window, even in broad daylight.

The really surprising thing about the growth of the town was the proliferation of new homes. There must, she decided, be at least a hundred of them, neat, one-story clapboard buildings, all of them whitewashed and each with its own small yard and vegetable garden. Looking at an old barn that had stood alone in a field, a place where horses could be bought and sold, Tonie saw that it was now surrounded by new houses. She scarcely recognized Independence.

Beyond the last row of houses was a field in which a number of covered wagons were scattered, their oxen and work horses meandering over a wide area as they foraged. Tonie realized at once that the people in these wagons were awaiting the arrival of the train in order to join it. She smiled a bit ruefully. These men and women had a great deal to learn, and she wouldn't be on hand to help them. Whip Holt would raise the devil with them until they began to arrange their vehicles in a tight, neat circle, keeping their animals inside the enclosure. She herself had questioned the need for these procedures, but experience had taught her their value. There would be no survivors of the assault on the bank of the Missouri if the caravan hadn't been arranged in a defensive position.

Tonie counted thirty wagons, then halted abruptly before she completed the task. She was torturing herself unnecessarily. The inhabitants of those wagons would remain total strangers to her. They would play no part in her life, so it didn't matter whether there were ten or fifty. She averted her gaze, then started off again in the direction of her uncle's ranch, which was only a short distance from what had become a boom town.

Two hired hands were sitting their mounts in the south pasture, keeping watch on the cattle there. Obviously they had been employed since her departure for Washington City, so she knew neither one of them, but she raised a hand in greeting and they returned the salute. From their subsequent conversation with each other, it seemed likely that they had guessed her identity. There weren't many young women in faded buckskins in the area.

The ranch house and its outbuildings were unchanged, perhaps a trifle smaller than they had become in Tonie's memory during the past year. She unhitched her team, then placed her work horses and gelding in the stable before she did anything else. Lifelong training had taught her that the care of animals came first.

But she could unpack her belongings later, and she broke into a run as she started toward the house. The wonderful couple who had reared her had truly become her parents. She had missed them even more than she realized.

Arnold Mell, white-haired and spare, met his niece in the covered passageway between the dining room and the kitchen out-building. He was overjoyed to see her. Tonie's cheeks were wet as they embraced.

"Thank God you're here," he said in his Russian-accented English. "I knew from your letters that you were traveling with the Oregon wagon train, but I didn't know how to get word to you."

"What's wrong?" She had a premonition, and her heart sank.

He put an arm around her shoulders as they walked to the large bedroom at the side of the house. "Sophie is ill, very ill. But she's clung to life because she's wanted so badly to see you again before she dies."

"What kind of illness—"

"We don't know. The only doctor in town left six months ago. There's another in Saint Jo, and I've written to him several times. He's promised to come, but so far he's been too busy to leave his own practice."

They opened the bedroom door quietly. Tonie was shocked by Aunt Sophie's appearance. The robust woman had lost so much weight that she was quite frail. Her skin was waxen and her dark, red hair had grown as white as her husband's. Tonie could feel the presence of death in the air.

Sophie Mell appeared to be sleeping, but she opened her eyes, focused with difficulty and then managed a tremulous smile when she recognized the girl who bent down to kiss her tenderly. Then she sighed and drifted back to sleep.

Tonie accompanied her uncle into the corridor outside the sickroom. "There's a doctor in the wagon train," Tonie said. "I'll get him, and come right back."

Arnold Mell knew his wife was beyond medical help, but he had no chance to tell Tonie not to bother. She was gone before he could speak.

Tonie quickly saddled two horses. Leading one while she rode the other, she headed at a canter toward the field at the edge of Independence where the newcomers' wagons had been parked.

When she reached the site the wagon train had just arrived. The vehicles were being moved into the usual circle and the place was a bedlam. People who had said their farewells to Tonie only a few hours earlier were delighted to see her, but she didn't return their greetings. Instead she rode straight to Robert Martin's wagon.

The physician had just finished unhitching his team, and looked up in surprise at the girl, whose face was tense.

"My aunt is very ill and there's no other doctor in town—"

Waiting to hear no more, Dr. Martin ducked into his wagon for his medical satchel, then mounted the spare horse. Tonie led him back to the ranch at a full gallop, making conversation impossible. When they arrived he went straight into the sickroom, while Tonie and her uncle waited in the parlor, a seldom-used room cluttered with heavy furniture. There the physician joined them a half-hour later.

"May I be blunt?" he asked. "I'm afraid there's no hope for Mrs. Mell. In fact, there's been none since the beginning of this illness."

Arnold Mell nodded. The diagnosis confirmed what he'd known all along.

Tonie averted her face. Robert Martin placed a hand on her shoulder. "Don't blame yourself for not being here these past months," he said gently. "There was literally nothing you could have done for her."

She turned and looked up at him, gratitude and something more—a great deal more—in her eyes.

So that's the way it is, Arnold Mell thought. Never

before had Tonie been interested in any man, and he told himself that something should be done about it.

Sophie Mell died later that same day, with her husband and niece at her bedside. Her funeral was held the following day at the Presbyterian Church in Independence, and virtually everyone in the wagon train was present. Arnold Mell, who had long anticipated the tragedy, bore up well. Tonie struggled hard to retain her composure, and was sustained by Dr. Martin, who stood beside her when her aunt was buried in the town cemetery.

Forty-eight hours later, the same church was the scene of a far happier occasion, the marriage of Claudia Humphries and Sam Brentwood. They were married by the church's pastor, with Cathy van Ayl acting as her sister's matron of honor and Whip Holt standing up with Sam. Again the people of the wagon train filled the church.

Tonie Mell insisted on holding a reception for the bride and groom, saying that by giving the party for her friends she'd be better able to put her sorrows out of her mind for a time. The members of the wagon train agreed, the women laying down the condition that they be allowed to prepare the food that Tonie and her uncle provided. A side of beef was barbecued in a pit behind the kitchen, and there were baked hams, fried chicken and a variety of cold meats. The ladies prepared mounds of potato salad, baked beans and several types of hot bread, and everyone drank hard cider made from local apples.

Claudia wore a dress of gray silk she had made for

the occasion, and Sam looked uncomfortable in what he called a "city suit" of dark worsted, worn with a high collar and white neckband. Soon he relaxed, however, because his bride kept a firm grip on his arm, and he grinned broadly whenever he looked at her.

Arnold Mell and his somber niece were part of a small group gathered around the wedding party, as was Dr. Martin, when Sam explained his current problems. "I figured I could rent a place to live and a warehouse in Independence without any trouble," he said. "But the town is growing so fast that nothing is available. It looks like we'll have to live in Claudia's wagon while I build a storage depot for the supplies that are already piling up behind the post office."

"Maybe I could interest you in this ranch," Arnold Mell said. "You'd have all the space you'd need here, and if you wanted, you could keep raising cattle so you'd always have meat for the wagon trains."

Tonie looked at her uncle in astonishment.

"Are you putting this place up for sale?" Claudia wanted to know.

"There are too many memories of my wife here, so I'd prefer to get rid of it. If Tonie doesn't mind."

"Whatever you say, Uncle Arnold." The girl could not hide her continuing surprise. Her family had been among the first to settle in the area, suffering many hardships as they'd tamed the wilderness, and she couldn't imagine Uncle Arnold living anywhere else.

"If you're serious about this," Sam said, "I've been authorized by John Jacob Astor and his partners to spend fifteen thousand dollars for a depot."

"For that kind of money," Arnold Mell said, "I'll throw in the livestock and most of the furniture. It's a good deal for everybody."

"Especially for me." Sam looked at his bride and squeezed her hand. "I'll be happier running the ranch, and Claudia can look after the supply depot."

"A perfect arrangement," she said, knowing he'd be far more contented working out of doors.

"Where will you and I go, Uncle Arnold?" the bewildered Tonie asked.

Her uncle smiled. "If Whip here will take us, we'll join the wagon train," he said. "Unless he thinks I'm too old."

Whip Holt, who had known him for years, protested vehemently. "You, Arnold? You may be in your sixties, but I'd bet on you any time in a free-for-all with men half your age. Besides, you've forgotten more about how to deal with nature than most of the greenhorns on the train will ever know. There's nobody I'd rather have with us!"

"Then it's settled," Arnold said.

Tonie was so ecstatic she couldn't think straight.

"So we'll have you with us after all, Tonie," Robert Martin said. "That's a grand piece of news."

Tonie could only nod. She was afraid to look at him for fear of revealing her innermost feelings.

Only Claudia understood the sacrifice Arnold Mell was making. She was able to penetrate his surface attitude and realized that, with his wife gone, he was willing to start anew for Tonie's sake. Somehow, he had gleaned that Tonie had fallen hopelessly in love with Robert Martin, and he wanted to give her the opportunity to let the romance develop on the long trail that lay ahead.

"This is working out fine for everybody," Sam said, and turned to his new sister-in-law. "Now we'll have plenty of room for you here, Cathy, for as long as you'll want to stay with us."

"I don't intend to stay, Sam," Cathy said. "Thanks all the same. I was waiting until after the wedding to tell you and Claudia that I've decided to go on to Oregon, too."

Whip reddened beneath his tan, and for an instant his gaze met Cathy's. That moment was enough for her to realize that the future was filled with promise.

In the twelve years that had passed since the first trading post had been established at St. Joseph, Missouri, less than sixty miles northwest of Independence, the rapidly growing town had grown accustomed to many strange sights. The recent acquisition of land by purchase from the Kiowa, Fox and Sac Indian nations had spurred immigration, new farms were being established and the town itself doubled its population every six months.

Rocky Mountain trappers mingled on the streets with Indians in loincloths, painted women from the local saloons and prim New Englanders. There were carpenters and bricklayers from the Eastern Seaboard whose jobs had vanished in the Panic of 1837, new arrivals from the German principalities and Scandinavia, who were just learning to speak English, Missouri River boatmen and adventurers of many stripes who were seeking a new life.

All stared in astonishment at the grim-faced man who plodded slowly down the main street, putting one foot in front of the other, wavering but somehow not falling. His face had been smashed to a pulp, his clothes were tattered and he clutched his side to ease the pain of broken ribs. Even his boots were battered, indicating that he had walked a great distance.

Smears of dried blood still on his face, Henry St. Clair made his way as far as the doorstep of the town's only physician, then collapsed. A thousand times he had been on the verge of giving up, but an inner force had driven him on, and at last he had reached his next destination.

His money belt was intact, the doctor would patch him up and his bones would mend. Then he would resume his mission. He hoped the worst was behind him, because one way or another he had to destroy the American wagon train that was bound for the Oregon territory.

The first half of the long march across the face of North America had drawn to an end, and the weary travelers who had spent months on the trail were enjoying a temporary respite. They had reached the last outpost of civilization in the United States. Beyond it lay the Great Plains, stretching toward infinity, the magnificent and terrifying Rocky Mountains and, beyond the continental divide, still more chains of mountain peaks to cross before they reached Oregon. Here their dreams would come true, if they had the strength, stamina and courage to survive.

**LYLE KENYON ENGEL,
THE ORIGINATOR OF THE
MOST SUCCESSFUL SERIES IN
PAPERBACK HISTORY CREATES
A NEW LANDMARK IN FICTION ...**

★★★★★★★★★★★★★★★★★★★★★★

Few stories are more stirring than the amazing success of the most famous book packager in America, Lyle Kenyon Engel, who created *The Kent Family Chronicles*. Engel, long a history buff, had been in publishing for 41 years when he originated the idea for the series authored by John Jakes. The first book was an instantaneous bestseller. The rest, as they say, is publishing history.

"I love America," says Engel, "and nothing gives me greater pleasure than novels, based on reality, that celebrate our nation and tell the astonishing stories of the men and women who made her great. In *Wagons West* we can look forward to a magnificent new series, spellbinding tales of rousing events by a bestselling author writing under the name of Dana Fuller Ross. Starting in Long Island, we follow the triumphant adventure of our nation's westward drive ... It is a saga that not only tells the story of America—but *is* America."

★★★★★★★★★★★★★★★★★★★★★★

FROM THE PRODUCER OF
THE KENT FAMILY CHRONICLES
WAGONS WEST—VOLUME II

NEBRASKA
by Dana Fuller Ross

Here is a special preview
of the exciting opening pages of the
second book in this sweeping saga of the
men and women whose lives were
caught up in America's westward drive.

1

Heavy clouds, thick and black, ominous in their intensity, blew eastward from the Rocky Mountains across the Great Plains wilderness, obscuring the moon and stars. The night air had been cool, but the ground was still warm from the early autumn sun that had shone down on Missouri the previous day, so a white mist, as impenetrable as a bale of cotton, rose from the broad waters of the great Missouri River, bathing the whole area in a blanket of swirling mists.

High on the bluffs of the eastern bank of the river, a short distance from the frontier village of Independence, stood the symbols of the future. Wagon after wagon arranged in a circle. Flexible wooden hoops were looped upward over their sides and covered with thick canvas to protect the inhabitants from the elements. There were scores of wagons, hundreds of men, women and children in the caravan, all of them asleep. They were the first pioneers who would blaze a path to the Pacific Ocean and, in the decades to come, would be followed by thousands of others making their way to the Oregon Territory and California.

Some had already traveled all the way from

the Eastern seaboard, to be joined by others along the way in a daring venture unique in the annals of the history of the young United States. Only optimists, only Americans, would have dreamed such dreams of the future or dared to make such a long trek into the unknown.

Inside the circle, the horses and oxen were asleep, too, as were the dogs. None stirred.

There seemed to be nothing to fear. Independence was a sturdy little community of ranch owners and farmers—people who took the law into their own hands when need be because no other law existed at this remote outpost. Bloodshed was not unknown, but violence occurred infrequently.

No one in the wagon train heard the two boats being rowed across the Missouri from the west bank with muffled oars. No one saw the little craft hauled ashore, beached and made secure. Certainly no one in the train knew that six armed men, frontier drifters who preyed on fur trappers or isolated farm owners, were finding the train a target too tempting to be left in peace. There were animals to steal, valuables to snatch—prizes for desperadoes who placed small value on human life.

The six men crept up the hill, pistols and knives in their hands. A shepherd dog stretched outside one of the wagons awakened and raised its pointed ears. The bandits crept closer, struggling quietly as they made their way up the palisade.

One member of the wagon train stirred. Tall and lean, dressed in the buckskins, he was sound asleep one moment, completely awake and alert the next. He reached for his long rifle automatically and rose to his feet with effortless grace, in a single move.

A glance told him the mist was too thick for him to see, so he listened intently, his head cocked to one side. Then a faint, grim smile appeared on his face. Moving silently, with the experience of one who had spent years as a hunter, trapper and guide in the Rockies, he went quickly to several key wagons.

In almost no time he was joined by a motley group of men, carrying rifles. The trio followed the man in buckskins to the lip of the bluff. No one could see much more than a few feet ahead—certainly no one in the group could hear anything untoward. Within a few seconds they were joined by an Indian brave, also clad in buckskins—a warrior who almost casually notched an arrow in his bow. Like the man in buckskins, he had no need to see the approaching menace.

The marauders came still closer. They were no more than fifty feet from the top of the bluff. A broad smile appeared on the face of the man in buckskins. There was no doubt that he thoroughly enjoyed the challenge of danger. He didn't need to speak; his companions had traveled far with him, and knew what was expected of them.

Now the robbers were no more than five

yards from the lip of the palisade, almost within reach of their goal. The man in buckskins nodded, almost laconically, and four rifles spoke simultaneously, the weapons deliberately fired over the heads of the approaching foe.

The startled bandits paused, then turned and fled down the steep slope, sliding and stumbling, falling and scrambling as they raced to the safety of their waiting boat.

Now it was the Indian's turn. He sent arrow after arrow toward the retreating enemies. The bandits saw the arrows dropping among them and increased their wild pace as they dragged their boat into the water and rowed off to safety.

The man in buckskins listened, heard the fading sound of oars, and nodded. His companions turned and strolled back to their wagons for another hour of sleep. He rolled himself in his blanket. The Indian followed his example. Within a few minutes they had drifted back to sleep.

The ears of the shepherd dog drooped again, and the mist was still thick. The men, women and children of the train were deep in slumber. Even those who had awakened briefly had mistaken the firearms volley for a crack of thunder.

The wagon train was secure.

As always Cathy van Ayl looked lovely as she emerged from her wagon, and as always she seemed unaware of her beauty. She paused on the back step to tuck some stray strands of her long, blonde hair under her sunbonnet, then tightened the sash of her dimity dress. She looked like a young girl in her teens rather than a widow of twenty-three, but that innocence wasn't accidental. Her elderly husband, Otto, a miserly farmer from Long Island who had died in a raid on the wagon train had never been affectionate toward her.

Cathy finished primping just as Whip Holt, the hired guide and wagonmaster of the Oregon-bound caravan, came into view. Tall and sinewy in his buckskins, he was armed, as usual, with a brace of pistols and the long bullwhip, wrapped about his middle, that gave him his name. His skin was leathery after a lifetime of exposure to the outdoors, and his eyes were hard. Then he saw Cathy, and when he grinned at her he suddenly looked younger than twenty-nine.

She smiled at him in return, her heart skipping a beat. When her husband was alive she'd had to conceal her interest in Whip, but all that had changed. Now she had no reason beyond her own sense of discretion to hide the way she felt.

Certainly Whip made no secret of his own feelings. "Morning, ma'am," he called, sauntering toward her.

"You're wearing a new buckskin shirt and trousers, I see," she said politely.

He was startled that she noticed what he was wearing. "Well, you know how it is. I get restless just sitting around Independence while we put in supplies and wait for the new folks joining us to show up. So one day I took me hunting." He cleared his throat awkwardly. "You look mighty nice, all dressed up for a day in the city."

Cathy couldn't help laughing. Certainly no one else in 1837 would dream of referring to the frontier town of Independence, Missouri, as a "city." The last outpost of civilization east of the Great Plains, it was visited by trappers, hunters and traders bringing their furs from the Rocky Mountains to the East. Now, with other wagon trains scheduled to follow Whip's caravan across the wilderness to the fertile Oregon country, Independence promised to develop into a major supply center.

"I told my sister I'd buy some things in town for her and bring them along tonight."

Only a few days earlier Cathy's older sister, Claudia, had been married to Sam Brentwood, the former leader of the wagon train. The couple would remain in Independence to establish a supply depot, sponsored by Sam's mentors, former President of the United States Andrew Jackson, and John Jacob Astor, a fur baron, leader of a group of wealthy businessmen who were encouraging the American settlement of the Oregon territory.

"Claudia and Sam asked me to supper tonight, too," Whip said, and shifted in embarrassment. "I—I wasn't so sure I wanted to go, seeing as how I don't sit me down at a table indoors very often. But if you're going, ma'am, I'll be happy to escort you."

"I'd like that," Cathy said. She smiled again before turning away, then added, "I'm not really dressed up, you know. All I own are a few dresses like this, except for the old woolen things I wear on the trail."

"Could you use a doeskin dress, ma'am?"

"I'd love it, Whip." Cathy hesitated. "But I wouldn't want you to think I was hinting."

"No matter. Stalking Horse," he said, referring to his close friend, a Cherokee scout, "has been pestering me to try our hands at hunting again, so I reckon I'll have some skins for you by the time we push off."

Cathy thanked him, discomfited by his generosity, then left the circle of wagons. Directly ahead, beyond the bend in the Missouri River, stood the limitless wilderness that stretched across the Great Plains, the Rocky Mountains and, on the far side of the Continental Divide, yet another chain of mountains which the wagon train would have to cross before reaching Oregon.

Otto van Ayl had given his wife no choice and had been determined to go to Oregon. But the widowed Cathy had an alternative and was free to make up her own mind. Claudia and Sam had offered her a home with them, right here in Independence. And she wouldn't be dependent on their charity, either. Her wagon was as solid as any made in

New England, where they had originated in the days prior to the War of Independence. The four horses which pulled it were strong, surefooted and healthy. She could get a substantial sum for the wagon and team if she decided to stay behind when the train moved out. In addition, Otto had left her the fortune he had saved in a lifetime of miserly living, two thousand dollars in gold. When they started on the journey; Otto had concealed the money beneath a false floor in the wagon, but after his death, at Claudia and Sam's insistence, she had moved it for safe-keeping to the enormous special wagon where the caravan's medicines, extra weapons and emergency rations were stored.

So Cathy was wealthy, at least by the standards of the emigrants who were heading out to Oregon. Certainly she could pay for her keep if she decided to stay with her sister and new brother-in-law. Fortunately she wouldn't have to make up her mind for a few days; there were influences pulling her in both directions.

Because of Whip she wanted to go on. But she was a grown woman, not a romantic adolescent, and she couldn't allow her interest in him to become too great a factor. It was true, however, that she believed in finishing what she started, and if any of the stories she had heard about Oregon were true, it was heaven on earth.

Tugging her in the opposite direction was the knowledge that powerful forces were at work trying to prevent the American settlers from reaching their destination. The ownership of the Oregon country was in dispute, with both the United States and Great Britain claiming it. A British agent, Henry St. Clair, had already made several violent attempts to halt the train, even inspiring a vicious attack on the caravan by Army deserters. Although that last attempt had failed, several members of the company had been killed. And the pioneers would not have been comforted, had they known the thoughts that were still going through St. Clair's head. By God, he promised himself, they're not going to beat me! Hell or high water, I'm going to stop that damn wagon train!

But the British attempt to sabotage the train wasn't the only one. Imperial Russia wanted to stop them from reaching Oregon, too. Russians had been the first to settle in Oregon. Although international pressures had forced the czar seemingly to abandon his claim, the government in St. Petersburg was actually doing no such thing. Cathy was one of the few members of the caravan who knew that attempts had been made by the *Cheka*, the czar's secret police, to blackmail a lovely, frontier-wise girl named Tonie Mell into working for them. Tonie's parents, whom she hadn't seen since early childhood, were still in Russia. She had been told they wouldn't be allowed to join her unless she committed acts of sabotage against the train. Thanks to her own courage and the help of

Sam and Whip, she had outsmarted them. But it was fair to assume that the Russians would try again.

In addition, there were terrifying rumors among the settlers about the hostile Indian tribes in the wilderness ahead. There were some pessimists who predicted that every last man, woman and child in the train would be murdered. But Cathy refused to believe such rubbish. No matter how great the menace of Indians might become, she had unbounded faith in Whip Holt's abilities. She had seen him in action, and she was confident he would lead the band of settlers, already four hundred strong and growing every day, to their Oregon destination in safety. She was convinced that no Indians could prevent Whip from reaching his goal—for that matter, neither could the British and Russians.

Tonight, perhaps, she would discuss the decision with her sister; it might clarify her own thinking.

The wagon train had made camp outside Independence, where the horses and oxen could graze, and Cathy headed toward the town. She passed log cabins and houses of whitewashed clapboard. Until the past year, Independence had been little more than a village. But now it boasted two general stores, a stable, and, on its main street, two brothels and at least a dozen taverns and saloons. When Sam and Claudia finished making changes in the ranch, their property would become the principal supply depot for later wagon trains.

The depot would sell both horses and oxen, as well as spare wheels, axles and yokes. Thanks to Claudia's experience on the long march from New York to Missouri, she planned to put in a full supply of such provisions as bacon, flour, beans and sugar—the staples that every immigrant family needed on the trek across the continent. Thanks to the generosity of Astor and his associates, as well as the official encouragement of President Martin Van Buren, Sam would have enough funds to put in a stock of firearms, gunpowder and ammunition, too.

The morning sun was warm, almost hot, the breeze was gentle and it seemed more like summer than the beginning of autumn. It was small wonder that Whip was eager to start the march across the plains as soon as possible. Cathy knew from her own experience in the past six months that the caravan could travel ten to twelve miles per day in good weather, but that progress was slowed to a crawl when it rained. When the rains were very heavy it sometimes became necessary to call a complete halt.

Pondering her decision, paying scant attention to her immediate surroundings, Cathy was suddenly aroused from her reverie by the sound of a man's harsh, deep voice.

"That there one is the prettiest I've seen since we got to this town. I claim her!"

"Like hell you do," another man, replied. "Maybe we'll draw lots for her, all of us, or maybe we'll leave the choice up to her. We got to be fair about this."

The startled Cathy saw eight or nine men who had just emerged from a tavern directly ahead. In spite of the early hour, they had been drinking heavily. Some of them were dressed in shabby linsey-woolsey and others in worn, greasy buckskins. They had not shaved for days and their hair was dirty and unkempt. All were armed with skinning knives, as well as either pistols or rifles.

These were the men Whip and Sam contemptuously referred to as "frontier scum," opportunists who earned a precarious living. Sometimes they bought furs from trappers down on their luck and sold them to traders. Sometimes they did odd jobs for local homesteaders. They were as unsavory as they were unreliable, and Cathy blamed herself for failing to see them in time to avoid them.

But she had little time for regrets. The group had spread across the road, blocking her path, and she was afraid, judging by their leers, that they would maul her if she tried to crowd past them. But she might be in even worse trouble if she turned and tried to flee; certainly that would encourage them in their game. There were no other pedestrians, no riders in sight, so it would be useless to call for help.

The best way to handle the situation, she decided, would be to keep moving forward, remaining calm, and ignoring the brutes. She was tempted to pick up her flounced skirt and run, but instead she continued to walk at the same, even pace, her head high.

One of her tormentors muttered something, and the group quickly surrounded the girl. The man with the rasping voice, appointing himself the spokesman, grinned at her. "You look like you need some lovin'," he said, "so take your pick."

"Let me pass, please." Cathy knew no escape was possible, but made an effort to speak calmly.

"Don't put on no airs with us, girlie," another declared. "You women up the road charge enough, so it's high time you give us somethin' free."

The stunned Cathy suddenly realized they had mistaken her for a girl from one of the brothels. Certainly they were in no mood— perhaps in no condition—to heed her denials. She was in real danger and she didn't know how to escape.

Follow the lives of Whip and Cathy, Claudia and Sam, and all those people who continue the hazardous journey from Independence to Nebraska. Their ultimate destination—Oregon. Read the complete book, to be available July 1, wherever Bantam Books are sold.

DON'T MISS
THESE CURRENT
Bantam Bestsellers

RELAX!
SIT DOWN
and Catch Up On Your Reading!

LOUIS L'AMOUR

BANTAM'S #1
ALL-TIME BESTSELLING AUTHOR
AMERICA'S FAVORITE WESTERN WRITER

☐	12354	BENDIGO SHAFTER	$2.25
☐	13881	THE KEY-LOCK MAN	$1.95
☐	13719	RADIGAN	$1.95
☐	13609	WAR PARTY	$1.95
☐	13882	KIOWA TRAIL	$1.95
☐	12732	THE BURNING HILLS	$1.75
☐	12064	SHALAKO	$1.75
☐	13680	KILRONE	$1.95
☐	13794	THE RIDER OF LOST CREEK	$1.95
☐	13798	CALLAGHEN	$1.95
☐	12063	THE QUICK AND THE DEAD	$1.75
☐	12729	OVER ON THE DRY SIDE	$1.75
☐	13722	DOWN THE LONG HILLS	$1.95
☐	13240	WESTWARD THE TIDE	$1.75
☐	12043	KID RODELO	$1.75
☐	12887	BROKEN GUN	$1.75
☐	13898	WHERE THE LONG GRASS BLOWS	$1.95
☐	12519	HOW THE WEST WAS WON	$1.75

Buy them at your local bookstore or use this
handy coupon for ordering:

Bantam Books, Inc., Dept. LL2, 414 East Golf Road, Des Plaines, Ill. 60016

Please send me the books I have checked above. I am enclosing $_____
(please add $1.00 to cover postage and handling). Send check or money order
—no cash or C.O.D.'s please.

Mr/Mrs/Miss _____

Address _____

City _____ State/Zip _____

LL2—3/80

Please allow four to six weeks for delivery. This offer expires 9/80.

Bantam Book Catalog

Here's your up-to-the-minute listing of over 1,400 titles by your favorite authors.

This illustrated, large format catalog gives a description of each title. For your convenience, it is divided into categories in fiction and non-fiction—gothics, science fiction, westerns, mysteries, cookbooks, mysticism and occult, biographies, history, family living, health, psychology, art.

So don't delay—take advantage of this special opportunity to increase your reading pleasure.

Just send us your name and address and 50¢ (to help defray postage and handling costs).

BANTAM BOOKS, INC.
Dept. FC, 414 East Golf Road, Des Plaines, Ill. 60016

Mr./Mrs./Miss_____
(please print)

Address_____

City_____ State_____ Zip_____

Do you know someone who enjoys books? Just give us their names and addresses and we'll send them a catalog too!

Mr./Mrs./Miss_____

Address_____

City_____ State_____ Zip_____

Mr./Mrs./Miss_____

Address_____

City_____ State_____ Zip_____

FC—9/78